DANCING

with the

AVATAR

Michael,

God bless you!

Joan Jones

ALSO BY JOVAN JONES

Descent Book One: Chasing the Avatar

—Available From Destiny Image Publishers—

DANCING

with the

AVATAR

DESCENT BOOK TWO

JOVAN JONES

DESTINY IMAGE® PUBLISHERS, INC.

P.O. Box 310, Shippensburg, PA 17257-0310

"Speaking to the Purposes of God for This Generation and for the Generations to Come."

This book and all other Destiny Image, Revival Press, MercyPlace, Fresh Bread, Destiny Image Fiction, and Treasure House books are available at Christian bookstores and distributors worldwide.

For a U.S. bookstore nearest you, call 1-800-722-6774.

For more information on foreign distributors, call 717-532-3040.

Reach us on the Internet: www.destinyimage.com.

Trade Paper ISBN 13: 978-0-7684-3271-8

Hard Cover ISBN: 978-0-7684-3497-2

Large Print ISBN: 978-0-7684-3498-9

Ebook ISBN: 978-0-7684-9047-7

For Worldwide Distribution, Printed in the U.S.A.

1 2 3 4 5 6 7 8 9 10 11 / 13 12 11 10

DEDICATION

To my Lord, my Knight in Shining Armor…Jesus.

How many times You save me!

Thank You…I am forever grateful.

ACKNOWLEDGMENTS

I thank my brother, Roderick, for always being there for me and for having the greatest sense of humor. Your memories of my crazy escapades during this time period make for some great Thanksgiving dinner stories. Man! You can keep us rolling!

I also thank my brother's wife, Nora, for being such a wonderful addition to our family. We are so happy to have you in our lives. You are such a blessing to us. Love you just like a sis'!

I thank Kamina Fitzgerald for coming into my life and being like a sister to me. You support me in everything and show up at *every* book signing and event. You are truly appreciated.

Thank you, Rebecca Marquette Tatum, for being a phenomenal friend. Girl! You know how to stick by a person through thick and thin. You have seen me through all of this and still you love me. Thanks for being my friend!

ENDORSEMENTS

Jovan Jones is an anointed woman of God with a powerful story to tell. In her page-turning account of Maya's descent into despair and profound spiritual darkness, Jovan vividly captures a mind-set and lifestyle that accurately depicts the experience of many people who have been involved in such groups.

As a person intimately involved in Cha Ma's group for many years, I see myself reflected in every page of Maya's story. For me, Jovan's words have provided an unsettling yet invaluable opportunity to critically view beliefs that I had clung to for many years. As a part of this group, I thought of Cha Ma as my "mother" and accepted her actions and words unquestioningly. My relationship with her was fraught with intense fear and an insatiable desire for her approval. No matter how hard I tried, I never found myself to be good enough and struggled for many years with the desire to end my life.

As I read of Maya's struggles with these same issues and the spiritual forces at work behind her thoughts and actions, I become even more convinced that leaving that group was the right choice for me. Maya's story also confirms my belief that it was the effectual fervent prayer of faith-filled Christians that enabled me to do so.

I pray that these books will encourage those caught in this type of group to think critically and to listen to their doubts. I pray that these books will help to educate the Body of Christ regarding Hindu doctrine and practice and thus give them insight into how to pray regarding these issues. Maya's story is a powerful affirmation to all that Jesus is greater than any obstacle or circumstance we may face (no matter how seemingly insurmountable) and that there is no darkness so impenetrable that the radiant light of God cannot shine through.

—Former Western renunciate who lived in the
India ashram for 18 years and who
wishes to remain anonymous

Wow! Once again Jovan looks past the seen and into the realm of the spirit, bringing us on a journey that we know exists but have seldom seen. Though this book is called fiction, it is perhaps more real than most would admit. Delivering great insight into a battle that has raged since the beginning of time...a battle that is already won yet is waged around us daily, unseen...*Dancing With the Avatar* is a must-read.

—Joshua Goodman
The Pursuit Church
Fayetteville, NC

There is no doubt that we all could benefit from the book, *Dancing With the Avatar,* especially those who are in search of the "absolute truth." Jovan does not simply hand you the answer, but rather takes you on a journey where you have to struggle in order to come to grips with life's most important questions. This book has inspired me, and I am confident that it will inspire all who read it.

—Bishop Paul B. Keeter, Jr., D.Min.
Rivers of Living Water Church of God
Fayetteville, NC

CONTENTS

FOREWORD

It is true: sometimes fact is stranger than fiction!

The events recorded in this series are based on real experiences encountered by the author, Jovan Jones. Being personally acquainted with her and her family for a number of years has been both an honor and privilege. I recall some of the initial meetings with Jovan's mother and the things she shared in regard to her daughter's experiences in India and her search for truth. We spent time together praying, laughing, crying, and experiencing God's awesome love and power.

I remember meeting Jovan for the first time in person. She had recently returned to the States and was just coming out from under the wicked powers that had sought to destroy her. To witness the wonderful work of God's grace and truth throughout Jovan's journey is nothing short of phenomenal. Today she is a powerful witness and positive influence on countless lives. Her worship of God is pure; and her passion for the Kingdom is real.

No doubt, Jovan's life is a gripping spiritual journey that is worth being told and read. This book will change your life and perspective on spiritual influences of good and evil, darkness and light.

The first book in the Descent Series, *Chasing the Avatar,* was indeed a genuine page-turner! This second book is even more revealing and compelling. I highly recommend that you read, experience, and share it with others.

Pastor Emory Goodman
Cliffdale Christian Center
Fayetteville, NC

INTRODUCTION

Dear Reader,

Again, I meet with you in sharing my journey. Thank you for joining me. As with the first book, I think an Introduction is necessary.

I am excited about all of the people my first book has touched. Thank you for contacting me and sharing your stories through your wonderful emails and letters. It has been immensely affirming to hear from, and meet, people who were in the same ashram (some even at the same time) and can attest to the things I have written.

Although I call this series a work of fiction, it is based upon my life—a fictionalized autobiography. It is a true account, from my memory and from that of my parents, of what happened over the two-year period in which I lived in India and traveled throughout India and the United States with the guru. I would say that 90 percent of the events in this series are true. I have written this book from my memory and according to my own perceptions and interpretation. I mean no offense or harm to any person, and I have changed the names of the characters and the location of the places out of respect for the people and to protect their identities. I loved them then and I still do love them. I miss them even now. They were vibrant, colorful personalities, beautiful in their idiosyncrasies. If my story has any purpose, it is that I may see them in Heaven one day.

This series is my story, the only thing I can give God along with my life. It is for Jesus that I write—simply because He saved me when I was beyond being saved, loved me when I was wholly unlovable, and because He was then, and is now, my Everything.

I will continue to pray that as many people as possible are touched by this series. My sincerest desire is for people to see Christ as He truly is. Intensely alive. Vibrant and passionate. He knows us so intimately, loves us so dearly, and has plans for each and every one of us.

As with the first book, enjoy!

Jovan Jones

P.S. Please remember to consult the glossary in the back of the book. By the nature of the subject matter, this story is filled with unfamiliar terminology, and I trust that my explanations in the glossary will help you. The glossary also gives the pronunciation of the various foreign words and names as they are unfamiliar to most readers.

PROLOGUE

"She will be fine." Archangel Michael spoke even as he materialized in the air. "Speak into her mind. Bid her peace. And then come." He commanded four angels as he took a position in the air above the Indian Ocean, a mile from the shoreline of a peninsula on the southwestern coast of India. On the peninsula, lush, green palm trees stood a slight distance back from a beach dotted with huts on the tree line periphery. Palm trees dominated the peninsula and extended far into the mainland. A slight break in the trees, right near the coastline, revealed a compound, a grouping of pastel-colored buildings, a couple of which stood above the trees.

His words moved through the air faster than the speed of light to the angels to whom he spoke. The four—Majesty, Awe, Brilliant, and His Strength—were standing in a tight circle about a woman within this compound, who, though devotedly and ardently attended to by them, was clueless of their existence. They were glorious and magnificent, awesome to behold, if only the human eye could see. Sadly, woefully, hers were not equipped to gaze upon such a sight. Her heart was turned inward and what she saw inside was a particularly dismal reality.

At the moment, though seeing outwardly, her attention was fixed on her internal reality—pain and frustration, self-hatred and despair, depression. Tears streamed down her cheeks as she mumbled nonsense about jumping. She stood on the roof of one of the pastel-colored buildings, the temple. She stood at the very edge. Listing forward. It was evident in her body that she wanted to jump. How she longed to jump! She leaned forward until she hung at an impossible diagonal, sure to tumble off if it were not for an objection.

"No, Maya…" Brilliant murmured quietly, more a breath than a sound. Yet, to be so quiet, immense power flowed forth from his words and arrested her. He stood in the air before her—commanding and glorious. Relaxed in his power. Brilliant was awesome to behold…they all were. His skin, his eyes, even his hair, shimmered with an iridescent brilliance. His tunic and pants hinted at all the colors in the light spectrum as the colors danced amongst themselves as if alive. His right arm was stretched forward, pointer finger barely touching her chest. Such a light touch from Heaven was all that was needed to keep her from careening over. So instead, she hung there. Even as he kept her from tumbling over, he reached forward and tenderly stroked her cheek with his left hand—his hand engulfing her entire face. "Ah, loved of God," he sighed and whispered in the heavenly language, "if only you knew how much He adores you…"

Of the four who surrounded her, Brilliant had been with her from before her birth. He was her guardian. Even when she had only existed as an impression in the Heart and Mind of God, he had been with her. From the moment the Lord had conceived her in His infinite Heart and Mind, before the beginning of time, he, Brilliant, had known his purpose given to him by the Lord—to protect and care for her, to ensure that she fulfilled her destiny. Her purpose, her destiny, and who she was, woefully brief and all-too-human, was intricately intertwined with him, an angel, a being almost eternal and certainly otherworldly. Who he was—a protector, a guardian, who lived for almost an eternity—was so bound up in her, a momentary, fallible vessel, that it was impossible to separate who he was from his purpose in serving the Lord through her until the day she died and the Lord released him from his purpose in her and sent him to another, assigned to him also from before the beginning of time.

Another of the four, His Strength, stood to the right of Brilliant. He had been called upon to assist Brilliant in caring for her. He stepped forward and placed his hand on her head. He was so large…or she so small… that her entire head nestled in his palm. He ran his hand over her head and part way down her back, allowing it to rest at her shoulder blades. Strength, the nature of who he was, began to thrum through her.

His nature was his name—huge and massive, his muscles corded and released beneath his pristine, white tunic and pants. He maintained his unimaginably powerful frame in perfectly controlled abeyance. His was power in a state once removed from actualization, always on the cusp of manifestation. Power tenuously poised to be unleashed. His Strength could, and did, release that explosive power at a moment's notice, always…solely… at God's behest.

The other two, Majesty and Awe, completed the circle. Their swords were drawn, glinting silver and shooting off silvery-blue sparks from the skirmish in which they had just been engaged. Majesty and Awe looked around them. Nothing and no one—physical or spiritual—was about, aside from the four of them and the girl, Maya. Yet they knew the others… the evil ones…were nearby. Hiding. Far enough away not to be burned by the Lord's Presence that constantly surrounded His angels, yet close enough to resume their taunting of the girl as soon as an opportunity presented itself. And an opportunity would do just that.

Majesty was bigger and brighter than the other three. Everything about him bespoke authority and power. He was massive and majestic, kingly and commanding. The other, Awe, was no less vibrant and massive; however, he willingly, joyfully, submitted his power. In his own right, Awe was simply awe-inspiring. Even at rest, everything about him stirred and glimmered with light; and when he moved it was as if an ethereal light show had commenced—light sparked and fired about him.

Brilliant spoke, a melodic sound rolling from his mouth, "Sit"— in a language, in a realm, to which most humans were not privy. Maya, although she did not hear in the physical, heard in the spiritual realm and acted in the physical. Awkwardly, she stumbled backward and plopped down on the cement roof. Surely she would have fallen had His Strength not been behind her, his hand bracing her shoulders.

Brilliant spread his massive hand over her chest, stepped closer to her and spoke, "Peace." He blew into her face. Sparkling, glittering light flowed from his mouth and over her. As it touched her body, it flowed into her.

The tears that had been streaming from her eyes ceased in a rush of bewilderment, for she no longer understood why she was so upset. She closed her eyes in meditation as an unusual peace settled thickly, swiftly, about her.

Majesty nodded to the others. He and Awe sheathed their swords at once, as they, as a body, moved to Michael. In less than an instant, they were standing a mile from the peninsula, grinning at him. Majesty and Michael clasped in a bear hug.

"Majesty!" Michael barked, "Awe, Brilliant, His Strength! It's always so good to see you!" He clasped the others in bear hugs, too. At the display of brotherly camaraderie, light shot out in different directions.

Everything about Michael bespoke his status in the Lord. Archangel. All of the angels were named after the nature that God had placed within them, a nature that they could not contain. Who they were and, more importantly, Who they served emanated from them. Of course, all of the angels were large and glorious. However, with Michael, there was simply *more* of everything. He was gigantic without being cumbersome and bulky. He was beautiful without a hint of weakness. He emanated pure masculinity. His muscles were alive of their own volition—rippling and flexing whether at rest or in action. His skin was a bronze hue that shimmered with a golden glow. His golden butterscotch hair seemed woven with gold and bronze threads that sparkled and glimmered. His face evinced a wisdom garnered throughout the ages and nurtured by his constant attendance upon the Lord of the universe. Kindness and delight sparkled in his eyes. Ah! He was beauty and pure masculine power. Every aspect of him attested to his archangel status—clearly, God had outdone Himself in creating His archangels.

Maya opened her eyes. An awareness dawned upon her that she faced the ocean. (She had been so overwrought, she had not realized that she had been on the roof or that she had sat down facing the ocean. She definitely had not been cognizant of the fact that she had been standing on the edge of the roof, poised to jump off.) She felt so at peace. Such a deep sense of well-being permeated her being.

She stared with rapt attention at the lightning in the sky, overwhelmed by the beautiful...odd...sight. Golden white flashes arced in front of her, yet there was not a cloud in the sky. Nor was there thunder. Nothing that spoke of a thunderstorm. Adding to the magnificent sight, the ocean roiled fiercely beneath the light. (The presence of the Lord's angels stirred everything near them.) The glorious light show was reflected dazzlingly, flamboyantly, in the play of the waves.

"It must be you, Kali!" Maya murmured full of wonder. "How else is the water turbulent with no wind? How is there lightning with no clouds? Or thunder?" She alternated her gaze between staring at the sky and peering at the ocean. "Or light reflected like it is on the ocean without the moon present? How amazing is your display...Kali!" Little did she know it was the divine, living light that the Lord's angels emitted from their bodies that caused the celestial light show. It was the raw, uncontained power that they radiated—when not in the presence of humans, they did nothing to conceal their glorious light and power.

With Kali on her mind, she began to chant the mantra given to her by Cha Ma, "Omm..." Upon the power of the mantra, something dark and sinister stalked slowly up behind her.

"Majesty, Awe, Brilliant, His Strength. I believe you have served the Lord with Hachao, Salaa, and Bredano before?" Even as Michael spoke, three other angels materialized.

These three angels were slightly different from the others in nature and appearance. They were commanders of the warrior angels and fearsome to behold. Each was easily 15 feet tall and looked to be a quarter ton (if angels actually had mass). As they moved, their muscles rippled under their golden-bronze tunics. They seemed to be living entities in and of themselves, pulsating and moving of their own accord—a quality that was had by some of the Lord's angels, but was present in all the warrior angels. Their shoulder-length hair undulated and twisted as if there were a breeze, for even it was alive and eager for battle.

Michael spoke, "The Lord has called Hachao, Salaa, and Bredano to battle in the Maya situation—they will go back and forth between Maya and her parents, depending upon the Lord's wishes."

"Do they need to be briefed?" Majesty asked, nodding at the three in greeting.

"No," Michael replied, "I briefed them earlier."

"The Lord has been cultivating Maya's destiny," Hachao spoke up. His voice was melodic, like all of the angels'; however, it was deeper and sounded like a bow being expertly drawn across the strings of the bass. "She is willful and curious. Impetuous and brilliant. All gifts He placed in her when He fashioned her. She is also dissatisfied—which is Satan's doing. The Lord has granted him great freedom in her life, permitting him to influence her, allowing him to drive her to where she is. Satan believes that he has full control over her. He's confident he will ruin her and her parents and all of those attached to her."

"Yes," Michael nodded his head, his eyes grave, "the soul count…for Heaven or for hell. How important and how so many humans never think of it. Each and every soul is of incalculable value. Each person priceless, who at the end of his or her life will be either gifted with an eternity with the Lord in true love and joy or doomed to an eternity far from the Lord, far from all love and joy." Michael paused and sighed, his eyes looking pained, "So quickly they grow so acclimated to their human life that they truly cannot fathom eternity, let alone truly believe it exists. They cannot fathom being forever separated from the Lord, living in hatred, fear, pain, and destruction, perpetually straining for their hearts' desires and never attaining them, forever burning inside with discontent, hatred, unrest, fear, and depression, every negative emotion conceivable with no respite, ever. Such a fate is much worse than even the burning of the body that they imagine is so horrendous. Each one is precious and so, so valuable to the Lord…

"If only they knew that all the resources of Heaven are mobilized to draw them to the Lord…are mobilized to take them away from hell. And yet," Michael shook his head sadly, "so many choose being forever apart from God. Free will…ahhh, but I digress. Continue, Hachao…"

"From what we understand," Hachao said, "this girl…woman… Maya, has no clue the battle that is around her. She has been gifted with so much from the Lord—internal attributes and external successes—all enticements by Satan to draw her away. And he has. There she was at Harvard, standing upon a pinnacle of success for most any human, when he dropped his lure before her face."

Salaa picked up, "Satan knew she could not resist. Of course, the Lord knew she could not resist. Given her nature, given all that she has been seeking and wanting, the discontent and unrest, Cha Ma was the perfect lure."

Bredano nodded, "Humans are always searching for something to worship and always so eager to worship another human. It's a wonder how so many humans are undeniably drawn to charismatic people; throw in some supernatural powers, and they can't resist. They begin to see that person as a god…Basically, that is what happened with Maya and Cha Ma."

Brilliant interjected, "So, she left everything behind and ran to India to be with Cha Ma. Although she tried, although all humans try, she couldn't leave herself behind—her pain, hurt, and struggles. They have followed her here."

"The demons have latched onto her pain," Awe paused, shaking his head slowly, which caused fiery sparks of light to shoot forth. "It did not help that she took a Kali mantra. Oh why, oh why did she do that?"

Brilliant chuckled, unexpectedly, "Leave it to Maya to go for the spiritual atomic bomb, to take a mantra of Chamunda Kali. The girl has no idea what she's taken within herself and is activating by repeating it so often. If only she knew…"

His Strength interrupted, "There she is now…" He nodded toward the set of buildings. "Chamunda Kali."

On the temple roof where Maya sat paced a macabre specter behind her. Perniciousness rolled out from it in waves. It was tall and gaunt and appeared vaguely feminine. Its skin was jet-black and hung as if from bones. They could see that she had her hungry, baleful eyes fixed on the girl, Maya. Every once in a while, those eyes would dart their way and then back to the girl. She…it…could not gaze upon the Lord's angels for long—the Lord's Presence surrounding them burned her, it burned all of the evil ones. They could hear her low, eerie growl of consuming desire. She was ravenous for the girl, but had every intention of toying with her before she killed her. All negative emotions—fear, despair, depression, hatred—fed her almost as well as death did.

"Chamunda is the head of one of the world's principalities…the cult of Kali," Bredano said, even as he kept his eyes trained on Chamunda. Something began to change in him and in his appearance as he looked upon the adversary the Lord had commanded him to confront. It was as though his body, his muscles, his skin, his hair, every part of his being began to gear up for battle. The same began to occur with Hachao and Salaa—their bodies automatically began *revving up* for battle. Clearly, they were created solely for warfare against Satan's minions.

Michael looked Hachao, Salaa, and Bredano over and chuckled, humor in his eyes, "Easy now! Our time will come. But first, we must allow everything to fall perfectly into place."

As one, Hachao, Salaa, and Bredano looked up into the sky…at the Lord, for they could see Him in the heavens. No matter where one was in Heaven, earth, or below, one could see the Lord—sitting exalted and glorious upon His throne…if, only if, one had eyes to see. As one, they took a deep breath, held it for a long moment, and exhaled. Upon the exhalation, they powered down and went to rest, even though their muscles continued to flex and release and their hair waved with subdued vigor. Even powered down, they were in a state of readiness for battle.

"For centuries, Chamunda Kali has held this area virtually unchallenged," Michael spoke. "Granted, there have been pockets of those who've loved the Lord, but they've never dented her supremacy here. Now is the time for this principality to sustain a real blow. The Lord will destroy this ashram, this temple to Cha Ma," Michael indicated the cluster of buildings, "who we all know is simply controlled…possessed…by Chamunda Kali. He will destroy her hold over many people. He will certainly destroy her hold over Maya and will wrap it all up rather neatly. As He always does."

"Ahh, there are the others…" Brilliance said as they all watched what unfolded on the roof of the temple.

At the prompting of Chamunda, several demons approached Maya. Their natures were distorted by millennia separated from God. It was almost impossible to conceive that, once upon a time, they had been as glorious and lovely as the Lord's angels who stood a mile away from them. They were rendered all the more hideous and ghastly because they understood the reality of being forever separated from the Lord, separated from the One who was the source of all that was good and lovely and noble. Their natures disturbed the atmosphere—it was akin to supernatural fingernails sliding down a chalkboard.

They were deformed and perverted. Despair, shrunken and folded in upon himself, was of an ashy, dull brown hue. Depression, being the opportunist that he was, moved in close and wrapped his putrid arms around Maya. Fear slunk about in the background, fearful, as was his nature. All were bent on feeding off of the girl. Any negative emotion—fear, depression, despair, self-hatred—was powerful food for them.

Finally, Suicide and Death approached. Because their natures were to destroy the human vessel and feed off their kills, they were larger than the others. Death, in his "natural" form, which was still vastly perverted from what the Lord had created, looked similar to a rhinoceros beetle—jet-black with a shiny exoskeleton. Two growths protruded from the top of his head. However, he had the ability, like Satan and some of the more powerful evil angels, to morph into a human form. This "talent" was a vestigial quality from when they were angels of the Lord, before the Rebellion.

Even as the evil ones crept close to the girl, they kept glancing at the Lord's angels a mile away. The Presence of the Lord burned them. None of the lesser demons and imps dared show themselves. In fact, they were simply unable.

After ensuring that the evil ones were only going to taunt Maya and not try to infringe upon the boundaries set by the Lord (at this time, for they violated the boundaries often enough, spiritual opportunists that they were), Brilliant turned to Michael and queried, "How are her parents?"

Michael smiled, "They are doing very well, although they probably don't feel as if they are. They are going through their testing and it is looking dark for them. Yet, they will stand strong. Mighty, Paul's guardian, and Jovial, Marie's guardian, are with them. The Lord has decreed the end from the beginning and all will be fine. All *is* fine. They must battle through and continue to pray for Maya.

"Marie's health is declining due to the effects of Sickness, Illness, and Disease. Doctors believe the debilitating headaches, the spots and webbing, and the loss of vision are due to a brain tumor and have given her two to six months left to live. We know what the truth is. It is Satan's plan to keep her so preoccupied with her own troubles that she will not spend time in prayer for Maya.

"The relationship between her and Paul is under attack, of course. For a house divided cannot stand. Satan knows this well and is trying to use it to his advantage. The enemy will continue to attack the bond between them because there is much power when they are in agreement and pray together. Definitely enough power to make sure Maya makes it home safe and sound."

"One can put a thousand angels to flight and two can put ten thousand," Brilliant agreed. "Humans really don't realize just how much power is mobilized when they pray, do they?" he asked, his question purely rhetorical. "They can't see that upon their prayers we move. They can't see that there are more of us than of them and that we are destined to win— with due prayer. I believe that if they were to truly know and *understand,* they'd pray much more." He stopped speaking, while the eight angels stood in the air watching the drama unfold upon the temple roof, a drama that revolved around the lone human girl who was oblivious to it all.

Depression sat on one side of Maya. Despair on the other. Each whispered into her ear. Their words wove their way into her and met the living Kali mantra that roiled inside of her. As they spoke, the peace that had settled heavily about her, dissipated.

Chamunda Kali whipped about in her pacing, "No! We need Delusion. After *them,*" she...it...cast a malevolent eye at the Lord's angels, "she needs to be reminded..."

Even as she spoke, Delusion slipped near.

"We need to remind her of why she's here, Delusion," Chamunda cackled as her skin darkened to a rancid blue-black. "We need to draw her in deeper..."

Delusion slumped down behind Maya and placed his hands (if they could be called hands considering how gnarly and misshapen they were) on her head. He growled suggestions at her, which in her weakened mental state, caused her to think the thoughts he desired for her.

Maya's mind slipped to when she first met Cha Ma and how she had been blown away. She had known...simply *known*...that Cha Ma was an avatar, one of those rare instances when a god or goddess took a human form in order to come to earth to help humanity, and as such, would lead her to enlightenment. Cha Ma would get her out of the reincarnation cycle once and for all.

Delusion continued, hissing into her ear, "Cha Ma is Kali. An avatar. She is your god." Maya thought the thoughts exactly as Delusion fed them to her—she was such a willing, open vessel—*Cha Ma is Kali. THAT I know. She is an avatar of Kali.* She felt a thrill of *something* chase down her spine. *It still blows me away to think that I live with an avatar!*

Maya recalled how in three weeks time, she had taken a leave of absence from Harvard and had run off to India to live in Cha Ma's ashram. She thought of her time at the ashram, how easy it had been to fit in with the hundreds of other devotees of Cha Ma who lived there. She thought of her newfound friends and acquaintances, some of whom were interested in enlightenment and others who were more interested in everything but—Radha, Sandi, Karuna, Alice, Anneshwari, Rukmini...Narayana. One thought of him flooded Maya with a rash of conflicting emotions—anger, fascination, hurt, obsession, resentment, desire.

Leading her mind on a string, Delusion rasped at her, "Heh heh... Narayana will *never* like you, you silly girl. He is so close to Cha Ma. He is so high and you are...nothing!" Quickly, Maya snatched her mind away from the painful thoughts of Narayana—*he doesn't like me. He is so close to Cha Ma and I am nothing.*

She thought of how she had had pot washing duty for a time—how hard and tedious it had been—*night after night scrubbing mountains of pots with ash and a coconut hull in that nasty, nasty kitchen*—and had graduated to cooking in the kitchen. Thinking of the kitchen caused her to recall the scathing tongue-lashing she had received from Cha Ma. *I deserved it. I'm blessed that I got it. I know it burned off so much karma*—Maya reassured herself.

She remembered how she had run to the roof of the temple after that excoriating scolding and had tried to jump off, but simply could not. *I am such a coward! If only I really wanted it...* She thought of the many nights (almost every night) that she found herself standing on the edge of the temple roof wanting to jump, but lacking the courage.

"You lack courage," Delusion muttered into her ear. "If you had courage...if you truly wanted enlightenment, you would have jumped by now. But every night you lose courage. You don't want it enough. You are weak and useless."

Maya sighed heavily, "I just don't want it enough. I am weak and useless..." As she thought about her frustration, her cowardice, her weakness and uselessness, despair and depression began to overwhelm her. The lump in her throat that had begun to dissolve in the presence of the Lord's angels came back. She felt hot tears sting her eyes. She sighed, deeply... heavily...and resumed her Kali mantra. "Omm..."

Fueled by the chanting, the insidious evil that had been planted in her by the mantra continued to grow. Feeling it burn vaguely in her belly, she stared at the glorious lightning that illuminated the sky. "Ahhh, Kali! What a show you're giving..."

MAGGOT-WORMS

Maya, or "Premabhakti"
India

I t was late afternoon when I found myself outside of the kitchen under the makeshift thatch awning idly stirring a pot of soup over an open fire. *It's been several weeks now—although it feels like just a few days—who would've thought that I would be spending so many hours a day in the kitchen cooking meals for the Westerners? And that I'd be one of only three Westerners allowed in the kitchen to cook... working alongside Brahmacharini Sita and Dirk. What two strange people to work with!*

My mind conjured up Bri. Sita and Dirk as I sat down on my favorite rock, gathering my navy blue work skirt, which hid stains so well, between my legs. I fanned myself with my white-turned-gray cotton shirt that was heavily mucked with soot, dirt, and everything-else grime.

Sita was one of the few Westerners granted the high honor of sannyasi. She was tall, rail-thin, and austere-looking with her brown hair pulled back into a painfully severe bun. She was fastidious and unreasonably orderly. Her yellow sari, which denoted her high rank, was perpetually wrinkle-free and appeared freshly ironed at all times. I could never understand how it remained so in the middle of hot, humid Southern India, when most everyone else went about looking wilted and crumply. When she smiled, it never reached her eyes. It looked fakey and hard; and she did nothing to disguise it. She did not seem to have a heart for anyone...Cha Ma included.

And then, there was tall, thin, bald Dirk, who was German and acted very much like a German. He had been at the ashram for over 11 years and knew everything about everything. He was a source of ashram information and could be great fun, if you were prepared for his searingly caustic sarcasm. Sometimes it was hard to distinguish between when he was serious and when he was playing. He always kept me a little *too* off-balance.

Granted I like sitting and shooting the breeze with Dirk...every once in a while, but...I don't enjoy his presence and company enough to work with him every day. And then...Bri. Sita. I sighed. *I simply don't like her at all. Something about her makes me uncomfortable. Deep in my bones I feel like she's "shifty."*

*Focus, Premabhakti...your Kali mantra...*I chided myself using the name Cha Ma had given me. I liked the sound of it a lot and I liked the meaning of it even more. *Prema* meant "divine" and *bhakti* meant "love." Divine Love. I could not believe that Cha Ma had named me "Divine Love." I probably meditated more on my Cha Ma name than I did on my Kali mantra. Cha Ma had given me the name when she had given me the mantra. The mantra frightened me a bit; I supposed that was because it was a Kali mantra and I had heard the mind-boggling tales of the devastating things that had happened to the people who took Kali mantras. Also, truth be told, it frightened me because it seemed to be a driving, overwhelming force with a will all its own. It felt like a living, breathing, *uncontrollable* thing. However, for all my fear, I was desperate to reach enlightenment as quickly as possible. If that meant I had to have a dangerously destructive Kali mantra, then so be it!

Keep chanting your mantra over the food...put the essence of Kali into it—I reminded myself again.

Being outside of the kitchen where the large fire pits for cooking were, all by myself (for all intents and purposes—as the brahmacharinis who cooked for the Indian canteen barely talked to me) should have made it easy; but it did not. My mind constantly wandered. I had to keep reminding myself to remember to chant. It did seem that the more I chanted the more the Westerners liked the "soup."

I was outside where a couple of the Indian girls were making rice for the Indian meal. I ignored them as I walked past. I did not know their names. Most of the brahmacharinis, the ones in white, remained anonymous as they kept to themselves and stayed in a close, indistinguishable group. It was hard to separate one from the other, and then to put a name and personality on any one of them? Next to impossible! There were only a couple I knew by name, but that was because they had stepped out of the larger mass and had distinguished themselves as individuals.

It was hot, very hot. I could feel the sweat dripping down my back, down my legs, and pooling in my cheap, plastic chappels. I could even feel it running down my arms. The heat from the three open fires did not help. The Indian girls were boiling rice in two humongous, blackened pots, and I was using another smaller, cauldron-like pot to cook the soup. The thatch awning over us was trapping the heat from both the day and the open flames—causing the air to be stiflingly oppressive, verging on unbearable.

Of course, my clothing did not help. I was not wearing the usual Indian female garb of either a sari or punjabi. I was wearing my favorite work skirt—a long, heavy-materialed, midnight-blue one that reached to my ankles and had to be tucked into my waist band to keep me from stepping on the hem—and a simple white (used to be white) top. Both of the pieces were indelibly stained with soot, grease, and dirt. The blue skirt hid the stains well; but the white shirt did not. These were my "working" clothes; I wore them for cooking, pot washing, toilet cleaning, temple sweeping, dirt hauling—you name it, they had "seen" it.

Today, I was making a lentil "soup." Usually, the "soup" I made for the Westerners was not soup so much as it was a thick, hearty, vegetable- and bean-laden gruel or stew. I made it with a base of pumpkin that when boiled down was like a puree. Pumpkin was great for thickening the soups as it had a full flavor and a nice, pea-soup consistency once boiled down.

I eyed the brownish-green "soup" that was boiling away happily as I stirred it. My thoughts turned to the difficulty of cooking in an ashram kitchen in the middle of Southern India. The greatest difficulty was bugs. I thought back to the first time I had encountered bugs in the food that I was prepping for dinner. I had wanted to throw away all the vegetables and beans that had bugs in them. Bri. Sita had stopped me short, speaking in a crisp, punctuated way, "We...*do*...*not*...*waste*...food here." I took note of Bri. Sita's words but not too much, as I did not like her enough to obey her.

Infinitely more "persuasive" than Sita was my confrontation with Cha Ma over some wasted, rotten tomatoes, which had come after Sita's sharp warning. The mere memory of the "dressing down" still stung my heart and mind. *Oh! If only I had listened to Bri. Sita!* I *never* wanted to cross Cha Ma like that again—she had frightened me beyond words.

After that time, I set about learning the rules of the kitchen concerning spoiled food and bugs. First: spoilage. If it was rotten through and through, we could throw it out. But that was in *extreme* cases when the vegetable was completely white or black from mold or rot. If there was a little bit of rot or mold, we could either cut it off or we could just boil all of it (including the rotten, moldy part) really well, until the germs were cooked off and the spoiled parts were indistinguishable from the good. Second: bugs. Nobody else knew, with the exception of Sita, Dirk, and the Indian girls who had to cook, that the beans and rice were full of little, black bugs that resembled fleas. The rule was to rinse and wash away as many of the pesky, little critters as possible and ignore the rest—because try as we might, we would never get rid of them all.

However, bugs in the vegetables demanded much more ingenuity. I had devised a special trick, of necessity, as I dared not throw away too much: take some onions, garlic, and some leafy spices and fry them with the buggy parts.

The onions and garlic went directly against Hindu beliefs. Early on in my Hindu walk—when I used to hang out with Manjula in her kitchen—I had learned the Hindu "food system."

Manjula had introduced me to Hinduism. You could say that it was because of her that I had met Cha Ma. I remembered Manjula so well—her long dreadlocks (so long that she could sit on them), how she could sit for hours in meditation, her vast well of knowledge about things esoteric. It was she who had taught me so much about Hinduism.

One of the first things she had taught me was the Hindu food system (probably because I spent so much time in her kitchen). The food system consisted of a hierarchy of foods and the "energies" that they emitted. It had three levels: sattvic, rajasic, and tamasic. Staunch Hindus would eat only sattvic food as it was considered of the highest vibration. Sattvic food was believed to influence people to be calm, focused, controlled, able to meditate, and inclined to a higher spirituality. Sattvic foods included milk and milk products, nuts, potatoes, carrots, raisins, and certain other foods. Hindus would eat the "second" tier of food (which was of a "lower vibration") but in limited amounts. This type of food was called rajasic. They believed that rajasic food influenced people to be excessively energetic, easily angered and upset, overly passionate, and attached to things of this passing, illusory world. Rajasic foods included tomatoes and spicy and hot food. As for tamasic food, Hindus avoided it altogether or tried to. Tamasic food was considered the "lowest" tier. Such food caused the eater to be slow, dull, lazy, completely disinclined toward anything spiritual, and drawn to negative thoughts and activities, at times even verging on violence. Tamasic foods included onions, garlic, and meat.

After I had received my excoriating chastisement from Cha Ma and thoroughly understood that I would be unable to throw away any food (no matter the bugs or the rot) but would have to cook it, I set about devising a method to disguise them, especially the bugs.

The best way was to fry…or sauté (however you wanted to say it)…the bugs. I would take one of the big frying skillets (which looked like a humongous wok with a blackened, oily-crusty underside) to the stone stove in the fry kitchen and melt some ghee. I would brown my spices (mustard seed, cumin, coriander, and a large helping of leafy spices—something that would, once sautéed, be indistinguishable from the bugs). Then I would throw in the onions and garlic. It was easy when the bugs were in the beans or peas, like chickpeas, because they tended to be little brownish-black things that, once combined with the browned spices, were indistinguishable. But, "pests" were harder to disguise in other things, say…eggplant.

I remember the first time I encountered Indian eggplants. They were miniature versions of the Italian eggplant—about four inches long and three inches in diameter. Really cute little vegetables. So cute that I did not want to cut them. But I had to, so I sliced one right down the middle. And there…*YUCK!*…writhing in the center was a handful of little white maggots. The wee critters were not more than an inch long, thinner ("skinnier") than any maggots I had ever seen. Someone had once remarked that the things were mealy worms. I had always believed mealy worms to be in flour and meal; and the ones I had seen, in the past, were never moving. These were different. These were moving. Vigorously moving. In the center of the vegetable, at that! Anyhow, mealy worms…skinny maggots… the name did not matter. They were gross! Disgusting! How they made it into the inside of the vegetable I could never tell—of all the times I encountered them, I never saw an entry hole in the vegetable. Not once. *Were they there from the beginning? Did the plant grow around the worms? (Yeah, stupid question, I know!)*

As I grabbed each eggplant and sliced through it, I found maggot-worm after maggot-worm—in *every single eggplant!* I knew I could not throw them away because I would have had to throw away the whole lot of them and *Cha Ma was not having that!* It was impossible to cut out the maggoty part because that left practically nothing of the vegetable. So instead, I had the kitchen cutters (those who had the stomach for it and did not rebel) cut the eggplants into little one inch, or less, cubes. Once I had browned all the spices, onions, and garlic, I took the eggplants—maggot-worms and all—and threw them into the frying skillet. With enough high-heat sautéing, the eggplant chunks cooked down into mushy, brown lumps and the maggot-worms shriveled up and cooked to a dark brown color. They looked exactly like the rest of the spices. When I was done with them, there was no way to tell the maggot-worms apart from the other spices.

Today had been one of those days—not a "maggot-worm" day—but a "little black bug" day. The diminutive, black, flea-like critters were in the lentils—some were crawling around and some appeared dead, as they were not moving. True to my newfound method of disguising the critters, I fried up a bunch of spices, garlic, and onions in a couple tablespoons of ghee. Sure, the garlic and onions made the food very "tamasic"; but the Westerners liked the food so much more when I spiced it heavily and used garlic and onions. Further, *What they don't know won't hurt them,* I rationalized. What I knew for certain was that I did not want to cross Cha Ma. I would rather deal with a couple hundred angry people who ate sautéed flea-like critters than one irate Kali avatar.

As I sat outside, stirring the sooty, black-bottomed kettle that sat upon a low circle of stones, I got up periodically in order to stoke the fire by adding dry, coconut tree branches. The branches, firewood, and kindling were stockpiled in a little lean-to just off the kitchen, a couple of feet away from the fire pits—*very convenient for the cooks, but talk about a fire hazard!* Sometimes the branches were not fully dry and then the fire would smoke heavily. Luckily, today was not one of those days. The fire burned easily, and the soup boiled vigorously. I kept an eye on it, sitting for over an hour, chanting my Kali mantra, and occasionally stirring the pot. Slowly the fire died down. The "soup" was ready. With a final glance before I headed into evening bhajans, I noted with satisfaction that it was impossible to tell that there was a bunch of dead bugs in the soup.

SAND SEVA

It's getting chillier now. I thought on the subtle change in the weather as I walked down the inside stairs of the ashram. I clutched my shawl about me trying to stave off the chill. The weather was definitely growing cooler. The seasons were changing, although just a little. It was not noticeable during the day. No, the days were as hot as ever. However, late at night—like tonight—the temperature had dropped enough that I had to wear a shawl.

It was late, very late—two in the morning—to be exact. I had been meditating on my favorite deck, which was a little 7 by 12-foot platform that sat over 12 feet above the regular meditation roof. (It was the highest place in the ashram.) A couple of people had started out the night watch with me, but by the time I came to, no one was there. I was not too certain why I wanted to walk over to the canteen; but I figured I would peruse the deserted ashram grounds one time before I went to sleep. I liked how the ashram was so peaceful and still in the wee hours of the morning when everyone else was sleeping.

As I came down the front stairs of the temple, I heard, "Cha Ma says that we are to do sand seva." I turned to my right and saw one the brahmacharinis. No one else was around. Clearly, she was talking to me, informing me of this unbeknownst-to-me duty. She had her little white sari hiked up to her knees. I had never ever…*never ever*…seen a brahmacharini expose more than an inch of ankle, and here was one with her entire calf showing. No! Make that two calves and her knees! Whatever they were doing I wanted to see—I *had* to see whatever it was that could get a brahmacharini to hike up her skirt to her knees!

"What is sand seva?" I asked as I observed another brahmacharini walking by. This one walked in the opposite direction of the one who first spoke to me. Like her counterpart, she too had her sari (obviously her work sari as it was a tie-dyed pattern indigenous to Kerala) hiked up to her knees. This calf-showing, tie-dyed brahmacharini was carrying an overfull plastic burlap bag—*I have never seen* plastic *burlap bags, rather oxymoronic if you ask me*—on her shoulder. The weight of it bowed her shoulders and back forward. She struggled under the weight, her legs staggering weakly for footing.

"Come! Follow me. We go!" commanded the first brahmacharini as she headed off toward the front entrance of the ashram.

I walked behind her. She moved slowly enough—that languid, graceful walk of most of the brahmacharinis (the brahmacharis, too, for that matter). It was a beautiful, leisurely walk. However, underneath it was the slow gait of a malnourished, underfed body—one that cannot hustle too much, one that must conserve energy at all times.

We walked through the front entrance and crossed over the little dirt road that passed right in front of the ashram. On the other side was a small clearing. Indians were all over the place. Westerners were, too. It was hard to believe it was two in the morning—so many people were about. *Where have I been to have missed this?!*

Outdoor lights were rigged at random places, shedding minimal light here and there. I could hear a generator running somewhere in the background—*I'm sure that's to power the lights.* Right at the entrance and along the road, many of the brahmacharis, as well as a couple of the swamis, stood lounging, talking, and watching the goings-on. Beyond the entrance, in the clearing, a large group of brahmacharinis was shoveling dirt, heaving it into burlap bags, and carrying it away. In the midst of that group was Cha Ma, barking orders in Malayalam as she, too, vigorously shoveled.

Hovering near Cha Ma were, of course, Rukmini, Anneshwari, and Alice. On one side of Cha Ma, Rukmini worked. Towering over all the women at 6' 3", I could not help but notice her first. Her dirty, white men's pants and shirt were too small for her thin, Amazonian body— but what could she do? She was simply too tall. Her wheat blond hair was pulled back in a bedraggled ponytail that only served to accentuate the harsh gauntness of her pale face. She shoveled away like a mad man, doing the work of several people.

On the other side of Cha Ma stood Anneshwari holding a shovel, but not doing anything. *It's hard to do much work when you're constantly staring at Cha Ma.* She was gazing at Cha Ma, with that adoringly idiotic smile upon her face. She was wearing a pale pink punjabi that was stretched a little too snugly over her short, pudgy body.

Behind Cha Ma hunched Alice. *Why is she hunching over? Hiding? Probably…* No surprise that she was not holding a shovel—she avoided work like it was a disease; instead, she paid close attention to what everyone else was doing. I was sure she remained so close to Cha Ma because Cha Ma was the center of ashram activity and Alice loved to be "in the know." As she stood there gazing about, she shoved peanuts into her mouth. She reminded me of a chipmunk—her overbite more pronounced because of the way she was chewing. She was wearing her usual crumpled and stained sari—*Does she even own more than one?* She was oblivious to everything but peanuts and gossip…and Cha Ma, but merely because she was the source of gossip.

As I stood there purveying the chaotic scene, one of the brahmacharinis, clearly exhausted from overworking, pushed her shovel into my hands and thrust one of the plastic burlap bags at me. The Indian shovels were unusual. They were shaped like "reverse shovels" with the "scooper" facing backward, so that in order to use it, I had to—we all had to—swing downward and stab into the ground and then pull toward ourselves to loosen and scoop up the dirt.

I joined a group of Western women who were shoveling away. Cha Ma continued to bark orders at us. The ground was tough as the dirt was dry and hard-packed. It was backbreaking work. Within a couple of minutes, sweat began to pour down my face and body. The night was not cool enough to counteract the intensity of the effort.

As I swung my hooked shovel into the earth, I queried, "So, what exactly are we doing?"

I paused to tuck up some of the fabric of my sari into my waistband, which would allow my legs room to move and some ventilation. I did not care overly much that my calves were showing. *The perks of being a Westerner! I don't have to mind convention. And hey! The brahmacharinis have their skirts hiked up, too!* It was true—almost all the brahmacharinis had their skirts hiked up to show ankles and calves. Something that under normal circumstances would have been impermissible; however, the demands of the work seemed to allow for greater freedom for the brahmacharinis.

"We're digging up the ground for the foundation of one of the new buildings," Radha answered as she dumped the dirt she had scooped up in her shovel into a plastic burlap bag. She rubbed her hands on her crumpled, dirty sari. She wore a Keralan sari—white with a sky blue, striped pattern around the bottom of it. It was her work sari. She pushed errant pieces of brown hair that had straggled out of the bun on the nape of her neck away from her face, leaving dirt smudges on her forehead. As always, her shiny blue eyes twinkled with some hidden giggle. In the months that I had known her, I had yet to see her truly sad or downcast.

"Uh, aren't there machines for this?" Chandy quipped, her Australian accent making her question sound like a song. Her long, brown hair was slipping from its ponytail. Her brown eyes turned up at the corners as if she were anticipating a hilarious punch line, which—knowing her—she was.

"Maybe...but not here. We do a lot of the work," Radha replied with a knowing smile.

"So, what do we do with the dirt once it's in the bag?" I asked as I clumsily tried to imitate Radha in dumping the dirt from my shovel into my burlap bag. Clumps of dirt slid to the ground. *Oh well...*

"We'll take it to the other side of the ashram and dump it into the backwaters. There's a section in the back that we're filling in. I'll take you there when you're done filling up your bag."

"OK," I grunted as I swung the shovel over my head. It was heavier than it looked. *How in the world do the little brahmacharinis do it?* It really was a mystery—they were so delicate and fragile-looking. *They must have muscles of iron. That figures! On top of being gorgeous, they're also unbelievably strong.*

For the next few minutes, our group of Western women swung in silence—the *whump-whump* of the shovels gouging the earth mingled with Cha Ma's bellowing voice. In no time at all, my back began to ache from being hunched over swinging.

"Why aren't any of the Indian men helping?" one of the Western women questioned, swinging mightily over her head with the shovel.

Devi laughed, her big, poofy ball of kinky-curly hair bobbing on the crown of her head. *It's crazy that she's one of the few white women I know with black folk hair!* She gave me a humorous elbow, "Indian men don't do this kind of work. Didn't you know that? Only women work. Especially here."

The Western women who were working with us laughed, nodding their heads in agreement. I could not believe that so many able-bodied Western women attested to this fact; yet no one protested or complained. We, like the Indian women, shoveled and carried all the dirt while the Indian men stood around watching. The Western men seemed torn—some worked, some watched, some did both (alternating between uncomfortably watching and frenetically working, as if driven by their guilt).

"I like doing the work," Sandi announced, her big, hazel eyes wide with excitement as she put her "big-boned" body into her swing. With each swing, her strawberry-blond hair fell farther out of its ponytail. *She's probably the only person really enjoying this!* She looked a little too happy to be working so hard while others (*all* the Indian men and some of the Western ones) did not.

Good-naturedly, Radha and Devi rolled their eyes at her, while Chandy snorted back a giggle.

After more long minutes of backbreaking swinging, Karuna nudged me. Her blue eyes sparkled with a joke. Her short, light brown hair had started to stick to her head from the heat, humidity, and the exertion. Her face had turned red as well. But, for all the redness and sweaty-head hair, she was still cute as a button. "Premabhakti, look!" she said with a slight, almost imperceptible, tip of her head.

I looked to where she was indicating and saw Narayana standing on the perimeter with Swami. *What a picture of contrasts and similarities!* Swami and Narayana stood at about the same height, both a couple of inches over six feet tall for Indian men—one very chubby, bordering on fat and the other slim. The poor lighting only accented their extravagant good looks—Swami with his long, wavy, dark-brown hair and almond-shaped eyes and Narayana with his slightly curly hair that hung just below his neck, his aristocratic features, and long, straight nose that sat just below large, expressive eyes. *Gorgeous men!* The two of them were laughing it up, more than likely, over some joke between them. Narayana seemed to have a great sense of humor around the brahmacharis...*and around Radha. I wonder...maybe he likes her...*

"Oh yeah, Narayana! I knew he was standing there. He was there when I got here," I mumbled as I kept shoveling, trying really hard to sound indifferent.

"He is so cute!" cooed Chandy, her Australian accent making his cuteness sound all the cuter. *I want an accent like that!*

"No, not cute! He's beautiful!" Karuna countered, her Australian accent heavy and lilting.

"And obnoxious!" Devi interjected to the snorts and chortles of the women in the group. By now, almost every woman in our group was

44

looking unashamedly at him—with the exception of me. I laughed with them but I refused to look at him.

"Obnoxious or not…I would put up with it for him. He is sooo beautiful!" Chandy gushed. We all burst out into peals of laughter again. Mine a little more fake than the others, I had to admit.

As soon as I had filled my bag, Radha, who must have been watching my progress, said, "C'mon, I'll show you where we dump the dirt." She smoothly threw her bag over her shoulder and headed toward the entrance. Trying to copy her, I flipped my bag onto my shoulder (with some effort) and followed. I kept my eyes down so that I would not look at Narayana. I was afraid that if I looked up, he might catch my eye and see… *I don't want him to see my feelings for him—not that he cares!* I walked past him uneventfully and hurried to catch up with Radha.

In silence, we walked through the wide front entrance of the ashram grounds and across the dark front yard. We skirted around the right corner of the temple building and followed its length. The dimly-illuminated temple cast weak light phantoms across our path—barely enough to see our way and not stumble. Once past the temple, we cut across the large, back lot and walked past the brahmachari huts in the back. All was dark here. Farther still, we picked our way through a grove of coconut trees behind the huts. *How come I never noticed this before?* I was surprised by the large area that was a part of the ashram but heretofore had been wholly unobserved by me.

Several yards into the grove, we came to a marshy, sticky mud area. The ground grew softer and softer under our feet until I noticed we were standing on the edge of a bog or swamp. I could not tell how deep the water was.

"We dump the dirt here," Radha instructed, finally breaking the silence. I laboriously swung the burlap sack from over my shoulder and dumped its contents into the water. She did the same. We walked back in silence dragging our empty bags along the ground.

On the way, we encountered a couple of brahmacharinis bearing full burlap bags on their shoulders. Their shoulders bowed, heads down. No one said anything. In the distance, I could hear Cha Ma yelling instructions. We walked through the entrance and into the dimly lit work area. Chandy and Devi walked past us carrying full bags on their shoulders. Of course, I noted that Narayana was still where he had been when we had headed off, only now his group had grown to include not only Swami, but also Swami Shivaramananda (who looked like an Indian Santa Claus with his pleasant face, pursed lips, wire-rimmed glasses, and his tall, almost fat stockiness) and several of the brahmacharis in white. They all stood in a cluster, swinging the bottoms of their dhotis as if to air themselves. *It isn't like they're working hard and need to cool off*, I thought somewhat resentfully. *Remember...this is India, not America. This is India...*

I picked up a shovel and recommenced swinging. It was easy to get into a rhythm. As we worked, we chatted. Time flew by. Whether I was busy stabbing at the dirt or lugging it on my back, I put all my focus into the task at hand—anything to avoid looking at Narayana—not that he was the only sight. It just seemed that my eyes had a volition all their own and, much to my chagrin, tended to find themselves straying toward him. I finally got enough of a hold on myself to keep my eyes looking downward instead of at him. *Kali! I'm not going to let him see me looking at him! I'm not going to let anyone see me looking at him—that's all I need!*

"Pssst! Prema...look!" Karuna whispered as she elbowed me.

"What's up...?" I asked distractedly. All the shoveling and dumping and walking and working was pushing me beyond tired...I was tumbling headlong into the realm of exhaustion.

"It's Narayana..."

"Yeah, OK...he's been there," I shot back, irritated—whether from her watching him so closely or from something else, I could not fathom.

"No! You don't understand," Karuna said as she hoisted a full bag onto her shoulder. "He's been watching you. Just look! Give it some time, you'll see! Look without being obvious about it." She headed off toward the dump pile on the other side of the ashram.

As I continued to stab at the earth, I kept my head down as if busily at work and peeked at Narayana through my lowered lashes. My heart skipped. He was looking at me! No, watching me! Obviously, he was not aware that I was watching him watching me. I was so embarrassed. I kept my eyes averted and continued digging.

I thought of our previous interactions—unpredictable, random, and contradictory. Every single time, he disconcerted me awfully. If we happened to lock eyes, which had occurred a couple of times, I was thrown off...dreadfully thrown off. My heart would pound as he looked at me, usually with an imperious look. Inevitably, he would say something mean to hurt my feelings—*not that he means to say anything to hurt me, I suppose.* He always acted as if he could care less whether I existed on the face of the earth or not. Nothing he *said* indicated that he thought of me at all—and I could have lived with that, if there had not been other times in which his behavior was in direct contradiction to his seeming disdain of me.

No, what told me he thought of me were the times, so random, when I would catch him staring, or someone else (*usually Karuna... What's she doing staring at him all the time?*) would point it out. In those moments, his eyes expressed an emotion the polar opposite of disdain or anything remotely similar. No, it was at those times when his eyes spoke of invitation and longing and desire. However, what look or what attitude I would receive—the tender, kind man or the haughty, condescending monster (*albeit gorgeous monster*)—I never knew. *That* was what disconcerted me. I could have taken him consistently one way or the other, but I could not take his unpredictability and randomness. My mind strained to remove myself from him, to get as far away from him as possible; yet my heart traitored me at every turn, pulling me near to him no matter the cost. I was fearful of my own nature. I was like a moth drawn to a flame—cliché? Yes, but oh so embarrassingly true.

Too soon, I was done with filling my sack. I scanned the group. *No one else is done. I'll have to go by myself.* I did not like the feeling of walking past Narayana by myself. I felt vulnerable. Transparent. But, go I would have to. I cast a quick glance over to where he stood. *Good! He's by himself at least.* The swamis and brahmacharis were gone—*probably left to go to sleep, not that they worked hard or anything.* If there was anything I disliked more than encountering him, it was encountering him with a bunch of Indian monks standing around—the prescription for an emotional nightmare perpetrated by the condescending monster I was beginning to adore.

I headed toward the gate, allowing myself to be bowed over by the bag. I kept my head down. *This time I'm not going to see what his eyes say nor am I going to give him an opportunity to say something mean*—I fervently promised myself.

"Premabhakti..." I heard a low, male voice say my name. Narayana's—I would know his voice anywhere. I doubted anyone else would have heard him hush my name. I ignored him. Again, "Premabhakti..." He was saying my name in his deep, slightly accented way. Highly personal. Just for me. So much said in just the utterance of my name.

I continued looking down, slowing to a halt when I saw his feet to my left. I looked up and was unexpectedly shocked. His gaze was fixed on me with a look of tender wistfulness that snatched my breath away. *What in the world does he have to say to me that would in any way correspond to this...look...on his face?*

"Yes...?" I asked in a whisper, my voice faltering with fear and hope. I was painfully aware of all the people behind me. *Kali, pleeeeease don't let Radha or Devi or Karuna be looking!* I could barely stand to meet his eyes. Somehow, he seemed to be standing much too close to me, although he was not.

"I...I..." he began in a low, husky voice, after clearing his throat. I had to avert my gaze from his eyes; they seemed to sparkle, almost liquid. A sweet, private smile touched his lips—just for me. *What is he thinking?* I stared at his throat in order to avoid his eyes. I could see a pulse beat at its base—*I'm staring that hard!! I can see his heart beat in his throat! Look away! Look away!* I screamed to myself as my heart thrashed crazily in my chest. I felt foolish and stupid...and hopeful and giddy. Something similar glimmered in his eyes. He inclined his head down toward me as if to speak.

"NARAYANA!" A hard voice sliced through the air. A woman's voice. Commanding. Cha Ma's voice. Narayana's head jerked up at the sounding of his name. In the blink of an eye, his entire demeanor changed, hardened. His jaw clinched, his eyes grew icy—I no longer existed to him.

"Namah shivaya, Cha Ma?" he asked eagerly, already striding over to where she was standing. He did not look back.

I stood there for a moment trying to regain myself. Finally, I resumed carrying my heavy load to the dump pile. When I had walked several steps and was certain that I was hidden in the shadows, I ventured a glance back at the scene.

And a chaotic scene it was! Nearly a hundred people were busily shoveling and carrying or standing around and talking. All, that is, except Cha Ma and Narayana. Cha Ma was speaking vigorously to him—her face and body language looked upset and angry—while he kept glancing in my direction, something uncertain and desirous upon his face. I turned and kept on walking—his face was too obvious and vulnerable for me to see for long. It was as though he were speaking his innermost thoughts aloud. Too much to bear. As I strained to harness my uncontrollable emotions, I thought, *she's going to get him for that!*

THICKENING WEBS

Marie and Paul
United States

"So, Mare, how was your day?" Paul asked his wife, Marie, as she stepped into the house—the empty house. Although Maya had moved out years ago to attend college, her recent disappearance had extended its intangible, depressing tendrils deep into her parents' house. It felt empty and hollow. Months had passed and the vacuity had increased. Paul was happy that Marie was home. Her presence helped dispel the dreadful emptiness.

Quickly he moved his large, an inch-over-six-feet frame from his favorite armchair to meet her at the door. Even though the strain of Maya moving out was affecting their relationship, causing them to grow distant and unable to communicate, he still looked forward to seeing her every day. He still yearned to hug her and hold her close, although it seemed that a vast gulf was forming between them. He looked at her closely simply because he enjoyed looking at her. She was smaller than him, full figured, beautiful after all these years.

To him, even more beautiful than when he had first laid eyes on her—that day passing each other in the school hallway when she had been 14 and he had been 17 and he had announced to his buddies, "I'm going to marry that girl." Decades later, he still loved her and found her lovelier with every passing year.

"So, tell me about the appointment," Paul urged. Marie had had her yearly eye exam with her optometrist. Paul had his thoughts about it, but he kept them to himself. He felt that instead of going for a routine eye exam, she really should have gone to her regular doctor to get her sinuses examined and to get a prescription for antibiotics. He was certain that her headaches were being caused by a sinus infection. However, she continued to hold off from getting her sinuses checked out, instead taking over-the-counter medicine, which really was not helping her very much. "How are your eyes? How'd the exam go?"

Marie put her purse and the bag of fast food that she had picked up for dinner on the table. She glanced at her husband briefly and then sat down at the table. "Well," her voice tremored, "Dr. Johnson's alarmed." She swallowed to get past the fear that was precipitously rising up her throat. "While he was checking out my eyes, he called his associate, Dr. Worthing, who's an opthamalogist, into the room. They analyzed whatever it was that they saw…"

Paul urged her on as he sat down across from her. "Well, what'd they say? What'd they see?"

She tried to collect herself. "They're not too sure what's going on…" Her voice dwindled away in doubt. *I've got to be stronger than this! Marie, get control of yourself!* She watched her husband empty the bag, putting the food on the table. *He seems so nonchalant. Doesn't he care?* The thought made Marie all the more fearful and anxious.

Taking a deep breath, she continued, "They said that I have a buildup of fluid behind my eyes. In fact, they believe it's the source of the headaches as well as the black spots and the webs I've been seeing."

"Webs?" Paul echoed. He looked up sharply from the food.

"Like cobwebs…I've been getting them in my field of vision."

"Black spots and webs?" Paul stopped setting out the food. His attention fastened on her. "What do you mean black spots and webs? I didn't know you were seeing black spots and webs. Don't you know that's a major sign that something's wrong with the eyes or the brain?" he chided her as if she were a child. His fear made him sound harsher than he actually felt.

"I know. I didn't want to worry you. And I had hoped they would go away." A long silence sat between them as they readied their food. "I was sure it was all because of a sinus infection and would go away with antibiotics…" She halted realizing that she had not even taken the steps to go to the doctor for antibiotics.

"But you didn't even bother to go get the antibiotics," Paul stated flatly.

Marie nodded. "I know…" she responded weakly.

Paul said nothing else; instead he put all of his attention into his food. They began to eat in a thick, loaded silence, discomfort and fear causing them to be unduly absorbed in the hamburgers before them.

After a couple of bites, Marie set her hamburger down. *I can't eat another bite. How can I eat? I'm so keyed up.* Her stomach was one huge knot that rose all the way into her throat and made her feel as though she would choke at any moment. She stared glumly down at her food as Paul continued to eat.

Finally, Paul urged, "So, what happened? What'd they say?"

She heaved a large sigh and resumed, "They ran me through all types of tests to see the source of my problems. Apparently, the headaches I've been having and the black spots and webs are all due to the fluid behind my eyes. They can see the buildup very clearly. I have to go back week after next for more extensive tests. And they've scheduled me to see a neurologist then, too."

"Week after next? What about this week? Or next week?" His questions erupted harshly from his mouth—clearly an indication of his being upset.

"It's Wednesday, Paul, there's nothing available for the rest of this week or next. Week after next is the soonest they could find. They gave me the next available appointment. It's not that far off. Anyway, Dr. Worthing prescribed some medicine to reduce the swelling. They believe it will help."

Silence. Finally, he asked, "So, what are the tests for…exactly?"

"They're worried that the buildup of fluid behind my eyes is a sign that something is wrong with my brain. In all honesty, they said that my symptoms have all the appearances of a…of a…" she struggled with getting the words out, "…of a brain tumor."

This last part hung in the air between them. Paul did not remove it by saying a word. Not of comfort. Not of understanding. Not of anything. Marie did not have anything more to say, except her fears, which she was afraid of sharing. She took a small bite of her hamburger. He washed down his last bite with some soda. The conversation remained in silence—each lost in his or her own thoughts. The pain, the fear, the uncertainty was too unbearable to give a voice.

As soon as he was finished eating, Paul announced, "I'm going to go relax." He pushed away from the table.

"Will you come with me?"

"Come with you where?"

I can't believe he's already shutting me out! "To my appointment?"

He stopped in the doorway, but did not look at her. "No, I have to work. I won't be able to get off in time."

As he walked out, Marie thought but did not say—*Won't be able to get off in time? The appointment will be almost two weeks away, if not more. And have to work? You could take the day off if you wanted to. In fact, you don't actually have to work there at all if you didn't want to.*

He went to the den and sat in his armchair. There he remained in silence for the rest of the evening. Brooding. Praying, or rather, *trying to pray.* He struggled in himself—the thought of losing his Mare after having lost Maya was too much for him. Although they would have been a relief, tears did not come. They had dried up a long time ago. *What is that Proverb? The one about hopes deferred makes the heart sick...was that it? And what happens when hope is deferred for too, too long and more and more dreams come crashing down? Does a man simply stop feeling? Thinking? What happens to his sick heart then?* His heart hurt so much.

He clenched and unclenched his hands. *I'd love to wring someone's neck, blame someone, take it out on someone... Whose neck would I wring? God's? No, God isn't the problem. Maya's? Well, definitely...if I ever see her again. Yes, I'd wring her neck after I hugged her for days on end. No, I'd wring my own neck. Surely, I've done something wrong.* And although he could come up with a thousand things he had done wrong with Maya, there was no way he could blame himself for what was going on with Mare, aside from not offering more support. *OK, maybe God...maybe I can blame God for this with Mare. But does that get me anywhere?* His mind whirled around.

Mare. A simple thought and his heart swelled with love and foreboding. *I know I need to go with her but I'm afraid of being there.* This admission was more an internal movement than it was a clear thought. *I'm afraid of going to her appointment because the doctor may say something that I just won't be able to bear.* His mind shot to a terrifying image of hearing that she was going to die and then to one of him breaking down and crying right there in the doctor's office. *No, I don't need to be there. I would be more of a hindrance than a help to her. How would my breaking down into tears help her in any way? She needs a strong man at this time, not one who's going to be falling apart crying. I'm not going to go. I can't go.* As he made up his mind not to go, he also decided not to tell Marie the reason why. *God! Help! How am I going to do this? I feel like I'm going through the paces of a miserable life. What else could go wrong?*

In his misery...in her misery...they were fair game for an attack. Marie's news—piled on top of Maya's disappearance—brought both Marie and Paul lower still and left them even more susceptible to the insidious whisperings of the evil ones assigned to harass and torment them.

Some came to Paul; others came to Marie.

Fear crept fearfully (as he was wont to do) into the house upon the news. His small, misshapen body, of a nondescript color, was unobtrusive and barely noticeable. He crept into their lives just as he had done in so many other people's—unnoticed and unchecked until he had already taken up residence for quite some time. He had joined Marie at the doctor's office, staying hidden, contracted in upon himself, so that he would be unnoticed when he attached onto her. The moment she had heard the prognosis, he had hitched a ride. An overload of bad news was an excellent vehicle for him.

Depression and Doubt had joined Fear at the house, intent upon spending time with Marie and Paul. The three fiends had slunk...or perhaps more accurately...had *oozed* into the house through the cracks and crannies. They did not have to take such indirect points of entry; they could have walked straight through the front door because they had been invited by the dismal words and depressed attitudes of Marie and Paul. These evil beings had legal entry.

As they entered the house, they found Sickness and Illness, both of whom embodied their particular brand of rebellious hideousness, attached to Marie. How did this sort of rebelliousness manifest? They were lumpy and misshapen; although their bodies had differing hues. Sickness was a vile, pinkish hue—a color that put one in mind of vomit. His body was lumpy and slimy. Illness had a frothy, greenish-yellow "exo-skin" that slid upon his misshapen mass. Their faces were lumpy, pulpy, pus-filled masses that no longer showed eyes, noses, or mouths; no, instead they had almost swollen shut orifices.

Sickness had a couple of his appendages stuck into Marie's head. As he inserted the essence of what he was into her, he sucked out her energy; her will...her life. Not enough to kill her, he did not have permission to do that, but enough to "diminish" and "weaken" her. As he fed upon her vital

56

energy, his slimy, lumpy body pulsed larger. His vile pinkish, vomitous cast deepened and grew rich, although no less vile and disgusting.

And Illness, with his frothy, greenish-yellow "exo-skin," slowly oozed onto and into Marie. He…it…made sure to spread some of the frothy mess onto her eyes. "Ah, the webs…my darling," he rasped into her ear, his voice sounding, even in the spiritual realm, disturbing and off-balanced.

Oblivious to what was going on in the unseen realm, Marie shuddered as gooseflesh crawled upon her skin. Immediately, webs appeared on the edge of her field of vision. She knew what would happen: the webs would knit upon themselves and grow until they filled her entire field of vision. It had not happened yet, but she knew it would one day come to that.

The evil angels had all entered easily enough for they had every legal right to be there. And yet, though they were opportunists, they did not feel 100 percent comfortable in Paul and Marie's home—too much worship had taken place in that house. Much too easily and often in the past, Paul and Marie had burst into explosive praise and worship, which had caused—unbeknownst to Paul and Marie—a legion of angels to swoop into the house. But now in this time of testing…

In perfect obedience to God's express command, the Lord's angels had "powered down" and stepped back. They stood away from the house. They were under the exact orders of the Lord to allow Paul and Marie to be tested, yet how they yearned to intervene. Even the atmosphere of the house drew them to intervene on her behalf—the years of loving God had created an atmosphere highly conducive to them. Under normal circumstances, perhaps, they would have stepped forward and would have intervened in some way…some minute way. Maybe they would have suggested…whispered…to Marie and Paul to pray, which would have released them to act. But, in this time of testing, they could not do anything.

So they stood back from the house powered down and waiting, urging in their hearts, "Marie...Paul...pray! Please pray! Release us!"

Marie was left to try to conquer her fears and doubts alone. Finally, she got up and cleared the table. What little dishes were in the sink, she washed. With Illness's unearthly "eye-bath," black webbing had slowly crept into her field of vision. By the time she was done washing dishes, her vision was greatly diminished. She blinked repeatedly to remove the webbing, to no avail. Finally, after she had straightened up as best she could, she went to their room.

She did not bother to turn on the light. She fell to her knees by the side of the bed and placed her aching head into her hands. She felt hot tears burning her eyes—tears she struggled to stop because she knew they would cause her head to hurt all the more ferociously. She gritted her teeth, working to stop the tears. She dug the heels of her hands into her eyes and gripped her forehead—useless, physical attempts to curb a pain that originated in the supernatural. She attempted praying; but her head hurt too much and her mind swirled about too much.

Further, Fear had come and joined her, leading and guiding her thoughts. He danced her mind around the "what ifs," his claw-like hands gripping her shoulders as he rasped into her ear: *What if it is a brain tumor? What if it makes you blind? Even worse, what if it kills you? What if Paul leaves you because it's too hard to deal with? What if you die before you ever see Maya again? What if Maya never comes back? What if she dies and, being that she's unsaved, goes to hell?*

That last one was the most sobering. She felt the awful tears, which she had gained tenuous control over, prickle her eyes again. *Well, at least, with me, I know that when I die, when I'm finally absent from the body, I will be present with the Lord. I will go to Heaven.* At the thought, she felt a deep thrum of reassurance course through her body. *But, where is Maya right now? What is she doing? What if she dies?*

After spending half the evening trying to sleep and being unable because of the pain and the worrying, Marie decided she needed help. She would have called her friend Connie, but she knew Connie and her husband, Jim, were on vacation. Even though she knew that Connie would have taken her call, Marie did not want to bother her—not on her vacation. So instead, she turned to someone who knew her from the time that she was a little girl. She needed someone who loved her and her whole family. She needed someone who would be stronger than she to stand with her. She needed someone who would not mind being leaned upon. She needed a prayer partner. She picked up the phone and called her brother's wife, Shanalee. It would be so comforting to hear from someone who knew her well and would help and love her without any judgmentalism or withdrawing.

"Hello, Shana? Will you pray with me? I got a bad report today…"

"Oh no! Not more!" Shanalee felt for her husband's sister whom she loved like her own sister. She was watching Marie go through all this stress; and it hurt her deeply. She did not understand why so much came against her sister-in-law and husband all at once. They prayed together often, but still it did not feel like enough. She was glad to help. "Well, what's going on? Tell me so that we know what to pray against."

Marie began to tell her. Quickly. Concisely. Without any embellishment. As soon as she was done, Shana began praying for her, lifting her up.

Soon Shana's petitions on Marie's behalf changed into the heavenly language. Melodious sounds flowed from her lips. Marie joined her in praying in the Spirit. Tears began to stream down their faces as their spirits lifted right into Heaven, right before the Lord. He smiled upon them. He was pleased. Very pleased.

The moment Shana and Marie began to pray, the Lord of Heaven commanded the angels of the Lord to act. Their prayer, as it was prayed in the

Spirit, was the perfect request. Heavenly angels blasted into the house. They had been waiting for an opportunity to enter. They sent Fear, Doubt, and Anxiety careening out, tumbling head over heels away from the house.

However, these evil tormentors did not go far. Sickness and Illness ceased meddling with Marie, although they did not lose their hold on her. They had permission to remain—for the time of testing was not complete.

MORE MAGGOT-WORMS

Maya
India

Another day in the kitchen, which was fine. I was growing to enjoy it more and more every day that I spent cooking. I was making mung bean soup, and Bri. Sita was making "something-or-other" salad. We were fortunate: in yesterday's shipment, a load of carrots, potatoes, and eggplant had arrived. Completely unexpectedly. Bri. Sita had gone into the kitchen as soon as the shipment was dropped off and commandeered the vegetables for the Western canteen, claiming that the Westerners desperately needed the food for their health. Her argument was that our systems were not used to living on the nutritionally deficient food that the Indians lived upon. She brought the goods over, clutching them as though she were afraid someone would take them away. She gave most of them to me.

Granted, the vegetables we received in the ashram were of much poorer quality than those we enjoyed in the West. Today's stash was no different. But, after the "scolding" from

Cha Ma—as many of the ashramites joyously proclaimed: the "karma-burning"—there was *no* way I was going to waste an iota of food if it were somehow, in some way, salvageable. No longer were my cooking methods up for discussion. If there were a problem with the bugs or the rot, I would handle it. I could, and would, deal with disgruntled, angry, vituperative Westerners but I could not, *absolutely would not*, cross Cha Ma again.

I had the Western sevites cut up some onions we had stashed away along with a portion of Sita's carrots, potatoes, and eggplant. The onions, carrots, and potatoes were no problem. I had the volunteers cut out the "horrid" parts and put them into one bucket separate from the "not-so-horrid." I set the horrid bucket to the side, to wait until the cutting crew was gone. Once gone, I would dump it all into a pot and let it boil for so long the good and bad parts would be indistinguishable.

However, as always, the mung beans were a problem—too many little rocks and too much sand and grit. No matter how many times I rinsed them, it was not enough. We would still grind our teeth on itty-bitty rocks, sand, and grit. I did the best I could and hoped no one would chip a tooth, although many of us (me included) had minute cracks in our teeth from crunching down on the sand, grit, and rocks. Molars were OK—those were hidden—I most feared for the incisors. I had seen a couple of people with chipped front teeth and more than I could count with visible cracks in their front teeth.

However, the worst—today and every day, of course—was the eggplant. I loathed the eggplant. For some reason the ashram buyers felt it to be their honor-bound duty to buy the pesky, little things. I began to believe that they bought them intentionally—to see how much they could irritate me. Every time I saw them in a shipment, I heaved a huge sigh of disgust and exasperation. They were such a problem.

Even today, the moment one of the volunteers sliced into the eggplant, she called for me, alarm evident in her voice.

"Premabhakti! Come see this eggplant!" she wailed.

"Ugh!" was the response of another as he looked at what she was talking about. I expected it…it never failed. I could hear the cutters starting up as they looked at the eggplant.

"Ew!"

"What is that?!"

It IS nasty, isn't it? I mentally concurred as I patiently made my way over. I knew what to expect. By the time I arrived at the table, I was ready. I peered at the sliced, purple-colored vegetable that was lying on the table.

Yep! That was the problem, maggot-worms, again.

"They have worms!" I stated matter-of-factly, using the word "worms" instead of "maggots." Maggots just seemed so much more disgusting and nasty than worms. A mass of the little maggot-worms wove their way through the inside of the vegetable.

"Yuck! We've got to throw these away!" declared one man cleverly.

"No, we can't do that. That's wasteful. What if there are some without worms?" I asked. I already knew the answer—they all had worms—they always did.

"I know!" suggested the woman who had cut open the crawly specimen. "Why don't we find out if they all have worms? Let's cut them all open. If they have worms, we'll just throw them away!" She was pleased with her suggestion.

Several of the Westerners nodded in agreement. A couple shook their heads in disgust. Putting down their cutting knives, they stood up and left the canteen. I smiled placidly. I knew what I was going to do! The real trick was to handle the problem in such a way that no one would be angry nor anyone really know what I was doing. I hated to rain on her idea-parade. Even more, I hated to lie to her—well, not really. Yes, we would cut open all of the ones we needed—but we would not be throwing any away. *They might throw them away—but not me!*

I gave them my instructions. "Cut all of the eggplant into little diced cubes. The parts…the cubes…that have no worms, put over here." I gestured to a bucket on the right. "And the cubes that have worms, put over there." I pointed to a bucket on the left.

They nodded their approval of my idea—we were going to throw away the wormy parts. I did not have the heart, and more honestly, the *nerve* to tell them otherwise. They swiftly chopped, filling up the buckets. As I had foreseen but had failed to tell them, there were no "good" eggplants.

The choppers proceeded on to the onions, potatoes, and tomatoes. With these, too, they separated out the good from the bad. In total, there were two buckets full of wormy eggplants and only one bucket of rotten, mildewy potatoes, tomatoes, and onions in comparison to five buckets of edible potatoes, tomatoes, and onions. I placed the buckets with the rotten, wormy vegetables over to the side, near the exit, as if I were going to throw them out. The choppers were satisfied. I thanked them as they left.

When the canteen was clear of all the Westerners, except Bri. Sita, I went to the huge cabinet in the canteen and grabbed several different bags full of dried, leafy spices—spices typical of the West. I grabbed indiscriminately as the purpose of the spices was to disguise rather than to flavor. Spices in hand, I headed through the kitchen and into the frying area in order to "do my black-woman's magic." I had to make several trips in order to get the Indian spices and ghee from the kitchen ammas and to fetch *all* the buckets of onions, tomatoes, and eggplants, good and bad. I grabbed a blackened pot that looked like a large, two-feet in diameter wok from a large pile of pots that were sitting on the kitchen floor.

Once in the fry room, I started a fire in one of the holes on the stovetop using the leaves and the dried hulls of the coconut trees that were in abundance. I poured a little ghee into the pan and dropped in a couple of handfuls of mustard seed. Within a few minutes, the seeds started popping, releasing their fragrance and flavor. I added a heap of ground coriander and a small pinch of cumin—the coriander added a "smoothness" to the exotic "kick" of the cumin. I tossed in a healthy portion of the leafy, dried spices. When the mixture was happily popping, I added the chopped eggplant. I sautéed them until everything was a nice brown. It was now impossible to distinguish the leafy spices from the maggot-worms in the eggplant, as they were both browned and shriveled. Pleased with my ingenuity, I added the onions and when they were sautéed to a light brown, I tossed in the tomatoes and allowed the mixture to simmer.

Bri. Sita walked past, commenting, "That smells great, Premabhakti!"

"Namah shivaya," I sang my thanks. *It does smell good! And it looks good, too. Black woman in the kitchen…better watch out! We can cook anything and make it look and taste good!* I was now ready for the rest. I went out back to where the brahmacharinis cooked rice in the six-foot-wide pots and made a fire with the help of Manoj.

Manoj was a big, beefy guy from the Maldives, who worked in the kitchen. Physically, he was not very cute. He always looked a bit disheveled, with wild hair and a short, untamed beard; however, his engaging personality added greatly to his looks. His habitual garb was a dirty, white dhoti that was tucked up in an insouciant manner. Sometimes he wore a white shirt, sometimes not. He was the only male allowed in the kitchen with the brahmacharinis at any time…all the time…very unusual, but he was in no way effeminate, probably because he was so beefy and carried a machete. Every time I saw him, he was either holding the machete on his shoulder or he was swinging it, whistling, and laughing. And he was usually laughing as he had an excellent sense of humor.

He was the kitchen "can-do" man. Whenever we needed something heavy picked up, we called Manoj. Whenever we needed a coconut opened, we called Manoj. The coconut-opening thing was most amazing. He would take his machete, heave it a foot or two above his left hand, which held the waiting coconut, and swing it beautifully, perfectly, into the cradled coconut. He never wasted coconut juice. He never sliced his fingers. Whenever we needed firewood or coconut tree branches, we called Manoj, and he would go fetch for us. Whenever we needed a heavy pot carried and were too exhausted to lug it ourselves, we called Manoj. Whenever I needed a good laugh, I called Manoj. He loved to talk and laugh and tease and shoot the breeze. He was great fun.

He had been in and out of the fry kitchen the entire time I was sautéing the maggot-worms, laughing and joking with me. Chances were he knew exactly what I was up to as he was very clever; but he did not say a word concerning it. No, he went about teasing me, and later, he climbed the woodpile (which was easily ten feet into the air) to get a few suitable branches of coconut palms for my outdoor fire.

Once the fire was going strongly, I took a big, black-bottomed pot and filled it with water using the buckets. I added the mung beans, noticing, even after having rinsed them many times over, a thin layer of sand and grit at the bottom of the bucket. *Ugh!* I added the potatoes. Finally, I had Manoj carry the maggot-worms-turned-spices-filled-wok outside and pour them into the pot. Of course, he spoke obliquely, "Good soup, Prema…good soup," and chortled. I pushed him, laughing myself, and sat down on my favorite rock. He pulled out his machete (he had slid it into the waist-fold of his dhoti in order to help me) and languidly strolled back into the fry kitchen, simultaneously whistling and laughing and swinging the machete. *How much does he know?* I wondered.

I sat outside with the soup for over an hour, chanting my mantra. The fire slowly burned away. When all but a few embers had died down, I made sure the pot was fully covered with a lid for fear of the geckos falling out of the thatching of the roof and into the soup (ashram legend was that geckos were extremely toxic) and left.

I went into the temple for the evening singing of bhajans. I sat down in the back of the women's side because I smelled of acrid smoke. I was still dirty and sooty from cooking. The lights were down low, which was unusual for the temple. Cha Ma was already there as were the residents of the ashram and many visitors who had come that evening. Cha Ma was in a "fierce" mood. She banged the stick she held against the edge of the peetham where she was sitting. She sang a bunch of slow, mournful songs, calling out to Krishna and Kali. Her skin, which was usually a "mild" color of brown, like café au lait, was dark, dark brown, almost black, as if it were made of a dark, bitter chocolate. She appeared exorbitantly, incalculably dissatisfied, upset, or angry—I could not figure out which. I did not understand her mood, except that it scared me. Horribly. Suddenly, in the midst of dolefully singing, whacking the peetham with the stick, and calling out to Kali, Cha Ma simply stood up and walked out the side door of the temple. Abruptly, the miserable bhajans were over, leaving us staring after her, stunned.

Slowly, we, all the devotees, meandered away from the temple, talking quietly amongst ourselves about what had gone on with Cha Ma. I headed out to the Western canteen, at a snail's pace, deep in thought. Karuna came along with me. She, too, was in regular "Western" garb, instead of sari or punjabi. Also, like me, she was wearing dirty work clothes. This month she had bathroom cleaning duty and was properly dressed for it. For some odd reason, I looked down at her feet, which were clad, like mine, in rubber chappels. Her toenails were dirty. Her heels were cracked, the crevices filled with dirt. I could not say much—my feet looked more or less the same.

"What do you think of it?" Karuna asked me, her Australian accent coming through, her face slightly flushed from excitement.

"I don't know! That was crazy! I've never seen Cha Ma in such a state. I wonder what was going on with her," I responded in bewilderment.

"I have no idea. I've never seen her like that either. I wonder if anyone has." She shook her head.

We stepped through the entranceway closest to the ashram of the Western canteen. Most of the people were already seated eating their soup and salad. A few sat at the tables eating the Indian fare of kanji and curry. Everyone was discussing the odd bhajan session. As I walked through, different people turned to me, praising the soup. Again, my soup was a hit.

"This is so good!"

"I love the flavor!"

"It feels so healthy!"

"Great soup, Premabhakti!" said a Western renunciate as she gave me a "thumbs up" sign.

"How do you get such flavor?" another Westerner, this one a visitor, asked me as she took another spoonful.

"I love your soups. They have helped my health here more than anything else."

I just smiled, as I always did, and said, "Cha Ma!" as Karuna and I headed toward the Indian canteen to get the kanji and curry. I actually liked the flavor of the Indian food, as did Karuna. Frequently I wondered, *Why come to India but then refuse to experience all that is Indian?* If I had to choose between the Western and the Indian food, I would choose the Indian every time. I preferred it…and not because of the bugs. It did not bother me too much if they were in the food. Hey! The bugs were in the Western *and* Indian food—no way to escape them. As for the grit and small stones, I hated them, but like the bugs, they were in everything.

Karuna and I stood in the Indian line waiting for the brahmacharis to serve us the kanji and curry—one ladleful of kanji and one of curry—the allotted amount. Manoj (definitely a partner-in-crime after the day's fry session) and another brahmachari, Raju, were serving.

I did not know Raju as well as I knew Manoj, but I thought he was a cutie through and through, even though he was very slim, perhaps too slim for my taste. He had an exceedingly nice-looking face that was framed by mid-neck-length hair fashioned in a blunt cut. His hair flipped up at the ends in a male, Sandra-Day-ish kind of style. Unlike Manoj, he tended to keep his face clean-shaven. However, similar to his serving-buddy, he wore a dirty, white dhoti sloppily tucked up and a white shirt (also dirty)—if, and when, he decided to wear a shirt. Where Manoj was beefy and thick in the upper torso, Raju was thin and, well…thin. What was most interesting about Raju was that although he was a brahmachari, and as such not supposed to talk to members of the opposite sex, he did. And clearly, he had no qualms about it. He was a heavy-duty flirter—*such a no-no, especially for the brahmacharis and -charinis.* Get Manoj and Raju together? What fun!

As I stood in line, I almost squirmed in anticipation of talking to them. I knew we would be in for a quick treat of flirting and light-hearted kidding. Finally, I made it to them and held out my meal tin. Manoj dished out the kanji and Raju poured out a ladleful of curry. Both of them, I noted, were "generous" in their helpings—another no-no in the ashram as there might not be enough food for everyone—a common problem.

"Namah shivaya, Raju! Namah shivaya, Manoj!" I said, throwing a toothy smile at both of them. They were some of the few—*only?*—brahmacharis with whom I felt comfortable enough to give a big, toothy smile.

Raju and Manoj grinned toothily back at me, heads bobbling. "Namah shivaya, Premabhakti! How are you doing?" they asked exuberantly as if they had been waiting to ask me that all week. They turned to Karuna, smiling heartily, "Karuna! Namah shivaya! What about you? How are you doing?" Their voices jumbled over each other, as they ladled out generous helpings to her, too.

"Namah shivaya, guys!" Karuna and I said, smiling back. Everyone was busy smiling at…everyone…

"How did your soup go?" Manoj asked as he winked at me and ladled another portion of kanji into my tin. *Oh, yes! Extra portions!* Faintly, I heard the rumblings of Indians behind us. We were starting to hold up the line.

"Fine," I responded, choosing to ignore the people behind us.

"Everyone loves your soup," he said, smiling an even bigger smile—if that were at all possible. He nodded with his head toward the Western side of the canteen, "Even the Indians are going to the Western canteen to get some of your soup."

I looked, and he was right! A few Indians were standing in the short Western queue!

Raju plopped another scoop of curry on top of the extra kanji. "Why aren't you having some of your own soup?" he asked innocently.

Covertly, I winked at Manoj. "I like the Indian food."

Manoj caught the intent of the wink and laughed gustily, throwing his head back, "I'll bet, Premabhakti!" I joined him in laughter.

Raju asked, "What? What's so funny?"

Manoj, smiling mischievously, leaned over and whispered to him in Malayalam. Immediately, Raju guffawed.

Karuna looked back and forth between us and cried, "I want to know! I want to know!" In response, Raju and Manoj dropped extra helpings on her tin.

"I'll tell you later," I promised. *Please let her forget! Please let her forget!* I did not want to tell her. *Time to change the subject...* "So, what did you guys think of bhajans?" I asked, grinning still.

"Yeah!" Karuna chimed in, smiling.

"I wasn't there..." Manoj said, holding down a giggle. "I was in the kitchen."

"Me, too," Raju replied. "I had to get the kanji ready. Nothing like fresh kanji. So much work!" He laughed.

He's so cute when he laughs, I thought. I sent a sideways glance at Karuna as she shot one at me—same thought. *Yep!*

"All you had to do was tip the pot..." I said, flashing yet another toothy, flirty smile, "...and pour the kanji in."

Manoj laughingly challenged, "Yes, but it takes a strong man. Have you ever tried to tip one of the rice pots?"

Raju answered Manoj's query, "Oh, yes! She has! She works in the kitchen, you know! Those pots are so *heavy*! Especially for you girls..."

"I know!" I replied. "That's why we *girls* need you big, strong men...to help us with those pots." Heavy flirting was on! I had almost forgotten that I was in an ashram flirting with two Hindu monks—*what was I thinking?!*

Raju and Manoj laughed, pleased with the compliment (so rare from women in the ashram). Manoj ordered, smiling at me, "Come! Give me your plate!" He ladled out yet another helping of kanji, although my tin was almost overflowing. *Yes! The compliment had worked.* "You, too!" Smilingly, he nodded at Karuna. Quickly she held out her tin for more.

"Thank you, Manoj and Raju!" Karuna and I said, almost in unison. Our voices unusually high and girly, definitely our flirting voices.

"No problem!" Manoj responded as he puffed out his chest.

"Namah shivaya!" Raju gave the Indian equivalent for "no problem," with a smile and a little head bobble.

I looked back and saw a long line of Indians—brahmacharis (the brahmacharinis ate in their little room off from the kitchen) and regular Indians visiting the ashram—had formed. Our chitchatting had severely backed up the serving line. The people in the front were completely engrossed in our conversation as they were staring intently into our faces, smiling with us. *I wonder if they think they're going to get extras, too?*

Karuna and I walked off, giggling to each other, and found a place on the cement floor of the Indian canteen. We put our plates on the long, narrow bamboo mats that ran the length of the canteen. We sat down cross-legged and began to eat using an Indian spoon.

"He is so cute!" Karuna sighed, as she took a spoonful of kanji and curry and cast a smiling glance at Raju.

"He who?" I asked, feigning ignorance, following her eyes to see Raju smiling back—innocence transparent in his eyes.

"You know…" she said.

"I know." *Raju.* We looked at each other in agreement. I continued, "You know what I really wonder?" My mind was still on Cha Ma's strange behavior.

"No, what?"

"What happened tonight at bhajans? Cha Ma was just so 'aggro'…" I mused aloud to Karuna as I ate a spoonful of kanji and curry. "Mmmm! I don't know why I like the Indian food so much, but I do." The bland saltiness in the kanji complemented the spiciness of the curry. The curry was nicely done today—it was dark brown with little green beans—Indian beans, not American green beans. What was so nice about the curry was that it was not too bitter. The kitchen Ammas had not put in too much asafoetida this time.

"You're right. It is nicely done," Karuna concurred. "It's not bitter at all." She took another bite. "They must've run out of asafoetida." She giggled.

I wrinkled up my nose. "I can't stand asafoetida. Well, when it is in moderation it makes the curry taste nice. But, I don't know why South Indian cooking has to have so much! It's so overpowering." I took another spoonful of kanji. Although Raju and Manoj gave us extra, I wanted more. "Have you ever noticed that it tastes like ear wax?"

Karuna burst out with a peal of laughter. Raju looked our way with an inquiring smile. "How do you know what ear wax tastes like?" she queried in between giggles. I shrugged noncommittally. Karuna leaned in to whisper, "Don't you think Raju is a little 'too concerned' with us?"

We kept our heads down and looked his way—under our lashes. Of course, he was still looking.

"He is so cute!"

"Didn't you say that already?" I asked with a grin and a sidelong glance at my friend.

She grinned back at me, blushing prettily, and shrugged helplessly. "Yeah! I did. Oh well! You know what I think?"

"Uh-uh. Tell me," I prompted as I scooped up the last of my meal with my spoon. Karuna had finished a few minutes before.

"I think he likes you. He's always watching you." She stood up, grabbed her metal plate, cup, and spoon and headed over to the huge metal tubs where used plates, cups, and spoons were dropped. If there were not enough utensils for all the people, the brahmacharis could quickly wash them off and put them back out. The only problem was that they washed them with water—tepid backwaters water, so perhaps "wash" was not the best word…"rinse off" was better—and put them back out.

I hopped up after her. "Really?!" I exclaimed a little too loudly. Raju looked at us again—*Had he ever stopped?*—smiling, of course.

"See? He's looking at you!" Karuna whispered loudly at me as I walked several paces away from her.

She was right! He *was* looking at me! And he wasn't hiding it! Very unusual. Very unusual, indeed! Raju was acting as if he was interested and he was not even attempting to hide it! He smiled at me and winked. *He winked!*

I smiled back at him as I walked to the garbage can—feeling flirty and cute. I did not have enough nerve to wink at him. Not in front of all the people. *Hmmm! An Indian guy! I wonder what it would be like to date one.* An odd sense of "conquest" arose briefly—*to get a brahmachari, a Hindu monk! Wow!* I chided myself as I hastily repressed it. *Stop that!*

Karuna grabbed my arm—*a mite too hard*—as she whispered, "Look!" and cocked her head to the left. I looked to the left and felt a wave of surprise and angst roll through me.

There was Narayana, outside the Indian canteen, leaning against the low wall—not a problem, except for the fact that he was watching me intently. His eyes—his entire countenance, from the set of his jaw to the deep furrows in his brow—appeared stormy and betrayed a host of emotions. Given his gaze, the source of his agitated emotions (the foremost of which appeared to be anger) had to be me. He did not look away when I looked at him. He continued to scowl and, simultaneously, look passionate, desirous of something and just plain *mad*. I found myself ensnared by his gaze, returning his furious, impassioned stare with my own bewildered one. After a few seconds of staring angrily, he snapped his eyes away and abruptly walked off.

"Oops, girl! Snagged flirting! By Narayana no less! Now that's something, especially because he was so upset! And at you! Why was he so upset? Do you think he likes you? I think so!" Karuna popped off a thousand questions, all of which she answered without even listening for a response from me.

I could barely hear her. My thoughts and emotions were tumbling around chaotically—*What did that mean? What did his eyes mean? Does he like me? Was he even looking at me? He had to have been, even Karuna saw it! But, why the look? Oh! He must despise me!* I walked along with Karuna as she chattered about Narayana. My head was spinning and I could not think. I was fine with her going on and on because I did not have to give voice to the crazy, fearful, excited, hopeful thoughts smashing about within me.

DEATH'S STING

Karuna and I headed up the back stairway to the women's dormitory where it was dark. For that matter, it was dark in the temple and in the brahmachari living area. Evidently, the power was off—we had used all of the electricity rationed to us early on. For the rest of the night, we would be in total darkness with the exception of flashlights and candles. The only place that had light was the canteen and the kitchen. Hopefully, the potwashers would get the dishes done by the time that power was turned off. If not, they would be washing dishes by flashlight. Luckily, it was a full moon. Its reflected light cast a surreal glow upon everything so that it was not as dark as it could have been.

Everywhere there was this *peculiar* hush. Silence—save whispered voices here and there as people stood in little groups talking. As we stepped into the women's dormitory and headed toward my bunk on the side closest to Cha Ma's apartment, I could pick up snatches of conversation.

"Cha Ma was so mad!"

"No, I don't think so. I think she was sad."

"I heard that Cha Ma said…"

On and on the conversations went—little clusters of women sat here and there whispering to each other in the gloomy darkness. Karuna and I sat on my wooden bunk, hunkered over because our upper bodies did not quite fit into the bunk—the top bunk was too low. I lit some incense and breathed in deeply. *Ahhh! I love the smell of Nag Champa.* We looked out the glassless window, its vertical iron bars (that kept out what?) unobtrusive.

"So, what do you think?" Karuna whispered to me. She stared at me in the darkness. Her eyes glimmered, reflecting the meager light from outside, from the moon.

"Honestly? I don't know. I've never seen Cha Ma act like that. And the look on her face…" I shrugged my shoulders and peered out the window at the dark brahmachari area. I could see a couple of faint lights flickering behind the window holes and the gaps in the thatching of their huts. *Must be candles.* "It was weird, really weird. It scared me, though."

I could see Karuna nod out of the corner of my eye. "Yeah! Me too," she assented. "I have an awful feeling that something is wrong."

We both sat in the dark, hunched over in my bunk, staring out the window. The air was barely moving. Voices were hushed all around.

"Look! Is that Cha Ma?" Anneshwari asked from her perfect-to-see-Cha Ma spot. I had not even noticed that she was there; but of course, she would be.

Karuna and I rushed off the bunk to Anneshwari's sleeping area. From her vantage point, we could see Cha Ma sitting in the garden just below her apartment. It was not the best view, though. Karuna and I went to the stairs to better see.

Cha Ma was sitting in her garden on a little concrete bench. It looked like a swami—*Swami, I think*—was sitting on the ground beside her. They were talking quietly. Karuna and I sat down on the concrete spiral steps that flanked the side of the building. It was cooler here—aided by a slight cross-breeze that blew by.

"Isn't it a beautiful night?" Karuna sighed, gazing up at the sky.

"Yeah…" I agreed as I looked up, too. "You're right! It really *is* beautiful tonight. I hadn't even noticed." I observed that the clouds were scudding by swiftly, like some sleight of hand. The light of the full moon reflected off the clouds as they slid by—shifting shapes quickly. The reflected moonlight gave the clouds an eerie and unusual, albeit beautiful, appearance. The sight was absolutely breathtaking! *The winds in the upper atmosphere have to be much stronger than what we're feeling here*—I mused.

Karuna and I sat there on the spiral staircase in the moonlit darkness watching the subtly-lit, shape-shifting clouds. The air was warm and balmy with just enough of a breeze to make us comfortable. We did not talk. There was not any real need to. The surreal beauty of the play between the moonlight and clouds, the intensity of the evening's bhajans, Cha Ma's strange behavior, the atmosphere itself—all hindered conversation. Instead, we sat and watched. How long? I had no idea.

Cha Ma sat with Swami whispering in the darkness. It was strange to have her around without her bursting out in raucous laughter at some point or another. The few brahmacharis who had been out—meandering, earnestly pursuing a given task, or chatting quietly—dwindled away. Sporadically, dim, flickering lights appeared and disappeared in the brahmachari and brahmacharini huts. The ashram grew increasingly more still. The hush deepened. I started getting sleepy, but I could not find the energy, the will, to muster myself to get up and walk ten paces to my bunk. So, I just sat there with Karuna.

And then, we heard—shattering the silence, the stillness, the calm—shrieking and crying. The sheer abruptness of it, the magnitude with which it disturbed the calm, froze me through. Terror and fear coursed through me. The awful shrieks were coming from Cha Ma's garden. Immediately, Karuna and I stood up and looked down into the garden as the other women rushed out of the dormitory to see the source of the angst.

Someone else was with Cha Ma—that much was apparent—and it was not Swami. He had left Cha Ma long minutes ago. By the cries, I knew it had to be a woman. In the eerie light of the moon and clouds, I could see only dimly. I could make out a distraught woman in a white sari. Because her skin glowed palely in the moonlight, I figured it had to be a very light Indian woman or a Westerner. The woman kept crying and shrieking and wailing. It was the most horrifically, heartrendingly, sad sound I had ever heard. It made my skin crawl. I wanted to cover my ears and run away. Yet, at the same time, I longed to cry out of pity for this woman who sounded beyond anguished.

"Who is that?" Alice whispered hoarsely, from behind me. She must have come from inside the dormitory. Even this late at night, I could tell by the gleam of the moon that she was munching on peanuts, her jaws feverishly working. Her profile, again, as always with her, reminded me of a chipmunk. The wan light faintly illumined her sari, which I could tell even in the darkness was wrinkled and dirty. The light breeze caused it to sag and flutter.

"I don't know," Karuna responded.

I peered harder into the darkness, trying to make out the person sitting with Cha Ma. Whoever it was kept wailing. The cries had died down from being shrieks to a kind of ululating wail. It sounded so forlorn and lost, so heartbroken and hopeless. The sound of her voice carried across the heavy, wet air and the weight of the cries caused the sound to hang there.

The woman had fallen at Cha Ma's feet and had put her head in Cha Ma's lap. It looked as if Cha Ma were rubbing her back, rocking back and forth herself, crying.

"Why do you think she's crying?" Alice whispered.

"Who is she?" I asked. "I can't tell from here."

"Me neither," Karuna responded quietly.

"I wonder what's going on…all I know is her crying is horrible," I said.

"I hate it," Alice muttered resolutely.

We grew quiet. Karuna and I sat down again after a few more minutes. Alice and a couple of other women found space to sit on the staircase with us. We sat there and watched in silence. The woman kept crying, her voice dying down to a quiet, heartbroken keening. Whatever it was that was hurting her so badly, I wanted to fix it. My heart went out to her.

I do not know how much time passed as we sat on the steps…watching…but it seemed like hours. The woman's crying never ceased. After what felt like an interminable amount of time, the woman shifted her body. From the angle of her face, we could all see who she was.

"Hey! That's Linda!" Alice said as she stood up and leaned over the concrete railing trying to get a better view.

"I wonder what's the matter with her," I mused.

"Hey! I wonder if it has anything to do with Doug. I haven't seen him in a few days and the last time I saw him I was really worried about his health. He's, like, steadily going downhill," Karuna whispered.

"I saw him just yesterday. He didn't look too good," Anneshwari joined into the conversation. Earlier she had come out and had kept vigil with us, not saying much, her short, pudgy body seeking Cha Ma. Cha Ma was always her focus.

"I hope everything's OK with him…" I said.

After that comment, our conversation died down. I noticed then that the entire ashram was pin-drop quiet. All of the lights in the brahmachari and –charini huts were off, not even any meager candlelight flickering within the huts. Overhead, clouds continued to scud by swiftly. The woman…Linda…kept on crying, her face still in Cha Ma's lap. It seemed as though the clouds rode upon her wailing and keening. Her keening grew softer, but in that softness it sounded more vulnerable and forlorn. Cha Ma kept rocking, almost in rhythm to the rise and fall of her keening. I could not move—I was lost in her pain—and I did not even know what it was about. I wanted it to go away. I wanted to *make* it go away.

Finally, I pulled myself together enough to get up. The other women followed suit. It seemed too intimate a moment for us to sit watching them, voyeuristically, in the midst of their pain. We walked back to our respective places. I lay down to the sound of her crying. I pulled my shawl, which also served as my blanket, over my head, covering my ears—and still the sound wafted up to me. I wanted to disappear, get away from the pain. I said a prayer to Kali for Linda as I wondered what could be so bad as to make her cry like that.

The next morning the answer was given. As I went down to chai after archana, I ran into Anneshwari.

"Did you hear?" Anneshwari asked in a hushed voice, looking around as if she were hiding something. Actually, it seemed that everyone in the ashram was looking around and whispering in the same way.

"Uh-uh…hear what?" I asked, my mind blank from the hour-long archana. *Nothing like an excruciatingly boring hour of the names of Devi to dull the mind. When Eastern religions speak of "stilling the mind," I don't think they have my type of "stilling" in mind.* I chuckled quietly at my own lack of spirituality.

"About Linda!" Anneshwari whispered loudly as we walked toward the canteen.

"Linda what?" Karuna asked as she approached us.

"You didn't hear about Linda…about why she was crying last night?" Anneshwari asked in astonishment.

By this time, Alice had joined us. We all stood in the line for the Indian canteen. "Yeah, I heard about it first thing this morning," Alice mumbled in between munching on a handful of peanuts.

"What happened? C'mon guys, tell us!" I pleaded as I stepped forward in line.

"Doug died," Anneshwari announced matter-of-factly as she picked up her metal plate and spoon.

"Doug died?" I parroted. "When did Doug die?" I felt a dull thud in the pit of my stomach. I felt like I wanted to throw up.

Anneshwari continued, shrugging nonchalantly, "Sometime yesterday…"

"How?" Karuna interrupted. We had stopped moving forward in the line—all attention on this. I did not want to eat any longer.

"He drowned in the ocean," Anneshwari replied.

"Doug drowned in the ocean?" I repeated in complete shock. "Oh no! That can't be!" *This can't be true! Oh no! How horrible!* Immediately, I felt the loss and the pain viscerally. My mind went back to Linda crying last night. "So, that's why Linda was crying?" I mused more to myself than to the group.

"Doug?!" Karuna asked. The shock of the news had slowed, tremendously, her ability to think, it seemed.

"Yes, Doug…" Anneshwari answered, rolling her eyes with impatience.

"What about Linda? What happened? Didn't Cha Ma 'see' this? Why didn't she stop it? What's Linda going to do now?" I shot the questions out, lickety-split. I felt my throat closing up. *I can't imagine what Linda must be going through—to lose your husband! Your new husband…they'd just gotten married! This is their honeymoon trip.* I felt like I was going to cry. I looked around at Alice, Anneshwari, Karuna, and the other people standing nearby. Although everyone seemed to be talking earnestly about "stuff," I could almost wager that they were talking about what had happened to Doug.

Alice held out her plate for a serving of kanji and curry. "It makes me think about what Cha Ma said about Doug being under a death star."

"Yeah, everyone's saying that he stepped out of her influence. That he went too far, and his death star got him." Anneshwari held up her tin for a serving of kanji and curry. "Namah shivaya," she thanked the brahmacharis who were serving.

Although I was worried about Linda, deeper thoughts, that I dared not even acknowledge, were trying to push their way to the forefront of my consciousness. They spun around in some dark recess of my mind, barely noted, though deeply and ferociously gnawing: *How could Cha Ma not have seen this? How could Kali or Krishna or Shiva—one of the gods we worship—not have foreseen this? Why didn't one of them…Cha Ma, especially…forestall this, stop this?* Somewhere deep inside, minute doubts that had begun to take root during my stay in the ashram, grew, especially when in the presence of such doubt-inducing events like this. I did not know it; I was not aware of it. Deep in the depths of me, I hurt from the scene of last night. Watching Linda cry on Cha Ma's lap, understanding that Cha Ma's "aggro" mood was because of Doug, but then knowing, somewhere deep inside where I did not want to admit it, that although Cha Ma knew, she could do nothing about it.

The questions swirled in my heart of hearts: *Perhaps she's not as powerful as we'd like to think, as she'd like to portray… Who has she really helped anyway? Who has she really saved? And what does it matter when push comes to shove and someone's life is on the line, she, with all her powers, with all her psychic abilities, can do absolutely nothing but be crazy-angry during the fact and cry afterward? What does it matter when all she can do is cry just like anybody else after the man's life is lost, gone…forever…? Doug under a death star…*

I thought of Doug and his boils and his announcement that he would be enlightened soon. *Did he think he'd die? Is that how he became enlightened? And if Cha Ma knew he was under a death star, couldn't she have done something? She said he had to stay near her in order to be protected…is that true? Could she…did she…really protect him here? It doesn't seem so, not when I think of his boils. And then, why couldn't she protect him even a few hours away? Isn't she powerful enough for that? She's supposed to be Kali…the Divine Mother…her power should extend farther than the ashram grounds.* These doubts burned and multiplied deep within me, and I handled these unacknowledged questions in the only way I could.

"Karuna, I think I'm going to skip breakfast. I'm going to go up to the roof to meditate. I'm just too upset." I ached to get away from everyone. I simply wanted to sit in my favorite place, the uppermost platform, and stare at the ocean and, hopefully, drop into a deep, deep meditation that would make me forget all this. Maybe I would have a vision of Kali or Cha Ma, something exciting and fantastic so that I could feel they were not failing me. Something that would distract me from the dangerous questions that swirled around inside of me. Something that would distract me from the doubts that I dared not hear.

"OK, Prema. I should go meditate, too, but I'm hungry," Karuna responded. She glanced up to the meditation roof. "I'll probably be up there after breakfast."

Alice (true to Alice-form, which is that nothing seemed to faze her nor did she *really* care about anyone but herself) said about Doug and Linda, "Man! That's so sad what happened with Doug, and Linda crying so." And then not even in the next breath, "Hmmm, I don't feel like kanji and curry today. I wonder what the Western canteen has to eat." Her voice was conversational and pleasant as if she had not just found out that someone she knew had drowned the day before.

I stood there trying not to show my incredulity at her callousness. I felt sick to my stomach realizing that to her...to many of the ashramites (as I looked around and observed)...Doug's death was nothing more than a curiosity, an "event" to break the monotony, a "happening" to pepper the experiences of life in the ashram. To many, his death was nothing more than an anecdote to share and gossip about. *No one seems to realize that Doug's not ever coming back!* I paused as I struggled to retrieve my untenable belief system. I recollected myself. *Oh yeah! That's right, we're Hindus—we believe that everyone is reincarnated. So Doug will be back...unless he reached enlightenment before he died.* But that thought did nothing to make me feel better. It felt like an ad hoc explanation at best and a flimsy excuse at worst.

Something deep inside challenged on (oh, if only I could shut it up!): *What if this is it? What if Doug has died and there isn't another life and another life and another...what if he's blown it? As for enlightenment and merging into Brahman, what if it's not true and we don't merge?* My Christian upbringing spoke to me. *What if he's dead and now he'll be in hell because he didn't believe in Jesus when he died?*

I felt my breath turning shallow. I simply had to escape my own thoughts. I turned to Karuna. "I'm out of here! I'll talk to you later." I strained to go into meditation and ignore, block out, chant out, chant away all the thoughts, the questions, the niggling doubts. As I walked away, still more thoughts wafted by, lighter than soft spring breezes, assailing me by their eternal import. *What if this is all wrong? What if we're banking on the wrong thing and there really is a Heaven and hell? What if they're right and the only way to get out of hell and into Heaven is through Jesus? What will happen to us? What will happen to me?*

I walked toward the temple feeling sick to my stomach—from the news of Doug or from my own chaotic questioning, I could not say. I began to chant my Kali mantra hoping that the mantra would dispel the rebellious thoughts and cheer me up. The thoughts dispelled; the upset did not. I grew more afraid and full of worry with each step that I took. The mantra felt like a living vise that slipped tighter and tighter, constricting with each syllable I chanted. By the time I reached the flight of steps to the fourth floor, I was running, trying to escape the mantra that rolled up from within me and spilled effortlessly from my mouth. I felt as though it were suffocating me from the inside out. I felt as if I were asphyxiating on a bunch of syllables that snaked about me, coiling tighter and tighter, refusing to let go.

THE UNSEEN BATTLE

Little did Maya know that as soon as she began to chant her mantra, Chamunda Kali knew and responded to the Sanskritic words—ancient sounds—that contained the essence of who she…it…was. Chamunda could *feel* the mantra…*her* mantra…calling her, beckoning her to come, to intervene in the ways in which only she could. She slipped through floors and walls to join the chanter of her mantra, Maya. As Maya chanted, Chamunda walked behind her and caressed her neck, slipped her fingers around Maya's neck…whispering insults, negative thoughts, fear, and worry into her ear.

"Stuuuuupid giiiiiiiirl, there is no real Heaven or hell." Chamunda hissed insidious words of spiritual foment, "There are only lokas of which Heaven and hell are a small part and you move through them. Of course, you don't have just one life, you have lifetime after lifetime after lifetime, until you merge into the ultimate Brahman…" As she talked, she leisurely stroked her long, gnarled fingers around Maya's neck and up and down her spine, causing the girl to shiver. "…the universal consciousness…the awareness of all that is and isn't. There is no real God. There are many gods, all of which are parts of the ultimate Brahman. All merge back into the universal consciousness. How can we be confined to *one* God? That is such a limiting thought….Why would this *one* God confine us to one lifetime…*one* chance…to get it right? And then, give us only one Heaven and hell for all eternity? Does that even make sense to you, giiiiiiirl?" She leaned close to Maya, hissing into her ear. Brownish black spittle oozed out of the corners of her mouth. "Why would a god condemn us to such an abominably horrible place as hell based upon one lifetime? That does not make sense…does it?"

Chamunda's words slid smoothly into Maya's soul, conflicting and warring with her doubts about Cha Ma. *No! I must be wrong. Cha Ma is good. There is no real Heaven or hell. There's not just one chance. But what if I'm wrong?* Confusion ensued. Maya spiraled quickly into a depression, aided by Depression who came to keep her company and whisper to her, as did Fear, Confusion, Despair, and others.

The war for Maya's soul continued on; and every little battle, every little skirmish counted. Every little doubt and moment of confusion tallied. Much toil—minuscule and Herculean, human and supernatural—went into the battle.

On the other side of the world, Marie was at work when she heard: *Pray! Pray now!* She felt an unction to pray. And so she did. In spite of her own troubles and problems, all of which threatened to dominate her thoughts, she obeyed the urge. She began to pray in the Spirit for her child. She did not know what exactly to pray for, so it suited her simply to pray in the Spirit. As she sat at her desk praying, she felt her spirit lift; she could not see that it was being carried right into the Throne Room of the Lord. As she entered in, she began to sing in the Spirit.

Immediately, the atmosphere on the other side of the world was disturbed, which in turn, affected Chamunda. "Ahhh! That awful noise!" Chamunda screeched as she wheeled around. Depression, Fear, and the others drew back. Chamunda loosed her grip on Maya and backed away, too. The simple prayers of Marie were enough to stay Chamunda's hand and her whispers.

Strangely for Maya, new and disturbing, yet at the same time, refreshing thoughts began: *Have I ever seen Cha Ma really heal someone or help someone? So many people here in India with so many ailments, diseases, and deformities—have I seen any healed, like I've seen with Christ?* Maya chanted harder, but she heard an answer from within her: *No.* Just that. Simply, "No." One word could have been enough to begin unraveling all her beliefs; but she did not allow the answer to penetrate her mind—it landed on rocky, inimical ground. She pushed it away.

Chamunda tried to get close enough to whisper in her ear but every time she drew near to the girl, the sound, *that awful sound,* was in her ears. She could not whisper to Maya. She could not even approach her. *Maya's blasted mother must be praying!* She hovered a couple of paces away from Maya, waiting for her opportunity. None came. *We must stop that woman!*

The day passed; Marie had stopped praying a long time ago. Work had engrossed her energy and her attention. When it was quitting time, she went home. Paul was there, which was unusual because with his new job he was rarely home when she got off in the evenings.

Although Marie had stopped praying and had resumed working, the warfare on the other side of the earth had not halted. The battle continued to swirl in and around Maya as she sat on the roof meditating and chanting throughout the night. Chamunda took the opportunity afforded by the girl's prolonged meditation and chanting of her Kali mantra and her mother's cessation of praying to redouble her attack.

In the dark of the night, a lone figure—Maya—sat on the roof. Wisps of something dark and sinister that shifted between a gaunt, hungry woman-thing and a tall, gnarly, knotty, tree-like specter, wrapped its fingers around her. It whispered, hungrily, into her ear as she fell deeper and deeper into a sepia-toned meditation. Figures spun and whirled toward and around and past her. As she observed herself involved in the drama unfolding within herself, she shuddered from the violence and brutishness of the beings populating her meditation. She saw acts too violent and hideous to mention. She saw herself not as a she but as a *he*, and she saw the man who was she committing acts too despicable and perverted to be even criminal. Longer and longer she sat. Deeper and deeper she fell. Her body listed to the side as that hungry monstrosity hissed into her and malevolently caressed her soul.

She startled to. Her mind, her emotions, even her sense of what was sensible and rudimentarily good was assaulted by her dark but vivid meditation. Her mind recoiled from the meditation. *What was that about?* She ruminated upon herself as she appeared in the meditation: *I was a man...I must've been this man in another life. Was I...am I...such a beast? Did I really do such...things...to others? Did I travel to another loka? Maybe the demonic loka that I've heard others talking about? Maybe I'm just burning off my evil karma. Oh Kali! Let me be burning off evil karma! Yes! That was what I was doing.* She was mortified by the evilness of what was hatched and executed within her own mind. Sheer depravity. *Is that what is lurking within me? Oh Kali! Help me! How I pray that this is my last lifetime...*

Her mind then settled upon one of her favorite, frequent thoughts that had recently taken a new turn in tenor: *I wish I were Doug. I wish I were dead. I wish I could die for enlightenment.* Her mind spun along, hungrily gravitating to this familiar and comfortable train of thought. *I wish I didn't have any more karma to burn. How I hate this life! How I hate being trapped in this human body...this awful body that keeps me bound to being reborn...* Half-thinkingly, she stood and walked to the edge of the roof. *No, it's not my body that keeps me bound,* she reasoned feverishly. *It's my thoughts, my words, my actions that keep me bound to this...samsara...my karma binds me...*

After hours of meditating and chanting her mantra, it seemed as if the words of the mantra beckoned her to the edge…to have courage…*If I truly want enlightenment.* Somehow…some way…like every other night she found herself standing on the edge of the roof.

Her toes poked over the edge. Again, she heard—

Jump!

She leaned forward. *I can do this…*

Jump!

"No!" Majesty, Awe, Brilliant, and His Strength spoke. With the utterance of that one word, a burst of radiant light, unobserved by humans, exploded from within and without their fully, purely divine bodies and undulated through them until it shot out of each of their mouths and united into one massive spark—a sublimely supernatural mixture of divine sound and light. All that was needed was one Word from the Glory.

"No!" Jovial and Mighty spoke at the same time. Even as they watched Marie and Paul talking—the stilted conversation of two people as far away and as distant as possible—they could see, at the same time, due to their divine nature, the battle that waged on the other side of the world as Maya stood on the edge of the roof. The Will of the Lord coursed through their bodies in much the same way as it did through Majesty's, Awe's, His Strength's, and Brilliant's. The force of His Will rolled out of their mouths—a powerful, destiny-altering spark—and shot through the atmosphere faster than a thought impulse, uniting and merging perfectly with the utterance of their angelic comrades on the other side of the earth. Even as that one word united with that uttered by Majesty, Awe, Brilliant, and His Strength and released its power, their eyes remained locked on Marie and Paul. ·

Marie and Paul tried to say a bit more to each other but soon the conversation died away. They sat in their armchairs in the den, not talking or watching the news. They stared at the screen and tried to blot out the fears and anxieties in their own minds. As the night passed, they fell asleep in their chairs.

The angels' hearts went out to Marie and Paul. They could see the pain and the fear, the upset. To their eyes, such things—aberrations in unnatural, *unhuman* hues of murky brown, dull mustard yellow, and sickly pink—were strikingly obvious and were, in fact, more real and tangible than anything of the physical world. As they gazed into Marie's body, they could see the effects of Sickness, Disease, and Illness—the fierce pain, the impaired vision, the internal swelling. They could see the effect of every action dealt against her body by the evil ones. And just as easily, because they were spiritual beings not bound by the physical, they could see the effect of every hurt, harm, and trauma that had been perpetrated against her heart, her mind, and soul during the course of her lifetime—those caused by simply living life and those deliberately perpetrated against her person by the evil ones. They could see the effects of worry and stress upon her, upon Paul, too—invisible (to the human eye) effects that slowly ate away at the emotional, mental, and physical material of their bodies, weakening them, deteriorating them, and ultimately paralyzing them (if the enemy had his way).

However, this was their, Marie and Paul's, test. They would have to press through and beyond to seize a prize that they could not see, a prize that they had to trust was awaiting them, especially when everything around them clamored that there was no prize. Such was the human condition in the spiritual realm. Rarely were humans given vision that included the future—that ability came only if the Lord allowed them access to a sliver of His divine perspective or if the evil ones (spiritual opportunists in the greatest sense) forced on a human their vision (a warped, distorted view that unconscionably excluded God and His Will and influence). Although, if the Lord gave a particular human access, then he or she could know the true, unquestionable outcome of the future, regardless of the personal, conscious choices of those involved—free will was a deeper, more subtle, more intricate mystery than ever could be imagined.

The same could be said of the Lord's angels: they did not always have a vision that held the future—such vision came only when the Lord allowed them a minute piece of His vision. However, they saw and understood much more than humans. They could perceive and observe the outworkings of the Lord's mystery concerning free will—how it was always admitted and functioning; yet it never ran contrary to the Lord's Will for each and every life; and in fact, it always conformed in some miraculous way to His Will for every life. Further, the Lord's angels could shape and fashion the future as the Lord deemed, circumventing and admitting complete and utter free will, solely through His express power—for to mold the future, a creative talent that only the Lord held, could only be passed from the Lord to one of His angelic proxies.

It was a skill, a talent that the evil ones did not have, *and never would*, having fallen out of His graces in the Rebellion. Satan, their lord, would never have that creative power and he certainly could not pass on that which he did not have. And then, of course, the evil ones simply could not perceive, let alone observe and understand, the outworkings of the Lord's vision. They simply were no longer equipped for that—they had existed for far too long outside the Lord's Presence. They were unable to shape and mold the future, unlike the Lord's angels, so instead, they usurped and manipulated in the hopes of gaining what they would never have.

Marie and Paul needed to pray together. They needed to come to a place of agreement because their unified prayers were supernaturally, exponentially, more powerful than their separate prayers. But, as they sat there, Despair and Depression wove an inertia-inducing web about their bodies. They no longer needed to break through *only* their own malaise; they would also have to break through a demonic web that was being woven to contain them.

Even as Jovial and Mighty watched, Paul muttered, in the midst of sleeping, "My God...help me!" The prayer, even uttered in slumber, flew to Heaven. Instantaneously, Jovial and Mighty received a message within themselves sent from Heaven. An order had been issued to stir Marie to join her husband in prayer—the Lord had heard and responded in His Throne Room. Further, He showed them, in a fraction of a second, a window of opportunity that He had opened in the spirit realm, which would have a profound impact upon Maya's situation in the future. Clearly Paul's words, however weak and unintentional…however slumberous…had power, for they were the catalyst. How much more would the two of them praying together have an effect?

"Marie! Now! Watch and pray! Watch and pray!" Jovial leaned his big, hulking, naturally protective frame over Marie and spoke in a whisper, of sorts. However, angelic whispers are not like human whispers, in that angelic words are generally not intended for, nor received by, physical ears. Jovial's whisper went past her ears into her spirit. He whispered again, "Marie! Pray now for Maya," and blew a thin stream of silvery light into her ear. Quickly it delved into her ear, swirled around within her head, and dove down to her heart.

Marie's eyes snapped opened and she sat up, "Huh?" Her eyes adjusted to the darkness of the den. Almost. Big, black spots were superimposed upon the indigo blue of the room, so that it seemed as though she were staring at irregular jet-black suns ringed with midnight blue coronas. *I was sleeping so well. I need to climb into bed and go back to sleep.* She felt her body and mind sliding back into slumber.

"Pray, Marie! Now!" Jovial commanded, fervently. As he ordered her in response to the Lord's command, divine power flowed into her upon his silvery breath. He saw the Holy Spirit well up inside of her to give her the strength, the energy, the desire to awaken and pray. He could see the Lord's Spirit moving within her, through her, around her—an awesome sight more vital and alive than anything physical. It was crucial that she pray. A window of opportunity had opened to "alter" the situation.

In response to the unction, Marie began praying in the Spirit as, simultaneously, the Holy Spirit welled up inside of her and she yielded herself to Him. As she prayed, she felt within her, "Awaken Paul, you need the power. Where two or more are gathered…" She did not know that Jovial was whispering those same words, silvery words gliding in upon silvery breath, as the Holy Spirit commanded from within her through her own praying.

Marie leaned over and shook her husband, "Paul...wake up...wake up..."

"What's going on? What's the matter?" Paul asked as she shook him awake. He pushed himself forward in the armchair as if he were ready to bolt.

"It's Maya! I just feel we need to pray, we MUST pray, right now!" Marie replied urgently.

"What do you mean? What are you feeling?" he asked, puzzled. His eyes searched the darkened room.

"I don't know. I was sleeping when suddenly I was awakened, almost as if someone had called my name or something and was telling me to pray. I'm sure it was the Holy Spirit or an angel calling me to action. There's such an urgency. I don't know what's going on, but I feel so strongly that I need you to pray with me and I need you do it *right now*."

"OK," Paul said. He slid out of the chair and onto his knees on the floor. He held out his hands to his wife. Marie joined him on the floor, facing him, holding his hands.

Paul bowed his head and waited for the Holy Spirit to move him to say what needed to be prayed. Finally, "Dear God...we pray for Your Will to be done." Paul paused, again, as if listening...sensing..."We ask for a legion, no...*legions*," he said this with unusual intensity, "to come and help Maya. We feel she's in trouble and she needs You to intervene, right now." He continued praying what he felt arising within him. "We feel that there is a window...a door that has opened in the spirit. We ask that You open it wide. We may not see it in the physical for some time... Oh God! Please give us the strength to wait patiently for You, trusting in You. Your Word says that we are those that wait upon You, Lord, and You renew our strength day-by-day. We mount up with wings like eagles so that we may run and not grow weary, so that we may, no matter the obstacles and how things appear...we may walk and not faint."

Marie joined him, quietly praying in the Spirit, expressing in tongues exactly what he was praying. Her words were melodious sounds that flowed like a song, weaving around and over his prayer. Her contralto voice danced around his deep tenor. They were in agreement, in complete unity. Theirs was a potent oneness that was borne out of their marriage covenant—the binding of a man's being with that of his wife that, when in agreement, could move Heaven and earth—a glorious mystery of Heaven revealed only minutely in the physical, the majority of its interaction within the spiritual. This mystery was rendered even more powerful and sublime when the man and woman were each other's God-appointed destiny, as Marie and Paul were—and not simply a wayward choice outside of God's Will that forced God to intervene and make it right after the fact—such an alignment of destiny was incalculably powerful.

As they prayed that night, the Lord's Presence grew within the room and in the house. Within minutes, they were overcome by the Holy Spirit. Tears began to stream down their faces. Paul's prayer in English switched into the language of the Spirit, a melodic, beautiful, otherworldly language, his tenor joining his wife's contralto. The Holy Spirit had been given His way—completely, fully. He prayed His Will through Paul and Marie. He was creating a window of opportunity that would be impossible for Maya to miss. It would be in the future, further away in time; but the seeds of it were being sown at that moment. Seeds, that once planted, would be hidden beneath a blanket of contrary events and happenings: events and happenings that would never once point to such a God-appointed, God-glorifying outcome.

Out of the house, magnificent, vibrant light radiated. It lifted higher and higher, as they prayed, soaring into the sky, reaching into the spiritual realm, and sparking out in all directions. Jovial turned to Mighty, a large smile gracing his face, "Yes! This is exactly what was needed. Help is on the way!" He looked toward the sky. From every direction, beautifully iridescent, glowing angels were descending upon the house. Such glory and magnificence radiated from them, from their very beings.

As they walked, ran, flew in upon the air…merely appeared, they began nodding their heads, uttering, "Yes! Yes! Thy Will be done! Yes!" They agreed in response to the commands of the Holy Spirit as He prayed His

Will through the mouths of Marie and Paul. The angelic host gathered. Literally, legions of angels were coming together at the behest of God, His Holy Spirit commanding them via the heavenly language. They ordered themselves by rank, naturally, effortlessly—for order was intrinsic to their nature for the Lord had made them so. They moved themselves smoothly into three legions.

Their beauty, their light—the Glory of God manifested in the angelic realm—filled the house with such color, radiance, and light. It was light that existed in spectrums unknown to man, even in theory. The light, their heavenly, glorious light, vibrated and undulated with the pure essence of pure, fiery, consuming love. Out of this undulation, this vibration (the source of a particle's wave and existence), a hum could be heard. A primordial, elemental rhythm pulsed. It flowed out from them and melded into the fabric of the universe, altering it for good, weaving it irrevocably with light. Upon this universe-altering, vibrational "sound," the angels sang a song to their Lord that rolled out from within their bodies—it suffused their beings, pressed out from them, and wove a divine vibrational fabric within and around them. They were enwrapped and intertwined with living light, vibration, sound, and song.

Jovial, as was his nature, flashed a jubilant grin as he looked around, reveling in the display of light and sound that was the vibrational sound and angelic song. All angels of the Lord, because of who they worshiped, could hear the sound of light and observe the brilliance of sound. As he gazed upon the Lord's handiwork in the angelic ranks, his spirit, already so high, soared even higher. He was beyond bliss. If only humans could understand that the nature of the angels...of all beings, including humans...was a divinely sublime and majestic mystery of vibration and light and sound.

If only Marie and Paul could have seen the power of their prayers! If only they could have observed the effect of allowing the Holy Spirit to pray through them! Such was the power and authority that manifested itself through them. Oh, to see all those that were for them—the beauty, the splendor, the brilliance, the *goodness* of the Lord's troops! As Elisha's servant was reassured and comforted when Elisha prayed to the Lord to reveal His troops and He did, they would have been tremendously comforted. If only they could have seen more were for them than were against them and that the battle was assured, they would not have worried.

But they could not see; thus, they were plagued with worries and fears. Their faith had not grown to the place that they could be fully confident in the Lord. Here in the crucible called "Test," the Lord would see to it that their faith grew. In this crucible, they pressed against the heavy weights of "Doubt" and "Lack of Faith" as the pestle called "Circumstances" crushed them. And so they prayed and warred in their minds. Yes, their hearts were steadfast—they loved their daughter, wanted her home, and knew that only God could help them; but their minds struggled and battled with doubt, fear, and anxiety.

At the direction of the Holy Spirit, the three commanders of the warrior angels—Hachao, Salaa, and Bredeno—stepped forward. The three were 15 feet tall and massive. The angels (warrior angels, too) positioned behind them were only slightly less tall and massive. All of their muscles rippled and pulsated under their golden-bronze tunics. They did not have on the full body gear used in all-out warfare with the enemy's principalities. They wore a sword on their hips, with several daggers tucked in here and there. No, this was not a call to all-out warfare, but rather a skirmish, an opportunity to play with the enemy a bit.

With unconcealed anticipation, Hachao, Salaa, and Bredeno separated, each stepping in front of one of the perfectly ordered legions. Without a word spoken amongst the angels, the three legions led by Hachao, Salaa, and Bredeno rose straight up into the sky and flew off in different directions. In less than a second, they disappeared altogether, only to reappear (to those who had eyes to "see") in India. To be exact, they reappeared above the Indian Ocean some one thousand feet away from the ashram. Still in rank. Perfect formation. In the instant in which it took them to materialize off the coast of India, they had pulled out their weapons.

They "stood" above the water. The very power of Who they represented flowed through and out of them, causing the water to churn violently. Anyone standing on the shore would have seen, out of nowhere, the ocean suddenly, seemingly without any provocation, grow turbulent and full of riptides. The bright light of the sun flashed and glinted on the water and on their brandished weapons. Their eyes blazed with a holy fire! Their hair undulated as though it were being caressed by the wind; however, the angels, of course, existed in a realm in which wind had no effect.

On the meditation roof, demon sentinels peered out toward the ocean, asking among themselves, "What is that? What is that glinting?" The Lord's angels had approached...*materialized*...so rapidly that the evil ones did not have an opportunity to note their arrival. The sentinels paced back and forth, looking, wondering...only rarely seeing such light in this part of the world. As they squinted out toward the ocean through one, two, and even three misshapen, deformed eyes, they noticed that a "force" sped toward them—awe-inspiring, glorious, powerful light—pure and radiant! Their bodies burned from the magnificent light although it was hundreds of yards away. In the blink of an eye, the light was upon them, cascading over them.

They careened backward—unable to react properly because of the swiftness and skill with which the Lord's army engaged them. Dar-Rek, one of the lesser imps, a guard, howled an alert into the wind, a signal, an alarm, to the others of the attack. Unfortunately, the fallen angels did not move as quickly as the Lord's as there was no longer light within them. They were bound by their own rebelliousness and disobedience, which led to a distinct disadvantage in warfare (the only way to overcome such a glaring disadvantage was through subterfuge, illegality, and opportunism). This time they would have to fight on the Lord's terms. As the evil ones mustered their strength and forces, the Lord's angels deftly overcame them—moving swifter than the speed of light, their skill and agility making them appear as if they were executing a beautiful dance.

Chamunda was taken by surprise, along with all the others. The Lord's angels were simply too fleet, careening in upon the very thought of the Lord. Chamunda had to make a choice (no choice really)—continue trying to coerce Maya over the edge, which was contrary to God's overarching Will and thus an immutable impossibility, or leave the girl and join her forces in battling the Lord's angels. She, knowing her chances, chose to leave Maya and go fight.

Immediately, Maya's knees buckled without the power of demonic suggestion holding her up. Majesty gently pressed his index finger into her chest. It was enough—she stumbled backward, away from the edge. She slumped to the floor, exhausted by the warfare that swirled around her and the dark, perverse meditation and suicidal thoughts that had preceded the warfare. She crossed her legs into a pseudo-lotus position in order to meditate. However, meditation was the last thing on her mind. She tried to focus on her Kali mantra. She tried to focus on her third-eye. Then, on the blue light. Nothing. All to no avail. Instead, the questions that had plagued her earlier, recommenced with a vengeance—*Has Cha Ma ever healed anyone? And then…psycho-ness aside, is anyone really, truly happy here?* From within, a "no" wafted upward. *And if they're not happy, do they get any happier while they're here? What if there really is only one chance around? Am I willing to bank eternity on it? What if I'm on the wrong side? What if there is a hell? Am I willing to remain forever and forever in hell?*

Further, as Maya struggled to meditate, the presence of so many of the Lord's angels disrupted her. Their glorious power and the Holy Spirit Who was with them ruined the atmosphere for any sort of meditation. As she sat there, the two eternally and diametrically opposed sides battled.

Swords of light glinted from an internally powered illumination in the hands of the Lord's angels. Some of them, in the midst of the battle, spoke Words, divine, God-ordained Words that shot out of their mouths, the most injurious of weapons. These inflicted the most damage upon Chamunda's minions.

Even one precisely uttered Word was enough—it would land upon their hideous, demonic flesh and hard, lumpy exoskeletons and begin to burn. It was the worst kind of acid. The burn from the Words of God would continue on for eternity—a forever wound that would always fester. A pain that would never be alleviated or lessened, but would worsen over the centuries, the millennia, and eons.

The atmosphere swirled violently as the demonic countered and parried to overcome the Lord's angels. They swung their weapons, which were more useful as instruments of torture or for bludgeoning—they used serrated sickles and battle-axes, clubs and maces, and wicked, jagged daggers. These tended to leave dirty, nasty mustard-yellow and sallow, brown streaks in the atmosphere as if they were sludging up the air itself.

Weapons rang against each other, punctuating the discordant grunts, groans, and shrieks of the demonic and the rhythmic, melodious voices of the Lord's angels. The battle did not last long (it never did unless the prayers that released the Lord's angels were lukewarm, half-hearted, and weak, or unless the evil ones acted illegally or tried, opportunistically, to preempt the Lord's angels). The demonic were speedily overcome. Their ranks fell apart one by one—Fear quickly bolted. On his tail scampered Despair. Dar-Rek, the lesser imp who howled a warning, held out longer than they did, but he, too, was rapidly overcome (no more could be expected of a mere lesser imp). To the end battled Death, Suicide, and Murder alongside Chamunda. Finally, they, too, backed off and ran away—overcome and burning, bearing forever the recently inflicted wounds in their bodies.

Maya was left on the roof with the Lord's angels. As had happened so many nights since she had arrived at the ashram, the Lord's angels clustered around her. Brilliant and Majesty of the closest circle, her assigned guardians, began speaking into her. The heavenly language flowed into her—a much-needed salve—healing and mending the emotional and mental damage inflicted by the evil ones. Majesty rested one hand upon her head and the other upon her chest—glorious, pale blue light swirled into her, entering deep within, giving her succor. Brilliant, glinting without from within, stood above her and breathed shimmery, golden light upon her. Quickly, it melted into her body—healing and restoring. Awe and His Strength stood with Hachao, Salaa, and Bredeno discussing strategy as the three legions formed progressively larger circles around her and around the ashram. They stared outward looking for the evil minions who had disappeared.

Maya remained sitting and slipped into a deep, dreamless sleep.

ANTYESHTI

Maya
India

"What's going on?" I asked as I joined Karuna on the women's balcony. She was staring out into the area of the brahmachari huts where a large crowd had gathered. From where we were standing, I could not figure out what they were doing. In the center of the crowd, I could make out a large pile of wood with something white lying atop it.

"I dunno," Karuna responded, puzzlement in her voice. "Let's go down and see."

It was unusual to see so many people milling about so early in the morning on a non-Kali Leela day. *I wonder what it's all about.* Karuna and I padded down the outside spiral steps of the women's dorm and cut across the field. As we drew closer, I noted that it was mostly a crowd of ashramites. They were hushed and reverential, many of them holding their hands in prayer fashion, palms together.

Quietly, we pushed our way forward until we halted at the pile of wood in the center of the throng. Just in front of us, forming a ring around the pile of wood, was a row of pujaris—male brahmacharis and sannyasis who were specially consecrated to conduct Cha Ma's religious ceremonies and rites—in white and yellow dhotis.

Karuna leaned over and whispered, "Isn't it odd to see the pujaris outside of the puja shrine?" I nodded. *It is odd to see them outside of the puja shrine.* The puja shrine was a tiny little building that consisted of two rooms—the main worship room and a smaller store room. It was set a few feet from the main temple. Its sole purpose was for the pujaris to conduct rites, ceremonies, and offerings to different gods and goddesses.

The pujaris were bare-backed, except for a thin piece of woven thread that hung over their left shoulder and looped down and around to the opposing hip—the Brahmin thread. Their dhotis were wrapped tightly about their waists and hung to the ground. They had cream-colored symbols—*more than likely made with tulasi*—written on their faces, torsos, and arms. They were standing in a circle, facing the huge pyre of wood, making mudras—hand gestures meant to have spiritual power—and chanting in deep monotones. My eyes swept over them unconsciously searching for the face I always sought. *Narayana! I didn't know he was a pujari!* I snorted derisively to myself. *It figures! Just one more thing "Ultra-brahmachari" can do!* I forced my willful eyes to keep moving. They moved on to the pyre.

Atop the pyre, which I could now see clearly, as we were only one row of bodies away from it, was...I stared...a *body* wrapped in white cloth. Understanding struck me at the same time that it did Karuna—

"Is that Doug?" Karuna queried in a high-pitched whisper.

"I think so..."

"Poor Linda," Karuna sighed deeply.

I nodded my head in agreement. It was all I would allow myself to do. I felt as though I were suddenly standing precipitously on the edge of a strange chasm. I was not too sure how I felt about sitting in on a Hindu funeral service, an antyeshti, especially when they were about to burn the body of someone I knew. It was one thing to watch the rites on a documentary on television. It was one thing to *talk* about burning the body. It was another thing altogether to *watch* a body burning. And then, the idea of burning the body of someone I had just seen a couple of days ago—someone who was nice and funny…someone who was recently married (*Poor Linda*, I echoed Karuna)…someone who was too young to die—was simply too unsettling and disturbing.

But, I remained anyway. Curiosity drove me…as did my desire to watch Narayana, who was busy performing the rites along with the others. I could not stop myself from remarking, "I didn't know Narayana was a pujari…" *How quickly I can get triflingly distracted—one minute I'm freaking about burning Doug's body, the next I'm thinking about Narayana.* I would have chuckled at myself if I had not been so aghast by the whole situation and my uncompassionate reaction.

Karuna nodded her head, looking over at him. "Uh-huh, I've seen him a couple of times in the puja shrine. Although it seems to me he spends so much time with Cha Ma that it's not really a duty he has to keep."

"Oh." I kept surveying the crowd. Directly across from Karuna and me stood Linda staring blankly at the body of her husband. Her face was swollen and splotchy, unimaginable anguish played fiercely across it. At the moment she was not crying, although she looked as though she had been crying non-stop since receiving the news. Even now, her swollen, red-rimmed eyes swam in barely-restrained pools that threatened to overflow and slide down her cheeks. My heart went out to her and then recoiled; her pain was too much for me to even begin to sympathize with.

Where's Cha Ma? She should be around here somewhere… I searched the crowd. She was nowhere to be found. How odd, at this time of great need and grief, she's not here! I looked back at Linda, who looked dazed and lost and in intense agony. It doesn't even matter to Linda. It probably wouldn't register anyway.

"I wonder if she had any idea when she began her honeymoon with Doug that it would come to this…" Karuna whispered over the subdued chanting of the pujaris.

One of the pujaris began walking around the body, holding a small pot. Over and over, as he chanted along with the others, he stuck his hand into the pot and flicked whatever was in it onto the body and pyre.

I shot her a castigating glance. "Of course, she didn't have any idea! Could you imagine going on your honeymoon and *this* happening?" I hissed back at her.

My mind replayed when I had met them. I had been standing in a rice pot scrubbing away in front of the Western canteen, when they had walked up, happy, smiling, excited about visiting Cha Ma. *Yeah! Who would have thought?* "This is a nightmare." I felt so sorry for Linda. "I can't even imagine what she's going through…although it would be great to be Doug…"

"Why do you say that?" Karuna sounded bewildered.

"Because he told me that Cha Ma had said that this would be his last lifetime, that he was going to reach moksha." Even standing in front of his funeral pyre, I felt a wave of envy wash over me, fighting with the part of me that rebelled against the idea of dying.

"Enlightenment! Really?" Karuna's voice was full of awe. "I wonder if this…his dying…was necessary in order to burn up his karma?"

"I don't know." I shrugged as I struggled to put the envy and rebellion in check. I watched the pujari who had been sprinkling the body, deliberately drop the pot at the head of the body. I heard it shatter against the ground as I felt someone jostle my arm.

"Namah shivaya." I turned to see Radha's smiling face. *Good! I can ask her some questions.*

"Namah shivaya," I greeted her in return. "What are they doing?"

"They're performing the funeral ritual. It's actually a several-day process…I'm not too sure how long," she whispered in a low voice. "The pujaris are doing a ceremony for preparing the soul and getting the body ready for burning."

"Can anyone do the ceremonies? Or just the pujaris?" I asked. I scanned the bare-backed brahmacharis, my eyes pausing on one in particular.

"Oh! Only the pujaris…and of them only the high-ranking ones can perform antyeshti."

"Wow," Karuna murmured.

I did not say anything because I did not want to give myself away as envy had, again, reared its nasty head. *I hate Narayana…Ultra-brahmachari!*

Radha continued, "All of the pujaris have been trained in doing the sacred rituals. They go through a special tapas…"

"Tapas?" Karuna interrupted.

"Spiritual practices usually meant to burn karma; but in their case it also keeps them in a high spiritual state. They have to maintain a very high level of purity so that they're able to do the pujas at any time without polluting the pujas with impurities or lower urges. This is especially important when it comes to antyeshtis. You don't want to mess up a soul's future."

"Oh," Karuna whispered for me.

"OK, so why did the pujari break the pot at the head of the body?" I asked, my attention again being drawn to the ritual. I could see Narayana carrying out his role; but as it was not one of the main roles, I watched the others. They moved so fluidly as they made madras—their hands flying through complicated, intricate gestures, in perfect unison—and performed the steps of the ceremony.

"I'm not sure. I think it has something to do with breaking ties with this life."

"Why do they burn the body instead of burying it?" Karuna asked.

"From what I understand, they believe that burning the body helps the soul let go of the body so that it won't stay around. If it's too attached to its body, it will linger." She shot us a wry smile. "Do you know what they call souls that linger around?"

"Huh-uh…" Karuna and I responded in unison.

"Ghosts!"

I felt my face frown up. *Not good!* Prickles slid up my neck. But then, somehow, standing beside a burning body has that effect upon people.

"So they burn the body in order to force the soul to let the body go. Hopefully, it will move on and be reborn…" She paused as a pujari grabbed a flaming stick from the fire pit nearby and stuck it into the wood of the pyre, near the bottom.

As I watched, I felt a shudder course through my body. *It takes a lot of getting used to—seeing a body set on fire.*

The wood caught fire easily, the flames hungrily lapping at the dry tinder. "But, if a person is done…if he's achieved moksha, the soul will easily go and merge into Brahman. Then, it's up to the soul as to whether it wants to remain as one with Brahman or if it wants to come back as an enlightened being to help the rest of us to enlightenment."

"Like Cha Ma," Karuna whispered—a strangeness pressing through her voice.

"Yes, like Cha Ma."

We lapsed into silence and stared at the pyre along with everyone else in the crowd. A peculiar stillness sat upon us—broken only by the deep, rhythmic chanting of the pujaris and the snapping and popping of the wood. I stared, entranced, by the flames overtaking the wood. *It's amazing how quickly it burns.* Smoke began to billow up from the pyre. With it, the distinctively sweet smell of burning spices grew.

I could see Linda's face in between the dancing fingers of the flames. She continued to stare at the enshrouded body of her husband as the flames began to lick up the white wrapping. Her face looked so distraught and undone. The devastating battle of conflicting emotions was all over her face. Tears coursed down her cheeks, again. Her arms were wrapped tightly about her body as if she were desperately trying to hold herself together.

A nervous fear grew in the pit of my stomach. *Please don't try to jump onto the pyre.* I recalled stories I had heard of wives throwing themselves onto the burning pyre of their husbands—sati.

I focused back on the pyre, where the flames were hungrily lapping away at the body. A hot breeze gusted our way, upon it rolled the putridly sweet odor of burning flesh. I felt nausea press up from my bowels.

"Karuna, I've got to go!" I clamped my mouth closed, clutched my stomach, and turned away without even looking at her.

"Yeah, me too. I can't take this." She turned with me.

I cast a glance behind me to see Narayana tossing something onto the burning pyre as he chanted. It looked to be flower petals. Slowly, his gaze slid from the fire to me, something deep and dark hinting through his eyes. Through the undulating waves of heat from the fire, his face was impenetrable and remote. His gaze shifted back to the fire, his face stoic and absorbed, unperturbed—beautiful—all the more so beside ugly, uncompromising death.

SANNYASA

"C'mon, Premabhakti! Hurry up!" Chandy and Karuna stood on the balcony outside the women's dorm, their heads poking through the glassless window by my bunk, the bars kept them from pressing their faces all the way in. "We don't want to be late for Kali Leela. We've got great spots!"

"OK! OK! I'm coming!"

They walked through the door of the dorm. "Come ooon," Karuna wheedled.

"OK! I'm ready." I threw my asana over my shoulder and headed out of the women's dorm via the entrance that opened onto the temple balcony. Karuna and Chandy led the way, practically skipping around the bodies of the Indians who were already populating the balcony. I knew that if the balcony were this crowded, the temple floor would be overly packed. I leaned over the balcony railing to see. *Oh Kali! It is packed.* "Do you think…?"

109

"No, we didn't lose our spot. I'm sure of it. Can't you see the space where it is?" Karuna asked as she stepped over an entire family. They watched us clamber by—Cha Ma's weird foreigners—always an interesting show.

I cast a quick glance into the masses of devotees waiting to see Cha Ma-as-more-Kali as I hurried behind Chandy and Karuna. "I don't see it."

"See? By Radha?" Karuna persisted.

I looked again and shook my head. "No, I don't even see Radha. But, that's OK. I trust you."

Within a couple of minutes, we were standing at the entrance of the temple—our journey taking longer than usual because we had to climb over so many bodies on the balcony. I stared into the women's side, which was utter chaos...again. As always. Women's bodies, legs, arms, saris, asanas, babies, and children took up every square inch of space. I ventured a glance to the men's side. It never failed to amaze and dishearten me—amaze me that the men could be so orderly, giving each other space and kindness; dishearten me because the women were the exact opposite, completely chaotic and boisterous, easily sparked into violence.

"Follow me," Chandy commanded as she determinedly began maneuvering over the obstacles on the women's side to get to the front of the temple, "namah shivaya-ing" the entire time. I followed behind her with Karuna pulling up the rear.

"Namah shivaya...namah shivaya..." I muttered my "excuse me's"—first, to the angry countenances of seated women, countenances which morphed into looks of surprise and awe when their eyes traveled the length of my body to rest on my hair—I could almost read their thoughts: *"Ahhh, so that's the black American woman?"* (It was really an "experience" to be a kinda-sorta infamous mini-celebrity.) Painstakingly, we filed our way through the mass of non-ashramite Indian women (who stared) and well into the thickly congested sea of white-clad, with a speck of sannyasi yellow here and there, brahmacharinis.

I pulled up beside Chandy, who had quickly plopped down near Radha, and sat where there was a foot of space between her and Radha. I half-expected the brahmacharini in front of me to turn around and give me a nasty look as I rammed my knees up against her back. She did not. *She's probably used to being squished like this.* Karuna plunked down, within nanoseconds of my sitting, slightly behind Radha and me. Her left knee pressed painfully into my lower back. *I'll bear it like the brahmacharinis*—I promised myself. We shifted our bodies back and forth, forcing the brahmacharinis to make room. I smiled hard at them and kept shifting. They were used to being squished, though, and quickly readjusted to allow us room.

After sitting for a while, Karuna awkwardly leaned over my body in order to whisper to Chandy. Her elbow dug into my thigh. I gritted my teeth. "Guess what I heard?" Karuna prompted, her Australian accent causing her voice to lilt in a cute way.

"Uh-uh, what?" Chandy asked with a slightly different Australian accent.

"What?" I inquired, inviting myself into the conversation. I figured that as long as her elbow was digging into my thigh the question was meant for me, too.

Karuna flashed a quick smile. "I heard...Narayana's taking yellow today!" Her voice bubbled with excitement.

"No! Really?" Chandy answered. "I thought Cha Ma doesn't give sannyasa to many."

"It's true, but...I heard that she'll be doing a special ceremony for a handful of the brahmacharis to become sannyasis," Karuna replied.

Radha interjected, "Yes, she's giving sannyasa to three of them today...Narayana's one of them. I'm so happy for him!"

"I heard that Cha Ma hasn't given sannyasa in a long time," Karuna remarked.

"Nope, I think the last time was over two years ago, maybe three," Radha said, her eyes glittering, a smile dancing upon her lips. "It's such an honor!"

I did not say anything. I could not say anything. I felt myself being inundated by a host of emotions and I struggled with making one out from the other—jealousy and envy were the most recognizable ones; pride was there too, although I had no clue as to why I felt proud. I also felt disappointment, hurt, and upset swirling around in the mix.

As I sat there, fighting not to drown in the massive whirlwind of emotions that the news of Narayana's initiation created, the conch shells began to sound and the bells to ring. The beyond-capacity crowd started chanting and singing loudly—we had commenced with a bang.

The noise halted our conversation abruptly, which was fine given the madness of my thoughts. I wanted to hop up, right then and there, and run away—just get as far away as possible. I did not want to sit and watch Narayana, a man I wanted, get something I wanted. But then, I wanted to remain in order to see the ceremony—it was such a special, auspicious occasion. Also (and I hated to admit it), I could not resist the urge to watch him.

I stayed and sang with the crowd, furiously swallowing in order to challenge the lump of tears that threatened to take over my throat. *What is the matter with me?* As I sang, I examined my erratic thoughts and emotions. *I wish I had been born an Indian so that I could become a brahmacharini and then, one day, a sannyasini (is that a word?).* I paused and delved a bit more deeply. *Or am I upset about Narayana? No! Narayana is nothing to me, just a cute guy.* My mind chomped madly upon itself as I sang harder and harder, trying to ignore the stabbing in my throat.

Suddenly the curtains parted, and Cha Ma came out amidst the waves of thick, pungent incense. The spirited singing and chanting died down as if upon some invisible cue (I had not seen anyone give an indication to stop). I peered through the fragrant smoke. In the back, veiled by the bluish smoke, I could make out the figures of three slim brahmacharis—one tall, Narayana, the other two not so very.

They walked forward, white dhotis wrapped neatly about their waists, hanging down to their feet. Their torsos were bare except for the Brahmin thread. They paced, slowly, measuredly around Cha Ma—four times diving down gracefully into a full pranam and then drawing themselves effortlessly back up to standing: *The four directions of the compass? North, South, East, West?*

My breath caught…*He has no hair!* All of the initiates were completely clean-shaven and bald with the exception of a tuft of hair that sprouted from the upper back portion of their heads and hung neatly braided down the back of their heads. *I'd always wondered what Narayana would look like without any hair. I'd thought (hoped?) he'd look ugly without any.* Narayana *should* have looked ugly. It would have only been fair for *something* to be wrong with him. Oh! How I *wished* that Narayana looked ugly; but he did not. Far from it—to my chagrin and paradoxical delight.

Narayana's bald head and clean-shaven face showed off his high cheek-bones, his soaring, aristocratic forehead—*even his forehead looks like he should be of the Brahmin caste!*—his full lips, his expressive, liquid, almond eyes, and his caramel skin. He looked gorgeously, mannishly beautiful, not in an overpowering way, but rather subtly. *Wow! Man!* I lamented to myself.

Chandy remarked thusly, "Narayana looks great with no hair!" to Karuna's and Radha's vigorous nodding in agreement.

"You're right! I was wondering what he'd look like without any hair," Radha stated.

"Yeah, not all guys can pull off bald," Karuna said, her voice sounding on the verge of awe or infatuation.

"But, he does, for sure!" Chandy simpered. Yet again, Karuna and Radha nodded vigorously. I clenched my jaw tightly.

I continued analyzing in silence as I stared at the brahmacharis on the stage. I did not dare say anything because I was afraid I would burst out crying. I noted that the initiates' shoulders, torsos, and faces had red- and cream-colored symbols and markings on them. I knew the markings were made with the cream-colored tulasi and the vibrant red kum kum—both powders noted to have significant spiritual powers, and thus widely used in Hindu practices and rites. I had observed the brahmacharinis mix the powders in their palms with a little water to make a paste, which they used to make bindis.

Karuna questioned, "What do the symbols written on their bodies mean?"

Radha smiled before answering, "Well, you know what the bindi means?" The initiates were wearing bindis—dots in their foreheads, concentric circles, a dime-sized red dot inside of a larger cream-colored dot.

Karuna and Chandy shook their heads—no. Karuna spoke, "I've seen the white and red bindis but I don't know what it means."

"Well, when there's a red dot inside of the white dot that symbolizes the union of Shiva and Shakti," Radha said. "The white is for Shiva and the red is for Shakti. You can see Shiva as the structure of the universe; whereas Shakti is the power within it. Structure and power. Form and energy."

"Ok," Karuna said.

"The other symbols are for Shiva."

The three brahmacharis sat down before leaf plates.

"What's going to happen?" I asked Radha.

"I don't know the full ceremony, but basically they have to go through a long initiation process starting now that will end tomorrow morning. All of it is about letting go of their old lives. They will become dead to the world. Tomorrow morning, they will participate in a fire ceremony, a yagna, which will symbolize the burning up of their old lives—all their desires, hopes, and dreams, thoughts and wishes…their old self. At the end of it, they'll be considered free of their old lives. Their lives will, then, be totally dedicated to service to the guru—to Cha Ma. She will be their lives. They'll be considered full sannyasis and will be given their yellow robes." I nodded, staring at the stage, staring at Narayana, who was focused on his part of the ceremony.

"After that, they'll be called Brahmachari Something-or-Other. Cha Ma will give them new names to match their new lives. No one knows what their names are yet. We'll all learn tomorrow." Radha stopped short as all the people in the temple began singing again. The noise was deafening what with the tablas *thom-thomming* underneath the strident voices and the kimini and bells *kaching-chinging* above them.

My heart picked up its earlier downward spiral. *Stop it, Prema! What did you expect? You crazy girl! And what is he? He's only some random Indian guy. And it's only a crush...a crush on someone you shouldn't have one on anyway. Let it go! Let it go!* I stared at him, entranced, battling against a fresh rash of insane emotions.

Out of the corner of my eye, I saw Chandy give me a quick, surreptitious glance and then look away. *What's the matter?* I looked down and saw a drop of water on my hand...a tear! Quickly, before thinking about it, I touched my face. *I'm crying!* Horrification swept over me about my own out-of-control emotions. I dared not wipe the tears away because I did not want my friends to see and guess what was the matter with me—*It wouldn't take a rocket scientist to figure it out.* I would hate for them to see that Narayana mattered that much to me. *I can imagine the teasing I would get—it would be merciless and unending.* I stared straight ahead and kept swallowing hard as I recommenced singing to Devi with all my might.

After a couple of songs, the singing died down as Cha Ma and the initiates chanted and went through a series of mudras. It looked like they were offering up the things on their leaf plates as they chanted. Their movements were so smooth and synchronized, in perfect time with the chanting, they looked like they were dancing. Finally, to my joy and disappointment, their movements abated as they settled their hands into mudras in their laps. The curtains closed as their subdued chanting wafted down to us and finally stopped. Soon, Cha Ma as "more-Kali" would emerge.

I sat in the crowd feeling bitterly alone and lonely. All around me, people talked and chatted, waiting for Cha Ma to reemerge. I could not join in. I sat and stared straight ahead, feeling wave upon wave of unbidden, undesired emotion wash over me. I could hear Radha's, Karuna's, and Chandy's voices talking about a thousand different topics. Finally the curtain parted, again to clanging bells, bellowing conch shells, and vociferous singing. Kali Leela had begun.

As soon as I could leave without drawing notice, I announced, "I'm going to go meditate."

"I'm going, too," Karuna said as she stood. "I have pot-washing duty."

"Luckily, I don't," I responded as we turned around and began picking our way through the crowd. I ignored the women who turned to stare at us, the crazy foreigners, as we walked out. After a couple of minutes, we made it to the entrance.

"See you later," I told Karuna as I headed up the stairs.

"Yeah, see ya!" she responded, her Australian accent pressing through.

I climbed the steps slowly, perplexed by my own behavior and emotions. As I plodded up the steps, I felt heavier and heavier as though one weight after another were being placed on my shoulders every time I took a step.

By the time I made it to the top of the roof, the tears that had vanished as mysteriously as they had appeared began again. On the tail of the tears pulsed the internal mantra that I heard every night, a mantra that compelled me to the roof just as often. *I should just kill myself! Jump! Jump!*

Some days a loud, demanding voice authoritatively commanded me to jump. Other days a quiet, unobtrusive voice hinted to me the benefits of removing myself from this body, from this world. Still other days it was a voice altogether different—a voice that, nevertheless, urged me to kill myself. I was comfortable with the voices. I had grown very used to them over time. I was starting to see them as my friend. In fact, I had begun to see the variation in the tonality of the voices to be variations in the moods of a friend.

I walked to the side of the roof that was closest to the ocean. It looked out over the brahmacharini huts, over the stretch of a hidden, thickly populated beach and, beyond the beach, the ocean. The ocean stretched out vast and beckoning—glinting darkly black diamonds upon black velvet.

I laid my asana and shawl down on the meditation roof and carefully looked around. *No one's here, of course. Everyone's at the Leela.* I walked to the edge of the roof. This time my toes were a couple of inches away from the edge. I stared at the ocean under the moonless night. Without the reflected light of the moon, the ocean's waters washed blackest black, glittering morosely. Yet, far out on the horizon, I could still perceive where the sky met the ocean—indigo meeting black.

Jump! I did not shift forward. I did not really feel deep inside the desire to die. Not tonight, at least. *If you wanted enlightenment. . . really wanted it. . . you would kill yourself*—the silky voice, my new best friend, murmured at me. Or was I simply talking to myself? Unconsciously, I inched back, just a little bit more, from the edge. I looked over. My heart caught in my throat as I imagined hurtling over the edge. I could see myself cartwheeling over, but not making a full turn, because the temple roof was not that high up. High enough that I would die if I jumped, but not high enough to make a full turn in the fall. The idea of hitting the ground caused me to flinch. I looked back out at the ocean, staring but not seeing. Its vastness and subtle hint at eternity drew me—I felt such a pull from deep within.

How long have I wanted to kill myself? How long have I thought about committing suicide? My mind rifled backward through my life. *Hmm. . . yes, at Harvard I thought about it. Yes, while at Carolina during my undergraduate years. . . high school. . .* I paused as my mind shrank back from its own internal investigation. *I've thought about killing myself ever since I was in high school!* My mind skimmed more vigorously through my memories. *I can't believe it! I've thought about suicide almost every day of my life since. . . since. . . I was a teenager. Sixteen! Why did I never actually do it?* Silence. I had no answer for myself. *Now. . .* that's *the question!* Not thinking about it, perhaps the shock of the realization caused the action, I lurched backward and plopped down on my asana. I was not sure which, the hard landing or the stark realization, one of them caused me to forcibly expel the air in my lungs. *Wow!*

COMPLICATIONS

Marie and Paul
United States

Marie and Paul sat down at a table in the corner of a restaurant. It was one of their favorites—low-key with delicious food. Traditional American fare. They scanned their menus although they knew what they were going to get—they were creatures of habit. When the server came, they gave her their food and drink order.

After she left, Paul asked, "So, how was the appointment today?" Marie had called him shortly after leaving the optometrist's office on the way to the neurologist. She had not sounded all that composed and she did not want to talk about it then. But, now, seated in the restaurant, they could talk freely.

"Well, Dr. Johnson and Dr. Worthing were there; but Dr. Johnson didn't stay for long. He said that given the results from the first set of tests, Dr. Worthing is better able to handle what is going on with me as he is a medical doctor who specializes in eye diseases and disorders. After that, Dr. Johnson left.

"Dr. Worthing first ran another series of tests on me. And then, we sat in his office and he gave me his opinion, which is that, right now, he's not sure what's going on. He said that the buildup of fluid behind my eyes is very dangerous. He feels that the medicine he prescribed last time will be effective in reducing the swelling and that even though I haven't seen a change yet, as soon as it works its way through my system, it'll begin to help.

"He says that if I hadn't come in when I did, I probably would've lost my eyesight. And at the worst, if the swelling has something to do with my brain, which he believes it does, I could have died from a rupture or from whatever is going on with my brain. In fact, that's still a danger. A big danger." Marie paused. Tears welled up in her eyes. Paul's heart twisted. He looked away. He could not bear to see his wife hurting.

"As it stands now, he's certain the medicine will decrease the swelling, which is the immediate danger, but he wants to get to the root of it." The calm manner in which Marie spoke obscured her anxiety and worry. Behind her words, she wondered how Paul would take this information: Would he be there for her or would he hide himself? She prayed and hoped he would be there for her.

Already, though, she could see the exact opposite. As she spoke of her doctor's visit, his eyes began to drift around the restaurant—looking everywhere and at everyone but her. He would glance at her now and again but he would not fasten his eyes upon her.

Paul really could not digest what she was saying. All he felt, deep within (too deeply to be understood), was that he had lost his son to California, his daughter to India, and now he was about to lose his best friend, his confidante, his wife…his everything…to some unknown illness. Unavoidably, he shut down.

Marie saw this. She knew this would be his reaction. However, she did not understand the reasoning, the thinking process, underlying the behavior, and so, she hurt. Even if she had known, she would have probably still hurt. *I will have to go this alone. THIS…on top of everything else.* Everything else—the many nights of troubled sleep and nightmares, of waking up and walking into the living room and seeing—literally seeing!—Maya lying dead in a coffin wearing a white dress. Once would have been one time too many; but it was so much more than once. Often, she woke up in the dead of night, walked into the living room, and saw…Every time, she froze, her heart stopping cold within her, her breath trapped against her spine. Even though she knew it was an attack of the enemy and she knew how to beat it, in fact, she had already, that knowledge did not keep her from dying inside every time a white coffin appeared in the living room with her daughter lying in it. So many days and nights, hour after hour, she would hear voices telling her to give it up, that Maya was dead, or at the least, long gone, never to come back. And still she fought; she *had* to fight. But, now this…*this*…the dangerous pressure in her eyes…threats that verged on promises that she might lose her sight at the best and her life at the worst…and her husband withdrawing even more, when she needed him so. It was simply too much.

Deep within, from a recess in her heart she choked out an almost silent groan, "Oh God! Help me!"

Even as Marie prayed those words, help was there. Help was always present for Marie and Paul, given the intimacy of their relationship with the Lord. Jovial and Mighty were sitting in the booth with them, listening to their conversation, observing their actions and reactions, profoundly aware of the Lord and His very explicit instructions concerning their charges, Marie and Paul, and perfectly obedient to His commands concerning the humans.

When Marie groaned, "Oh God! Help me!" instantaneously, Jovial and Mighty—at the behest of the Lord who, unconstrained by time and space, had issued an answer before she even asked—placed their hands upon her and Paul's head and heart and allowed their light to flow into them. They began to speak the words they were hearing from the Lord,

Who sat in Heaven. They spoke words of blessing and peace, of stillness and strength. The words, unheard by most in the earthly realm, danced and wove dreamily, gracefully, from their mouths into the atmosphere and into the humans.

They did not do more. They did not undo the damage, although they easily could have. They did not intervene or change a thing. No, this was Marie and Paul's test. One they would have to take alone, with minimal help. One that—once they passed it—would bring great glory to the Lord.

When the server brought Marie and Paul's food, company...unwanted company...came and joined them. Sickness, Disease, Despair, and Doubt. Sickness slumped up behind Marie and hunched over her.

Despair—trying to reclaim a small amount of the power that he had had earlier, power that Chamunda Kali had snatched away from him—muttered at the Lord's angels, "We can be here." Even though Despair tried to sound strong and courageous, his nature seeped through the sound of his voice. "Our dark lord said we have a right to her." He cast furtive glances at the Lord's angels from under his atrabilious brow—for their light was too radiant, too pure for him, for *any* of the evil ones, to look straight at them.

"Your dark lord..." Mighty retorted with a snort. The slight movement of disdain caused his prodigious muscles to bunch and shift underneath his white tunic and trousers. Even when he was still, his muscles rippled minutely.

To Mighty's rebuff, Sickness shrank behind Marie. As if a human could protect a spiritual being!

Jovial, smiling graciously, joy glimmering in his eyes, continued, "Our Lord, the Lord of the heavens, the Lord of the universe, has given Satan permission to test Marie and Paul. *Only* because of the Lord's permission are you even permitted in this room. Do what you must, but...remember your bounds. All is in His Will and He wins."

The evil ones nodded their acquiescence reluctantly. Still smiling, Jovial blew a wind of icy, glittering light around the table at the demonic entities. The light-wind that blew past them caused them to forget that it was all according to the Lord's Will. It caused them to sink deeper into their own delusion. Instantly, they felt bold in their delusion, confident that they would win.

Jovial and Mighty looked at each other and stepped back several paces, allowing the evil ones room to maneuver. The demonic ones moved close to the humans and began to do their work upon Marie and Paul. As the Lord's angels did nothing, Sickness gained a little courage. He began to stick his grotesque appendages into Marie's head, spitting into her eyes and smearing the nasty goo in. He had been given the right to. Granted, her prayers and those of her church were strong; however, the Lord had issued an order to allow the testing to continue.

As they worked, the strain of being in the presence of the Lord's angels affected them. Sickness's pulpy, vile, pink face, which on a good day resembled vomit, turned a lighter shade of pink, thus looking all the more putrid and sickly. He kept his eye slits turned away from the Lord's angels; they were so buried by lumpy flesh that there was no way much of the light of the Lord's angels could have reached his eyes anyway. Nevertheless, he turned away.

Near him stood Despair and Disease looking ill at ease. They shifted back and forth on their legs, casting nervous glances at the Lord's angels.

When the Lord's angels did not move forward to stop Sickness, Despair gained a sketchy confidence. He pulled himself right next to Marie and began hissing into her ear, "It's no uuuussssseee… She's going to diiiiiiie, and you're going to die, toooooo."

Mighty cast a glance toward Jovial and cocked his head toward Sickness. Jovial caught his look, a smirk flashing across his face. Mighty moved forward and placed his hand on Marie's head again, just a fraction away from Sickness's tentacle, which was embedded in Marie's head. Hastily, Sickness snatched his appendage, his tentacle, away from Mighty, a shudder coursing violently through his body.

The jerky movement of Sickness withdrawing his offensive appendage from her head so quickly and abruptly caused Marie to flinch. Instinctively she pressed her fingertips delicately against her temples. "My headache just stopped! How in the world did that happen? One second, pounding so hard, another second, nothing…absolutely nothing…?" Marie voiced wonderingly.

Paul looked up at her, "I don't know…are you OK?" Fresh worry seized his heart.

Jovial chuckled at Sickness, "Still burns, eh?" He was never one to miss the humor in a situation. His eyes glinted with mirth and something else. His hand remained on Marie's head.

Sickness hissed a curse at Jovial and then refocused his attention on Marie. Mighty and Jovial noted that he did not put his appendage back where it had been on Marie's head—for that would've been much too close to Mighty's hand. Finally, Mighty removed his hand and stepped back beside Jovial. Seizing the opportunity, Sickness reinserted his append-age into Marie's head.

Despair left Marie and moved toward Paul, stealthily slinking around Jovial and Mighty (as if he hoped they would not notice him). This time, Jovial winked at Mighty, although they did nothing.

Despair leaned near Paul's ear and began to hiss, "You'll neveeer make it. You know Marie's going to diiiie. Heh heh…she's going to leave you all by yourself. You have no children anymore and now yoooou have no life. Your life is worthlessss."

As he spoke a sulfury, yellow smoke wafted from his mouth. And his skin did a strange thing…it shifted between a rich, muddy brown and a washed-out, tepid beige as his skin tone shifted along with his thoughts. As he warmed to his subject, his skin reflected the effects of his morose musings, thus appearing richly hued, but the moment he thought of the Lord's angels, or was caused to think of them because they shifted (Why would they shift about, when they could hold themselves perfectly still in obedience to the Lord? Perhaps to disturb and agitate the evil ones?), the richness of his skin quickly dissipated. His mood swings, made bla-tantly apparent by his skin—shifting from brown to beige to brown— were rapid and erratic.

As Despair whispered on at him, Paul clenched his teeth against the thoughts that bombarded him, thoughts he was all too ready to claim as his own. These thoughts taking root were the opening for yet another to come: Condemnation. Oh! How Paul struggled. He was too wrapped up in his own struggle against despair and doubt, and now condemnation, to even notice the emotional state of his wife.

Across the table from him, Marie stared down at her uneaten food. From nowhere the headache had come on (she found no rhyme or reason behind the timing of the headaches). But then, it had disappeared... only to come back, minutes later, with a vengeance. This time, the pain came low and throbbing and quickly built up to a massive spike of misery behind her eyes. She sighed because she knew what would come next—the spots and webs. They would not fail her now. She was not sure how much time elapsed as she stared down at her uneaten food. The pain had spiked so quickly and was so tremendous that it was hard to even mouth the prayers.

Jovial and Mighty shifted restlessly, but they knew they would not act. The Lord had said no. So, they stayed and watched and did nothing more to taunt and tease the evil ones.

The tension in the room was unbearable. Two fundamentally opposed sides, intrinsically designed to war, were too close to each other to do *nothing*. A skirmish seemed to be on the verge of breaking out.

However, it would not be because of the Lord's angels—they knew their orders. Protect Marie and Paul, support them, make sure the demons maintained their boundaries; but they, the humans, would have to battle for every piece of ground they gained. Faith would have to be etched into the places of their beings where there was none. A painful, arduous process. A terrifying process.

Finally, Marie and Paul, encumbered by their thoughts and their spiritual squatters, slid out of the booth and trod heavily out of the restaurant. They spoke minimally to each other—their unwelcome company said too much. They were not even aware of their own lack of communication. Too deep was their misery.

NAILED!

Maya
India

Another day in the kitchen. I liked it though. It suited me. It gave me time to sit by myself and just…be. There was something very grounding about cooking, about sitting by a kitchen fire, tending to it. As I sat there, I chanted my mantra.

As I chanted, my thoughts strayed toward enlightenment. What would I do to be enlightened? Would I have enough nerve, enough desire for enlightenment, to die for it? I contemplated all the different ways I could die for enlightenment. Jumping off the temple would be the easiest…Drowning in the ocean? No, too painful and drawn out. Too great a chance that I'd try to save myself. I chanted on with my Kali mantra. I tried to keep my mind on the mantra; but it was not easy. Not at all. Usually, my mind wandered all over the place. At least today, it fixed on something, even if that something was how to kill myself. *Isn't there some way to kill myself without it being painful and difficult?* I chuckled to myself. *I need a coward's way…*

The fire began to grow low. *I've got to get more wood.* I was making pumpkin "soup." Because the ashram buyers picked tons of pumpkin (*I have NO clue why!*), it had become my job to use as much as possible. I had tried cooking chunks of it; but the Westerners did not like the texture of pumpkin cubes, floating around like little islands in one of my broths. And then, they were not very tasty that way either. So, I had thought to make a puree. First, I had tried pureeing the cooked pumpkin in a blender—Bri. Sita's idea. Too time-consuming and too unpredictable. I was never sure when the ashram power would be on. Then, I had found that if we cut up the pumpkin into little one-inch cubes and let it boil for a long time, it would all boil down into a thick, even consistency—not unlike orange pea soup. But, the process took a lot of wood and time, easily two hours of boiling. Fine by me. I had the time. And although it meant that on pumpkin days, my kitchen time ran over into bhajans, I did not mind. Some days I just did not want to be there watching *him* (even though I had not seen him since his sannyasa initiation, no one had, for that matter) sitting with Cha Ma and the swamis.

Today, all I needed to do was make sure I had enough dry wood. It was easy to cook the pumpkin into a smooth consistency, if there was enough wood and if it was dry. *Time to get more wood.* I headed over to the woodpile. I climbed atop the unsteady mini-mountain, moving gingerly as the branches and pieces of wood slid underneath my cheap, plastic chappels. I found some old, dry wood—coconut palms and blocks of wood that I figured were the remnants of old two-by-fours. As I was stacking wood into my arms, something pushed up, sharply, under my right foot. I felt a pinch of pain, but I did not think anything about it. *Probably just my arch falling . . . climbing around in woodpiles would do it.* I kept stacking pieces of wood into my arms as I chanted my mantra. It was not until I moved to climb out of the woodpile that I noticed: *A board's attached to my foot!* Literally, a board was attached to my foot!

I tried to lift my foot to check it out but I could not keep my balance standing precariously on top of the pile of sliding wood. I half-climbed/ half-slid the foot with the board attached to it down the woodpile, still holding onto the bundle of wood in my arms. I was amazed that my foot did not hurt. When I made it to the bottom of the pile, I dumped the wood in my arms onto the ground. I lurched, hobbled, and slid my foot over to the kitchen's exterior wall, and leaning against it, carefully lifted my "blocked" foot to examine the situation.

A foot-long section of plank, four inches wide and about two inches thick, was solidly attached to my foot. It did not fall off when I lifted my foot. I shook my foot—*to test how well the board's attached?*—nothing. *It's firmly attached!* That was when I noticed the blood dripping...*lots* of blood dripping. It was generously running down the side of the chunk of plank that was attached to my foot and then splattering onto the hard-packed, dirt floor. *Why had I not noticed it before?!* I looked back toward the woodpile and saw a thin, drippy trail of blood. Luckily blood did not alarm me very much, especially my own. I stared in wonderment at the oddness of it all.

Strangely enough, I did not freak out or anything. Accidents rarely ever fazed me (although Cha Ma yelling at me could make me psycho). Instead, in an accident everything seemed to whittle down into a sort of myopic, "slow-mo" vision thing as my brain grew intensely thoughtful and calculating. This time (as in times past), I rapidly, albeit methodically, considered the situation before deciding what to do.

Apparently...the situation was that I had stepped on a small—small being relative, of course—piece of two-by-four, which had a very long nail hammered through it. When I had stepped down on the board, the exposed tip must have punctured my chappel and gone straight into my foot. I could not tell how long or how thick the nail was as the wood was flush against the sandal, even though I could guess that it had to be rather thick and long in order to hold a foot-long piece of two-by-four snugly in place.

I pulled against the board, trying to take it off my foot. No luck—it would not budge. *It must be in deep.* I sat down in the dirt and pulled harder, with all my might—nothing. *I'm going to have to work it out.* I began twisting the board left, then right, then left again, back and forth, back and forth, trying to wiggle the nail loose. After much working back and forth and much blood, I finally pulled the board off my foot. I was amazed! The nail was very thick and very long. Almost two inches had been fully buried through my chappel and into my foot.

I looked at the bloody puncture hole that was between the arch of my foot and my heel. *That hole* has *to be deep! Thank Kali it went into the meaty part of my foot or it could have gone straight through. For that matter, it could have run into a bone!* I stared at the gushing blood. *Kali! What am I going to do?* I sat for a minute watching the blood run from my wound and pool on the dusty ground. *I'd better go wrap it up.*

I hopped on one foot into the fry kitchen, where a couple of brahmacharinis were busily frying. "I stepped on a nail," I remarked as their eyes traveled downward. "Do you have any bandages here in the kitchen?"

Shock evident, they replied, "Oh Premabhakti! That's awful!"

"You are hurt. You need to see Cha Ma!"

"You need to see the doctor." They had many comments but nothing with which to wrap my foot. I hop-hobbled through the main kitchen area, leaning on iddly-makers and pots. Once I made it to the Western canteen, I saw Bri. Sita, who was putting the finishing touches on her cucumber (bitter Indian cucumbers) and chickpea (with bugs) salad. I showed her my foot, to which she sighed pseudo-sympathetically, and I told her, "I'm leaving to doctor my foot." My foot was starting to throb.

"Are you coming back?" her voice threatened panic. "You know I don't make soups as well as you..." Her look said that she did not *want* to make the soup.

"Yes, I'll be back. Just let me wrap my foot. Stop the blood." I glanced backward and saw a trail of blood marking my path. Nasty. *I wonder what's nastier? That I've trailed blood through the whole kitchen area and not a thing will be done to clean it or that my foot had touched the yucky floor earlier today?* I thought of Radha's words, so long ago it seemed, when I had first arrived and she had shown me the kitchen telling me that the Western doctor and nurse refused to enter because of how filthy it was. A cesspool of germs.

"OK." She nodded, disinterest already evident on her face, and returned to her salad. I hobbled off.

By the time I sat down on my bunk, my foot was throbbing horribly. The pain shot through my foot and leg—simultaneously dull and strong, sharp and deep. I wondered if I could take the pain. *I don't have any painkillers— well, some ayurvedic drops and some herbal stuff, but I need some real medicine.* I bit my lip, determined not to cry. Deep inside I was starting to feel a little like a wimp. *No time for that! Just think, you're burning karma!* I gritted my teeth and pulled myself in check.

I found one of my raggedy, but clean (beat-against-a-scrubbing-stone-with-cheap-detergent-and-dried-on-a-rock-clean) petticoats and dabbed at the wound. It *was* deep…and ugly. It had been hard to figure just how deep it went while the blood was gushing out of it, but now that I had pressed some material against it to staunch the flow, I could see more clearly. *Do I need stitches?* I figured it was a good thing that it had been bleeding so profusely. *Hopefully, it will flush all the germs out.* I pressed the piece of petticoat against it. The blood rapidly saturated the cloth. I tore another piece and pressed. After the fourth piece, the blood flow was not so heavy. I pressed more material against the wound. I tore another strip, wrapped it around my foot—binding the wad in place—and tied it snugly. I was ready to go back to the kitchen.

As I hobbled into the kitchen, thoughts flitted through my mind: *I wonder if I need a tetanus shot or antibiotics? Tetanus? I don't think so.* I remembered that I had had all my shots updated at school before I had left in pursuit of my guru. *Antibiotics? Now that's another story…I'm sure I need them. Oh well! Kali will just have to save me…*

Majesty stood beside Awe. He smiled at Maya, "She's pretty amazing, you know." His arms were crossed over his chest. He beamed at her like a proud parent.

"You're right. I can't believe she just stepped on that and reacted so little." Awe nodded, his hair letting off ephemeral sparks with the movement.

"So many humans would have been so upset."

"Given the bacteria and disease that is in that wound…there is enough there to make her very ill."

"Definitely, enough present to kill her."

"Chamunda would like that, wouldn't she?" Awe asked as he and Majesty strolled leisurely alongside Maya as she went about finishing the soup. Their large bodies cut through the low ceiling. They walked, but not on the floor. They had to concentrate to remember to observe the laws of the physical realm and stay earthbound.

"But Chamunda can't kill her," Majesty responded. "She can try…she does try, just like in this case. And things will happen; but she will not be allowed to kill Maya. We ride upon the wishes of the Lord and, as we know, His wishes supersede everything, everywhere, and at all times."

Maya sat down on her favorite rock outside by her soup and examined her foot. The rags were rather bloody. And dirty from the kitchen floor. Gingerly, she unwound the rags in order to see how her foot was doing. The wound continued to seep blood, but not as much as before. It was obvious that she needed stitches. She clenched her jaw against the pain that throbbed along with her heartbeat—with every beat, it felt as though a spiked sledgehammer slammed against her foot.

Awe leaned over and tapped her foot, ever so lightly. The blood flow stopped. He looked at Majesty with a slight grin, "I know, I know, we're not to do too much…" He paused, looking longingly at Maya. Oh! How he desired to heal her of the pain, nullify the effects of the bacteria, close the wound.

"No," Majesty shook his head as he sat in the air.

"I know. She must deal with the fruits of her own choices…"

"To an extent…if she were to deal with them completely, she'd be dead." Majesty flashed a grin at him. "But, you can remove the bacteria in the wound, she's not supposed to lose a limb. That's definitely not in the Lord's plans."

Awe chuckled and blew on the wound and a shower of iridescent light that radiated between gold and pink flowed from his mouth. "She'll be just fine."

WHEN IN INDIA
DO AS THE INDIANS DO

"Have you heard the news?"

"Huh? What are you talking about?" I reluctantly opened my eyes. I felt as if true sleep had deserted me a long time ago. It felt as if sand had been glued under my eyelids and as if someone had tied my limbs down with heavy boulders and then had thrown me into the ocean. A deep-down tiredness plagued me, not just a body fatigue, but whatever the tiredness was, it also assaulted my spirit and soul. *I wonder if I'm feeling this way because of malnutrition or a protein deficiency. Everyone keeps telling me that we'll crave sugar when we have a protein deficiency. They also say that we'll feel very lethargic. Well, I'm definitely feeling lethargic.*

"Get up, Premabhakti! Get up!" Karuna's voice cut through my sleep-induced reverie. I felt her shaking my body. I was trying to get up, but I just could not seem to push myself wholly into a conscious state. I felt myself drifting…off…

"C'mon, Premabhakti! Get up!" More forceful shakes this time. I cracked open an eye. "Have you heard about Rukmini?" Karuna asked in a whisper, leaning over me.

My eyes snapped open—it was near impossible not to get my attention with some scintillating gossip. I shook my head—no. "Uh-uh! What happened?"

"You mean...*you*...don't...know about what happened with... *Rukmini?*"

I knew she was not talking this way to make herself sound melodramatic; "drama" was not her thing. No, she was trying to get some really important piece of information across to me.

"No, tell me." I felt reasonably awake by now. I swung myself around and sat cross-legged on my bunk. Karuna was sitting on the edge, half-in and half-out of the mosquito netting. I fought the urge to tell her to either get in or out of the netting, but not halfway. Halfway let in mosquitoes. The dreaded mosquitoes. *What time is it anyway?*

The sun was bright and hot. From the amount of heat it was giving off and where it sat in the sky, I could tell that it had been up for some time. I swung my head around, puzzled. It was too late in the morning for the sleeping forms of all the women; the dorm should have been clear. *Oh! That's right—last night was Kali Leela.* Everyone was sleeping in. It had been a long night, which had poured over, with its usual excessiveness, into the wee hours of the morning.

Karuna interrupted my thoughts, "She's in the hospital!"

"The hospital? For what? For how long? Why?" Questions shot out of my mouth, rapid fire. I was WIDE awake now.

"Get this!" Karuna said as she ducked her head under my mosquito netting—*thank you!* She spun around on her bottom and crossed her legs as she faced me on the bunk. She pulled the netting into place behind her. *Good! No mosquitoes now.* She leaned in close, hunkering over to fit into the tight bunk space—the top bunk was so low.

Her voice dropped low, "Well, the way I heard it, last night…well, early this morning…during Kali Leela some of the Indian men got to her."

"Got to her?!?" Immediately my mind went to Rukmini being raped. *Ugh! Ugly thought.*

"Yeah! They beat her up."

"Beat her up!" I paused a beat. Hesitating. "Anything else?" I asked with trepidation. I could not stand the thought.

She shook her head. "No."

Whew! I was incredibly relieved that they had not raped her—that would have been absolutely horrid.

Karuna went on, oblivious of my concerns, "They say about eleven of them jumped her and beat her up."

"Yeah! That's right!" Right then, Alice walked up to my bunk.

Karuna and I peered at her through the mosquito netting. *Does she ever sleep?* She stuck her hand to her mouth, as always she was munching on a handful of peanuts. *Old, filthy peanuts*—I suspected. *How can she eat peanuts so early in the morning? What about breakfast?* I felt my face screw up with the thought of her not-so-tasty, grubby breakfast.

"So, Karuna's telling you about what happened with Rukmini last night?" She sat down on the other side of me on my bunk. Outside of the netting. *On* the netting. I frowned. Her body pulled the net tight. "Hey! Do you have any peanuts?" she asked completely unaware of my mosquito netting angst.

What do you need more peanuts for? You're eating a bunch already! I did not say these things, instead I answered, "Yes and no. Yes, Karuna's telling me about what happened with Rukmini." I looked at her pointedly. "What all did happen? You're close to her, Alice, you'd know. And no, I don't have any peanuts. Hey! Wait a minute! I have some, but they're old and stale…" I wrinkled up my face at the thought of stale peanuts. "You know where they are." I gestured toward the row of clear, plastic containers that lined the backside of my bunk, stationed against the wall. One of the first things I had learned about India was to store all of my food in airtight containers in order to keep out the ants, roaches—no, waterbugs (*they're waterbugs when they're in your own place and roaches when they're in someone else's*)—flies, and a whole variety of other pests.

"You don't mind if I eat them, do you?" Alice asked, already tugging against the netting she was sitting on in order to lift it up. I felt my face frown up again. *If she stretches my net...* With her free hand, she reached toward the plastic jar that held a couple of handfuls of old, stale peanuts. "I mean, since no one else will be eating them, being all stale and all..."

"Sure, Alice. Just tell me what happened with Rukmini...and climb under the netting. I don't want you to let any mosquitoes in."

"Yes, Alice! Tell us, because I've just been hearing bits and pieces," Karuna agreed with me.

"OK." Alice climbed in. Karuna and I moved over to make room for her. We sat in a tight triangle on the narrow bunk, knees touching, hunched over. "Well...I wasn't there, either," she said, while she unscrewed the jar of peanuts. "But, I did talk to Rukmini this morning at the hospital."

"This morning? What time is it?"

"Almost eleven," Alice answered, all of her attention focused on rooting around in the peanut jar, trying to catch a handful of them.

I shook my head. *I didn't know it was that late! How'd I sleep so late?* I yawned. *I guess I don't have to worry about the mosquitoes.* It was well past the "mosquito-hour."

"So, you were at the hospital?" Karuna prompted.

"Uh-huh, I just got back."

"Well, what happened?" Karuna pressed.

"I'm getting to it! Give me a moment!" Alice paused a moment to chew and swallow her peanuts. "Well, apparently," she began in a hushed voice, "while Rukmini was sleeping last night, some of the Indian men came into her hut."

"You know she lives out with the brahmacharinis, right?" Karuna interjected for my sake.

"I didn't, but now I do. OK. Keep going," I urged.

"Well, she lives out in the huts and last night…actually it would have been early morning when Kali Leela was wrapping up…she'd gone to sleep early because she was so tired. You know usually she stays up, but last night she just couldn't do it," Alice meandered, lost in her stream of consciousness. "Well, while she was sleeping, a whole group of Indian men went into her hut, dragged her out behind it, and beat her up."

I could not help but be appalled. "What do you mean?" I struggled to digest the information.

"What do you think I mean?" Alice retorted through the peanuts, chewing rapidly like a chipmunk. "They beat her up. Real bad, too. She said that they began punching her and hitting her with sticks and clubs and when she fell to the ground, they began to kick her. She passed out from the beating. A couple of brahmacharinis found her."

"How many were there?" Karuna asked, her voice subdued.

"Eleven or twelve. At least, that's how many Rukmini remembers."

"Did they…did they…?" Karuna asked hesitantly.

Alice saved her the question, "Did they 'do' anything to her? No. Nothing like *that*. They just beat her up real bad. She has a lot of internal injuries and bleeding. She's going to have to stay in the hospital for a while."

I felt a surge of anger shoot through me toward the Indian men. *How could they DO that to a woman? As a group? Go beat a woman up? To get together and agree to hurt her? Plan to do it? And then, do it?* I felt disgusted. And afraid. My emotions pinged all over the place, slamming against any object. My first object was Rukmini as my anger attacked her for being so focused on Cha Ma and for being so careless of Indian customs. Within seconds it flowed over to Anneshwari and Alice. *If they were more careful, if they were more thoughtful of the customs, then the men would not get so angry and want to beat them up.* I especially felt anger toward Rukmini, because…to be here in India and to be as tall as she was, as *blond*, as *gaunt*, as "aggressive" as she was—she stuck out like a sore thumb. On top of it, she antagonized the men and women with her behavior and did not care that she did. She and Anneshwari were infamous for being obviously obnoxious.

"No one heard them beating her up?" Karuna asked, looking aghast. "C'mon now, a person getting beat up, even by one person, let alone eleven or twelve, and NO ONE HEARD?"

I nodded my head, vigorously, "That does sound like an impossibility! How in the world, given all the people who live in the ashram and all the people who visit the ashram, especially on a Kali Leela night—how in the world could a woman getting beat up not be heard?"

Alice nodded in understanding. "I know! I thought the same thing, too. But they beat her up during Cha Ma's grand finale…and you know how loud that is!"

I nodded, "That's right! Kali! That's rough!" *Cha Ma's grand finale? Where was I?* I had been dancing outside by the brahmacharini huts for months now. *Where was I last night? Oh yeah, that's right—sleeping.* For days, I had been fighting this mind-numbing exhaustion. Last night, I gave into it and went to sleep before Kali Leela was over. I told myself that I would get up in time for the end, but I did not. I slept right through the noise, the singing and clanging and banging and bellowing of horns. Another thought struck me: *What if I had been out there?* The place where I danced was only a few yards away from the brahmacharinis'…thus, Rukmini's…hut. *What would have happened?* Chills shot down my spine.

"Do they know of any of the guys who beat her up?" Karuna asked.

"Yeah, she says that one of the guys is the policeman who always comes to get darshan from Cha Ma," Alice said.

"Wow! You've got to be kidding me!" I exclaimed. I could not be more astonished by all the news and then…this! "One of the guys is a policeman?!" I heard my surprise squeak shrilly out of my throat.

"Nope! I'm not kidding you! And two of them are householders who live here and two of them are brahmacharis," Alice said in a chatty voice.

How in the world can she sound so nonchalant? I marveled because once again, just like with Doug, she sounded so "OK" about it all. As if it were simply a funny, interesting story rather than people getting awfully beaten up and even dying.

"Two householders and two brahmacharis? Who live here?" I asked incredulously.

"Well, what are they going to do? Is she going to press charges? Especially since she knows who they are…" Karuna queried rapid-fire.

"No. No pressing charges…everyone's saying just leave it be, that she's in India and as they say, 'While in Rome do as the Romans do.' Well… here in India, it's do as the Indians do…that if she'd been acting the way a proper woman acts she would not have made them so angry that they would've wanted to beat her up. They're saying…"

"They who?" I asked.

"They, the brahmacharinis and kitchen ammas…" Alice answered, reaching into the almost-empty canister.

"How many people know already? It's what? Eleven?" Alice could barely squeeze in a nod to Karuna's volley of questions. "It's still so early."

"All the Indians know…everyone's up with the exception of the Westerners. It's all people are talking about," Alice said.

"Well, what are they saying?" I prompted Alice.

"They're saying that she should've known better. That she can't bring her Western behavior to India, but that she should've acted like the Indians and that it's her own fault for getting beat up. She brought it on herself…"

Alice shrugged, popping the last couple of peanuts that she had scraped from the bottom of the canister into her mouth.

"Wow! It WILL be interesting to see what happens."

Chamunda Kali called her underlings to her...It was time for a meeting, an organizational, *hierarchical* meeting. She wanted to know one thing, "Who authorized the beating of Rukmini?!" She paced back and forth, back and forth. Oddly, the wind whistled around her physically nonexistent, jet-black, skeletal frame as she ghosted from one end of the meditation roof to the other and back again. She clenched and unclenched her hands—claws may have been a better word—either in an effort to curtail her rage or because she was acting out in her mind what she wanted to do, no one could say. Her face was a hideous mask of fury. "Who?!" she bellowed when no response came.

Terror and Violent hung their lumpy, misshapen, grotesque heads. "We did, our liege. We thought...we thought..." Violent spoke up for himself and Terror; however, the frozen look of contempt that Chamunda threw at them made his voice whimper away into nothing but a high-pitched whine that only dogs and bats could hear. In the distance, dogs started barking at the disturbing whine.

"Who told *you* to *think?*" Chamunda spat back. Frosty, ugly, and bitter. Sulphurish spittle flew out of her mouth. She was *not* pleased. She clenched her claws so tightly her dagger-like nails gouged into her hard, leathery, black skin. She did not flinch as a black ooze, which resembled oil and must have been demon blood, goozed from the gouge sites. Absentmindedly, she scowled down at the wounds and impatiently flicked her hands, causing thick droplets of the black, oil-like demon-blood-ooze to scatter across the meditation roof. She looked back at the lesser ones and growled, "We do *not* run our ranks this way...perhaps humans function amongst themselves with freedom of thought...perhaps God's human Kingdom functions with freedom of choice...but...OURS DOES NOT!" She finished her thought in a high, shrill bellow that made the others cringe. Fear slunk down several feet into the roof floor, unsuccessfully attempting to hide himself from Chamunda.

Chamunda continued to pace back and forth, peering over the ledge of the uppermost meditation deck. Ten or twelve demons, lesser demons, and imps stood nearby, watching her warily—she was much too volatile and horrifically dangerous not to. One lapse in watching her could have disastrous results—a face covered with the burning, viscous, acid-like substance that she spewed from her mouth or an eye gouged out by her claws. When she strode near, the lesser ones shifted backward, not caring that fear and terror wove about them as obvious and thick as a constricting carpet. Odd how the characteristics of the demons affected each other...

In the midst of the demonic "conference," humans meditated. A couple of the more "aware" humans had "visions" in which they saw Chamunda, Terror, Violent, or one of the others. However, this night, most of them had "nothing" meditations because Chamunda and all the others were too preoccupied to "guide" them into anything "visionary." Later, they would come out of meditation, with no memorable visions or sightings; instead, they would emerge cranky and aggravated for having sat in the presence of such pure, unmitigated evil that did not even bother to disguise itself.

"WHY DID YOU DO IT?" Chamunda shrieked into the air. Terror and Violent shrank back further as did all the others summoned to the roof. Chamunda's voice cut into them. How could mere words cause a painful slice? But then, one had to remember that God created all that exists, including the earth by speaking...simply speaking. Such is the power of words, always potent, whether inadvertently or not.

"We...we...we wanted to do something to create fear. We wanted to do something that would...that would fright—fright—frighten the people...all of them," Terror stuttered out of terror as he talked about fright.

Fright chuckled sinisterly, his icy, obsidian eyes squinting almost closed in diabolical contemplation. *If only I could get to him...*Fright drawled to himself, thinking not of the people, but of Terror. *How I hate him! He needs me in* *order for his power to function, but he never wants to acknowledge it. One day, I will reveal him for the fraud he is, not that it will matter. If only I could destroy him . . . but I can't.*

All demons understood the limits of their power, the boundaries of their sphere of influence, the extent of their effect. They could not truly destroy anything that was spirit. Only God had the power and capability to create and end spiritual life—it was all left to God's judgment. And demons, no matter how diabolical and evil, were still ultimately controlled and bound by God. They could hope, they could dream of destroying a spirit—granted they had such power over the physical—but never would they have *that* power. The only one who could wield *that* power, would not; instead, He would, at the end, only send them to an eternity of the absence of anything good and light, an eternity of no God. Even then, He would not destroy them (or any spiritual being). Destruction for them, the ending of an infinitely evil and nasty existence, would be a blessing. No, they would never get such a blessing. This knowledge of what was their lot forever fueled their rage. Nothing, no matter how perverse and evil, wants an eternity of pure, unmitigated evil and darkness, an eternity without an iota of God.

"Fine job that YOU did!" Chamunda bellowed, her face contorting further causing her to look even more like what she was—an *it*. She flung her arms wide in exasperation—inky, thick drops of black demon-blood flew off her hands. Caustic, mustardy-yellow spittle dribbled down her chin, burning rivulets into her flesh. As it was her own spittle, her body would absorb the acidic gooze and repair itself of any injury, leaving one among countless many disfiguring scars. "Sure, you frightened the people! But, we don't want to scare them away!" she shrieked a series of curses that caused the atmosphere to waver and go dim from evil words spoken by an evil being with evil intent. "What are we going to do if we scare them away? What happens if they leave before it's time?"

"And *Rukmini!*" she spat the name out as if it tasted nasty on her tongue. "Why her? She's one of ours! She's so lost, we could kill her tonight and she would not even care! She's so *unloved*, not a single person would care!"

Chamunda was working herself up into a fury. Her ranks shrank back out of fear, sliding down below the floor and ducking their heads underneath. Why? It was not as if the floor hid them from her in the least. And although they understood that nothing in the physical realm offered them any real protection, still they could not help shrinking back from her, moving away from her—dangerous and perverse as she was. And then, they were afraid that she was about to fly into one of her infamous rages—one of her "Rages of the Ages"—as her underlings liked to say (but not in front of her). They happened only once or twice a millennium. It was easy enough to joke about them when they thought that there was no possibility of one happening. It was easy enough to make fun when eight or nine centuries had passed and the last one was fading from memory. But, with her…it…right in front of them, working itself up into a slathering, baleful rage…No! They did not want to see one. And they most certainly did not want to be the cause of one.

One of the last times was so devastating that it had become memorialized as a myth. That time, she had been so engrossed by her destructive, all-consuming rage-lust that she began attacking all of her "own," a legion of lesser demons, the Indians called Raktabija. So outrageous was her outrage. So intense was her intensity. So lethal was her anger. She had wiped out almost every single one of them (injuring them for millennia) until Shiva—a demon of equal standing in Satan's kingdom, mythologized as her consort—had stepped in. He had lain down in front of her, which had forced her to desist. Satan had ordered him to intervene—she, in warring against her own, had been destroying her own principality, that of the Queen of Heaven, and thus Satan's kingdom. A house divided will surely fall—Satan knew this to be Truth. Certainly, tearing apart all the lesser demons under one could be considered a house divided.

This was when Satan, Shiva, and all the others realized just how powerful and cruelly lethal she was, even to her own. She was like a rabid, hungry mama dog that would eat its own pups not even out of spite, but just *because*. And of course, she had no remorse. In fact, she had no real inducement that would keep her from doing the same thing again. The best thing was to keep her from teetering…careening…over that invisible ledge of self-control.

The lesser demons peered about nervously. They did not understand why she was so angry. They did not know what she knew. They had not been briefed by Satan as she had been. She knew the scope of his vision: this girl (*Stupid, insipid thing that she is!* Chamunda snorted derisively to herself.) was obviously integral to some plans that God had. Satan had seen that in the way in which God had "grown" her. *Like some sort of special hot house flower! Always watching over her. I despise her!*—Chamunda thought venomously. Satan meant to thwart God's plan. She knew the crazy girl was key to the plans Satan had for an area in the United States. If she died, that would pull down her parents and, hopefully, their church. And there was no way, NO WAY, this silly girl was going to ruin all she had built—her kingdom on earth, her Eden—here in India. No! It was not going to happen! They did not understand all that was riding on this particular girl in this particular place at this particular time.

She, it, stood on the edge of the roof, looking over. "There they are now...the women..." she muttered about the clusters of women who were on the ground, walking by. However, she was watching one woman in particular, "That stupid girl! On her way to get chai." Her voice dripped with disdain, but underlying, hidden deeply, was another sound—a sound not often heard from her. Could it be? Fear? Yes, fear. Chamunda was afraid of Maya, or rather she was afraid of the Lord's Presence in her life, a Presence bidden by her parent's prayers. The other evil angels could have sensed, could have *smelled*, her fear had they not been overcome by their own fear of her, their capriciously violent leader.

Of course, what do demons do when they are afraid? They do not admit their fear, no, they twist it around so that it becomes anger. Or if it is great fear, they pervert it into RAGE. No wonder, then, that one nano-second Chamunda was watching the Western women walk by, and then, in the next nano-second she had *flown* from the edge of the deck to where Terror and Violent stood mostly submerged and cowering under the floor of the meditation roof. Her claw-like fingers wrapped around their necks, her face beside theirs, dripping venomous malice. This was what she wanted to do to the girl, but she could not. How she burned to kill her. Strangle her. Thrust her over the edge of the roof.

However, the prayers surrounding the silly girl, protecting her, were too strong. Further and more delimiting, the stupid thing's death was simply not in the Lord's plan. It was next to impossible—*Argh! Fully and eternally impossible!*—to go contrary to the Lord's plan. *Not that we won't try, anyway...* The evil ones failed to understand that the Lord's Word and Will were perfect and complete and whole; there was no loophole through which they could subvert it.

"Come here! Come here!" she commanded, dragging them behind her, their bodies still partially, yet unaffectedly submerged in the roof. She held them by their necks, their heads hanging over the edge. "See those women! Do they look afraid? See the girl, Premabhakti! Oh! What is that? You can't look? You can barely stand to be anywhere *near* her? And you can barely even *look* at her? What is that? *Why is that?*" Chamunda forced them over the edge to look, against their desperately struggling bodies. She pressed ruthlessly down on their necks as if she were punishing two unruly dogs (in some way she was). Their eyes bulged and ooze dripped from their oversized pores like nervous sweat. They strained to get as far away from Maya as possible. They kept their heads turned, eyes cast away.

"Oh! She burns you, does she? Is it her? Or is it the prayers, the protection, the Lord's angels...that infernally *good* Presence...surrounding her that burns you? Well, burn then...BURN! Chamunda shrieked in rage, bit a chunk of Violent's ear off (as Violent's nature overcame her), and spat it out violently. She continued, her voice dropping low and furious. The others stepped farther away—a Rage for the Age was definitely brewing. "Does she look afraid? Is she afraid enough to leave? Does it even matter?"

She let Terror and Violent go. They skittered backward on their claws, their bodies smaller now, darker and more shriveled, than before. Violent nursed his injured ear. Light greenish puss dripped from the wound, causing ethereal smoke to rise from the roof as though it were being burned away by a caustic acid. The wound would heal, but unlike the Lord's angels who healed perfectly as they stood in the Presence of their Lord, Perfection Himself, he would heal even more torn and misshapen, the wound promising to smart and burn for eternity.

Chamunda flew at the rest of them, running on all fours. She looked like a huge, skeletal hound from hell—grotesque and perverted. Her otherworldly body passing through the humans sitting in meditation, causing a few to shudder. Her nails clacked on the cement of the meditation roof—a sound that could only be heard in the spiritual realm. Yet, it was nevertheless highly disturbing. Acidic spittle flew in the air behind her and dribbled down her chin. The lesser demons and imps hunkered down in fear of her loathsome madness. She pulled up short before them, crouching down as if to pounce. Their muscles contracted, anticipating the attack. She paused, locked tight, furious energy in abeyance, and hissed, "Yes, it matters! Let me tell you WHY!! If she leaves before everything takes place, our plan is ruined! Satan's plan for her life…the one he has orchestrated from the moment she was born will be ruined! His plan for her parents and for all the people tied to her will be ruined! My world, my kingdom, *my Eden*, will be ruined!

"When you *compelled* those men to beat up Rukmini, did you ever think that it just might scare her away! And no! I don't mean Rukmini! Rukmini means nothing except that she should cast her worship upon me until I feel ready for her to forfeit her life at the right time. However, this…" Chamunda searched for the proper word, "this…*event* just might scare that stupid Premabhakti away!" Her voice dripped vile hatred. "And then, where will we be? As it is, we are walking a tightrope—everything must be delicately balanced…precisely and perfectly executed. There is no room for mistakes. There is no room for you acting of your own accord. There is no room for you to act with idiocy. There *is* no room for you to think. You were not made to think."

Chamunda's gaze swept wrathfully across the lesser ones. "Her mother is ill. We'd like her to believe deathly ill. We can't kill her but we can talk her into speaking death over herself, which will kill her. Her parents are distant and growing more distant. We are trying to ruin their will, their determination, their prayers. If we can get them and keep them in disagreement, then their prayers over Premabhakti will be useless.

"Right now, our plan is working. The delicate web that Satan has been weaving is closing in on the stupid girl. Soon she will be ready for snatching up completely. She will be ours forever! Unless…she leaves! Then everything will be ruined!" Chamunda's size grew with her rage. Her face distorted beyond its usually mockery of anything even slightly human. The features slid into each other. Her black "skin" darkened…*deepened*… until it was a deep, shiny, jet-black obsidian.

Abruptly she stopped. In the midst of her baleful, malevolent diatribe, she lifted her face (if it could be called a face—such was the hideous distortion) and sniffed the air. She wagged her head, slowly from side to side as if she were examining something. The demons about her began to shift back and forth. Yes, they felt it, too—in their bodies. The burning was increasing. Yes, they had been burning from the moment the blasted girl had arrived on the peninsula, but they had grown used to it. But this was greater, increasing in horrid strength. They dared not say anything. They dared not *do* anything. They stood there burning in increasing agony. Fear of Chamunda kept them locked in place, though they yearned to run, to scatter…they ached to get away from the God-awful-burning.

"I HAVE NO CLUE WHAT GOD IS DOING!!" Chamunda erupted. "Although I do know her parents…and others," she hissed, "are praying for the girl. Right now! I can feel it! You can feel it, too!" She spun around, livid. "God's Presence is getting stronger every moment, thus we burn more. You can barely take it now, because you are so puny….Soon, if they keep it up, I won't be able to take it!

"As it is, I can barely stand to be in the girl's presence when they're praying—too damaging!" Chamunda seemed to be muttering to herself rather than speaking to the others. She kicked at the face of one of the imps who was still submerged beneath the floor. "Agh! I'm seeing more of God's angels sent on the prayers of her parents. They're moving much more quickly than us, they're much more powerful than us, there are so many more of them than us…it has never been like that here."

Chamunda flew straight up into the air, leaving a smudgy, smoky plume that betrayed her angst behind her. "This is my arena! How can this be…?" She shot back down, she knew why, although she would not tell the others. The Lord's Presence, riding in on the prayers, hindered her. She was losing power. She was growing befuddled and confused. "Yes, prayers are going up…" She lost her train of thought. *I must maintain some semblance of control.*

She decided to re-embark upon the topic of Rukmini, though the beating of Rukmini was not the *worst* issue. Rukmini would be fine. She was one of theirs and not yet due to die. She continued on that safer, less revealing vein. "You take it upon yourselves to have Rukmini beat up in order to scare them…" *No good.* She was not able to focus on Rukmini.

Her mind circled unwillingly…painfully…around the Lord. She glared at her minions shifting in pain. She began pacing back and forth to alleviate her own pain…the burning….it was getting too intense even for her stronger, more seasoned body.

Her mouth opened and she spoke—she did not like the words she heard from her own mouth, but she could not help herself. "Of course, God's Word is correct," she mumbled to herself as she stalked to and fro on the meditation roof. "His Will will prevail in that what we intend…*everything*," she spat the word out, "we intend…for our dark lord's purposes, He uses for good."

The lesser demons peeked at each other, the unspoken question evident in their expressions—*What is she talking about?* Her words had taken a decided, rebellious turn. They *knew* that what she spoke was true, they *all knew*, but rarely would one of the leaders of an entire principality have dared voice what they knew to be true. It was spiritual foment!

"Don't you know that all things that happen to them that love the Lord God…work for good…*His* good…simply because they love Him," *What am I saying?!*—Chamunda was horrified by her own words but unable to stop, "and because they are the Called according to His purposes?"

"The Called"—how the evil ones hated "the Called"—the ones chosen for eternal life by God for no particular reason, simply because He wanted to. They understood that being "called" was a possibility for every human; however, what set the Called apart was that they chose Him in return. Humans—by simply being His created object of love, intended from the beginning to enter into a true love relationship with Him (for how can love be truly love unless it is chosen time and again?)—were hated. "The Called"—by accepting Him and stepping into that love relationship of choice, by becoming *His special treasure, His pearl of great value*—were deeply, irrevocably hated. "The Called"—fundamentally faulty, driven to gross error, and incalculable mischief—were free to choose time and again and were free to receive unwarranted, inconceivable Grace (something that they, the evil ones, would never experience). "The Called" were an eternal, uncompromising reminder of God's Absolute Sovereignty and the angels' "otherness"—for the evil angels had chosen rebellion one time and would pay eternally; whereas, "the Called" could choose, and keep on choosing, rebellion and yet were offered eternal, inestimable Grace over and over. "The Called" were a constant, glaring reminder of all they had forfeited, all they would never have, and most painful of all, *all they would never be*. How could the evil ones *not* loathe them?

"It will be interesting to see how we play into His hands with this one!" With that accurate, yet supernally inflammatory soliloquy, Chamunda stopped, entirely aghast and taken aback by her own admission. The lesser demons looked no less dumbfounded and disturbed. She could not deny it. She could not retrieve it. All was silent about her. Her rage, and her subsequent admission of evil's subordinate place in God's Will, had rendered them silent. Even the atmosphere seemed stilled by her statement of an absolute Truth. Almost everything was silent…except…except…

"That infernal praying…in tongues at that…" Chamunda muttered to herself. She seemed to shrink into herself, to darken and diminish. The power of the prayers (the words themselves of a higher, lighter vibration) traveled across seas and land, through time and space and slammed against them. Over and over like a battering ram.

"Your liege…what do we do now?" Fear asked barely above a whisper, his voice trembling. He dared not creep near her out of fear of her anger; instead, he drew himself into a tighter knot trying to avoid her gaze and, even more, the burning of the prayers. He kept all but his eyes below the cement of the roof's flooring as if he were hiding from her, not that it mattered—nothing physical could ever protect that which was spiritual.

Chamunda just shook her head and stared off toward the horizon over the ocean. Seeing…sensing…something. "I…don't…know…" she responded after a long while, her voice trailing off. "I…I…suppose I need to go see Satan…see what he has in mind. Tell him that what he's doing to her parents is not working, that they are praying even more and that their prayers are even stronger." She heaved a great sigh as if she knew the penalty of such an admission, "He has to change something, increase the assault...do *something*." She dreaded seeing Satan and informing him that they were not succeeding. He hated admitting when he was wrong or when something he did was not working. Her rages were nothing in comparison to his. She knew he would not be happy.

"Did you know Rob's coming home?" Marie asked Shanalee as they talked on the telephone. Rob was Marie and Paul's son, Maya's older brother. He had moved to San Francisco right after college and had grown distant over the years. Marie's heart ached for her son and she knew that her husband's heart ached all the more. Rarely did he mention Rob. Even more rarely did he call him. Over the years, a gulf had grown between her husband and only son. When Paul wanted to know what was going on with Rob or wanted to ask him a question, he generally directed it through her for it was she who called Rob most of the time—just to check up on him, see how he was doing. It was easier, perhaps, being the mother and breaching such bounds. She knew when Paul sat in the dark and brooded and prayed that both of his absentee children weighed heavily on his heart and mind, so heavily now that it about crushed him.

"No, you didn't tell me that!" Shanalee exclaimed. "When did that come about? When is he coming home?"

"He called last week and told me. He's planning to come home for Christmas," Marie replied. Even as she said it, she strove to contain the excitement she felt bubbling up inside. She just could not take another letdown, another piece of bad news, not again. *If Rob doesn't come...*, she pushed her mind away from the thought.

"Ah! Paul must be so happy!"

"Yes, he is. I am, too. I think Rob coming will be so good for Paul. I'm hoping he and Rob get to spend some time together. He needs Rob..."

Shana finished her thought, "And Rob needs him. More than either of them know!"

WHAT TO DO?

Maya
India

I was in the Western canteen, hanging out with Dirk and Devi. We were drinking some chai—the ashram version—watered down, boring, no spices, lots of water, just a smidgen of tea and even less milk. *Packet milk at that! Why keep cows if they don't produce milk?*

The ashram kept cows—old crotchety, skin-and-bones beasts that had ceased giving milk years ago. *What use are they? Aside from eating up the best vegetables?* I looked over at the cow shed as I ruminated on the animals. The cows ate better than the ashramites. *We could eat them.* An option my strict vegetarian sensibilities rebelled against—not to mention that they were thought to be sacred and thus were not considered a viable food source. Thinking of cows made me think of Rukmini, the ashram cow-tender, the "cow-herd-girl"—*rather a misnomer to call her a girl*—*more like hulking woman…or cow-he-woman.* I chuckled to myself and quickly extinguished it. *Don't be mean!*

"How's Rukmini doing?" I asked. It had been a couple of days since she had been assaulted.

Devi took a sip of chai and then responded, "They say she's getting better. The internal bleeding has stopped. But, the doctors say that she will probably never be able to have children. They kicked her pretty badly in the stomach."

I shook my head and stared down into my chai. Dirk did not reply; instead, he got up from his chair and went to the cabinet, muttering something like, "I need some milk for this chai."

"Milk? You keep milk in the cupboard?" Devi asked.

"No. Not real milk. Powdered milk," he answered brusquely.

As he rooted around in his cupboard and Devi and I sat there sipping, Radha approached, carrying her own chai cup. "Are you going to the meeting?"

"What meeting?" Devi and I asked simultaneously. I took a long sip of my watery chai.

Dirk turned around from rummaging through the supply cabinet. "Meeting? Meeting? For whom? About what?" he asked, his German accent stronger, his already harsh voice harsher—a clear sign that he was agitated about something, whether it was Rukmini, the meeting, or the chai needing milk, I could not tell. With an irritated "humpf," he turned back toward the cabinet.

"You know…the emergency meeting! For the Western women. It's about what we should do about what happened to Rukmini." Radha sat down. "I have some time. The meeting doesn't start for thirty minutes."

"You want some milk for your chai, Radha?" Dirk asked.

Radha shook her head, smiling, "No, I don't drink the chai here. Actually, I don't drink tea or coffee. I had to lay off the caffeine years ago. It's bad for me, my body."

"What're you drinking, then?" I asked, curious about what she was sipping.

"Oh, the boiled water that the brahmacharinis prepare." She took a sip upon answering. "It helps my stomach and I like the taste of it," she stated matter-of-factly.

Ewww! I thought of the reddish-brown tinted water the brahmacharinis cooked up. The first time I had seen it, I had been in the kitchen cooking buggy lentils, trying to figure out how to disguise the bugs that time around. A brahmacharini had peered into one of the steamers, which was filled with a boiling liquid that looked like very weak tea. When I asked why she had made the tea so weak, she had replied that it was not tea but boiled water with caraway seeds. (Obviously, the boiling was for the Westerners—20-plus minutes to cook off all the bacteria, viruses, amoebae, and parasites—not that the brahmacharinis boiled it that long. They could care less if we Westerners perished from dysentery. In fact, they would probably be overjoyed to have a few less bodies crowding around Cha Ma. The longest I had ever seen them boil the mixture was for five minutes...maybe; while boiling it, they would quickly grow disinterested and turn off the steamer.) The brahmacharini had informed me that the caraway seeds aided digestion. I personally abhorred the taste of caraway, so I had a hard time imagining voluntarily drinking it. I had simply nodded my head, attempting to hide my overwhelming sense of disgust. Very, very rarely did I drink the stuff, only when I did not have any filtered or bottled water on hand and I was thirsty. *And to think Radha drinks it because she likes it! Yeech!* It made my stomach tighten up and my mouth water in pre-vomity-vomitous. I could imagine the amoebae attaching to my gullet. *Oh no!*

"Ah! Here we go!" Dirk announced as he took the powdered milk he had finally found and sat down with us. The milk looked highly suspect— the plastic bag it was in was old, holey, and not very sanitary-looking. "Anyone want some?" he asked magnanimously.

"Oh yeah!" Devi responded, quickly extending her cup.

"Uh, sure..." I said, somewhat dubiously considering the bag.

Dirk sat down and after pouring some of the powdered milk into his cup—*Such a gentleman, always ladies first*—began to pour some into our cups.

Radha picked up where she had left off. "Some of the Western women are concerned about what happened with Rukmini. So, they've called an 'emergency meeting'"—she made quote/unquote marks with her fingers—"of the Western women to discuss what to do."

"Oh! I heard about that," I said. I took a sip of my lukewarm, powdered milk with weak chai. "Hmmm, it's interesting, though. I don't know how I feel about it."

I was lying. I *did* know how I felt about it; I was just cautious to whom I said what. I did not really want to say too much contrary to the sentiments of the other women...the *Western* women, that was. At times, they could be so overbearing. It was easier to go with the flow. The problem lay when going with *their* flow was in direct contradiction with the ashram's flow, which could possibly—*more than likely*—be the case here.

"I know that when in Rome you do as the Romans do," Devi shrugged her shoulders. She swirled her chai around in the metal cup and then sniffed it deeply as if she were a wine connoisseur enjoying a heady bouquet. Furtively, I imitated her, sniffing into my cup—*Nothing. Doesn't smell like chai, that's for sure!*

Devi continued, "...meaning, Rukmini knows how to act here. She's been here in India long enough. She knows how men are about women. She knows how Indians are about Westerners. So, then, she should know how they are about Western women. In fact, she has been told over and over. Yet, she constantly acts contrary to the culture—going so far as sitting on the men's side and even hitting them. What was she expecting?" She shrugged again in resignation. Then, she took a sip and exhaled a huge, loud sigh, "Ahh! Good chai!"

"I'm going, but only to watch the action," Radha remarked. As she spoke, Karuna stepped through the entrance of the Western canteen.

"Hey guys! Are you going to the emergency meeting?" Karuna asked excitedly. Her mischievous grin and twinkling eyes made it apparent that she was going for entertainment purposes alone and she said as much. "This is going to be so interesting!"

"I'm going, but I really don't have much of an opinion," Radha said.

"I agree…" As I spoke, I saw myself only watching.

Gangama presided over the "emergency meeting." Gangama looked like the sort who would preside over such a meeting. She was a tall woman, nearly six feet, and heavy. Very, very heavy…OK, fat. She looked like a female Buddha. She had long black hair that she wore in a topknot atop her head—like Buddha. She could sit cross-legged for hours, hands in a mudra, eyes half-closed, immobile. Her manner was slow and deliberate, measured. Never did she do anything out of haste. In fact, she was so meticulous she seemed to consider every step she took before she took it, literally.

Gangama ran the meeting with incredible impassiveness and managerialism—a unique blend of Eastern detachment and Western bureaucracy; and it seemed as if she had an agenda that she wanted to put forth before the meeting ever began. The women discussed and debated back and forth: how did we feel about the situation (a lot of discussion went into that issue), what did the *assault* of Rukmini mean for us Western women here in India, what were we going to do about the situation, how should we support Rukmini (our Western sister), to whom did we owe allegiance, etc. At one point, in the midst of all the intense discussing and sharing of feelings, a woman I recognized as a "newbie" meekly raised her hand (*we're not back in grade school*—was my first thought) and asked for solid background.

Gangama and the other "old-timers" explained the Rukmini situation by giving her history at the ashram, her interactions with the Indian men and women, etc. Gangama began, "Well, the story starts a ways back. You know how it is with Rukmini and the men?" The woman shook her head, no; but Gangama's question was more rhetorical, more of a device by which to begin describing Rukmini's life in the ashram than it was a means to elicit an actual response. Ignoring, or not seeing the newbie's head-shake, Gangama continued, "It's so many things but mainly it's been a blatant disregard for Indian customs and norms." She shifted a bit, presumably to settle more comfortably into a full lotus position. She arranged her hands into a complex mudra in her lap. We sat in silence waiting for her. Once she was settled, she continued, "In order to be close to Cha Ma, she'd sit on the men's side. Now, we all know that it's taboo for a woman to sit on the men's side. That was one strike against her. And then for that woman to be a Westerner? That was another strike against her." She paused, her eyes falling to half-mast, before recommencing, "The Indian men were only going to sit around for so long letting a woman do whatever she wanted whenever she wanted wherever she wanted to do it."

Helen, a householder renunciate with two daughters and a husband, all of whom lived in the ashram, joined in, "And then, if the Indian men said anything to her she'd ignore them. Of course, that infuriated them. So, they'd try to forcibly move her, which caused her to punch them and even beat them up. The men...everyone, Cha Ma included...kept warning her that her behavior was WAY OFF and that she'd need to tone it down majorly."

Gangama picked up Helen's thread, "She never did tone it down. She just didn't care what the Indians thought—the men or the women. She might now..." The implication of her words was clear. "The only person she cares about is Cha Ma. *If* she really cares about *her*...she ignored Cha Ma's warnings, too. I knew she'd have trouble—one day. I wasn't sure when. But tell me, how often can a woman act as a man, ignore the men, fight them, beat them up, and not have troubles with them? Especially in such a...*misogynistic*..." Gangama, who had spoken so impassively throughout the entire meeting thus far, hurled the word out as if it were a conviction of a heinous crime. A random thought wafted through my mind: *I wonder if she's a feminist? Probably...hmm, the question is: How much of one?* "...country as this—how'd she expect not to have problems?"

The newbie asked, "How many men has she beaten up?"

"Many," Gangama replied, the word falling heavily in our midst. "I can't even say how many because I haven't been around for them all. And

I can't say how often…but imagine…a Western woman beating up Indian men!" Episodes I had observed of the towering, Amazonian Rukmini hitting and pushing the smaller men, while ignoring their weak and futile shoves flashed through my mind. "It's no surprise that she got beat up—it was coming to her—eventually." She sighed deeply, signifying the inevitability of what happened. She seemed so "Buddha-ish"—her sturdy, rotund body sitting there in full lotus, her hands in her lap, her eyes at half-mast. *Even while she talks, she's so still. How does she do it?*

Chandy interjected, "OK! But whether Rukmini had it coming to her or not, the question is: 'What should we, the Western women, do—if anything?'"

Maneshwari, a long timer by many years, asked, "What does Cha Ma say?"

Gangama replied with a wry smile, her eyelids lifting a millimeter, "Cha Ma says that we are all 'like her little children. If a three-year-old boy hits his little sister, does his mother go and cut his hand off?' That's her dilemma. To her, the Divine Mother…Kali…we are all like little children behaving badly." I looked around—several of the women murmured in assent; but more than a few looked as troubled and puzzled as I felt.

The line of reasoning bothered me. *Wow! Kind of rough way to see things.* I felt a hint of agitation arise within me. *Why? Is it because it's an easy way to get out of making a decision that would make either side angry—take the spiritual high-road or act so esoterically "high," so spiritually "advanced" that real issues can't reach you? Is it because someone has been injured to the point of being in the hospital for several days, and never being able to have children, and our guru, who has the power to manage and control us, has nothing to say about it except that we're all like little children and thus she's not going to do anything about it? Is it because her putting it on the level of children tacitly puts her stamp of approval on it?* I could not put my finger on why. I would have to go and think about it when I was quiet (already knowing that I would not; instead, when the meeting adjourned, I would put my troubling questions out of my head, if I could).

Into the thoughtful silence left by Gangama's pronouncement, a woman spoke up. Another followed her. Many views were aired. Many positions were given. After an hour, the meeting ended with no real reso-lution. The Western women agreed to come back together to continue the discussion another time.

CHRISTMAS
WITH THE AVATAR

"Come on! Come on!" Anneshwari and Alice pulled on my arms.

"I'm coming. I'm coming! I don't understand what all the fuss is for…" I responded somewhat irritatedly as they pulled me out of my bunk. *They're pulling kinda hard. What could be the big fuss?*

"It's Christmas! You've got to go to the Christmas celebration!" Anneshwari blurted out, her face crinkling up around the eyes with gleeful anticipation. "We get to celebrate Cha Ma!"

"Celebrate Cha Ma?" I felt confused. "At Christmas? Christmas is about Jesus." I felt a strange mixture of dismay and confusion as my tenuous, Christian roots momentarily asserted themselves. Not for many years now had I been concerned with Christianity, let alone with defending Jesus's claim to Christmas. I squelched my spiritual territorialism as I leapt out of the bed to keep up with them.

"Yeah, well," Alice replied as she led the way out of the women's dorm, "many people believe that Cha Ma, in one of her lifetimes, was Jesus."

You're kidding me! Cha Ma? An incarnation of Jesus? Again, something deep within me rebelled—it was an automatic, unconscious impulse. I squelched the pesky thing and rolled the thought around in my head. *Cha Ma was once Jesus. Hmmm. Now, that's interesting...*

We stepped out onto the balcony. The temple was dimly lit. A few people were sitting, spaced randomly, around the balcony. They were sitting close to the wrought iron railing, peering through the curved, intricate ironwork at the activities below. By far, most of the people—mainly ashramites as there was only a sprinkling of visitors—were sitting on the temple floor.

"You guys go ahead," I urged Anneshwari and Alice on. "I want to sit up here and watch everything."

"OK!"

"See ya!" they called as they headed toward the stairs that led to the temple from the balcony. Clearly, they did not need me to prod them a second time.

I settled down on the balcony, close to the inner temple and women's dorm, in an area that was clear of bodies. Sitting cross-legged, I pressed my knees through the bars as I gently placed my forehead against them. They felt cool against my skin. I could see almost everything that was happening on the floor.

It looked to be several hundred people—mostly ashramites. *It seems like everyone knew about the Christmas festivities except for me*—I thought, not really caring one way or the other. The temple floor was a sea of white—*All the brahmacharis and -charinis are here.* In a tight cluster in the center of the "sea of white" sat a narrow band of gold—the sannyasis. Within the sannyasi circle were the swamis in burnt orange. Smack-dab in the middle of it all was Cha Ma. The crowd had clumped up close—all attention on her. *Of course!* I felt an involuntary shudder of revulsion. I never liked to be "all up in it." It tended to make me feel claustrophobic and unnervingly overwhelmed. I preferred to sit on the outskirts and watch what was happening.

I stared down at Cha Ma. She was wearing her usual heavily starched, immaculately white sari and was sitting on…a lawn chair. *How odd!* She looked like she was camped out—ready to enjoy a "show on the lawn." At the sight, my mind flitted back to the many warm, humid nights in Boston, back to the Half-Shell, where people would gather to watch movies and performances. Many a night I had been part of that fun, boisterous crowd. A starry sky. A blanket spread out. A cooler stocked with snacks. *Kali! My life has changed so much!* I focused back on Cha Ma.

She was leaning over in her chair, talking to—*I should've known!*—Narayana…Brahmachari Narayanan, now. *I wonder why Cha Ma kept his name the same. He's the only sannyasi to keep his own name. Figures! Even with his name, he gets special treatment. He's such "her favorite"!* I felt a rush of jealousy flash through me. *I've got to have better control than this!* Telling myself to have control did not furnish it. I stared at him as he chatted with Cha Ma. Something he said made her guffaw in raucous laughter, throwing her head back with abandon. Leaning in closer, he shot her a roguish grin, which made him all the more gorgeous. *I wish it were me he was talking to!* I caught myself sighing. *Stop that!* I was tempted to smack my own cheek in chastisement. I forced myself to look elsewhere other than at Brahmachari Narayanan.

I looked to the stage—the curtains of the inner temple were drawn to. The show had not yet begun. *I wish it would hurry up and start. Give me something to look at other than him.* I watched Anneshwari and Alice pick their way through the crowd—slowly but steadily moving through the people in white. *I can't believe it! They're going to wedge themselves up close to Cha Ma. You'd think that after what had happened to Rukmini, they would act better, not be so pushy.* Finally, Alice and Anneshwari had waded and climbed and pushed their way close to Cha Ma; but the sannyasis and swamis would not part to let them beyond their circle. *That's as close as it's going to be for them tonight.* They plopped down on the periphery of the sea of white. The movement of the brahmacharinis, to allow them space, was like a ripple in a thick, viscous, white pond. I observed them a couple of seconds longer and then shifted my attention…

…to Narayanan, of course. My heart skipped a beat—he was looking up toward my area of the balcony! *Is he looking at me?* I looked to my left and right—*I can't believe I just did that! How goofy can I get?*—to see who was beside me and could be attracting his attention. No one was in my vicinity. Our eyes locked. I could not tear my eyes away. *No need to really, no one else is paying attention to us*—A more rational part of my brain whispered (How it could be considered rational while condoning a stare-down with Narayanan, I had no idea!).

Distantly, I heard the first strains of music. My subconscious registered it—*The show's starting!*—while I continued staring at Narayanan, ensnared by his eyes. If I had had any ability to step outside of myself, I would have noticed that he was just as ensnared by me. What we looked like to others was unfathomable and far from my thoughts. I was certain that no one (with the exception of Karuna, who always seemed to notice our interactions) was even paying attention to us as the show had begun.

Vaguely, I perceived the lone warbling of a sitar. Three slowly plucked notes undulated across the temple, rising like a set of diaphanous stairs into the air. The third note was long and drawn out, the air molding itself about the sound. The undulating tone wove a web around my mind and my senses...in harmony with the keen, but now familiar longing for Narayanan that wove ever more tightly about my heart. The note hooked my heart and drew it out of me, while holding my mind in abeyance...

WAP! Cha Ma swung the little stick she often held for keeping rhythm and smacked Narayanan on the leg. Hard. Immediately, his gaze snapped away as did mine. I could not withstand the pull...I peeked a glance back.

He was looking at Cha Ma, his face oddly unreadable. Her face was a dark bitter chocolate rather than her usual cappuccino hue. She frowned as she spoke forcefully at him and then suddenly, in that peculiar but lovable Cha Ma fashion, she changed up and smiled at him, caressing his cheek. I looked at the others. The swamis and sannyasis sitting nearby were watching and grinning, obviously enjoying the show of Narayanan and Cha Ma (and me?). Only Swami was not watching; instead, he stared up at me with a look both serene and disturbing. I could tell he did not approve.

I looked to the stage. The skit was under way. It was the story of Christmas and opened with the announcement of Jesus's birth. Several of the young Western children who lived in the ashram were dressed in white gowns with angel wings, fashioned out of wire and a white, gauzy material, attached to their backs. They ran up to a teenage girl, a Westerner, who wore drab, brown and tan robes and worked hard to look serious and sincere. *Mary, I would imagine....It's amazing that even here in India, miles and miles from any real Western Christianity, you'll still find Westerners who have to do the Christmas story.* A teenaged Western boy, wearing white robes bordered with gold trim, stepped through the little angels—*Archangel Gabriel?* He announced to Mary that she would give birth to an exalted child, the Savior.

I watched and listened, noticing that they presented a version that was close to the traditional Christian one, with only slight variations that incorporated Hinduism: the teenager, who was Archangel Gabriel, added in speaking to Mary that the son she was to bear, Jesus, was an avatar of Vishnu. He shared that in the past Vishnu had come in the form of Lord Ram and Krishna and now, he was coming as Jesus. A young brahmachari stepped out as John the Baptist and shared that he was the reincarnated Elijah. And at the end, a teenaged American boy came forward dressed as Jesus and, facing the audience, reiterated Archangel Gabriel's words that yes, he was Jesus, which was just another form of the god, Vishnu, and that he had come centuries ago in the forms of Lord Ram, Krishna, and now had come as Cha Ma. He shared eloquently how he, as Vishnu, chose, every so often, to come down in a human form in order to help ailing humanity.

I dared a glance over at Cha Ma. She was engrossed in the play. Her hands clasped under her chin like a little child. The swamis were another matter—they looked insurmountably bored and covertly kept peering about the temple. And then, there was Narayanan. *Don't do it! Don't do it!* Needless to say, my eyes had a will all their own! I ventured a glance his way in spite of myself. *I make my own self sick! I can't control myself to save my life!*

He was looking back up at me. *Does he realize that he keeps looking at me? Can he really not control himself at all? Is he that drawn to me that he can't stop himself from staring? Is he even aware that he's staring? What'll happen if Cha Ma catches him again?* I looked around and noticed that Swami was watching him watching me. I could not tell what Swami was thinking, his half-mast eyes veiled and distant. His jaw set firm; his full lips pressed into a thin line of disapproval.

At the end of the skit, a large group of Indian girls, Kathak dancers, ran out and danced a version of a Krishna dance, this time singing, "Hare Jesus, hare, hare Jesus!" They wore bright, vibrant costumes of royal blue and rich purple. Thick ankle belts of bells jangled in rhythm to the tablas.

They danced beautifully, in perfect time as they executed complex moves. Everyone in the temple, including Cha Ma and the swamis, joined in singing vociferously. The celebration ended with everyone calling out, "Jesus! Cha Ma! Jesus! Cha Ma!" amid much clapping and cheering.

Even as the boisterous merrymaking went on, the crowd parted to allow the participants of the show to line up for darshan with Cha Ma. Quickly, she gave them a hug as Br. Narayanan and a very pretty, chubby brahmacharini in yellow passed the people to her. When she was done giving darshan, a man and a woman stepped forward out of the group bearing a heavy flower garland and a large thali—a round, stainless steel plate about two feet in diameter. From my vantage point, I could see what was on the plate: four small piles of powder—red kumkum, cream colored tulasi, yellow turmeric, and gray vibhuti (ash), three small silver cups—one filled with thick almost transparent, brownish-yellow ghee, another with creamy, lumpy curd, and the last with thin, watery coconut milk—and a pile of flowers petals.

Br. Narayanan held the large thali as the couple placed the huge garland about Cha Ma's neck and then pranamed. After they stood, Br. Narayanan handed the thali back to them. Throughout the crowd, I heard a murmuring. I could only make out something that sounded like, "Pahduhpoojja... pahduhpoojja..." I watched closely so that I could understand.

The swamis began singing a soulful bhajan to Kali as Br. Narayanan and the yellow brahmacharini placed Cha Ma's feet into another large thali. The crowd joined into the singing. I noticed that most everyone's hands were like mine—clasped together in front of their mouths in a position of prayer. The couple worshipfully poured first the ghee, then the curd, and finally, the coconut milk on Cha Ma's feet, dipping their hands into the run-off in the thali and pouring it back onto her feet. Next, they dabbed her feet with the kumkum, tulasi, turmeric powders, and vibhuti until the piles were gone. I could see their lips moving, but I could not hear their voices below the singing. I figured they were chanting a special mantra just for the occasion. Next, they took the flower petals and offered them to Cha Ma before throwing them gently on her feet. When they were done offering the flower petals, Swami approached them carrying a large, ornate arati lamp. The lights in the temple were dimmed even further. Only the faces closest to Cha Ma were illuminated.

Swami shifted into singing arati. Solemnly, the couple waved the lamp before Cha Ma, whose hands were clasped together in front of her chest, her eyes closed. Everyone in the temple sang arati along with Swami. The song faded as Swami took the arati lamp. The couple pranamed again and backed away from Cha Ma, a look of intense reverence upon their faces. The temple was so still. In the dim light, everyone waited on Cha Ma.

After several minutes, she opened her eyes and whispered something to Br. Narayanan. He took her elbow and helped her to stand up. The crowd parted as he led her out of the temple through the side door closest to her quarters. The swamis trailed closely behind her. Everyone else slowly filtered out of the temple. A few of the non-ashramites, devotees who had traveled to see Cha Ma, spread their light, threadbare blankets (or nothing at all) and laid down where they were. Soon all was quiet.

I continued to sit on the balcony, thinking—*Cha Ma an avatar of Jesus? Then who is she really...if not Kali? Is she Krishna? But then, Krishna is an avatar of Vishnu.....So, is she really a Vishnu avatar and not a Kali avatar? Is Jesus simply a Vishnu avatar? Cha Ma was Jesus...Wow!* I continued to roll the thought around in my head. Deep inside something said, "No!" to the idea of Cha Ma being Jesus, of Jesus having been reincarnated. *He's just more special than that*—I felt the whisper. Slowly, consumed with my thoughts, I rose and headed into the women's dorm.

As I unwound my sari and prepared to lie down, Anneshwari and Alice approached me carrying a huge thali. *The* huge thali. In their wake were several Western women.

"Look what we have!" Alice announced. "We have..."

"Cha Ma's pada puja!" Anneshwari interrupted her triumphantly.

"Pada puja?" *So, that's what I was hearing...pada puja!*

"Pada puja is the worship of the guru's feet," answered Anneshwari matter-of-factly. "You saw it..."

When I did not answer, Alice explained, perhaps taking my silence for ignorance, which it was. "Hindus believe that the feet of the guru are charged with great spiritual power. They are a reservoir of spiritual energy…" I looked at her blankly, so she continued, "…you know, the kundalini shakti…the kundalini, the shakti, the energy…flows powerfully out of their feet. It's considered a rare treat to be offered the liquid run-off from the worship of the guru's feet, the pada puja juice. It burns away our karma and increases our spiritual power." She sounded surprisingly, strangely, like an encyclopedia. *Maybe there's more to Alice than I thought…*

"So, why are you carrying it around? What are you going to do with it?"

"Oh! We drink it." Alice produced a small silver cup (from where, I had no idea). She and Anneshwari carefully tipped the thali and poured a little bit of the pada puja juice into it. "We've all had some. We're now looking for people who haven't had any." She extended the cup to me. "Here, have some."

Pada puja juice…hmmm…well, anything for enlightenment! "Sure!" I took the cup, threw my head back, and drank. It did not taste like anything in particular. The odd mixture of curd, ghee, coconut milk, kumkum, tulasi, turmeric, ash, and flowers had no distinctive taste. Not yummy. Not yucky. It just was.

Alice took the cup out of my hand and moved on with Anneshwari and the crew of women behind them. I lay down on my bunk and thought about the strange Christmas I had just celebrated. In the midst of my musings, I fell asleep.

Marie, Paul, and Rob
United States

It's 12:01 A.M. Christmas Day. We made it. Paul looked from his wife to his son and felt his heart swell with joy and peace. A part of him could not believe they had made it to Christmas. So many times it had felt as though they were not going to make it, that the enemy, Sickness and Pain, were going to eat them up. But, here they were. He held up his miniature communion cup, "To Christ," he said as a benediction to the communion prayer he had just prayed.

"To Christ!" Rob said as he held up his cup.

"We love You, Jesus!" Marie said as she held up her cup.

They smiled at each other over the cups. The soft glow of the lights on the Christmas tree illumined their faces. The atmosphere of the house was wonderful.

They could not see into the spiritual, but if they could have, they would have seen angels in the house saluting the recognized birthday of their Lord—they took every opportunity to celebrate their Lord. They sang joyous songs of His Glory and Majesty, their voices rolling out from their bodies and reaching far into the atmosphere.

Paul felt such a feeling of peace, one he had not felt in months...actually, not since Maya had left. He thought back to the conversations he had had with his son during his stay over the Christmas holiday. *We've talked more in this past week than we have in the past five years!* He marveled over the closeness and honesty that was between them. His mind went back to one particular conversation; it had helped his heart so much.

"You think she's coming back, Dad?" Rob had asked about Maya as they sat in front of the television. It was well past midnight. Marie had gone to bed a long time ago. They had sat together and watched an action movie. After the movie, they had started talking. Sometime during the course of the conversation, Paul had turned the television's volume low. They stared at the screen as they talked.

"I don't know, Rob," Paul had shaken his head. "I pray she does..."

"Whatever you do, Dad," Rob paused as he cleared his throat, "don't blame yourself." Paul did not say anything, but he was listening. "And I know you are...but you've done the best you could...by me and Maya."

Paul shook his head, "I don't think..."

"No, really, Dad! You did your best with me and Maya when we were growing up. And your best was more than enough. You were a good dad. You always have been." Rob paused, then resumed, "You probably think that you did something wrong with me and that's why I live so far away and don't call a lot. But, Dad, that's me...not you! As for Maya, she's my little sister, but you know how she's always been..."

Paul nodded. He *did* know how she was—a thrill seeker, excitement hungry, fearless, and always pushing the limit. She had been so difficult as a child. *What was that? Ahh! The strong-willed child. She gave new meaning to strong-willed.*

"You can't blame yourself for choices she and I are making as adults. And, look at me...I've not turned out badly. I've got a great job and a good life. I'm a responsible man. As for Maya...she'll come around. But, you... you just can't blame yourself. You've been a great father." Rob gave a tentative smile. "Heck, I want to be like you when I have children."

As Rob spoke something in Paul's chest broke. He felt something rise up in his chest and threaten to erupt into tears. He stared at the television and swallowed rapidly. Finally, he replied, "Thanks, Rob. You don't know how much I needed to hear that. I just want you to know that I'm so proud of you. I know I don't say it all the time, but I am."

"Thanks, Dad," Rob responded. "All I've ever wanted to do was make you proud." The room was silent as both sunk into his own thoughts. Finally, Rob announced, "I think I'm going to go to bed now." He rose to leave.

"OK," Paul rose, too. "I love you, son!"

"I love you, too, Dad."

Awkwardly, they embraced—each too manly for his own good. Then, Rob walked out of the den as Paul sat down and stared at the silent television. Tears of relief and release coursed down his cheeks. He had not felt so good and free in a long time.

KOVALAM BEACH

Maya
India

"You can come with us if you'd like," Gangama offered with a smile, which did not do much to alter her Buddha-esque stature. I was in the Western canteen and had caught the trailing end of a conversation that Gangama and her friend, Priya, were having.

"Yes, I think you'd enjoy a trip to the beach a lot," Priya added. She, like Gangama, was a long-time Western renunciate. She was tall like Gangama, but much slimmer, and where Gangama looked stoic and serious, she looked pleasant and too normal to be in an ashram in the middle of India. She kept her brown hair at a medium-short length and wore glasses.

"Are you sure? I'd hate to be a bother…" *I can't believe that Gangama and Priya, Gangama especially, want me to go with them.* Gangama was an icon (of sorts) of the ashram—more distant and inaccessible than Cha Ma, even. She was one of the long-time renunciates and many believed she had been around as long as most of the swamis. In fact, gossip around the ashram (amongst the Westerners) was that she was already enlightened.

"Oh no, not at all. Kovalam beach is large enough to hold the three of us," Gangama answered congenially, with another smile. "We'll be doing our own thing." Priya nodded in agreement. "We'll probably meet up for meals…you'll have a lot of freedom and time to yourself."

"C'mon, you'll enjoy it," Priya urged again. "We're leaving tomorrow morning. Our taxi's supposed to be here at nine." She gestured at Gangama. "Gangama doesn't like riding the buses or trains."

Gangama gave a curt nod in the affirmative. "It's all been arranged."

"OK, I think I will." I had never been to Kovalam beach and had only heard snippets about it. A few of the Westerners had gone and it seemed to be a hub of rest and relaxation from the intensity and craziness of ashram life. I was curious and was suddenly aware of the need for a break from the ashram.

Thus began my one and only trip to Kovalam beach. The taxi ride was uneventful enough. The driver let us off on a side street nearby.

"We'll have to walk from here," Priya told me.

Even as I thought—*Why?*—Gangama answered my question. "The access roads to the beach are too narrow and poorly made. They're just not good for cars. The taxi could easily get stuck."

"Oh," I replied. I threw my duffel bag over my shoulder, glad that I had packed lightly. I figured that as we would only be gone for a couple of days, a few at the most, I did not need to carry too much. If I needed more clothes, I could wash what I had.

I had the feeling that we would have to hike some distance to reach our lodgings. I was right. Gangama, Priya, and I walked single file down the narrow street as it wove its way to the beach. We marched about a half mile until we came to the beach. From there, we walked down the length of the shoreline for another half a mile. As we walked, we passed low-slung buildings—hotels and eating establishments, mostly. Some were pure white and looked cool and refreshing; others were colorfully pastel and reminded me of the ashram. All were stained with mold and mildew.

Gangama turned left into a long, low, white building. It was our hotel. It looked to be good quality—not a four-star hotel or anything, but adequate, and definitely better than what we lived with in the ashram. From what I could tell, the rooms opened onto balconies that faced the ocean. *How nice!*

We stopped in the lobby. Gangama walked forward to get our room key. I leaned over to Priya, "I don't know Indian hotels very well, what would this be considered?"

"What do you mean?" Priya asked, peering at me through her glasses.

"Like in terms of hotel ratings, what would this hotel be rated according to Indian standards?" I looked around. *The décor looks OK. Kinda like a Motel 6 in the U.S.*

"Oh, I don't know...probably a four-star..." Priya looked around with me.

"A four-star? Really?" *Wow!* I continued looking around as Gangama checked us in. Soon enough, she was done.

"OK, we're ready," announced Gangama as she approached us. A young Indian guy who looked to be a teenager approached us in order to take our bags. "No, thank you. We can carry them." He walked away as Gangama headed off. Priya and I followed her.

We had to go back outside as all of the entrances to the rooms were adjacent to the patios and faced the beach. We walked several doors down to the second to the last door.

Gangama unlocked the door, pushed it open, and moved aside so that Priya and I could walk through. We stepped into a smallish, common room. Its furnishings were two plastic chairs and a table centered between them. A glass door to our right opened onto the balcony. A door was the only thing in the wall adjacent to the balcony. It led to one bedroom. Against the far wall was a sink with spidery crack lines. Next to the sink was the door that led to the bathroom. The bathroom was tile and white-wash—clean, but not immaculate. One side of the bathroom boasted a showerhead above a slightly downward sloping floor that ended in a hole about five inches in diameter. The other side was the toilet, which was a squat hole (oval-shaped, with foot tiles on either side). Next to the squat hole was a bucket and scooper under a faucet. In the wall to our left was a narrow hallway that led to two other bedrooms. All the bedrooms were clean and neat. Each had a narrow cot in the corner and a small table with a chair. *OK, this is do-able.*

We agreed that they would take the adjoining bedrooms. I would take the one on the other side of the common area. As soon as I dropped my bag on the table in my room and was thinking about washing up after the hours of traveling, Priya popped her head in. "We're going to get something to eat, you want to come?"

"Oh yeah!" I answered. My stomach rumbled in response to her question. I had not thought about food for the entire journey; now my stomach was calling to me most hungrily.

We headed off down the beach away from the direction we had arrived. With the ocean a few yards away—it was a nice scene…kinda sorta—OK, not really. Already I did not like the beach, it was rockier and stonier than most of the beaches I had enjoyed. And rocks and stones aside, the sand itself was not fine, granulated sand so much as it was rocky and pebbly. I compared the beach to the ones I had visited in the Carolinas, the Yucatan peninsula, the islands of Malaysia, Italian beaches…*Nope! Not the same.* Seaweed had drifted onto the beach and was tangled everywhere. Gnarled chunks of driftwood lay about. *Definitely doesn't call me to come and walk barefoot on the fine sand. Huh-uh! Doesn't beckon to me to come and lay on its sandy shores. Definitely not the type of beach to be laid upon.* Not that I was planning to. However, the condition of the shore was not my biggest problem. No, I was to encounter a bigger problem than the pebbliness of the beaches.

As we walked, Priya remarked, "Why are all the men staring at you?"

Whew! Outside proof that I'm not mad! I had grown used to being stared at in the ashram and when I took little trips to Trivandrum or Ernakulam, especially when I let myself act like a foreigner, an American; but this was something altogether different…something…more.

Gangama answered for me, "I would imagine it's because she looks like an Indian but she's hanging out with us and is dressed like a Westerner. Further, if any of them listen to her talk, they'll notice that she's not Indian. And…she's pretty, what do you expect?" Gangama's succinct analysis of the situation made me want to go hide. I felt embarrassed for myself.

"No, she's not pretty…she's beautiful!" Priya fawned, as she gave me the once over as women tend to do when they are sizing each other up. "Do you think they can tell that she's an American?"

"Probably…if they hear her speak. Her accent is definitely not British, and India was once a British protectorate," Gangama paused, pondering. "And then, I suppose the way she looks figures in. She just doesn't have that 'British' feel."

British feel? What's the British feel? Do I have an American feel? Now I did want to crawl underneath a rock, although, at the same time, I felt pride swelling within me. "OK! That's enough, now! Let's talk about something else."

"Well, here we are…" Gangama announced as she gestured to a restaurant that sat on the edge of the beach.

It was one of the low-slung, pastel affairs. Palms and vegetation grew lushly and haphazardly all around it, giving it an air of wildness. Gangama led the way inside. Priya followed closely behind her as I slowly trailed, busily taking it all in. Inside was just as lush and "vegetatious" as the exterior. A fair-sized crowd sat inside on cushioned bamboo chairs pulled up to intricately carved tables. The lighting was low and came from candles on the tables and elaborate, wooden sconces on the walls. Soft music played in the background—flutes and tablas. The atmosphere was one of relaxation and leisure—a place where friends could sit for hours eating and drinking and enjoying.

We were seated near another group of Westerners and before long we had pulled our chairs over to their table—everyone eating, drinking chai, talking and laughing, and just acting like foreigners, very touristy foreigners. The hours slipped by as we sat and talked and laughed. Finally, we walked back to our hotel. Tired, I fell into bed and dropped off to sleep listening to the sound of the waves crashing against the shore.

That first day was illustrative of my visit to Kovalam beach. I met many Westerners while we were there. I ate a bunch of yummy food, usually with Westerners. I drank prodigious amounts of tasty chai while we sat talking and shooting the breeze. I meditated a little. I swam not at all—the water was dark, not necessarily murky but too dark for my tastes, and choppy with white caps. It looked unpredictable. It spoke of riptides. And then, when I considered the driftwood and seaweed that constantly washed up onto the beach from the water, I had no desire to touch the dark, danger-ous, watery stuff. And sunbathe? On a rocky, stony, pebbly beach in India?! With the leering Indian men who found me to be a Western novelty and something to stare at and even follow—*Oh no!* In fact, I had no desire to even go near the beach. I walked along it often enough, usually on my way to some restaurant or café. I preferred, by far, sitting in a beach-side restaurant drinking chai and watching others walk by. *Hey! I've always been good at sitting in a café, drinking a hot, caffeinated beverage—coffee…chai…it made no difference—watching others go by!* This was no different.

What was most remarkable about the whole Kovalam beach trip was the response of the men to me. It was one thing to be stared at by men and women, which happened all the time in the ashram and whenever I traveled about. I was used to that. Now that my hair was growing out and I was wearing it in twists, I garnered a lot of attention and surreptitious hair tugs. It was another thing altogether, the "odd" encounters I experienced while at the beach.

The first time I had an unusual encounter, I was walking along the beach by myself (*hurrying myself along* would be a more apt description be-cause I felt like a sitting duck to walk along the beach by myself). A middle-aged, not too bad looking Indian man approached me, "Excuse me! Excuse me, miss!"

I stopped, "Yes?"

"You're not Indian, no?" I shook my head no—I was not Indian so no head bobbles for me. "I have heard about you. You are the black American woman!" He made his pronouncement with an air of unconcealed delight as though he had made a remarkable discovery.

"Uhhh, OK…" I began to ease away from him.

He grabbed my arm. "Marry me!" he exclaimed, his face earnest.

"What?" I snatched my arm away from him.

Before I could say anything else, he said it again, "Marry me, please! I will pay you…" Furtively, he looked to his left and right and then proceeded, "I will pay you $15,000 to marry me!"

Had I been a money-grubbing woman, I might have considered him. I was not. Quickly, I walked away, "No thank you! I don't even know your name!" He started after me. Luckily for me, Gangama and Priya were approaching from the other direction. I practically ran to them, hoping against hope that Mr.-Marriage-Buyer was not running behind me. I would not have put it past him—something in his face made me nervous.

"I'm so glad to see you guys!" I squashed the overwhelming urge to give them a hug just for being at the right place at the right time.

"What's the matter?" Priya asked, as she looked past me to the guy. "Is he giving you trouble? We can handle him!"

I looked behind me to see if he was still pursuing me. He was not, although he was not walking away. He appeared to be trying to stand nearby unobtrusively. *He needs a tree to hide behind like Rukmini.* "No, I'm fine."

"We're on our way for some chai, you want to come?" Gangama asked. I nodded my head yes. "Good, then you can tell us what's up? What happened with that guy?"

I fell into step with them. "He asked me to marry him…offered me $15,000." Gangama nodded with an air of understanding and something that seemed almost like forbearing pity. "He said he'd heard that I was the black American woman," I said this with a poor version of an Indian accent. "What do you think he meant by that? 'He had *heard* that I was the black American woman'?"

Gangama nodded again. "I'd thought that word would get around about you. I just did not think it would be so…much. But, I can see the attraction—you look like an Indian woman, definitely someone from Kerala or Southern India, but then, with a Western passport. No, even better—you come with an *American* passport."

Priya added, "Hmmm, I can see that…despite all the bad press about Americans and America, we are really blessed to be Americans. So many people would do *anything* to get into America. And to get an American wife, who looks like an Indian? Wow! I *bet* they would be after you."

"Hmphf! It's all a little overboard to me!" I said in dismissal as we sat down in a cozy, beachside café for chai.

I thought that was the end of it; but it was not. After the third marriage proposal—business proposition—we began counting. I received seven marriage requests over the course of four days. All the men stressed the fact that I was a Westerner and that they wanted a Western woman. Several mentioned that they had heard about me—*the black American woman*—like I was some rare, exotic bird that could be caught or bought. A couple offered me nothing but their undying love. *How can they love me? They don't even KNOW me!* A couple stated matter-of-factly that I would make them a good wife—*Ha! Ha!* (Gangama, Priya, and I got a great laugh out of that one— my independent Western ways would surely drive them crazy. Hey! Any woman who would move to India at the drop of a dime, would probably be a little too free-spirited for the average Indian man reared in traditional India.) Most offered me big dollars to marry them, ranging from $15,000 (the first man's bid was the lowest) to $40,000. A couple even had the nerve to pull out their wallets to "show me the money." One wanted to write me a check right on the spot. Initially, I was flattered; but quickly my feelings turned to extreme "botheration"—it was simply too much *weird* attention.

By the end of our four days, I was ready to go. In fact, I would have gladly sat in the taxi waiting for Gangama and Priya to get packed and ready to go, if I had not had to walk the length of the beach to get to the access road alone. When we finally climbed into the taxi, relief flooded my being at the thought of going back to the ashram—back to the rules that forbade any real interaction between the sexes, back to uptight brahmacharis and repressed sannyasis, back to intense stares and unfulfilled desires.

CLANDESTINE
(RUINOUS) DESIRES

"See, that's the one…" I hushed at Radha, as I indicated with my head toward a brahmachari, sitting in half-lotus. His hands rested lightly, palms down, on his thighs. His spine straight, his head sitting strong and erect upon his shoulders, eyes closed. *Not like me! I'm always listing like an abandoned ship or, even worse, my head'll loll to the side, giving away the fact that I'm sleeping.* Not him—he looked to be in a comfortable state of deep meditation—calm, serene, engrossed.

It was late afternoon. The sun was past its zenith. It was sinking flamboyantly into the ocean in front of us—as if it could not get enough of its own splendor. Its rays caused the ocean water to sparkle brilliantly. The rippling waves appeared to be playing a game of hide-and-seek with the light. The light, glancing off the few clouds, had painted the sky brilliant shades of pink, lavender, magenta, and purple.

I and Radha, and several others, were on the meditation roof facing the ocean and the setting sun—it was a fantastic sight to behold. She and I had positioned ourselves side-by-side with the intention of a good meditation session. Now, over an hour later, I was done. I supposed hers was good. Mine had been full of sleep (my excuse being that I was tired from cooking in the kitchen). When I awakened from my deep and edifying "meditation," I surveyed the roof and perused the other meditationers. That was when I saw him. He must have come up to the roof while I was "out" in meditation *(sleep)*.

He was good-looking. No, he was more than good-looking. He was *insanely* gorgeous. He was tall, especially for an Indian man, nearly six feet and slim (most of the brahmacharis were). His long, wavy hair reached just past his shoulders and was not in the usual color range of dark brown to black and all the hues in between that I was used to seeing in India; rather, it was a very light brown with sun-blond streaks. It was layered and slightly unkempt-looking, not so much from an intentional cut as from hair neglectfully grown out. His skin and eyes were almost the same color as his hair—a strangely, beautiful combination—all a rich light brown, like butterscotch or toffee. He kept himself clean-shaven (which was unusual, for the brahmacharis tended to grow mustaches and beards unless they were too young), which when coupled with his untamed hair, lent to showing off his chiseled cheekbones.

Given all that, what was most extraordinary about him, though, was his eyes. There was something distinctly…peculiarly…*feral* about his eyes. They gave him an air of wildness and unpredictability. He reminded me of a wild, dangerous animal that was momentarily caged; although nothing in his behavior indicated anything other than the usual brahmachari temperance. In behavior, he was like all of the brahmacharis—fastidiously controlled and mindful of boundaries. However, his eyes shouted that he was a caged, hungry animal that would soon find its way out. He was not around very often—he must have lived in another of Cha Ma's ashrams. I figured he was a brahmachari, though, because he remained with them when he was here.

What held my attention about him, aside from his wild, outrageous good looks, was that I would catch him looking at the women in the ashram a little too often, not in the way Raju or Manoj would look at us, which was more like sisters or just wanting to talk and maybe flirt. Rather, there was something knowledgeable, even bordering on predatory, in his gaze.

Of course, my curiosity was piqued (fire always has an inexplicable allure for pyromaniacs). I wanted to know about him, but I had not had the chance to ask anyone. He was around so rarely, and I always forgot to ask about him the moment he was out of sight. This was the first time that I saw him (and thus remembered to ask) when there was someone around to whom I could ask my questions. I knew Radha would give me the truth. If there were anyone who would know the *real* story, untarnished by gossip and conjecture, it would be she.

I waited until she opened her eyes in order to accost her. "Oh him…" She smiled and stretched. "That was a great meditation! I and Cha Ma were…"

"Raaadhaaa! The guy? *The guy?*" I whispered at her in mock exasperation.

"Oh yeah! I've heard snatches about him here and there. What I've gathered is, first and most importantly," she gave me a knowing look for emphasis, "it's best to stay away from him. Far away."

"Why do you look at me like that?" I asked with feigned innocence, knowing full well why.

"Why? Because you know how it is with you and the brahmacharis!"

"Yeah? Well, anyway…" I decided to ignore her. I did not want her to touch upon my ashram-monk-issues…my *male* issues. "What's up with him? Is he a brahmachari?" My curiosity could not be contained, especially when it was growing by the second.

"Yes, he's a brahmachari…one of the first ones. He came to Cha Ma when he was very young a looong time ago. If he had stayed with it, had not let his lower nature take over, he would still be in yellow or maybe even in orange, by now."

"Still be in yellow…? Be in orange…!" I yelped.

"Shhhh!" Radha scolded me, while her smile promised more. I leaned closer to her. I was all ears (and eyes as I stared at him).

"A few years ago, he turned yellow. He used to live in the ashram then. He was very close to Cha Ma back then, too."

"Were you here then?"

She nodded the affirmative. "Um-hmm, I saw him but I never knew him." She resumed the story. "Apparently, Cha Ma warned him that something was 'not quite right' about him—within him—and to beware. She told him to stick close to her in order to avert disaster." Our eyes remained upon him as she spoke. It did not matter as his were closed. Our talking about him did not disturb his calm.

"Disaster? What do you mean?"

"Well, all of this is what I heard after the fact. At the time, I did not know any of this. But, people say that he had a problem with the female persuasion…we were his temptation….one he couldn't resist." I did not say anything, I just stared at him—all eyes for him, all ears for her. "Well, at the time, there was a brahmacharini here, I don't know her name. Everyone who has been here over the years knows who she is, but no one will talk about her. They won't even say her name. They say that she and he fell in love…and began to see each other clandestinely…Now, you know that has never happened before or since with Cha Ma."

"Why is that?" I asked. I glanced at her and then resumed staring at him. He seemed to grow wilder, untamable, and much more attractive (if that were even possible) before my eyes.

"Well, because Cha Ma knows everything. She can look…she *does* look…at us and know *everything* about us. Our thoughts. What we do. What we say. You know…" I nodded because I *did* know. Cha Ma had an uncanny, actually…*frightening*…ability to know everything about everyone at any time. It was just a question of *if* she would say anything to us about it.

"No one knows how it all started. They…he and she…never said. They began to meet just a little on the roof—right here. It probably would not have progressed very far—too many people around all the time. But, for some strange reason the two of them were sent to the Madras ashram. There they had time to be alone. That's where they got to know each other…and fall in love."

"Well, what happened? I guess it all turned out wrong?" I prodded.

Radha nodded, her face grim. She flashed a sad smile. "It turned out horribly wrong. Soon, Cha Ma called them back to the ashram. Not because of what was going on with them. It seems that it was still under wraps." Radha frowned. "Although I don't know how anything's ever really under wraps around Cha Ma." She bit her lip in thought. "How'd they slide under her radar?" She seemed to be talking more to herself than to me. After a moment, she resumed, "They came back to the ashram in a quandary about what to do. They loved each other. But, he had never prepared for a life outside of the ashram. All his life he'd trained to be a brahmachari. And she was just an Indian girl who had forsaken her entire life and family to come to Cha Ma. Before coming to Cha Ma, she had given up the one offer for a husband."

"Had she gone to school or did she have anything to fall back on?"

Radha shook her head hard. "Premabhakti, this is not America or Europe. No, she had nothing. She hadn't even finished school beyond a couple of years. Because she rejected the arranged marriage and chose to come to the ashram, she basically exiled herself from her family and from Indian society."

"Oh!"

"Well, one night they were on the roof…"

"This roof?" I asked interrupting.

Radha nodded, "Yes, this very roof—right here! A couple of brahmacharis came up to meditate and saw them kissing…and that was it! They grabbed her and dragged her down to Cha Ma."

"For kissing?" I was horrified. "That's nothing!"

"Yeah, well, not for this ashram. Not for the vows the sannyasis make. Don't forget it's much more serious because this is India...there are men and women living together. Female monks are very rare, and then, to have them living with male monks? Unheard of. Many people watch Cha Ma, the ashram, her brahmacharis and -charinis, looking to discredit what she's doing. They're looking for illicit affairs and broken vows.

"So, Cha Ma demands the strictest observation of the vows of sannyasa. She cannot afford to do otherwise. To have a violation would ruin everything she has done and is doing. And until then and since, no one... that anyone knows of...has violated their vows."

Wow! I had never thought of it like that! It makes sense. I finally began to understand all the rules regarding separating the sexes, mainly keeping the brahmacharinis away from the men, that I had seen imposed so diligently around the ashram. *I can understand why Cha Ma keeps the brahmacharis and -charinis so separate and is so strict about their interactions (or lack thereof). It would be all the more difficult given that they are all of a young age — the age for falling in love.* "So, what happened when they dragged her down to Cha Ma?"

"Cha Ma was furious. Now, I was around for that. I was sitting in the inner temple when they brought her before Cha Ma. Cha Ma went into a rage. An awful, frightening rage. One of the worst, if not the worst, that I had ever seen. After Cha Ma flipped out," Radha looked over her shoulder as if she half-expected Cha Ma to suddenly appear—*Couldn't put it past her!* "she told the girl to go..."

"What did the girl do?"

"She began to cry like a baby. She said she had nowhere to go, no one to go to. Where would she go?" My heart went out to the despondent, unfortunate girl—*All over a kiss!*

Radha continued, "Cha Ma said that as she, the girl, had embraced Kali, she would have to suffer whatever Kali decided to give her. She told her to leave her presence...that she never wanted to see her again." Radha stopped and looked away to the ocean. I swallowed hard against the lump in my throat. *Why do I feel like crying over the sob story of some girl!* Although I chided myself, I knew the answer to my own question: because I could relate to her. I could relate to doing stupid things for love, for falling madly for some guy, and getting myself into a doomed relationship. Hoping against hope and betting against the odds that I could somehow bend the rules and get the guy. I hated the ugly thought of her losing everything over a guy. No, even less, over a kiss (because she certainly did not get the guy!).

"So what happened?" I prompted.

"She wouldn't say another word to the girl. Immediately, the girl was kicked out of the ashram and he was sent to one of Cha Ma's other ashrams—I don't know where. They were kept separated and didn't have a moment to speak to each other. They never saw each other again."

"Well, what happened with her after that?"

"No one knows except that her family would not take her back, of course. She had abdicated from an arranged marriage, ran to an ashram… not the best choice for a girl…and then, went and broke her vow of celibacy. Basically, she ruined her life. I'm sure she dropped in terms of caste— probably shudra or dalit."

"But, why?"

Radha sighed and shrugged her shoulders, "I don't know. It's just something about their society, especially concerning ashrams and brahmacharis and -charinis. Don't forget—Cha Ma's one of the few gurus who has male and female monks…*young* male and female monks. It's considered too dangerous and too much of a temptation to have men and women together, especially celibate men and women. It's an accident waiting to happen. Many people look for Cha Ma to fail at this." She thought for a while. "So I'd imagine that she had to deal with the two of them severely in order to keep any others from getting involved in a relationship and sullying her reputation and perhaps ruining, because of desire, all that she has built."

"But, this girl's life is ruined…all over a kiss…" I protested. I felt awfully sorry for her. Radha shrugged noncommittally. I pressed, "It doesn't seem right."

"Welcome to Indian society…" she muttered, a tinge of bitterness rising in her voice. With that, she stood and threw her asana over her shoulder. Pointedly, she looked at the dangerous brahmachari and back to me and shook her head as if signifying, "No, don't even think about it!" Then, she winked at me with a wry smile and left the roof.

I remained where I was. I wanted to ponder all she had said. I looked at the brahmachari. His eyes were still closed; so I was free to look without any hindrance. *Is that the reason he looks so wild? Was she anything to him? What was between them? Did he have a broken heart? I know she had to have had one. Does he miss her? Does he regret what happened?* My mind swirled with questions, none of which were answered by his closed eyes.

SHE HEARS
EVERY WORD YOU SAY!

By the time evening came around the story had roiled around in my head much too much. I had ruminated far too long on the clandestine and ruinous affair. *How's the girl doing now? Is she OK? Is she a shudra now…a dalit? Does he ever think about her? Was the kiss worth it?*

As we sang bhajans, I thought about Cha Ma's jealous, territorialistic rage as I watched her sing. Radha's account of the affair was diametrically opposed to the sweet, singing guru who was in front of me. I knew of Cha Ma's unpredictable anger. In fact, I had been scathed by it myself. The time with the tomatoes was one time too many. I marveled to myself the vast difference between the gentle, smiling satguru and the fearsome, baleful Kali incarnation. On the one hand, I loved it—*I'm sure she will get me to the goal of enlightenment;* on the other hand, I was terrified of her. And I could not put any words to it. I could not even begin to wrap my mind around my fear of her. As I sat there singing bhajans with the rest of the ashramites and devotees, I marveled on how Chamunda Kali had decided to put herself into a body. *Oh! That she would be so kind and care about humanity enough to take on a body!*

"KRIIIIIIISHNAAAAAA!" Cha Ma, in the midst of singing a bhajan to Krishna, called Krishna's name aloud. Her eyes closed. Head thrown back. She sat in full lotus on her peetham, swaying from side to side with the rhythm.

"She's going to go into samadhi!" Radha leaned over and whispered into my ear.

I nodded, anticipation quickly rising within my chest. In the months that I had been at the ashram, I had not observed Cha Ma go into samadhi. I had heard a lot about her deep states of absorption into herself...into Kali. I had heard that it was nearly impossible to pull her out of the deep trance. In such a state, her breathing slowed drastically, as did her heart rate. She became impervious to exterior stimuli. I had heard stories of her falling into the backwaters and the ocean; and had no one hauled her out, how she would have drowned. I had heard of how, in this state, she would go without any nourishment—food or liquid—for days and weeks on end.

However, such "high" states were the norm for divine beings and enlightened masters. In my spiritual quest, I had heard many stories of how the enlightened masters would go into samadhi. In fact, I had heard some Hindus assert that that was how Jesus had fasted in the desert for 40 days—he had simply gone into samadhi. There were levels of samadhi—from simply the state of trance-like absorption to the final, irretrievable state. It was said of a few of the greatest masters, that when it was time to die, they *knew* it and would put themselves into that deepest, most irretrievable state—mahasamadhi. Death.

"She used to go into samadhi so much in the 'olden' days, when she was much younger. She'd be in it for days, even weeks on end," continued Radha as she wrapped her shawl more tightly about her body.

"Really?" I thought of the snatches of the stories I had heard. I knew whatever Radha said about it would be as close to the truth as possible. "What about the bathroom and having to eat? Drink?"

"She'd do none of those things," Radha leaned in close as she whispered. "Even now, when she goes into samadhi, she doesn't do any of that. The trance consumes her. Haven't you noticed? She goes into a kind of samadhi during Kali Leela."

"I didn't know that..." I remarked, my voice hushed with wonder. "I had wondered why she never stops to go to the bathroom or to eat anything during Kali Leela."

"Yeah," Radha nodded, her eyes glittering with some sort of emotion, "well, it's a kinda...mini-samadhi. A lower-level one. Not so deep. She has such a mastery over the human state that she can function while in samadhi. Most gurus are unable to do that—it's a sign that she's a divine being...an avatar."

Right then, Cha Ma threw her head back and punctuated our conversation with another deep, yearning cry to Krishna. "KRRRIIIIIIISHNNN-NAAAAAA!" It lasted for several long seconds. She stopped swaying by the last exhaled note. Whatever hushed noises there were in the temple ceased completely. Cha Ma's eyes remained closed. Slowly, she lowered her head until she was looking straight ahead (if her eyes had been open), settled her hands into a mudra, and went completely immobile. It was a strange immobilization...a "still-ification"...as if her body were being set with stone right before our eyes. A sense of massiveness loomed about her, almost as though she were a spiritual black hole so dense and massive she threatened to suck all of us into her.

"There! She's gone into samadhi," Radha said with an air of satisfaction.

Wow. So, that's it? "How long do you think she'll be in it?"

"Oh! It's hard to say." She bit her lip in thought as she considered the question. "Nowadays she doesn't tend to stay in it very long. For that matter, she doesn't enter into it as much as she used to. She has too many responsibilities to be gone for days and weeks on end. She may be in it for the rest of the night, though...maybe tomorrow. The swamis and swaminis will run things while she's out."

As if on cue, Swami picked up leading bhajans. He led one more song, this one doleful and heartrending, to Krishna. I felt tears prick my eyes. Deep yearning pressed up inside of me. *I want to go into samadhi! How wonderful it must be to be able to just leave this place...to be able to leave wherever I am whenever I want, just check out, and be with my ishta-deity.* I wondered if I could bear the pain of yearning. Oh! How Cha Ma drew me! Even more, her *state* drew me—*To be so totally absorbed in Kali as to leave your body behind...* Bitter, vibrant longing swept through me as I stared at Cha Ma...as we all stared at Cha Ma. She had not moved. She sat as immobile and still as a rock, a faint smile on her mouth as though she were privy to a wonderful secret at which we could only guess.

When the last strains of the Krishna bhajan painfully died away, Swami stood to leave. The other swamis—Swami Shankarapranatman, Swami Shivaramananda and Funeral Swami—and the brahmacharis and -charinis who had been singing with them stood to leave soon after him. Swami Shankarapranatman looked angrier and more irritable than usual, which was no easy feat. The atmosphere was subdued and quiet. The lights that usually illumined the temple were turned low as we, the ashramites and visitors, slowly vacated the temple. As we were following the crowd out, I looked back and saw Swami, Swamini Ma, and Swamini Atmapra-nananda hovering over Cha Ma's seated form. *What are they going to do? Leave her there? Move her? How do you move a person who is sitting solidly like a rock?* I did not have enough nerve to stand there and keep watching. I could just see "Irri-table-Swami," Swami Shankarapranatman, yelling at me. Slowly, I walked to the Indian canteen deep in thoughts about samadhi.

There I joined Karuna in the line for the Indian fare. It seemed every-one's mood had perked up upon exiting the temple. The canteens were boisterous—the Western one more than the Indian, as usual. After we re-ceived our kanji and curry from two of the brahmacharis (I did not recog-nize them), we went to sit on the floor in the Indian canteen.

I ate quickly, in silence, in a hurry to get to the roof in order to med-itate. Watching Cha Ma go into samadhi made me hungry for my own spiritual experiences. *I want to go into samadhi. I want to know what it's like. They say it's the most blissful, enjoyable experience.*

As soon as I was done, I raced to my favorite haunt, the uppermost deck on the roof. I spread my asana, pulled my shawl over my head and around my shoulders, and tried to meditate ("tried" being the key). I could not focus. Too much "stuff" roiled around in my head, the foremost of which was the pitiable tale of the exiled brahmacharini and dangerous brahmachari that danced around in my mind. After trying to meditate for as long as I could, I gave up. I stood, hefted my asana over my shoulder, and went down the stairs in search of someone who could give me some tasty tidbits of gossip.

The temple was dark with the exception of a few meager lights here and there. Few non-ashramites were around—the crowd had been small today, not a Kali Leela day. As I walked along the interior balcony to the women's dorm, I did not have to pick my way over a bunch of prone bodies. No one was sleeping on the balcony. *A very small crowd tonight.* I meandered into the women's dorm, which was dark, too. I could discern the forms of many of the women already in bed, asleep, ostensibly. As I laid my asana and shawl on my bunk, I could hear the giggling voices of several women. I padded over to the outside stairwell to see who it was. Given the sound of their hushed voices and rifts of laughter, I figured they could be a source of interesting news.

As I neared I could make out the voices of Karuna, Alice—*Good! Someone who will know all the gossip*—Chandy, and a couple of women who were short-term visitors. I noticed that they were all looking over the concrete stair wall. I stepped onto the stairwell to join them.

"Namah shivaya, guys?" I namah shivaya'ed my "what's up."

"Not much," Karuna whispered. "Cha Ma's come out of samadhi. She's in the garden talking with the swamis." I leaned over the edge to see the sight. Sure enough, Cha Ma was sitting on her stone bench with Swami, Swami Shankarapranatman, Swami Shivaramananda, and Funeral Swami sitting at her feet.

"And Br. Narayanan," Chandy added, her voice lilting on the last syllable, because of her Australian accent or because of her excitement about him, I could not guess. I squelched a faint twinge of jealous possessiveness—*He's not mine! He's Cha Ma's!* I squinted into the darkness and saw that he was sitting on the bench beside Cha Ma. His sannyasi-yellow-clad body partially obscured by the palm trees that bowed over them. *Why do the palm trees bend over like that? I'll have to ask someone.*

"Why is the one in yellow sitting with her and the swamis?" one of the new women asked.

"He's really close to Cha Ma and might as well be considered one of the swamis given how they...*she and the swamis*...treat him," Alice whispered conspiratorially. I could tell by the sound of her voice that she would be willing to share whatever bits of information she might know. *Good! I'll have to hit her up later with my questions.*

Karuna giggled and whispered, "I bet Swami Shankarapranatman is looking really irritable right now." When she said that, an image of his hyper-aggro face popped into my mind.

"There's never been a time when I've not seen him looking angry," Chandy remarked.

"I know," Alice assented. "Has anyone ever thought that Swami Shivaramananda looks like Santa Claus?"

"Yeah, you're right! I've always thought that!" I agreed.

"I know," Karuna nodded as she continued leaning over the cement banister. "He always looks so jolly and pleasant."

Where is Anneshwari and Rukmini? I knew that with Cha Ma out and about they would have to be somewhere nearby. I searched the trees and bushes surrounding the garden. Sure enough! There was Anneshwari and Rukmini...both of them trying to hide their big bodies. Anneshwari was standing straight and tall behind a skinny palm tree. It looked like she was attempting to suck her gut in—but she poked out from both sides. Rukmini was crouched behind some shrubs. She poked head-and-shoulders above the top of the shrubs—her tall frame simply would not fold up tightly enough. *You'd think she would've learned...after getting beaten up so.* But she had not. She still chased behind Cha Ma. Granted, I had not seen her beating up any brahmacharis lately.

As we bantered back and forth, joking and laughing and whispering, Cha Ma and the swamis...*and Narayanan*...stood. With Cha Ma leading, they made their way across the empty yard in front of the brahmachari huts. As they walked, Cha Ma barked something in Malayalam over her shoulder.

From the shadows near the brahmacharini huts, two brahmacharinis in yellow stepped out and immediately began trotting to catch up with Cha Ma and the others. I did not recognize one of them, although the other I did. Her name was Brahmacharini Durgamma. She was a full brahmacharini as signified by the yellow sari of sannyasa. She was an older (she looked to be in her thirties, however, it was so hard to gauge their ages) brahmacharini. She was small and slender—wiry and compact, to be exact. Pure, tight muscle. Strong. I did not know Bri. Durgamma too well except for the fact that I knew her to be as mean as a snake, as hard working as a horse, and as mercilessly demanding as a slave driver. Her sole focus was Cha Ma. Any and everything else was entirely expendable and a waste of time. Bri. Durgamma and "No Name" followed at a distance. *Probably called to be available to fetch whatever might be needed*—I reasoned. They all went into the grove of trees on the far side of the brahmachari huts.

"Hey! That's where we dumped the dirt when we did sand seva..." remarked Chandy.

"Uh-huh," Alice replied, nodding. "That was some hard work!"

I heard myself, "Hmphf!" as Karuna and I exchanged a mirthful glance of understanding. *Not that she did any work that night.*

With our immediate source of entertainment gone, we all went back into the candle- and flashlight-lit dorm, still laughing and joking and giggling. I figured it was the perfect time to ask about the illicit affair.

"Hey, Alice! Do you know anything about the brahmachari and -charini that were caught kissing? Do you know what happened to them?" I asked.

"Yeah, but I'm not going to say anything without a little bribe. Do you have any peanuts or cookies?" In the dim light, I could see her head darting left and right as she looked around for her favored munchies.

"Yep! I've got peanuts *and* cookies," I offered. I was ready to sell my right arm to hear more salacious tidbits.

"OK, I'll tell you…" Alice conceded, as she plopped down on my bunk, already reaching her hand under the mosquito netting for the plastic canister of peanuts. *Never fails! She'd better not mess up my mosquito netting, though!*

"So, what is this about a brahmachari and -charini kissing?" Chandy asked, her accent making the hint of a tasty morsel of gossip sound absolutely delightful…and scandalous.

"Radha told me about this brahmachari and -charini who got involved with each other and kissed…which caused Cha Ma to fly into a rage," I volunteered.

"Ahhh! Cha Ma's rages…" smirked Karuna. "Prema can tell you a bit about them. She's been the victim of one of them. I heard it was intense." She was baiting me—I knew she was. She knew I could not resist talking about Cha Ma, especially her Kali-esque fits of anger. She also knew about the tongue-lashing I had received in the kitchen the time I had not used the spoiled tomatoes, as she was one of the first people I told after I had finally pulled myself together.

"Tell us! Tell us!" A few other Western women had gathered around. Their eyes shone expectantly in the darkness. I shook my head, smiling, knowing they would prod the story out of me soon enough.

"See," Karuna began, "Cha Ma had found some buckets of tomatoes…"

"No…one. Just one bucket of tomatoes," I interrupted. I could not resist my own drama.

"Yeah…one bucket of tomatoes that Prema had hidden in the Western canteen. She didn't use them in the evening meal. So, they were wasted." Karuna had begun recounting a brief and slightly fallacious—*She makes those tomatoes sound like they were good when she knows they were rotten!*—version.

I jumped in, "Yeah! Cha Ma went crazy! She went off on me! Kali came through!" I giggled. "Everyone likes to think she's so sweet and kind…"

"Yeah!" Alice interjected, ready to gossip now that she had peanuts in hand. *How old are those things?* I had gone out and bought them in the village after she had eaten up my last store of peanuts. I thought of the tiny store where everything had been covered in a thick layer of grimy dust. *I can't imagine how long they sat on that shelf.* "That's the public persona! In front of the public, the outside world, she's this cute, sweet, little, chubby mommy-type. But…"

"…in reality, she's Kali, through and through!" I added.

"No!" one of the newbies gasped, disbelief in her voice that her beloved Cha Ma…her sweet, cute Cha Ma…could be so…*Kali.*

"Yes!" I responded. "In reality, she's hard-core!"

"Uh-huh!" Alice added, nodding vigorously. "Have you ever seen her hit Anneshwari?"

"Anneshwari? Really?" Chandy interrupted, wonder evident in her voice. "I've never seen her hit anyone."

"Oh! You've got to watch closely—she'll smack the daylights out of the brahmacharinis and a couple of the Westerners, especially Anneshwari…" Alice popped a couple more peanuts into her mouth, chewing vigorously as she talked, "…but it's when no one's really paying attention."

"She's hit you before, hasn't she?" I prompted Alice.

"Yep!" Alice announced as if she were proud that she had been hit. She dropped another peanut into her mouth. "It was Kali Leela and I was sitting…"

"STOP IT!"

I heard her, before I saw her—Bri. Durgamma. She shot into the women's dorm from the outside stairwell yelling fiercely, "Stop it! She hears every word you say and she says to stop it!" Fright and upset showed on her face. All giggles and chortles instantaneously died in our throats. Fear clutched my bowels. I knew the expression I saw in the other women's faces was mirrored in mine. "Stop it, right now!" she ordered again, her face dead serious, her hands clenched in fists at her side. Her wiry body tight with anxious tension. She whirled around and disappeared back into the blue-black night.

Silence. No one dared utter a sound. In fact, no one dared move for a few seconds. Finally, our little cluster of women drifted apart…most to their bunks, one went out into the temple area…Karuna, Chandy, Alice, and I, and a couple of others who had enough nerve, went to the balcony. From there we could see Durgamma hurrying back to the grove of trees where Cha Ma was. No further word had been spoken amongst our group. The silence and stillness in the air oppressed us like a heavy, dense blanket. My mind choked around one simple thought—*How could she have heard us from so far away?* Surely, every other woman who was with me was wondering the same thing.

I stood on the dark balcony listening to the silence for a long time. I strained to hear something, anything. However, it was odd…there were no nighttime noises, no music blaring, not even the distant sound of the ocean rolling in upon the air, nothing at all. For the first time that night, I noticed that the sky itself was a deep, solid navy blue—no moon in sight. An unusual night sky…an Indian night where the depth of the night, its very color, seemed to ingest all that approached it, including sound. It was so still and silent.

Slowly the other women all went to bed. Little by little, the faint light from the women's dorm behind me grew ever fainter as the last of the women put out their candles and flashlights. I remained on the balcony staring into the dark long after the last light was snuffed out. Finally, I, too, turned and went to bed, feeling my way with my hands. The last thing I thought before I drifted off to sleep was—*Alice never did tell us what she knew about the sad relationship. What would it be like to be in love with one of Cha Ma's brahmacharis in a doomed, Kali-cursed relationship?* In the distance, I heard a snippet of Cha Ma's laughter…riding in on the silence. It sounded eery—otherworldly, non-human.

DREAMS

Marie and Paul
United States

"I've never heard that before," Marie said to Connie in surprise. Her face flashed a quick smile, most of it because of a few minutes respite from the headache. *It feels so good not to have a headache.* "So, you're trying to tell me that dreams have meaning…or rather, that Christians believe that dreams can have meaning? I thought all of that was just some crazy New Agey stuff."

Connie gave a gentle laugh to Marie's New Age remark. "Oh yes, dreams are very significant. And so many things can have meaning, *Christian* meaning, in our dreams." Connie sat back on the couch rubbing her hands together as she winced— her arthritis was acting up worse than usual.

Marie settled in across from her in the easy chair, gingerly cradling a cup of coffee in her hands. "OK, here's one for you…what does it mean when you dream about a house?"

she asked a bit skeptically, a slight grin touching her face. She took a sip of her coffee.

"Well, mind you, when you're interpreting dreams, you've got to do it in a way that corresponds to the Bible."

"What do you mean?" Marie could feel herself growing intrigued.

"Think about it…there's many, many instances of significant dreams in the Bible." Connie paused to think. "Off the top of my head—there's Joseph in the Old Testament and then, there's Joseph—Jesus's father, Nebuchadnezzar, Daniel…Most Bible scholars who interpret dreams tend to say that the dreams we have are usually windows into ourselves. Sometimes they can be prophetic dreams. They can even be visions, but that's more rare. From what I understand, visions are much more straightforward and clear-cut in terms of interpretation, but seeing that vision become reality is usually difficult and hard. Whereas, dreams can be difficult to understand and interpret, but seeing them come to pass is easier."

Marie took a slow sip, her eyes narrowed in speculative thought. Finally, she remarked, "That's interesting. So, if what you say is true, then dreams from God are more common and easier to have come to pass than a vision?"

"Yes," Connie replied. "But, remember that dreams may be more difficult to interpret."

Marie nodded. "OK, so tell me more about dreams then…"

Connie smiled and continued, "Well, when we have a dream the first thing we have to do is figure out its source. There are soulish dreams, demonic dreams, and dreams from God."

"Soulish dreams?"

"Dreams that come from our own minds and souls—basically noise from living our lives."

"Oh, OK."

"And then, of course, there are demonic dreams sent from Satan."

"Demonic dreams?" Marie asked, looking wide-eyed over her coffee. "What do you mean?"

"Dreams that come from Satan or from a demonic source."

"How can we tell the difference?"

"Well, demonic and soulish dreams will be dim in comparison to those from God. Think about it: The Word says that God is the Father of lights with Whom there is no variation or shadow of turning. Being that He's the Father of lights, He's the source of light and all that is good. Further, as there's no variation or shadow of turning, that means His Light doesn't change or go dim. So, it stands to reason that dreams from Him would be full of color and bright and vibrant."

"I could see that," Marie responded. "Given that line of reasoning, then, a dream from Satan would be dark and dim." Marie bit her lip as she thought.

"Yes." Connie nodded her head. "For myself, dreams not of God are often sepia colored…"

"Sepia colored…" Marie murmured. Her mind shifted uneasily to the disturbing dreams of her daughter lying in a coffin in her house. *But, sometimes I'm not fully asleep; but still the air seems tinged with a brownish-yellow light. I'd always thought it was because I was half-asleep. But, maybe it's not because of that…*

"Mmm-hmm, dim, yellowish-brown, dull, dark. But, it's important to distinguish whether a dream that's not from God is from the enemy or from our own minds."

"OK, so tell me about dreams from God." The idea of demonic dreams made Marie uncomfortable, to say the least, so she sought to place her mind on God.

"Dreams from God? Aside from being bright and vibrant? I know that usually they'll bring peace. Even if I'm going through a hard time, the dream will give peace. Even if the dream's not full of joy, perhaps it's a warning to me to stay away from something or a caution to not do something, it will still have a calm air and will give me peace. If it's disturbing and frightening—I tend to write it off as not from God."

"So, what do you do about dreams that aren't from God?"

"Hold on, though, Marie. I have to give you a major caveat—a lot depends on what's going on with a person. Basically, I believe that if a person feels really badly during and after the dream, then it's not a dream from God—unless it's a warning. But, even then, there should be a certain peace and calm during and after the dream.

"As for your question: What do I do about dreams that aren't from God? Me personally? I don't pay much mind to dreams that are dark and heavy... my job isn't to be about Satan or myself, my job is to be about the Lord. So, when I have dark, heavy dreams, I will usually pray immediately and give the dream to God, cover it in the blood of Jesus and ask Him to do His Will with the situation. And I ask Him to make me forget the bad dream."

"So, what about a dream about a house?" Marie redirected back to her first question.

Connie smiled again. She took another sip of coffee, moving slowly and deliberately because of her rheumatoid arthritis, before speaking, "Many say that when a person dreams about a house, the house symbolizes that person—their personal life, their emotional, mental, and physical well-being."

"What does a dream about a car symbolize?"

"A dream about vehicles usually says something about the ministry or work a person is in. The larger the vehicle, the greater, or far-reaching, the ministry. So, a bicycle would mean one's own personal ministry with a very small sphere of influence. A car would symbolize a larger realm of influence in a personal ministry. A plane would symbolize a huge, fast-moving ministry that would touch many people."

"How interesting!" Marie leaned forward to put her empty cup on the coffee table. "OK. Here's one for you...snakes. What does it mean if you dream about snakes?"

Connie prompted Marie through the answer to her own question, "Tell me this—what do snakes symbolize in the Bible?"

"Evil. Satan," Marie answered. "Satan came to Eve in the form of a snake."

"Exactly. So it makes complete sense that a dream about a snake would, more than likely, mean Satanic attack or the presence of evil." Marie nodded her agreement. Connie asked, "OK…how about bugs?"

"I don't know…" Marie's voice petered out. "You tell me."

"Usually? I would say dreaming about bugs would mean something negative. Small bugs that bite may symbolize someone being attacked, criticism, backbiting. Larger bugs and large infestations of bugs could mean demonic manifestation."

"Demonic manifestation? Really?"

Connie nodded. "Think about it: when God came against Pharaoh with the plagues, a couple of times it was with bugs. Locusts and gnats. They were a negative, destructive thing." She rubbed her arthritically gnarled hands unconsciously. The rheumatism was always present, always painful. "Are there any bugs that are seen positively and in a good light in the Bible?"

Marie thought to herself and said, almost more to herself than to her friend, "Cockroaches?…No. Definitely no! Are they even in the Bible? Ants? Aside from being organized, hard workers, which Proverbs talks about, they bite and sting. Mosquitoes? No. Beetles? No. Flies? No. No, I can't think of any bugs that are seen positively, aside from ants."

"Given such a context, it would stand to reason, then, that dreams of bugs can usually be interpreted to mean demonic manifestation."

Marie thought to herself—*Well, it's a relief that I don't have dreams about bugs. That's one good thing, at least…"* She laughed ruefully to herself. *No, I just have waking dreams…visions…hallucinations…of Maya lying in a coffin. Hallucinations so vivid and real.* She felt an urge to tell Connie about her hallucinations, but for some reason, she was ashamed of them, as if having them was a sign of her own spiritual failure. She was not ready to admit spiritual failure to anyone, not yet. She took another sip of coffee, lukewarm now, before asking another question. They sat well into the night discussing dreams.

GREAT LOVE

Maya
India

"Some Westerners are such a pain! Wanting to sit around and meditate and not do seva!" My exasperation was coming through.

"Yeah, I know," Radha chuckled gently, "but what are we to do?" I rolled my eyes and shrugged my shoulders in response. I was thoroughly annoyed by the lack of seva-mindedness among the Westerners.

Radha and I were sitting at the seva desk. We were busily talking as we poured over the charts of who was assigned to what. The ashram always had more work than workers, especially when it came to the tough and dirty, low-visibility jobs like pot washing, toilet cleaning, and temple sweeping.

"Cha Ma was talking about you…" I heard Br. Narayanan's voice before I saw him. *I'd know that voice anywhere.* My ears had become attuned to the sound of his voice. My stupid heart leapt involuntarily into my throat. *My body is a traitor! Kali! I hate when I jump to the sound of his voice! Why can't I act like I don't care?* I looked up.

There he was—*When had he approached? How long has he been standing there? Weird.*—head peeking around the corner, fingers tapping out a rhythm on the dingy, whitewashed wall. I could almost *see* the kimini in his hands, so animated was he. I remembered our last conversation...our last *good* conversation (Oh! He was great at flying out of the Foreigners' Office and yelling at me to grab something or do something. And sometimes, very rarely, when I was busily working at the seva desk, I would happen to look up to see him walking toward me, an indescribable look upon his face. Our eyes would meet for a long second before he looked away and turned into the office, shutting the door behind him. I encountered him countless times a week; but a good, *positive* exchange with him that did not leave me wanting to cry either out of hurt feelings or out of yearning? Now, *that* was rare and memorable)...had been at the seva desk. That time, too, he had been busily beating out a rhythm on the wall. However, that time, there had been no Radha and he had sat down in the teeny-tiny space and had talked with me.

Not this time. This time, there was Radha...who was so perceptive and who, at the moment, seemed to be studiously observing *me* responding to *him*. I cast a desperate prayer up to Kali that she would not notice anything amiss.

"What did she say?" Radha asked with a big, inviting smile. I marveled to myself that she and Br. Narayanan had such an easy relationship. *How can she interact with him so freely?* Inevitably, I felt like a deer caught before headlights whenever he came around. *He always turns me into an idiot! I hate him!*

Although Radha had asked him a question, he just kept smiling at us, tapping out a rhythm on the wall. He was the only man I knew who could be asked a question and not give an answer *and* it be absolutely unnoticeable. As always, he began to lose himself in the rhythm. His eyes got that "faraway" look, his head cocked to the side as if he were listening to some internal beat thumping away or as if he could hear some instrument in the wall, which was imperceptible to Radha and me. Regardless, he did not answer Radha's question.

*He is so gorgeous...*I do not know how much time passed before I realized that I was staring at him, tapping away, and he was staring at me staring at him! Radha was completely forgotten, until I noticed movement out of the corner of my eye, and it dawned somewhere in the hidden recesses of my smitten consciousness that it was she. I could see, with my peripheral vision, her head going back and forth between me and him as though we were some enthralling tennis match. I forced my disobedient eyes away from him and looked at her. She winked a big, glossy, blue eye at me and gave me a huge, toothy grin to boot. I looked down, embarrassed at being caught. *Ugh! Snagged! I'll never hear the end of it.* Br. Narayanan kept banging out a rhythm, oblivious, so it appeared, to the nuanced drama that was unfolding with him in the center. I liked him so much more when he was like this...happy—bordering on silly—and playful. *Oh yeah! That's right...*

"So, what did Cha Ma say?" I prompted him. In response, he smiled pointedly at me—the most beautiful, open, generous smile he had ever given me intentionally (or unintentionally, for that matter). He snagged my heart...again.

"I know what Cha Ma said about yo-oou! I know what Cha Ma said about yo-oou!" he teased in a singsong voice, keeping rhythm with his tapping.

Heeeelllllllppppp! I'm a sitting-duck when it comes to him. What is he doing anyway?

"Well! What did she say?" I asked in mock exasperation while loving the attention at the same time.

He smiled at me, his big, almond eyes gleaming laughter. "I'm not going to tell yo-oou! I'm not going to tell yo-oou!" he sang at me, still teasing and joking and tapping away on the wall. Staring.

I dared a glance at Radha. She was smiling an even bigger, toothier grin, looking from Br. Narayanan to me. *At least she's not saying anything.*

As this was going on, who should approach but Karuna? *Oh man! That's all I need! If Radha doesn't tease me, Karuna will be sure to.* She always had an eye for seeing when Br. Narayanan was looking at me and for telling me about it, much to her sheer delight. And now, with the two of us, me and him, within five feet of each other and the two of them, Radha and Karuna, privy to the drama and having each other for reinforcement? I could not even begin to imagine the glee and joy they would have in teasing and goading me if, and *when*, they started bouncing off each other! *Oh Kali! This could get excruciating…excruciatingly fun!* I had to admit it.

"What's going on guys?" Karuna's eyes flitted between the three of us, easily assessing the situation. A smirk snaked across her lips. She squeezed past Narayanan as his body was blocking the narrow entrance to our little "alley" and sat down beside Radha, who had moved over in order to share her chair.

I don't know why she even bothered to ask! I thought with an irritation that was buoyed by pleasure.

"Ha! Ha! Br. Narayanan started telling Prema about something Cha Ma said to him about her, but he just won't get it out. I think he's teasing her!" Radha explained with a twinkle in her eyes and a grin stretching from one end of her face to the other. *She looks like a Cheshire cat.* Although admittedly, I did not resent the teasing too much—I liked the fact that the source of their teasing was Narayanan's attention to me. Further, I could not believe the fact—although I loved it—that this deliciously handsome brahmachari in yellow (a full sannyasi!) was busily teasing me—a woman! In front of others, at that! *Talk about breaking every celibate taboo known in the ashram!*

"Oh no! I'm *not* teasing Prema! That wouldn't be right, now would it?" he queried as if he did not believe his own words. His almond eyes grew wide in mocking delight as he smirked at me. I gawked at him incredulously. I had seen his eyes twinkle more in the past five minutes than I had the whole time I had been living in the ashram.

Radha and Karuna dissolved into giggles, falling upon each other in their mirthful glee. *Aww, man!* "Weeeeellllllll," Radha drew the monosyllabic word out for days, "c'mon, tell us! What did she say? What did she say?" she asked in between rifts of giggles.

"Well, Cha Ma said," Narayanan singsonged in between taps, "that Prema has"—*tap, tap…tap, tap, tap*—"so much bhakti." *Tap, tap.* "That she loves God so much"—*tap, tap, tap…tap*—. He stopped tapping—*unconsciously?*—his fingers arrested mid-tap and simply stared at me. Hard. He seemed to have gotten…lost…in staring at me. Then, after several long seconds, as though he and I were the only ones there, he whispered, the timbre of his voice low and husky, "I suppose that is why she named you…Premabhakti…" His tongue rolled over my name, his accent making my name sound like something yummy to eat.

Snort! Snnnrrt! I heard raucous snorts beside me, killing the moment— *Dadnabit! Radha and Karuna!* Out of the corner of my eye, I saw they were desperately straining to control their laughter, tears streaming from their eyes. Karuna had wrapped her arms around her waist trying, in vain, to hold in the laughter. Her face was red—whether from the exertion of laughing or from trying to keep it in—I could not tell. Radha was busily wiping the tears from her eyes. Even as I could see and hear their delight in our conversation, I could not pull my eyes away from him.

Radha snorted—*again!*—as she continued to try, unsuccessfully, to hide her mirth. I kicked her under the table, which elicited a surprised yelp from her. She shook her head as though she just could not help her-self. Karuna leaned back, surrendering herself to the giggles. I threw them a fierce "I'm-going-to-get-you-later" look. To no avail. They just laughed harder—snorting and chortling and wiping tears. Karuna indicated with her head toward Narayanan.

I looked back at him and saw that his stare had shifted into an intense look of—*What is that?*! His gaze upon my face was decidedly male and ap-praising; and whatever he saw he liked. Definitely not chaste and celibate. My heart and lungs stopped altogether, boycotting me at the most inop-portune time!

Too much for me! Time for me to go! "Hey guys! I'm going to have to catch you later!" I jumped up and, squeezing past Br. Narayanan's yellow-clad body, which continued to block the little entrance to the seva desk, sprinted out of there. I threw back much more casually than I felt, "Yeah! Cha Ma says I have a lot of bhakti—that's crazy!" *I can't believe I'm walking away from Br. Narayanan! How crazy! But, I just can't take it!* My heart had found itself and had resumed thumping madly. Surely, someone could have, should have, seen it pounding under my choli. *What does all of this mean? Br. Narayanan and Cha Ma talking about...me? Me? Why would she be talking to him about me? Is he interested in me? I wonder if she's burning his karma? And then, what's this about me having so much bhakti? That she named me Premabhakti because of my great love for God?!* My mind whirled with question upon question, thought upon thought.

I practically ran around the balcony and into the women's dormitory. It was almost empty, just a few Western women here and there—women I did not really know, not residents but visitors. I continued on to the back stairs and down to the inner temple. Totally high on my conversation with Br. Narayanan, I decided I would sit in the inner temple, watch Cha Ma give darshan for a little while, and bask in what had just transpired.

I stopped at the entrance to the inner temple. The problem: the inner temple on the women's side was absolutely jam-packed, there was no place to sit at all. The only space was standing room in the back. I took a position along the back wall beside several other Western women who had stepped in for a few minutes to watch Cha Ma.

As we were standing there, I saw Alice and Anneshwari saunter in, both with their customary single-minded focus upon Cha Ma. Anneshwari, her lime green punjabi stretched tightly over her wide girth, strode forward. She stepped over some women and trod on others who did not move out of her way in time, using the women's heads to balance her progress. When she was within arm's reach of Cha Ma, with no one in between her and her object of obsession, she sat down. Plop! Right there. The Indian women—most of them visitors in brightly colored Keralan saris—scrambled out of her way, frowning and looking extremely put-out. She smiled at Cha Ma with a look of unmitigated adulation. Cha Ma, head bobbling, beamed back at her.

Alice remained standing along the back wall, surveying the scene for a good spot, asana draped insouciantly over her shoulder. As always she looked crumpled and bedraggled, her grayish sari splotchy with rust spots. Her limp, brown hair pulled back into a messy ponytail.

As Alice's eyes scanned back and forth, a plump Indian woman who was sitting in the second row from Cha Ma began to stand up in that ungraceful way that only certain Indian women could do. Her hands and feet were firmly planted on the ground, rear end pushing up higher and higher into the air. The move was something akin to a baby standing up from a sitting position. As the woman struggled to upright, her toes snagged in the front of her sari so that she could not stand up completely. In the few ungainly seconds that it took her to "unstick" her toes from her sari, I saw Alice's body shoot out from a standing, locked leg position along the back wall. While diving in midair she took the asana from off her shoulder and put it out in front of her. The woman continued to struggle against her sari edge with her toes. Suddenly! Luckily! She was free! She stepped back to gain her balance. In the split second that she lifted her right foot, Alice slid in underneath her on her asana—in a half-pranam on her knees, head to the ground.

Alice held the half-pranam longer than necessary. *Probably waiting for the woman to leave.* The poor Indian woman tottered on one foot for a few seconds before regaining her balance and shuffling off. Alice sat up, settled cross-legged, and began looking around at everyone but Cha Ma. She was astoundingly oblivious to her own madness at claiming a place to sit. I shook my head—*Ahhhh! Such was life in the ashram! To be in the "love" of a saint; I've never seen such unsaintly, ungodly behavior.*

ADIPARASHAKTI

"I need to write Cha Ma a letter," I informed Karuna. We sat hunched over on my bunk, making sure to keep our fingers and toes from getting caught in the mosquito netting that was hanging down. It was late morning and the probability of mosquitoes still flying around was minimal; but Karuna respected the fact that I did not like the netting being lifted up for fear of a random mosquito flying in during the day and remaining there to feast on my entrapped body later that night. *Sometimes I think all I do is obsess over mosquitoes.* I would have laughed at myself had I not been so earnest about the mosquitoes.

"What for?" Karuna asked, her Australian accent causing her voice to lilt on the question. She shoved a couple of errant strands of straight, brownish-blond hair away from her face. She had decided to grow out her hair and it was now long enough to catch up in a mini-tail; although a few pieces managed to evade mini-tail imprisonment. She leaned over and grabbed a cookie—a permitted fats and solids cookie—from the package. *Karuna's the closest thing to my best friend here so she doesn't have to ask to eat my cookies. Unlike Alice.*

"I want to tell her that I want to be a renunciate. That I have a little under $10,000 to give and that I'd like to stay here for the rest of my life," I said as I grabbed one of the cookies and began to munch. It was dry and not very flavorful, sort of like a very stale, very flavorless, shortbread cookie. *Hmm, permitted fats and solids*—I mused as I glanced through the ingredients listed on the side of the cylindrical package. I had read the ingredients a hundred times over, and every time it never failed to bemuse…stump… me—the permitted fats and solids thing. *What does that mean anyway? What's a permitted fat or solid? What's an unpermitted fat or solid? Lard?*

"Almost $10,000, huh?" Karuna mumbled through the cookie.

"Yeah, I was told that it costs $10,000 to become a renunciate."

"Why does it cost money to become a renunciate? Do the Indians have to pay as well?" She voiced the same questions I had asked Radha when I had first begun to seriously consider it—the renunciate thing. I had received an answer—a not very satisfying answer—but it had to do.

"No, the Indians don't have to pay…" I paused and glanced away to avoid Karuna's look and to halt her next question.

She asked anyway, "Why are the Indians free but the Westerners aren't?"

"I don't know…" my voice dwindled away with uncertainty. "Anyway, I've been told that we, the foreigners, have to ask if we want to be a renunciate and if Cha Ma accepts, we have to pay $10,000. The money stays in a bank account and we live off the interest." I pulled another cookie out of the pack. I did not feel much like eating it, but I crunched on anyway.

"Hmm, that's a pretty large chunk of money for India." She was unknowingly, but accurately, shooting into the same assiduously ignored holes that dampened my own enthusiasm for being a renunciate. "Think about it…how much does the average Indian household make in a year?"

"A little over $1,000 per year…" I answered weakly.

"See what I mean? Ten thousand is *a lot* of money to have invested...for India, that is." She took another bite of her cookie and smiled.

Wanly, I smiled back as I felt her observations about the renunciate process resonate with my own reservations. Unintentionally, she was crushing my sketchy confidence and resolve. I decided to try to divert her attention, "I didn't..."

"Yeah, well, I think Cha Ma makes a nice profit off us Westerners."

I felt a dull thud in my stomach but did not say anything.

She stuffed the rest of the cookie into her mouth and mumbled around it, "Well, come on. I know who to ask!"

"Who?"

"Brahmacharini Lakshmini. She'll definitely translate your letter." Karuna ducked under the netting and slipped her feet into her chappels.

"Who's Bri. Lakshmini?" I asked quizzically, getting caught in the netting that she let fall on my head.

"Oh! You know her...the really pretty Indian brahmacharini."

Mentally, I countered—*They're all really pretty. How can one be singled out based on that quality?* I placed the netting carefully on the bed, making sure that none was hanging off and thus, inadvertently, leaving a little hole for some bloodthirsty mosquito to sneak through.

Helping me position the netting, Karuna continued oblivious to my thoughts, "She's chubby which is unusual because most of the brahmacharinis aren't. And she's really, really pretty." I shook my head—I could not recall her in my mind. "When you see her, you'll know who I'm talking about. She's really pretty. She has curly hair that reaches to her shoulders. She usually wears it back with a headband. She's really nice and friendly, always smiling. And you know how the brahmacharinis are. They don't smile a lot and they're not very friendly," Karuna said matter-of-factly.

I thought of the pretty brahmacharini who helped Narayanan with the Christmas pada puja. "I think I know who you're talking about." I slipped on my chappels. "Oh! I almost forgot!" I reached under my pillow and pulled out a folded sheet of paper, trying not to lift the netting too much—*You never can tell when those little buggers will slip in.* "I have my letter written." I brandished my handwritten letter before Karuna. "I just need it to be translated into Malayalam for Cha Ma to read. Come on. Let's try to find Lakshmini."

"I think I know where she'd be right now." Karuna and I walked through the almost empty temple (it was still morning and a non-Kali Leela day), chatting as we went along. As we neared the Foreigners' Office I wondered if Narayana—*No, not Narayana, but Br. Narayanan. . . why didn't she change his name?*—was there.

Karuna voiced one of my thoughts, "I wonder if Br. Narayanan is there," and added, quite randomly, "He looks even better as a sannyasi!" *Yeah, whatever! Arrogant snob!* I hated to agree with her; but the sannyasi yellow really suited him. *He does look even better now that he's yellow. Maybe it's the confidence, the assurance, of rising so high in the ashram?* I checked myself. *Whatever! His promotion just made him an even more insufferable snob.* Even with all of my disdainful thoughts, I could not help but hope to get a quick glimpse of him. Sneakily, I shot a glance out of the corner of my eye. The door to the office was closed.

"Looks like he's not there..." Karuna sighed. "I wonder what he's doing..."

"Definitely not meditating," I quipped. "I've never seen him meditate except once or twice."

"True, true...but he probably doesn't have to, being that he's so close to Cha Ma and spends so much time with her."

"Yeah, you're probably right..."

"You know," Karuna mused, "I've heard it said that just being in the satguru's presence will take a person to enlightenment. So, think about how close he is to her, how he serves her, and is around her all the time...he must be so close to enlightenment. If he's not already there." I nodded in agreement but did not say anything. I could feel envy bubbling up inside. *Stop it…stop it…*

We trotted down the stairs and paused at the wide entrance of the temple. I turned to face the inner temple, quickly half-pranaming—Cha Ma was not in the temple; but the Kali murti was.

Only a few devotees were sitting on the temple floor waiting for Cha Ma to come out for the day's darshan. I figured the crowd would not grow beyond a couple hundred, at the most. Numbers were always low on non-Kali-Leela days.

Karuna kept walking as I bowed. I hustled after her as she went down the temple steps and cut a sharp left to go to the brahmacharini huts. I followed her. Already the sun was beating down mercilessly on the ashram. The air felt heavy and wet. *Another hot day in India*—which was nothing surprising or new. Every day was hot. And wet. *I have never sweated so much in my life. Not perspire, which has some dignity; but sweat—even my sweat sweats!* We wove our way around a couple of small, dilapidated buildings—one a mildewed, used-to-be-whitewashed affair, the other a ramshackle, wooden shack—before reaching the brahmacharini huts.

"Namah shivaya!" Karuna greeted two brahmacharinis who appeared to be enjoying a moment of quiet. They were sitting on a low step in the doorway of one of the huts brushing their hair. Unlike usual, their hair was damp and loose so that it hung carelessly…gloriously…about their shoulders and down their backs. They were beautiful with their hair pulled back in buns and absolutely gorgeous with it cascading loose and free down their backs. They were sitting in their petticoats and cholis. It was apparent from their uninhibited freedom and carelessness that they did not expect any males to venture over into their area (which they never did). I stared at their rarely-seen, unbound beauty.

"Namah shivaya," they responded in unison, heads bobbling languidly.

"Do you know where Bri. Lakshmini is?" asked Karuna.

One of them gently gestured back in the direction we had just come with the brush in her hand. "You look in kitchen?" Her accent rolled around the words, her voice husky and rich. I recognized her as one of the brahmacharinis who often sung for Cha Ma during bhajans and Kali Leela. *Wow! Her voice is so deep and throaty.* Her voice was even more incongruous because of her petite frame—she looked to be barely a couple of inches over 5', thin and waifish, an Indian-fairy. Incongruously, fascinatingly beautiful—*Hmphf! Even her voice is beautiful! How does she get her voice so high when she sings?*

"Namah shivaya!" Karuna nodded, saying good-bye and thank you with the same phrase.

"Uh…yeah…namah shivaya," I muttered, having been pulled out of my enviously admiring thoughts.

The brahmacharinis smiled and bobbled their heads, "Namah shivaya," they good-byed us as they continued to slowly brush their hair.

"The kitchen?" I asked, skeptically. Karuna and I headed back in the direction we came. "In the weeks…months…" I halted, stumped by my own confusion. "Uhh, how long have I been cooking in the kitchen?" Karuna shrugged as we walked across the open dirt space in front of the temple. *Time really does slip by us here in the ashram…* "Well, in the time I've been cooking in the kitchen I don't think I've *ever* seen a yellow brahmacharini in there cooking."

"What about Bri. Sita?" Karuna questioned conversationally rather than confrontationally.

"She doesn't count." We both giggled; but I was not sure why. "She's a Western renunciate anyway." A mental image of Sita flitted through my head, with a thin sliver of resentment and dislike attached to it.

Karuna chuckled again as she wiped sweat from her brow with the trailing edge of her sari. "How does she keep her clothes so perfect?" she voiced one of my points of resentment. *How does she keep saying exactly what I'm thinking?*

I shrugged and chuckled with her, "Beats me! I couldn't keep myself looking so neat if my life depended on it."

"Me neither!" she agreed. We both looked at each other in our white saris and erupted in laughter as we were both rumply and stained and the morning was not even over. We looked like we had been wearing the same sari for the past three days.

We stepped into the kitchen going through the brahmacharini room. A couple of younger brahmacharinis—*Pre-teens, probably*—were in there. They were sitting on the little *coco-denutter* stools, grinding out the insides of coconuts with the jagged edge. A metal bowl sat underneath the round, jagged blade in order to catch the shredded coconut meat. A heap of meaty coconut halves sat beside them. On the other side, was a smaller pile of de-coconutted coconuts. They did not look up. I stuck my head into the fry kitchen, which was as black and sooty as ever. It looked even blacker and sootier with no one in there cooking. I turned right in order to walk through the main part of the kitchen with Karuna on my heels. A few more brahmacharinis in white were in there, prepping for lunch.

Karuna stopped and asked, "Namah shivaya, do you know where Bri. Lakshmini is?"

One barely glanced at us, shyness emanating from her. "In the temple…with Cha Ma," she whispered.

"Well, back to the temple!" Karuna announced.

We walked through the rest of the dank, moist kitchen, going around haphazard piles of large pots and cauldrons, and cut through the Western canteen, which was empty. I cast a glance over to the Indian canteen—a couple of brahmacharis were sweeping the floor with bundles of twigs. We headed toward the back of the temple, skirting around the edge of the building.

Over by the cow shed, which was to our left, Rukmini was working. It looked like she was cleaning out the stalls. Karuna and I looked at each other but neither said anything. The whole-Rukmini-getting-beat-up in-cident was still a fresh and tender wound. I did not know what to think about it all. So, I tended to push it out of my mind when I could. I think most of the Western women did the same thing as nothing had ever happened with her beating. There had been no apology on the part of the men and, definitely, no punishment. It seemed they had not even been forced to acknowledge that they had played a part in it or that it had been wrong.

At the back of the temple, we cut over to the back stairs that led to the women's side of the inner temple. I could hear faint chords of music— *Funeral Swami's playing already?* Darshan had begun. *Have we been meandering around looking for Lakshmini that long?* At the balcony door of the inner temple, we peeked our heads in, and then hastily pranamed at the threshold before entering.

Cha Ma was hugging a woman and speaking into her ear. Br. Narayanan was at Cha Ma's elbow, passing men to her. At the moment, he was preoccupied with holding, at arm's length, a squirming, screaming little boy in cloth diapers. The child was staring at Cha Ma and shrieking for all he was worth. His eyes flitted around her as if he saw something horribly frightening. Br. Narayanan looked like he could not put the child down soon enough, misery all over his face. Cha Ma, laughing heartily, looked at the child and chucked him under the chin. He just screamed harder. *I wish he'd stop screaming. Why is he screaming so?*

"There she is," Karuna said, pointing. I looked to where she was pointing—a pretty brahmacharini in yellow was standing against the wall, farther inside the inner temple. She was average height and nicely full-figured. Her skin was the color of café au lait. Her curly brown hair was pulled back with a brown headband. A smile played across her lips as she watched Cha Ma with an enrapt look.

"You're right! I do know her."

Bri. Lakshmini looked our way, smiling, as always. We beckoned to her. She bobbled her head in assent and headed toward us. We stepped back out onto the balcony. She followed us. We all sat on the stairs.

"Namah shivaya," I began. "I have a letter for Cha Ma. Could you… would you…be willing to translate it? It's long…" I said apologetically.

Bri. Lakshmini's head bobbled gently—a yes that looked like a soft no, "Of course, I will translate your letter." Her delicately accented voice was lovely. I handed her the letter. She quickly scanned it. "Oh! This should take no time. I will have it done for you by dinner. I will give it to you then?"

"Oh! Namah shivaya!" I exclaimed very pleased.

"Namah shivaya!" Her head bobbled gently as she smiled at me.

We headed our separate ways.

"She is so cool!" Karuna said what I was thinking as we went up the stairs and into the women's dorm.

"My thoughts exactly!" I concurred. If there was any one brahmacharini I wanted to be most like, it would be her. She was beautiful *and* friendly *and* nice *and* smart.

"Here! You! Westerner! You stand right here." One of the brahmacharinis monitoring the line gestured for me to skip to the front of the line. Lakshmini had had my letter translated by dinner. She had found me in the Western canteen, getting ready to get my kanji and—*let's be honest here*—listening to the rave reviews on my soup. She had slipped up to me and handed several folded sheets of paper to me. When I had opened them, I saw that there were two pages worth of tightly written Malayalam and my own letter in English. My first thought had been—*Her writing is so beautiful....*My second had been—*How did my one page letter grow in size!* It seemed that for every word I had written the translation had called for four. *Wow! That's a lot!*

Karuna pushed me forward, "Go ahead and skip! If you don't, you might be here all night!"

Leaning against her hands, I shook my head, "I shouldn't..."

"Go *ahead!*" She urged more emphatically, pressing even harder against my back.

"OK!" I took a place five people away from Cha Ma, quickly clambering down onto my knees. Rapidly, I scanned the crowd in the inner temple. The women's side was, as always, pure chaos. Women, children, and babies were all over the place. Uncontrolled, "aggro" chaos. The men's side was—you guessed it!—orderly and calm, smiling. And there, directly in my line of vision—Br. Narayanan. *Oh no!*

I began to chant my Kali mantra, to try to get, and keep, my head "in line." *Definitely don't want Cha Ma picking up the wrong thoughts...and then, telling someone. Ugh! Not good.* It seemed as though Cha Ma kept looking at me over the heads of the people she was hugging. *It's probably my imagination.* Everyone felt that way—that she was looking at them over the heads of the people she was hugging: as if she could not wait to give you your own personal, special hug. However, an even stranger thing was that while you were being hugged, you felt like the most important person in the world.

I rapidly closed the distance between us—moving forward on my knees—as she was giving quick darshan. I worked to remember to chant my mantra—*Omm Kali...,* to pray to Kali—*Oh, please let me stay,* and to try not to look at Br. Narayanan. *That's the last thing I need, her saying something about me thinking about him with him here!* Before I knew it, it was my turn. That was when I noticed that the brahmacharini who was helping her was mean, old Bri. Durgamma. *Figures! Here's my special moment with Cha Ma and I get mean ole' Durgamma. She's as crotchety as her name sounds! Oh! I better stop before Cha Ma notices and says something.* I waited, almost paralyzed with fear that Cha Ma would read my mind and say something about my like of Narayanan or my dislike of Durgamma.

Roughly, Durgamma shoved my body around so that when my turn came, I would be in place. *Why does she have to be so rough?* I watched Cha Ma hug and whisper into the ear of the man in front of me. As she did, she peered around his head and looked at me, smiling, her eyes crinkling at the corners. *She's so cute, just like a ma!* When she was done with him, she kissed his cheek and gave him a wad of vibhuti and prasad—a sweet offered up to a deity. Usually, darshan prasad was a piece of hard candy, today it happened to be ladus, which was a yellow, sugary ball of, well...sugar, and was one of my favorite sweets. *How Kali that on my special darshan day the prasad is ladus!* The brahmachari helping on the men's side (it was no longer Br. Narayanan—*when did he leave?*), carefully assisted the man out of the way. *Why are the brahmacharis gentler and kinder to the men than the brahmacharinis are to us women?*

Immediately, Bri. Durgamma pushed me against Cha Ma's knees. I tried not to touch her feet as I had been told that they ached badly—*probably all the kundalini shakti coursing out of them.* Durgamma roughly grabbed my forearms and placed them around Cha Ma's waist. I resisted against Durgamma's forceful positioning in order to hold up my note. I knew from watching other darshans that Cha Ma would not read it during darshan because one, it was so long and two, she tended to read notes later in her apartment when she was alone. Cha Ma grabbed me and positioned my forehead on her shoulder as she started whispering into my ear. Out of the corner of my left eye, I could see that she was unfolding the note. The pages rustled as she arranged them in her hands.

When she began reading, she pressed my head down into her lap. *So, she is going to read my note! Now,* that's *unusual.* I kept my head down and just chanted, "Ma...Ma...Ma..." quietly to myself. I was afraid to breathe for fear of what she might say or not say. I was afraid she would say no to my staying and being a renunciate. I was afraid she would say, yes, I could be a renunciate. I was afraid she would say that I had to go back to school, that my "destiny" was not to be found in India. So, I waited with baited breath, hardly believing that she was reading my letter in its entirety... now *that* was totally unheard of. As she read, I heard her chuckle and laugh and say something aloud, ostensibly, reading a portion of my letter to Bri. Durgamma and whoever else was standing nearby. At one point, I heard, "Rumble...*rumble*...*rumble* (the way Malayalam sounded coming out of her mouth)...Harvard...*rumble*...*rumble*..." Laughter followed. *Harvard? She just said Harvard! I heard laughter. What is she saying about Harvard that's so funny?*

Finally, after what seemed like several minutes of her reading with one elbow dug into my spine as she held my letter and the other hand rubbing my back, she pulled me up to look at her. She smiled at me, kissed me on the cheek, and started speaking, her head bobbling in that unusual, but now-familiar Indian way. She stared at me intently as she spoke, smiling. The entire time that she spoke, she played with the mala around my wrist.

(I had had a handcrafted astrological mala set—a necklace and a bracelet—made especially for me that I wore religiously. The set was made out of my astrological stones: gold veined, cobalt blue lapis lazuli beads for Saturn and vibrant, rich green tourmaline beads for Mercury. These stones were interspersed with clear, round crystals—for Venus and in order to magnify the energy of the other stones—and were prettily fashioned on thin, delicate silver wire. Such astrological malas were considered conducive to moving the wearer along to enlightenment. It was believed that the arrangement of the stones and the fact that they were tied into one's astrological chart caused them to hold significant spiritual power within them. Further adding to the power of these malas was that while the women made them, they chanted powerful mantras into them. I used them for doing japa with my Kali mantra—embedding even more power within them. And I had to admit—*They're really pretty, too, and they look great on me.*)

As Cha Ma spoke, she played with my malas—alternately fingering the stones around my wrist and those hanging about my neck. *Is she aware that she's playing with my malas? What does it mean…what will it do…to have a Kali avatar play with my malas?* I wondered these things as she spoke. Her voice, as usual, was deep and gravelly. She said a lot. *What is she saying? She's probably saying that I can't stay and be a renunciate.* I felt my heart take a downward turn.

Durgamma leaned in close, her hand covering her mouth (as a sign of respect to the deity of Cha Ma), and brusquely translated, "Cha Ma says that everything will be fine. You stay in ashram. Be brahmacharini. Don't worry about school." Cha Ma kissed me on the cheek and then ducked her head down as though she were shy or was looking into her lap. After several long moments of looking down into her lap, she looked back up at me.

SHOCK!! ABSOLUTE and STARK! coursed through my body. CHA MA HAD MORPHED! SHE WAS JET-BLACK AND HARD AS A ROCK! In the time in which she had looked down and then had looked back up at me, everything about her had transformed. Literally. Her body had changed completely! It was hard, hard as a rock. I could not say…had become…because I did not feel a *shifting*, a *changing*. No, just one moment she was soft and pudgy—this I knew because I was kneeling at her feet, my arms around her waist (as much as possible as she was a plump woman), my hands lightly touching her back—and the next moment, she was rock hard, stone cold. There was not an iota of softness or warmth to her. It felt as if she had no flesh at all. She was no longer warm and inviting. She no longer felt like "mommy." Her body, through the sari, was cold, hard, impenetrable. She had become like a statue or a murti made of iron or stone.

Granted, her soft, chubby body turning rock hard freaked me out; however, it was her face that shocked…frightened…*terrified*…me the most! It was no longer mocha brown, smiling and pudgy, sweet and cute. It was no longer…Ma. The moment she looked up, her face was black—jet-black, coal-black—and hard and shiny. It looked like something out of a comic book or a science fiction graphic novel. It looked like she had become a piece of polished rock—like obsidian or black opal—its surface highly polished and reflective. Her eyes glinted gray. *Gray! Am I really seeing this?* I questioned myself of the unbelievable truth I was witnessing. I struggled to digest it. And if the shift in the color and consistency of her body, face, and eyes was not enough, she was now looking at me with a frown…and speaking. Rather, *growling* out an answer. True, she had always had a deep, gravelly voice, but this gave "deep and gravelly" a new meaning. She growled fiercely at me, her voice octaves lower. She was frowning, angry…so it seemed.

Pure, unalloyed fear coursed, bucked, and reverberated through my body. I was too stunned and too weakened by terror, to even think of running. I just stayed there. Kneeling before her but wanting to run. Gripping her…no! She was no longer a "she" but rather an "it"…gripping *its*…hard, cold body. Terror kept flooding through my being. I wanted to pull away. I was too petrified to move. I could not swallow or breathe or think, even. At the same time, another emotion began to shoot through me—entirely unexpected and irrational—*exhilaration!*

She…*it*…leaned forward and kissed me on the cheek. A thought, a single, terrified thought flew like a trapped bird through my brain and smashed against the bars of terror—*Kiss of death!* Another wave of fear heaved through my body, more powerful than the first. On its heels came another rush of exhilaration. Sheer and stark. The ultimate thrill seeker had met her match!

Bri. Durgamma leaned in even closer. She was so close to Cha Ma... Kali...it...and me. Her eyes were wide, shock registering in them. I knew that she was seeing what I was seeing. Still, her hand covered her mouth, in awe and respect and fear of angering *whatever* it was that was speaking. She translated in a hoarse whisper, her accent choppy, "Cha Ma says that you, Premabhakti, do not have to worry. She will...take care of everything. What is your school...your life...anything...before her?" Cha Ma...*it*... continued to growl words at me, frowning, shaking its shiny, black head, ferociously. Her eyes glinted gray again, my breath rolled in on itself—*Did her eyes just flash gray again? No, no...couldn't be...* Durgamma continued, "She says, 'She is Adiparashakti. She is the ultimate energy of the universe. Everything arises, is sustained, and dissolves in her. What is your school... what is your life...to her?'"

With that, Cha Ma...*it*...abruptly stopped speaking and ducked *its* head. After a moment, it looked back up. To my bewilderment, she was no longer a frightening, profoundly monsterish "it" but was, again, a "she." And she was that plump, cute, mocha-brown, smiling ma that I knew, not the scary, hideous, hard thing that I *seemed* to have seen. For a nano-second, I wondered if I had, perhaps, imagined it all—*But I did see her! I felt her!* I looked around and everyone nearby was staring at Cha Ma with their faces exhibiting expressions that mirrored my feelings and was surely reflected in my face, too. Countless emotions—fear, awe, wonderment, terror!— danced madly across our countenances, undeniably displaying the chaotic emotions at what we had seen.

Cha Ma, back to her cute, little, chubby self, fingered my malas again. She took my right hand and pressed a packet of vibhuti and a ladu into it. She smiled again at me, so endearingly that I could not help but wonder if what I had seen was what I saw. I smiled back, pressed my hands together in praying fashion before my lips and full-pranamed at her feet. I got up, namah shivaya'ed her good-bye and thanks, and left. Awestruck!

What Maya did not see was the events of the darshan that unfolded in an entirely "other" realm…the spiritual. Brilliant, His Strength, Awe, and Majesty watched Maya as she approached Cha Ma with her note. They were fully aware of her intentions. They tended to keep their distance from her in order not to alert Chamunda and the others to the fact that something was going on in the heavenlies. They strove to appear as a protective unit and not one of deep intervention. To that aim, they watched the scene unfolding in the inner temple from the vicinity of the meditation roof.

"So, what will Chamunda say to her?" Brilliant asked Majesty as they stood in the air.

"That she may remain, of course. Chamunda would love to keep her here and eventually kill her. What a conquest that would be!"

"Hmmm," Brilliant responded, understanding fully that Maya would not remain. No matter what, they would succeed in pulling her out.

They began talking strategy, their voices sinking into a melodic hum as they spoke in the heavenly language amongst themselves. The lesser demons that were as close as the vibrational pain would allow, backed up even farther. The heavenly language burned their already burning bodies. A couple of meditators on the roof had fleeting visions of dark, dense, ghoulish beings and glorious light beings that resembled humans. The demons would have liked to play in their meditations but the pain of being around the Lord's angels was too much. They kept their distance.

Abruptly, the Lord's angels broke off their conversation, holding themselves still, listening, perceiving. Majesty nodded; and they disappeared, only to reappear that same instant in the inner temple.

Already swinging his sparking sword in a full arc as they appeared, Majesty commanded in a booming voice that caused the atmosphere to reverberate, "You have no right!" His sword sliced between Maya and Cha Ma as he landed in a kneeling position to the right of Maya. The other three angels moved as he did, completely unified, as they were of one mind. One appeared on the left side of Maya, the other two on either side of Cha Ma. Their swords arced in the air and sliced down between Cha Ma and Maya. Iridescent sparks shot from their huge swords. Their righteous indignation caused their bodies to radiate light. Heavenly fire shot from their eyes as pure, white light.

In less than the next instant, Majesty spoke, "It is written that the Word of the Lord is living and active. Sharper than any double-edged sword, it penetrates even to the dividing soul and spirit." The words flew out of his mouth rapidly, meant only for those who dwelled in the spiritual realm.

Chamunda Kali, in the midst of manifesting herself in Cha Ma, was caught off guard, although she understood and immediately obeyed. She ducked Cha Ma's head and after a moment, permitted Cha Ma to look back up at Maya. In her upset, she relinquished her hold on Cha Ma—for the time being.

Cha Ma placed something in Maya's hand, smiled at her, and let her go as Chamunda whirled to standing from her seated position within Cha Ma. Belligerently, she faced the Lord's angels. Her gaunt, skeletal, black frame was vibrantly shiny, like highly polished obsidian—she had been feeding off the adulation of her devotees. As she trained her eyes on the Lord's angels, her frame turned a dull black. Their proximity sapped her strength—it never failed that the nature of Who and What the Lord's angels worshiped overwhelmed and overpowered all others.

Her ire was up. "How dare you infringe upon my domain?" she spat the words at the Lord's angels as she waved a hand before her face. From her fingers, rapier-like claws grew. She lunged at the angels, swinging her rapier claws outward.

Awe executed a spectacular spin, light flying off him, and easily parried her move with his sword. "We'll have none of that here. Now is not the time. You'll not win. You'll not even slow us down." As he spoke, his hair undulated, shooting sparks into the atmosphere. Chamunda flinched as a few of the sparks landed upon her body—they burned.

Majesty glanced at Awe, who nodded and stepped back. Deftly, Majesty moved forward and spun his sword, sliding Chamunda's rapier-claws up against her heaving chest, effectively pinning them to her body. "We're not here to battle. Sorry, Chamunda Kali." She moved as if to push away from him. He stepped forward into her as he spoke, his narrowed eyes beaming fierce, white light into her face. "Later. We're simply here to ensure that the orders of the Lord are observed."

Chamunda slowly retracted and extended her claws. "What have I done that is out of order?" she asked. She attempted, with no success, to look innocent; instead, she looked devious and dangerous. She knew her illegality.

The Lord's angels chuckled. Majesty responded, "You know you may not manifest yourself to her."

"And why not?" Chamunda hissed. She peered at the Lord's angels through her rapier claws as she clacked them against each other before her face. "She is here of her own volition. She is such a stupid girl...such a waste..."

Majesty stared at her, the bright light of his gaze slowly raking over her visage. Wherever it touched began to smoke. He smiled before speaking slowly as though he were talking to someone of limited understanding (but then he was). "She is not stupid...far from it. And you know that or Satan would not spend so much effort with her. Nor is she a waste. No human, no matter how far gone, is ever a waste to our Lord. But that you will not ever understand. It's not in your nature."

Chamunda shook her head to move from the burning rays emitted from Majesty's eyes. Stealthily, she stretched toward Maya (who was just standing up—human and spiritual time was vastly different), her ethereal body grotesquely elongating, in order to touch the girl with the tip of her rapier-like pointer finger. "Why should *she* receive special treatment from the Lord, when He has given all the others that are here to me?"

Awe shook his head at her and gently swung his sword, pinning her rapier down as if he were toying with an overly playful animal.

"You know the effects of the prayers of those who live their lives for God. Her mother and father pray for her constantly. You know that..."

Majesty said this slowly, as if he were chiding a child. He paused a moment and then looked her up and down, his eyes evaluative, their light turning golden. "I can see the effects of their prayers upon you. Your color is waning."

Chamunda snorted, "Hmphf!" But, it was patently true. The effects of the parents' prayers and the effects of the Lord's angels were sapping the evil ones. At the least, they were losing the vibrant sickness of their color; at the most, they were losing their essence, their will, their substance. Even as she stood beside the Lord's angels, in all their glory, she could feel her essence rapidly seeping away. What was most frightening was that no matter how much she lost, she could never bottom out, she could…and one day would—all those who chose the Rebellion would—simply spiral lower and lower as she lost all of what she was but would never reach the end of losing it. To lose oneself, but never completely, spiraling and dissipating away for an eternity, with no opportunity of ever recouping it? She abhorred the Lord's angels for it and even more, she abhorred them for What and *Who* they had chosen and how it had, over time, made them more beautiful, more powerful, and vibrant. They would grow and increase over time, while she and hers would devolve upon themselves, dissipating and reducing, spiraling deeper and deeper into fear and misery, humiliation and doubt, anguish and hate, never as powerful or strong as they were the moment before.

Brilliant shook his head, causing golden light to fly across the inner temple. A few of the sparks flew through Chamunda, causing her to tremor with pain. She struggled not to show it. He remarked, "Tsk, tsk… that you chose the wrong side."

"Yes, well…" Chamunda faltered, he had hit a chord. No matter how evil she was, still a part of her yearned to return to what she used to be when she was good, noble, obedient. They all did. But, she…it, like all the evil ones, had made an irrevocable choice against her very nature. Unlike humans, the angelic did not have free will. To shun God and follow Lucifer, to choose to rebel: the act of making a choice, by a being created without a choice, was an act of supreme rebellion. To choose against the Creator of them, doubled the magnitude of the Rebellion. They had acted wholly contrary to their nature and the purpose for which God had created them. In that choice, the dye had been cast. Their lots given. Their natures warped and perverted to meet the Rebellion. And yet, a mite of goodness remained. *If only…* She hardened her heart—or what used to be her heart—again, as she had incalculable times over the millennia…*there is no "if only"!*

She shook herself, "Back to the girl!"

"Yes, back to Maya," Majesty responded as he scrutinized her. He was fully aware of her thoughts as he was receiving knowledge directly from the Lord. "You know the rules. The Lord will not brook you manifesting yourself to her."

"But she gives herself to me…"

"You have no right to remove the boundary between the physical and the spiritual for a child of God."

"She's the one who's trying to remove the boundary," Chamunda objected, her voice evincing a whiny undertone. Majesty cocked an eyebrow and glanced at the others out of the corner of his eyes. Awe smiled as Brilliant snorted derisively. "And…and…she's no child of God…she's mine."

Majesty and the others chuckled as if they were thoroughly enjoying the joke. Then, Majesty responded quietly, "You can think what you like. You will see. You know what you can and cannot do with her. As the Lord limited the actions of Satan with Job, as the Lord allows only what He chooses, you may not remove the boundary between the physical and the spiritual and you may not manifest yourself to her. You did just now. Silly, presumptuous mistake! Be glad the Lord did not put you in the pit before your time."

A stricken look involuntarily flashed across Chamunda's visage, which she quickly hid with a stony glare. "He wouldn't?!"

Majesty stared her down in silence—his eyes boring into hers. It took all of Chamunda's self-control to not shrink back from the burning light in his gaze. "Remember yourself!" Majesty commanded. Chamunda gave a quick, sharp nod of assent, unaware of concurring. Majesty looked around at the others and nodded in agreement—it was time to leave Chamunda

Kali. Immediately they removed themselves, leaving Chamunda Kali to carry on with her darshan.

I meandered out of the inner temple, still stunned…*Kali*…in a haze of spiritual inebriation…unable to focus on any one thing in particular. As I ambled along the second floor balcony of the temple (*How did I get here?*), I noticed that Bri. Lakshmini was walking behind me, calling to me, "Namah shivaya! Namah shivaya, Premabhakti! Namah shivaya!"

I halted and nodded my head at her, trying to find my focus. *Kali!*

She caught up with me, "Where are you going?"

"To the meditation…roof…to think on what just happened…" I stumbled upon my words. I felt high as a kite.

"What happened?" She stepped closer to me, beaming. Her voice was soft and gentle, the words tilting sweetly around her accent.

"Did you notice anything significant about my darshan? She read the letter." Something crazy…mad…felt like it was wanting to punch through my chest.

"That is significant enough! She rarely reads a letter during darshan. But, yes," she nodded emphatically. "I did see your darshan. What happened? What did she say to your letter? To your request to stay?"

"C'mon, I'll tell you. You want to go with me up to the meditation deck?"

"Oh yes!" she exclaimed and walked with me along the balcony. She talked of Cha Ma. I remained silent. My thoughts were too full of my strange and frightening darshan. *She shifted…she showed me herself as Adiparashakti!*

Once we got to the meditation deck, we walked to the section that looked inland. Standing there, gazing at the endless expanse of green— palm trees upon palm trees for miles around on three sides of me, to my back was the ocean—I told her about my darshan. She already knew parts of it because she had translated my letter. I told her what Cha Ma had said.

"That is amazing! Cha Ma said *that?* I have never heard of such a thing…" Her voice was breathy and excited. Her smile broadened.

"And then, the way she changed…"

"The way she changed…?" her voice trailed off questioningly. Her eyes widened a bit, wonderingly.

"Oh yes! Most definitely, I saw that. I have never seen that before. Cha Ma turning so…so…she looked so strange and dark and…" I paused, for a thought or out of fear, I wasn't too sure, "…scary. She scared me a bit. It's hard to explain!"

"Cha Ma!" she exclaimed.

"She called herself Adiparashakti…What does that mean?"

She grabbed my arm and leaned in close, her face inches from mine, barely able to keep her voice under control, "Adiparashakti? She called herself Adiparashakti?" I nodded. "I cannot believe that she revealed herself to you as Adiparashakti. I have heard her say, so often, that she refuses to reveal more of herself because it would scare us and everyone would leave her. She says that she keeps who she is a secret and doesn't reveal that information to anyone because we could not take it. But, to you…she did!" She clasped her hands together under her chin, like a little girl, smiling a wide smile of joy. "How fortunate you are!" she breathed.

"But, what does Adiparashakti mean?" I persisted.

"Adiparashakti is the name of the ultimate energy of the universe. It underlies everything. It is all-powerful. Cha Ma has shown you that she is the power of the universe!"

I did not say anything. I dared not.

"Come on! Let's dance! Let's sing a song to Cha Ma, in celebration of what happened!" she urged.

I started singing the first song that popped into my head—a song about Kali in one of her fiercest forms, Chamunda Kali. "Chay-mun-dai-yay kali-yay kali-yay kali-yay!" I started dancing around the roof. Bri. Lakshmini joined me singing and dancing. We twirled around and around. I grabbed her hands to stop her and said, excitedly, "Can you believe Cha Ma revealed herself to me?"

Bri. Lakshmini looked at me wide-eyed and exclaimed, "I've never heard of her doing that before nor have I ever heard of her saying who she is. Kali! To show and to say? Never!" We kept twirling about, laughing and giggling, high on the experience. "You are very special, Premabhakti! The satguru has blessed you! Oh! You will experience moksha in this lifetime... you must!"

As they twirled about, they could not see into the supernatural realm. If they had been able, they would have seen Chamunda Kali whirling about in delight—she, it, had left darshan to drink in the sweet taste of two devotees caught in the thrall of her. She was terrifying: jet-black, skinny and emaciated, skin hanging from her face and body as there was no fat to speak of. She had manifested ten arms and each of them brandished a weapon. One arm held a machete. One held a sickle, while another wielded a butcher knife. Still another held a sword and one, a trident. The bottommost hand on the right side held a sloshing bowl full of deep red blood. Above that bowl, another hand slung about a decapitated head by its long, jet-black hair; which dripped blood profusely. She was waving her arms and moving about in a crazed dance. As she danced, she insanely shrieked along with the two devotees, singing the song to herself, abandoned to an diabolical, ghoulish glee. As she whirled, light snaked from the bodies of the two into hers—she was drinking up their spiritual energy.

Near to them whirled and danced other demonic beings. High on the adoration of their lord—for anything—be it attention, focus, love... worship—that did not go specifically to the One True God went to theirs. A macabre celebration was underway. Farther away stood, perfectly still and at peace, yet diametrically and fundamentally opposed in their nature to the demonic, the regiments of the Lord's angels. They stood in perfect formation in the air. Their armor and weapons of silver and gold glinted from within. Light in various hues streamed from their eyes into the sky, for they all were gazing upward. They were receiving instructions from the Lord Himself. And from Him streamed a burning, iridescent light that flooded them and pulsed into their very being and fiber. They were being prepared, empowered, and directed.

"Shanalee, I don't know how long I can keep this up…"

"You will have to, Marie. Maya needs you to. Remember, though, the Lord never gives us a load we can't bear. You can bear this. You can see this through."

Marie sighed on the phone, "I just don't know…"

"Where's Paul?" Shanalee thought to change the conversation.

"At work. I don't know why he's even doing this. He doesn't need the money and definitely not at the cost of his health."

Shanalee's heart went out to her husband's sister. "Let's pray…"

"OK…but, I'm just so beat. You won't mind if I don't pray? Will you pray for me?" Marie's head hurt tremendously. *How long has this been going on? Months now…*She could feel herself swiftly growing depressed on that single thought. She forced herself to think more positively—*The doctors had said that the headaches would subside and the webbing would diminish as the medicine took effect… IF the medicine took effect…It has to work!* She clung to this. She did not want to consider the other possibility.

Shanalee began, "Dear Lord, we don't understand Your ways…" As she prayed, Jovial touched Marie's head. The headache lightened. It was all he was permitted to do. He yearned to do more for her. He yearned to allow the Lord's healing power to flow straight through his hand into her, so easily she could be well; but it was not yet time.

Marie lay down upon the bed, closed her eyes, and let her sister-in-law—her true friend through thick and thin—pray. Her mind examined the many doctors' visits she had had in the past couple of months.

Just today, the neurologist, Dr. Rushman, had called her to his office to discuss the results of the latest battery of tests she had taken over the past several days at a state-of-the-art university research hospital in a neighboring city. Paul went with her. The receptionist had showed them into a small conference room. Dr. Rushman was already there, seated, as were three others.

After they were seated, Dr. Rushman, a young man who looked to be in his thirties began, "Marie...Paul...I have asked my colleagues, Drs. Worthing, Steele, and Webster, to join us and give their medical opinions." All three were in white lab coats and looked suspectly grim. "You remember Dr. Worthing? He is the opthamalogist who was called onto your case by Dr. Johnson. As you know, Dr. Johnson transferred your case to him because he is a medical doctor who specializes in ocular pathologies. Drs. Steele and Webster are also neurologists. Given the situation, we felt, Dr. Johnson included, that it would be best if we took over the management of your case."

Marie and Paul nodded. Dr. Rushman continued after receiving their vague consent. "Marie, may I be frank with you?" he asked hesistantly, kindly.

"Of course, please..." Marie responded. She tried to swallow around the lump in her throat. She noticed that her heart was pounding rapidly out of fear. Her palms were clammy.

"I'll say it in layman's terms because I don't want to confuse you with a bunch of medical jargon. You need to be perfectly clear and understand all that I am about to say to you and your husband."

"I appreciate that. Please go on…" Marie sounded more collected than she felt. She glanced over at Paul. He smiled bleakly and then looked at the wall.

"You know we were suspecting a mass in your brain?"

"Yes?"

"As we've said before, you have all the symptoms of a brain tumor in an advanced stage. That's what we've been searching for. We're fairly certain that it's rather large because of the amount of fluid that has built up around your brain and because of the unusual amount of pressure this fluid is causing. This buildup of fluid is pressing against the top of your spine and against the nerves in your eyes, the optic nerves. It's this buildup that's causing the headaches and the black spots and webs, at least in part. But, we have to allow that the tumor itself could be causing these symptoms, depending upon its location."

"What does this mean for me, doctor?" Marie tried not to cry. She swallowed hard. She reached out and grabbed Paul's hand. He clutched hers. *I feel like I'm drowning. It's not supposed to be this way!* Marie's heart protested.

"We have some effective therapies for your condition. There is medication to reduce the buildup of fluid, which we've been giving you. It's effect has been minimal, as you well know. We're still hoping that as the medicine works its way through your body, it will grow more effective. If that happens, then it should stop the headaches and impaired vision—*if* that is what's causing the buildup of fluid. As for the brain tumor…" he paused.

"Please go on…" Marie urged, praying that she would not start crying. *Not here. Not the place for weakness.* And she was afraid that if she started crying, she would not ever stop.

"We'll continue to try to locate it. Once we find it, we'll be able to say what we can do for you. However, we sense time is of the essence." Dr. Rushman looked around the table at his colleagues for confirmation. They all nodded in agreement, frowning. "We just have a problem because we can't seem to locate the mass."

"Can't find the mass?" Marie murmured.

Dr. Rushman shook his head, "No. We will continue looking."

"Is it life-threatening?" Paul asked. His voice sounded strained. He was gripping Marie's hand so hard it hurt. She dared not look at him.

Long silence. The doctors shifted uneasily. Dr. Rushman finally spoke up, "Yes. We believe it is. We feel you may have a few months left to live unless we are able to successfully intervene."

"A few months...?" Marie's voice came out as a whisper.

Dr. Rushman gave one curt, grim nod, his eyes looking sympathetic. "We really need to find the tumor and remove or destroy it."

Marie swallowed and swallowed again, vainly attempting to push down the fear that was lumping up in her throat so that she could speak. "Doctor, please forgive me...what about a second opinion?" she asked her voice barely above a whisper. Suddenly, she felt like fragile glass—any sudden movement or jarring noise and she would shatter into thousands of little pieces.

Dr. Rushman sighed. "I am sorry, Marie. That is why I have turned to the medical opinions of my colleagues, Dr. Steele, Dr. Webster, and Dr. Worthing," each inclined his or her head, "Not to mention your optometrist, Dr. Johnson. This is a very serious matter. I don't like to give such information without obtaining a second opinion myself. In this case, I have sought three different opinions outside of my own."

One of the other doctors spoke up (Marie felt so overwhelmed she could not distinguish one from the other), "I am Dr. Worthing. All of the tests Dr. Rushman ordered were sent to us." Dr. Worthing gestured to Drs. Steele and Webster, "and were independently evaluated by our labs. We concur with his diagnosis. The question is what do you choose to do?"

The discussion with the doctors continued. Finally, exhausted from the flurry of thoughts and fears that assailed her and the pounding headache that drained her energy, Marie agreed to take a couple of days to think on her options. Before she left, the doctors reminded her that she did not have much time—they would have to act fast if they hoped to save her life; even then, they feared that if they could not find the mass, she would die.

On the other hand, they feared the possibility that even if they did find the mass, they would be unable to do enough and she would die still.

After the visit, Marie went home. Paul went to work. As she sat alone, her mind revolved around the question, "What do I choose to do? What do I need to do?" She had no clue. After much struggling within herself, she picked up the phone and called Shana. She needed her friend, her sister-in-law's strength.

EXPLOSION!

Maya
India

Kali Leela night and I was aggro. Very, very aggro! I had no clue why. It was as if something had gotten under my skin or had gotten on me or *into* me…*something*. I was beyond angry, beyond red-eyed rage, beyond baleful. For some reason, *everything* made me eyeball-popping, "cuss-you-out-like-you-was-a-dog" angry. I could find no outlet, no release.

Feeling hyper-aggro and destructive, I washed pots, my normal, late night Kali Leela duty with the other Western-ers—*that* made me irritable. All of the Indians staring at me, pulling my hair, and touching me everywhere—*that* made me aggravated. Simply walking around made me angry. I tried to stay to myself; I *knew* I was too aggro to be around anyone. I would have surely picked a fight. I longed to have a knock-down-drag-out-beat-somebody-down session.

Finally, I found myself sitting on the roof, seething, staring out over the ocean, but not enjoying it. Its beauty enraged me. I was too angry and agitated to meditate. I was too angry to even fall asleep while trying to meditate. Toward the end of the night, Karuna ran up to the roof to tell me, "Cha Ma's giving darshan to the residents. Come on!"

"Already?" I snarled, my nasty attitude instantly surfacing.

"Yeah, go figure!" she grinned, not acknowledging my nastiness. "She finished with the people early and called for us."

I set my face and turned my back to her, refusing to speak. *I don't want to go! I don't want to see her!*

A long pause of silence. "Well, I'm heading on down," Karuna announced cheerfully, as she started toward the stairs.

"Alright!" I spat out at her happily retreating back. I sat for a bit, staring at the ocean, but not seeing. I huffed out an explosive sigh of exasperation. *I'm going! She's the guru, she should be able to handle my anger!* I lurched to my feet, slapped my asana over my shoulder, and strode down.

In the temple, the crowd was singing lively, energetic bhajans with the swamis. Swami had come back to lead, with Swami Shivaramananda and Funeral Swami singing backup—Kali Leela was soon to be over. There were no long lines filtering along the sides of the temple, another sign that Cha Ma was almost done. I hustled along the length of the temple, now eager for darshan, yet still feeling incredibly volatile and moody. *What's the matter with me?*

I entered the inner temple by the side door and joined the very short queue, only seven women were waiting—all ashramites. *She'll be done in less than ten minutes.* I looked around. On the men's side, two men—Western renunciates—waited for darshan. The men's side looked, of course, orderly and happy. The women's side was as it always was—crowded, chock full of shoving, cramped women, children, and babies. Asanas, shawls, and saris were scattered all over. There was Alice and Rukmini, right beside Cha Ma. Alice was being Alice, busily looking at everyone but Cha Ma. Rukmini sat even closer, cross-legged, her hands resting lightly on her thighs. Her pale, gaunt face ghostly-still, her bluish-lavender eyelids half-closed. *Is she meditating?* I wondered if she had learned her lesson. *At least, she's not sitting on the men's side anymore.*

Several industrial-sized fans violently stirred the air in the inner temple. Anneshwari stood to the side of Cha Ma, right at her left shoulder, spritzing the air with rosewater from a water bottle. The air, blown gustily about by the fans, picked up the rosewater droplets and scattered them throughout the inner temple. It had a definite cooling effect. A delicate fragrance of roses wafted throughout the inner temple.

I watched Cha Ma, who was wearing a lavish, purple sari bordered with ornate, gold embroidery and a tall, golden crown, talk to an Indian man as he knelt in front of her. He seemed to be asking something—*probably some favor or blessing*—as his head bobbled beseechingly, endearingly. He held his hands, palms touching, in prayer fashion before his mouth. She sat, smiling at him, nodding. Her right arm rested on his shoulder nonchalantly. A couple of times, she pushed her heavy hank of hair back with her left hand, irritation momentarily flitting across her face.

Suddenly, with no warning, she whirled around and smacked Anneshwari, speaking angrily at her. Then not missing a beat, she turned back to the man, smiled at him, drew him close, and whispered into his ear. He grinned back at her, his head bobbling furiously as she placed a wad of vibhuti and prasad in his hand. Nobody seemed to even notice that she had slapped Anneshwari. I was stunned by her violence (although I had heard about it) and Anneshwari's complete calm—she had not flinched even though she had been struck so hard (already her cheek bore a fiery, red hand mark). The brahmacharis and -charinis helping her did not seem to notice. *Or maybe they had noticed. . . .* Well, I had noticed but I did not care. Mentally I shrugged. *Cha Ma is the avatar.*

I waited—alternating between feeling aggro and wanting darshan. Before I knew it, it was my turn. A thin brahmacharini in yellow, her peaked face looking unusually youngish next to the thick streaks of gray in her hair, pushed me forward. I recognized her well enough but had yet to learn her name. I was too angry to place my hands together in prayer fashion.

Cha Ma grabbed me firmly by the shoulders and stared searchingly into my eyes. I felt raw, explosive anger surge within me. Deliberately, she thumped my chest hard with the back of her fist, one time, and smiled at me. I felt my lips mash together full of ire. She paused and then hit me hard in the chest again. The anger swelled precipitously beyond the violent, pernicious rage. I gritted my teeth together as I tried to contain the angry, *unhuman* growl that wanted to erupt from me. She struck me one more time in the chest (this time even harder) and let go. I launched backward almost as if I had been shoved. The thin, graying brahmacharini grabbed my wrist to steady me, placing her other hand behind my back. I shrugged her off. *That's it? No hug? No back pat? No vibhuti or prasad!? This isn't a darshan! This is junk!* I was incensed, so livid I could barely see.

I shoved myself up and stalked out of the back exit. I felt myself push past women's bodies, but I did not bother to say "namah shivaya"—I could care less. I could barely make out where I was going as my vision had narrowed myopically. I felt like I was trying to find my way through a graying tunnel with swirling red and orange walls. I went straight to the women's dorm, cursing under my breath. I scared myself, but I could not stop. The bhajans were blaring and clanging. They matched and stirred up the chaos in my mind. *Maybe I'm going mad? Like crazy Kartika. . . How often do people go crazy here?* Still breathing curses, I sat on my cot.

My eyes spied my Kali doll lying against the wall. I snatched her up and glared at her. *Kali!* Rage—fiery red, icy white, combustive orange—pounded and shrieked for release from within me. I drew back my arm—*Kali!*—and swinging it forward, I released the doll, madly screaming my rage at the top of my lungs. No one heard, of course—the bhajans were too loud as Kali Leela was ending. As I launched the doll, I felt as if eons of pure, icy-hot rage—bellicose, ferocious, and destructive—poured... flooded...through me. Engulfed me. I watched as the doll flew across the room, struck the wall, and...

EXPLODED!

Pieces and chunks of fabric and stuffing and jewelry and hair flew everywhere! Immediate satisfaction shot through me. I stared at the destruction. After a couple of seconds, my mouth dropped open. I was stunned as my mind registered what I saw. Wreckage. Mangled doll. I stood and continued to stare at the wreckage. *How does a soft, cloth doll EXPLODE into hundreds of little bits? The question coursed over and over through my mind.* I did not move. I had ceased hearing the music, it was dying away anyway—Kali Leela was over.

"Prema…" I heard someone murmur my name, a hint of fear hidden within it. "What happened here?" I turned my head and looked. It was Radha, standing in the doorway. Looking at the debris, she queried, her voice low and full of…something, "Did you…cut up your Kali doll?" She cast a strange look at me. I could almost read her thoughts—*Prema's cut up her doll. She's highly unstable. She's gone crazy.*

"No." I lifted my hands and shoulders in a shrug and gave her a bewildered look. All the anger had dissipated, in its place were the wreckage and a yawning emptiness with no answers. "It's crazy…" I proceeded to tell her what had happened.

"Your doll *exploded?*" Skeptically, she surveyed the wreckage again. "All by itself?"

I nodded. I bent down and began to pick up all the little pieces of the doll. She joined me. Snatches of black and red cloth, smaller than an inch, were all over the place. Tiny skulls were scattered over the floor and under the bunks. We picked up strands of hair and pieces of gold-plated jewelry. Tufts and chunks of stuffing were strewn about.

"How in the world…" she whispered, perplexity evident in her voice, her forehead creased in bewilderment. I know my face matched her voice. *How in the world, indeed?*

Maya could not see into the spiritual realm. She could not see Majesty, Brilliant, His Strength, and Awe watch her as she went about her Kali Leela night duties in a terrible anger. She did not see them sit beside her as she tried to meditate on the roof—all the while singing and speaking over her. She did not know that they observed her as she went down for darshan, the words they were singing over her weaving a divine web about her. The words had power—all the more because they were uttered in the heavenly language. As the words wove about her...delved deep into her...they caused to rise up the part within her that belonged to God.

That *God part*—King Solomon wrote in Ecclesiastes that God places eternity in the hearts of men. In the heart of *every* man...lies *His eternity*... that part that belongs solely, completely, incontrovertibly to Him. That part that seeks and yearns for Him and Him alone. Nestled...sometimes buried and hidden so deeply it appears virtually nonexistent, sometimes erringly and ignorantly placed in things other than Him (as in the case of Maya) and sometimes rightfully and wonderfully satiated in Him— *That* God part rose up (stroked and succored by the divine Words laced in the heavenly language spoken into her) within her. *That* God part—as it arose—met and battled the urges, the desires, the will within her that clamored for Cha Ma, for Kali...that clamored for all that was demonic and *not God*. *That* God part confronted and overwhelmed the Kali mantra as it pulsed insidiously within her. *That* God part was not to be defeated, it was not to be stifled and suppressed, rather it clashed and battled and warred within her against all that was *not God*...with ensuing confusion and chaos, anger and rage. All of this, building up...building up...in the human vessel, to finally spew forth in a messy, ugly mixture of violent and volatile emotions.

And then, the moment she had released the doll—the cloth murti, the soft idol—Majesty, who had been closely watching the internal struggle within Maya and had stood poised for just the right instant, called, "Now!" Immediately, he, Brilliant, His Strength, and Awe had sent powerful streams of living, fiery light right through the doll—although not just a *doll*, rather a cloth murti, an idol. The instant it struck the wall, the light smashed against it—smashed against the evil that lay hidden within it— with the force of a divine sledgehammer. The Kali doll, the cloth-murti... the soft-idol...exploded as the pure, divinely powerful light decimated the evil within it.

Majesty turned to the others, satisfaction playing upon his face. "They really don't understand the power of an idol, even if it is in doll form…"

"They really don't, do they?" Brilliant murmured as bits and pieces of the Kali doll floated through his…their…ethereal bodies. Awe shook his head in response, which caused iridescent light to shoot from his hair—vibrant, fiery light that when it touched the bits of the cloth-murti caused them to erupt into intangible flames.

Simultaneously, while Maya climbed the stairs to the women's dorm and felt herself being consumed with that explosive, sense-obliterating rage, Cha Ma, who was now finished with giving darshan, proceeded through the final stages of the night's Kali Leela. Reveling in the din of the bells, the blowing of the shells, and the passionate singing of her devotees, she stood triumphantly on the edge of the inner temple stage, directly underneath the women's dorm. Just as the devotees sang the last jubilant notes of their song to Kali with Swami leading them over the precipice of spiritual inebriation, his voice undulating, "Kaaa-aaa-aaaa-liiiii-iiiii," Maya launched the cloth-idol, the Kali doll. In that instant, Majesty called, "Now!" and the Lord's angels shot living light to destroy the murti. In the moment that the Lord's light decimated the evil in the Kali doll—an immense and potent act in the spiritual contained within an infinitesimally small human instant, Cha Ma flinched. She closed her eyes…momentarily…as she swayed.

Swamini Ma, ever watchful of Cha Ma, leaned over to Swamini Atmaprananananda and voiced her concern, "Did you see that? Is she OK?"

Swamini Atmaprananananda reassured her, "It's probably that she's tired. You see how she works during Kali Leela…" Swamini Ma nodded in agreement.

Of course, they had not seen, could not see, that a piece, a nugget, of Chamunda Kali had been smashed—the effects of which were felt deep within Cha Ma. Thus, Cha Ma was incalculably weary, weary beyond the demands of the nightlong Leela. Chamunda Kali, a piece of herself destroyed, shrank back, and ran away. Cha Ma was left to manage her exhausted body and battered soul by herself—no pick-me-up was to be had by the possessing deity.

Brilliant, His Strength, Majesty, and Awe looked upon Maya. Directly behind them stood a legion of angels. Their bodies soared to the ceiling; many soared *through* it. Bunks and other objects cut through their ethereal bodies. In the midst of one of Kali's nights, in her lair, they stood, and they had every right to be there. No demons were nearby. With the blatant decimation of a piece of Chamunda Kali and her ensuing retreat, they had run away, too.

They did not question why the Lord's angels had moved so mightily and decisively within a realm that, millennia ago, Satan had initially claimed. A territory that he had immediately passed on to one of his fellow insurrectionists, Chamunda Kali, to rule. They knew the reason. Yes, they owned the territory, had owned it for millennia. Yes, Chamunda's principality had been largely undisturbed for centuries, since the days of Thomas the disciple. (In fact, Satan tended to neglect the territory, so long had it been undisturbed. He wanted to believe that the Lord would allow him this place until the end of time. He was having difficulty perceiving the fact that the Lord was back in this area, so he continued to leave Chamunda to herself.) However, that "ownership" was solely because the Lord allowed her…them…this territory, this principality. Further, they knew that even in the midst of their permitted principality, deep mysteries of free will, intercession, and legal entrances prevailed. Mysteries, all of which they could glean glimmers, but never gain any real understanding. But then, how could they who were so far removed from the Lord, so unlike Him in thought and heart, ever understand that which was hidden from, and had to be diligently sought out by, those who loved Him madly and strove continually to be like Him? The demonic would *never* understand the mysteries of God. (Certainly, they understood the Bible and the Laws of the Lord. But not the mysteries. Never the mysteries.) In fact, their consciousness could barely even register that such mysteries existed. However, they knew enough to figure out that *something* much beyond them was happening and that that something had *everything* to do with legal entrances into a powerful principality.

Without a doubt, the Lord's angels had legal entrance into their domain: they had been bidden through the prayers of Maya's parents. Every day, Paul and Marie prayed Psalm 91 over Maya and asked for a legion of angels to stand guard over her and to protect her. The Lord was pleased to oblige. And so, there they were upon the orders of the Lord. The Lord had commanded them to destroy the Kali doll, the soft-murti—enough was enough! It had greater power than Maya knew or understood. Most idols did. It was just so long that the Lord would tolerate the influence of an idol around one of His.

Majesty smiled tenderly at Maya, as she stood talking to Radha. He placed his hand upon her head. Light began to radiate from his hand and flow down into her. Their eyes could perceive the glow spreading, flowing throughout her—her head, her chest, her arms and legs, even her fingers and toes.

"She is in great confusion. As you know, she gave her life to the Lord when she was twelve and, as the Lord promises concerning those who give their lives to Him, He holds them in His hand and He will not lose a single one. Never. Ever. Every single one of His will remain with Him. It is His Will and intention. This *thing*," he cast a dismissive glance about the dormitory, "that she is going through is exactly that—a *thing* she is going *through*. In the end, she will, she *must,* return to the Lord."

He paused and walked about—although his feet did not touch the floor—looking around for the demonic. It was second-nature for him to check, although he knew they had departed. He knew the evil ones had to flee from the bright presence of the Lord's angels—their very natures could not help but dispel darkness. He did not worry whether or not the evil angels overheard him, as they were incapable of understanding the heavenly language. Having been cast out of Heaven they had lost all ability to hear the truly, divinely angelic.

He stood beside Maya as she knelt down to pick up the bits and pieces of the dollish murti. Light emanated from him, from all of their beings. He continued, "She is going through such turmoil right now. Ah! The mysterious ways of humans—so much of her is committed to this. Almost to the depths of her being, she has embraced this…way…these demons. But deeper still, in her spirit, in a place only the Lord can see, she loves the Lord…has always loved the Lord…will always, and only, love the Lord. That deepest part, that most powerful and precious part, belongs to Him still. It is from this place that she is repelled and repulsed by all of this…" He waved his hand about, indicating the ashram and the Hindu life. A flash of disgust touched his face, almost imperceptible. "And yet, what draws her into this, but truly…her search, her yearning, her deep, intrinsic need for God? And He knows this. He placed this within her. As the Word says, 'He has placed eternity within the hearts of men.' Eternity…His eternity… eternally spent with Him. *That* is in her heart. She will not rest, she will not be at peace, until she returns to Him. And return she will. He will see to it—He swears upon Himself."

"And He is not a man that He should lie," Brilliant interjected. The others nodded, sparks of iridescent light shooting from their hair and eyes.

"What erupted in her!" Majesty asked rhetorically, his light pulsing gently through different soft colors, colors not of the human spectrum, the closest in the human realm being pastels although these were stronger and more potent than any human pastel. "A massive confusion of righteous anger meeting demonic rage. The eternity in her heart and the hell into which she has placed herself conflicts violently." The angels, a legion strong, nodded. Their weapons and shields glinted and sparked in the darkness. Even in a place shrouded in darkness, they reflected the light of God.

"And yet, she will be just fine," Brilliant added, placing his hand on her back. His and Majesty's lights met within her, meshing, melding, and growing brighter. "She cannot go too far. There is nowhere she can go to escape Him. No place too far, too deep, or too wide. No place too god-less or demonic.

"Here we are at His command and here we will stay to see her through," Brilliant sank into silence. Even at rest, his hair undulated as if from a power all its own. It gave off a faint iridescence. Majesty, Awe, and the others in the legion were silent, too...thinking. As they pondered the mysteries of God in relation to humans, their beings glowed brighter—various shades of ethereal yellow and orange and magenta. They loved pondering His mysteries.

Majesty nodded in agreement with Brilliant and continued, "*Such* a mystery exists—a beautiful, obscure, known-only-to-God mystery concerning human will and the redemptive power of God's grace. Ah! Throw into it true, fervent, fiery love and unflagging, heartfelt intercession... absolutely incredible! Oh! The things humans experience and are blessed to know, if they choose to look into them." He sighed audibly. "The saddest thing is that so many of them choose not to. They have the mysteries of the universe and beyond at their summons and they refuse to delve into them."

COBALT-BLUE-SARI LADY

I loathe that girl! Why can't she just leave? She is becoming the bane of my existence. Her parents' praying is burning me...burning all of us. You would think that we would grow used to it over time, but we haven't. It just burns and wears us away. How long can we burn and wear away? That was a rhetorical question. All the evil ones knew that, one day, they would be herded together and thrown into the lake of fire, forever tormented, forever burning and being worn away, forever desiring and never attaining. Truly hell...

Chamunda, being a perverse, destructive spirit, did not need rest like humans. No, spiritual beings rejuvenated differently than humans. And then, of spiritual beings, the dark ones reenergized differently than those of the light. The evil angels needed to feed off of human emotions and actions. The darker, the more perverse, the more devastating and destructive the emotions and actions, the better fed they were. She... it...could no longer recall how she rejuvenated when she had been one of the Lord's angels. She vaguely remembered that it had been inconceivably glorious and fantastically enjoyable and had something to do with directing thoughts toward the

Lord. The mere thought of the Lord flooded and infused them with joy and love, thrilled them unimaginably. Actually, she could barely remember that she had been a "he" as one of the Lord's angels—everything that had to do with that time, all of it gloriously lovely, had all but vanished from her mind. Early on, after the Angelic Rebellion, she had been able to remember well and oh how it had burned to recall and yearn for all that had been lost. But, time and God had faded all her memories away. She… he…it…had chosen its side.

At the moment, she "rested" in the Kali murti in the inner temple waiting for morning archana to begin. Nothing revived and energized her more than worship directed toward her. Archana was a big refresher. Kali Leela was an even greater one—*Aaaah! I could stay high off Kali Leela for quite a while.* The night before had been Kali Leela and she had relished it. She refused to admit that she was happy the Lord's angels had stayed away… somewhere. She was not too sure where. Sometimes she felt that they were still around but that they had "dialed down" the radiance of the Lord's Glory that flowed through them so that they were not very discoverable. *I'm sure they would not leave that idiotic Premabhakti by herself. Stupid girl! Without them, I'd have her completely and she'd be dead by now. How I hate her. How I burn to hurt her, but I can't…at least, not right now. However…I can play with others…I need to play. I'm feeling low.* In spite of the previous night being Kali Leela and thus a great energizer, Chamunda's energy was low, every day the steady drain of the Lord's angels and the parent's prayers took a little bit more of her essence.

"Madness! Insanity! Where are you?" Chamunda sang in a ghastly voice from her inanimate dwelling. "I need you…"

The others heard and immediately came to her, excited about a prospect. Crazy Kartika was getting boring—how long can one expect to get thrills out of a lost soul that merely shuffled back and forth before the bathroom stalls, its mind decimated years ago? There was nothing in her to play with—such an empty, depleted vessel. Nothing to feed on. Definitely nothing exciting.

I stepped into the temple, it was still dark outside—the sun was just beginning to peek over the horizon. Through the temple windows, I could see the heavy fog as it lay like a dense, gray blanket over the palm tree shrouded region. Tendrils of light nipped at the edges of the fog far in the distance. The air was still cool—relatively cool.

The temple was dim, with only a few lights burning, ostensibly to aid those pilgrims who had come to see Cha Ma and either lived too far away or were too exhausted after the night's festivities—*Kali Leela is always such a party*—to go home. Spent after an evening of spiritual excess and inebriation, most lay sleeping on the temple floor.

I walked...no, *shuffled* in, asana thrown carelessly over my shoulder, head hanging. Eyes aching. Dead tired. I moved oh-so-slowly between and around the prone bodies. A few of the more ambitious pilgrims were rousing themselves for archana, which was due to begin in a couple of minutes. Most, however, were still sleeping right where they had been sitting during the Leela. Last night's festivities had run, as usual, into the wee hours of the morning (granted, it had ended at 4 A.M., which was much earlier than the usual 6 or 7). Everyone, with the exception of the brahmacharinis and kitchen ammas who had to prepare breakfast, had been able to get a couple of hours of sleep before archana time. Faintly, I could hear the kitchen girls and ammas in the kitchen busily preparing breakfast—they never seemed to sleep.

I looked up toward the inner temple and saw the brahmachari who was to lead the archana drowsily arranging his asana and mantra book before he sat down. I did not recognize him, which was a good thing, perhaps. And he was not too cute, which was an even better thing, most definitely. *At least I won't be sitting here during the entire archana ogling him and daydreaming about having some poor, yawning guy as my brahmachari boyfriend.*

I chose a place to sit on the women's side, two-thirds of the way into the temple, close to the center aisle. Wearily, I spread out my asana and clumped down. Tiredness made me stumble. Everyone seemed to be moving in slow motion, clumsily, as if at any moment they could pitch over into sleep. Tiredly, I drew my shawl over my shoulders and head and huddled down within my snug little "shawl-hovel." *OK! I can tell that I'm already planning to go to sleep.* It was one thing to "happen" to fall asleep during meditation; it was an entirely "other" thing, to burrow deep into one's shawl with the intention of getting some good zzzz's. I could feel the anticipation for a snooze welling up within me. *Mmm hmmm...*

The brahmachari began the chant, "Om..." His voice was slow and thick with exhaustion.

I mumbled the reply along with the other few archana participants, "Ommm, blah, blah, blaaaah..." *Oh, help me! I'm so sleepy I'm going to fall asleep right here. How in the world am I going to make it through this entire archana?* I mused to myself not even trying to stifle a big, mouthy yawn. *I'm not going to make it! I admit it.*

The brahmachari intoned the next name of the goddess, "Omm shree..." Sure enough, the chant had chugged off in its own lethargic way.

After a couple of minutes, I peered from under my shawl cocoon at the few people still sitting for the chanting. It seemed that even of the brave few, more than a couple had caved to sleepiness and had lain back down. The dense air of spiritual lassitude was growing thicker by the second. Lazily I rocked back and forth, as I responded to the languid intonations of the brahmachari. Time sluggishly passed, as we seemed to be caught in a thick, non-thinking fog, when suddenly...

BOOM!

And then, *BAM!*

The stillness-shattering noises exploded in the back. Immediately, everyone who was awake for the archana whipped around to look and some who were asleep popped up to look, so loud was the noise. The "BOOM" had come from the large, wooden, front doors of the temple as they had been shoved open and had whacked against the walls. After slamming against the walls, they swung back and hammered into each other with a loud "BAM!" The initiator of the heaving doors was a lovely, classy-looking Indian lady who appeared to be in her mid-twenties and who was, at the very moment...*sprinting*...down the center aisle toward the inner temple.

Involuntarily, I sucked in a surprised breath—*this* was a sight I had never seen while living in India: an Indian woman—a BEAUTIFUL, appearing to "have-it-all-together," probably of the Brahmin caste Indian women—in a fastidiously ironed, perfectly fitting, absolutely GORGEOUS cobalt blue sari. (Let me pause to talk about the exquisite sari because even as she ran in my direction, intent upon the inner temple, I could not help but be impressed—it was an incredibly deep cobalt blue, with large splashes of vibrant orange, yellow, and red flowers. It had a golden, embroidered, filigree-ish border. It had to have cost a pretty penny. And it fit perfectly. Simply lovely!)

And there she was! Cobalt-blue-sari lady! Running through the temple…right down the center aisle, between the men and the women's sides. Her bare feet pounding, *Thoom! Thoom! Thoom!*, as she sprinted the length of the temple. Even as she ran, her sari did not fall out of place—the gold, embroidered edge, drawn over her tightly-knotted bun so that her shoulders were covered (not unlike a cape), stayed in perfect position. It was such an oxymoronic sight—a beautiful, exquisitely dressed, and pulled together Indian lady running for all she was worth down the length of the temple. Her face determined. Her jaw resolute.

I could not help but be transfixed. For that matter, *everyone* was transfixed…captivated…by her—cobalt-blue-sari lady! When she came to the sound system that sat halfway to the inner temple in the center aisle, she leapt…*hurdled*…over it effortlessly. Her right leg shot out in front of her, straight, high, parallel to the sound system. Her left leg followed, bent, as if she were a professional Olympic hurdler. Her form was beautiful. Her right foot hit the floor and she kept running—the sound system had not slowed her mad dash one bit.

Strangely enough, we—the brahmachari and morning chanters—did not stop our chanting. That was because of the rule that archana, once begun, must never be stopped—*that* rule was a given. So we did not stop. We chanted, now fully engrossed in what she was doing, from memory. Excitedly. Vociferously. The names of Devi rolled off our tongues with no thought. I know I continued to chant and did not even glance at the chant book the moment cobalt-blue-sari lady had slammed through the front entrance. Little did we know that the chanting itself, the *very* sound, was stirring up what was inside of, and around, her.

I watched in rapt attention, curious as to what she was going to do, when she reached the inner temple. I did not have time to ponder. She approached the three steps of the temple at full-tilt. Right before her feet hit the steps, she hurled herself forward. All I could think was—*Superman!*—as she launched herself into the air. The momentum gained from running propelled her body forward in a prone position into the inner temple. Her arms were stretched out in front of her, her legs behind. The edge of her sari still sat on her shoulders, the tail of it, which would normally hang behind her to her thighs, was now floating behind her—like Superman's cape. I could not help but marvel—*Wow! She looks like Superman! She's so graceful!*

She hit the ground in the same prone position and slid on her belly into the murti of Kali. Right before she reached it, she pulled herself up to her knees. The gracefulness of her movements, the *unusualness* of her movements, seemed weirdly "*unhuman.*" On her knees, she immediately began to pull the jewelry and clothing off the murti, screaming, "KALI! KALI!" at the top of her lungs. Her voice evinced an unmitigated wildness...an untameable franticness.

"OM SHIVA SHAKTYAIKYA..."

"OM SHEEVUH SHUKTEEYAYKAY ROOPINYAY NAWMUHHUH!" we thundered as we kept chanting...by now, *screaming* the names—completely carried away by the excitement and craziness.

"OM PARA SHAKTYAI NAMAHA!" The brahmachari, who was wide-eyed with amazement and screaming the names in a frenzy, was at the same time, frantically gesticulating toward her. It was evident in his face and gestures that someone...*anyone*...needed to come get her, needed to come and rescue our beloved Kali murti from the psycho-woman.

Some of the men jumped up and ran onto the stage (not in any way as gracefully and beautifully as her!) to come and help, but they stopped in their tracks. They looked from the woman to the brahmachari to the woman and back again. They were constrained by the hard and fast rule of the ashram—MEN ARE NOT TO TOUCH WOMEN!! and vice versa. Their bodies seemed frozen into positions of "wanting to help, willing to help, but do not dare."

"KALI! KALI!" she screamed.

The men backed up a bit and looked back into the outer temple where we all sat, panic and confusion plastered upon their faces, as the woman continued to rip off the murti's clothing (bits and pieces of cloth and jewelry were flying *everywhere*) and scream, "KALI! KALI!"

We in the outer temple continued to shriek the names of Devi at the top of our lungs as the brahmachari continued to lead us by screaming the names while at the same time motioning wildly at her. Pure pandemonium had broken out!

"OM SHEEVUH SHUKTEEYAYKAY ROOPINYAY NAWMUHHUH!" we screamed.

"KALI! KALI! KALI!" she shrieked back as she snapped one of the skull malas off the Kali murti's neck. Large flesh-colored beads carved to look like human faces shot into the air. The brahmachari ducked.

"OM SHREE LALITA . . ." he hurled out.

I looked around the temple for an answer. *Who's going to help? What's going to happen? She can't continue ripping the murti to bits!*

"OM SHEEVUH SHUKTEEYAYKAY ROOPINYAY NAWMUHHUH!"

Out of the corner of my eye, I saw a flash of white! My head snapped to the back of the temple! *Ah! Yes! The kitchen ammas! I didn't even know they were in here.* They were running down the length of the temple. *I didn't know they could run!* The "mothers" of the ashram—the older, matronly, much more mature, sedate, settled women, the "mamas"—had come to save the day. It looked to be 10 or 12 of them. Saris gleaming white. The trailing edge tucked in neatly at their hip—a sure sign they intended to do some work. They came running from behind us on both sides.

"KALI! KAAAALI!" The woman howled as she shook her head ferociously. She had grabbed the limb-skirt on the murti and was pulling for all she was worth.

The brahmachari yelled, *"OM MAHA KALYAI NAMAHA!"*

The kitchen ammas leapt over the three steps into the inner temple in single bounds. They grabbed the screaming woman's arms as she continued to "arrange" what remained of Kali's clothes and jewelry. She howled, "KAAALI!" as if she were a wild, rabid catwoman and easily threw them off her. They fell back, looked at each other, and redoubled their efforts, resolution set in their eyes.

"OM SHEEVUH SHUKTEEYAYKAY ROOPINYAY NAWMUHHUH!" we called in a frenzy.

They pounced upon her again. This time, their hold held. They were able to drag her away from the murti and, half-staggering/half-dragging, pull her to her feet. She kept lurching toward the murti—intent upon rearranging—*destroying*—it. It was hard to say what was going on in her mind.

What *was* going on in her mind? A war…and it was raging all around her; however, not really a full-on war as there was no opposition. The demons were in a vicious frenzy—something about the scent of a human on the brink of madness—insatiably drove their thirst. They were rabid with a desire for an unseen, intangible, all too real blood—the blood of a mind ruined…a heart torn…a life, still living yet on the brink of being forever lost. They screamed at her, "Kali! Kali! Kali!"…a discordant chant, deafening in her mind, obliterating all other sounds, yes, even all other thoughts. Swirls of deep, richly disturbing tones and colors shot past and at her. All had a pervading, underlying tone of darkness and despair—mustardy and ruddy, muddy and gray.

"Kali! Kali!" they shrieked and pushed images into her weak, on-the-verge-of-irretrievable-chaos mind. They felt their power growing, enlarging. More and more evil beings came and began to swirl about her. Such an invitation! A fragile mind teetering on the precipice of utter destruction.

Suicide, Despair, Hatred, Insanity, Deception, and many others were embroiled in spiritual bloodlust. Leading them was Madness. The others gave a berth around Madness for it was a creature that even *they* did not care to have around because of his penchant for deluding...*seducing* a mind...*any* mind (and spiritual beings have minds)...into chaos; and no one, *no thing*, no matter how diabolical and evil, wants to lose its *own* mind. As the morning crowd chanted loudly and fiercely, unwittingly caught up in the drama that unfolded in the inner temple, the demons sucked in deeply of the power-laden words and increased their activity.

"OM SHEEVUH SHUKTEEYAYKAY ROOPINYAY NAWMUHHUH!" Thoroughly engrossed in the excitement (my eyes, surely, the size of saucers), I screamed along with the others. The kitchen ammas struggled with the woman from one side of the inner temple to another. They would disappear from view and appear again as they fought her. I was entirely spellbound, and oddly, found it humorous and entertaining to see the way they struggled back and forth with her in the inner temple.

They were finally able to wrestle her to the women's side and onto the back balcony. Once on the balcony, they continued to struggle back and forth with her. I could see them here and there as they fought.

Our chanting began to die down as we were on the last couple of names of Devi.

"Om chamundayai namaha," the brahmachari said.

"Om shiva shaktiyaikya rupinyai namaha," we responded.

"Om shiva shaktiyaikya rupinyai namaha," the brahmachari muttered, his focus still on the woman and the kitchen ammas.

"Om shiva shaktiyaikya rupinyai namaha," we replied.

As our chanting died away so, too, did her stringent cries for Kali. She struggled weakly against the kitchen ammas. She, who had been herculeanly strong, was as weak and pitiful as a newborn kitten. The kitchen ammas easily lifted her up, carried her down the back stairs, and away. A queer hush descended upon the temple as we finished up the chanting—the atmosphere itself felt exhausted and spent. Random images of the lady kept going through my mind for the remainder of the archana.

As soon as archana was over, I ran upstairs to tell anyone who would listen about cobalt-blue-sari lady. "You should have been at archana this morning," I told a sleepy Karuna after awakening her in great excitement. I launched into my rendition as the other Western women who slept in the dorm gathered around to hear the unfolding of the morning's strange events. Yes, in less than ten minutes, cobalt-blue-sari lady had become an anecdote.

Soon it was time for chai, then breakfast…then the morning Upanishads lesson with Funeral Swami. The day picked up its pace as the afternoon slipped by quickly, the end of which found me outside sitting by a fire, nursing one of my "soups." Somewhere in the activities of the day, I had forgotten all about cobalt-blue-sari lady—she was simply another person among many.

"Hey! Premabhakti! I need your help." It was Clyda. She was a character unto herself. Strong-willed. Domineering. American. Although she did not tower over the men physically, in masculinity and aggressiveness she dwarfed them.

Clyda approached me as I sat on my favorite rock out behind the kitchen. She eyed my pot warily as she put her hands on her hips, elbows akimbo, feet planted wide apart in a masculine power-stance. Every time I looked at her, I could not help but marvel at her courage (boldness?… sheer craziness?).

In the midst of a very traditional Southern India where the usual garb for a woman was a sari (even a punjabi set was a little on the liberal, rebellious side), Clyda chose to wear a pair of white punjabi pants (by traditional

Indian standards—female underwear when uncovered by the long punjabi top) and a man's white, short-cropped top (unheard-of on a woman!). The punjabi pants hung on her hips and did not quite meet the man's top so that two inches of her midriff was exposed, which left her looking starkly, peculiarly, half-naked. She finished off the ensemble with a five-inch wide, Iron John, deluxe-sized leather toolbelt—full of hammers, screwdrivers, wrenches, and the like—which hung off her hips as well. The toolbelt served only to accentuate the gathers of the punjabi pants and emphasized the fact that she was wearing underpants (pantaloons, if you will) as a pair of pants.

Clyda has come into the kitchen! I could not...did not even *try*...to hide my incredulity at her entering the kitchen. That was something new. Clyda *never* set foot into the kitchen, the women's domain. Clyda abhorred all things female and tended to stick with the males. She was handier with tools and carpentry than any man in the ashram. Thus, she had gained the not-so-highly-coveted spot of ashram handy man. She was a spectacle, a curiosity, in everyone's eyes.

This must be serious! Clyda did look serious, and somehow, slightly reminiscent of John Wayne, the way she had swaggered in, her thumbs caught in her work belt.

So, there she stood, with her hands hooked into her belt, eyeing me.

"What's up?" I asked, wiping my sooty hands on my sootier blue work skirt. I stood up and stirred the soup. I did not need to stir it too much as the fire was dying down. The soup was almost done.

"We have a situation and we need someone strong. We figured you'd be a good one to help," she said as she slid her hands back and forth over the top of the toolbelt and rehooked her thumbs in the front of it. *John Wayne female-style.*

Someone strong? What about all the men in the ashram? "What about all the men in the ashram?" I asked.

261

"Well, you know the Indian men…they're not too strong. Not for what we have to do. And besides, no man can help. This has to be a woman. You'll see."

"Hmmm…well…" I hesitated for drama's sake because I was certainly game. *I wonder what's up?* I put down the large spoon. "Are we doing crowd control?" *I don't want to do crowd control.* Often, the Western women were called to do crowd control because we tended to be so big and strong in comparison to the Indians. Why were the Western men not called to crowd control? I had not a clue. *Probably has something to do with women needing to ground themselves.*

"Ha! Ha!" Clyda belted out a deep laugh, throwing back her head in mirth. "Oh no! Something infinitely more interesting," she said cryptically and winked at me.

"OK." I wiped my hands, again, on my sooty skirt. "I'll help."

"Good! Just follow what I do and do exactly what I say to do," she ordered mysteriously. She definitely had my interest. She turned and quickly strode away, toolbelt clanking. I did not give another thought to my soup as I ran to catch up with her.

We passed through the Western and Indian canteens and walked the short distance over to the temple. We took some side steps that led down into the first floor, or basement (depending upon how you looked at it) apartments.

"Here we are…the cells…" Clyda murmured. That was what we, in the ashram, called the little first floor rooms. The windows were level with the ground: small rectangles about a foot high and a foot and a half wide. Vertical bars covered the windows to protect those inside from outsiders. Or perhaps…to protect those outside from whomever was inside.

We took a couple of steps and halted in front of the first door on our left. People, Indians, were standing around, whispering to each other. Hands over their mouths in a gesture of respect…or of fear.

Bri. Durgamma stood in front of the door. She looked to be guarding it. Clyda stopped in front of her. She leaned forward and whispered something to Durgamma, who, in turn, looked over her shoulder at me. Her eyes narrowed as she sized me up, not at all trying to hide it. I must have passed the test because she stepped away from the door, which was padlocked.

Clyda fished a key from many that were on a huge, overladen key ring attached to her toolbelt. "Here we go…" she mumbled more to herself than to anyone else as she unlocked the lock. "OK, now, don't forget…just follow my lead," she commanded as she entered the room.

I stepped in behind her, excitedly…gamely, surely not expecting to see what I saw. Immediately, an intense sense of dismay and sadness coupled with a strange sort of disgust washed over me at the sight that greeted me.

The room was small, as were all the basement rooms, no more than ten feet by ten feet. It was completely bare. Empty. Cold, although it was hot outside. The walls were whitewashed and had faded to a dingy, nondescript, light gray. The room felt lonely and forlorn. The late afternoon light filtered in from the small, dirty window that was near the ceiling, but it did not seem to touch the sallow walls. *No wonder they call these rooms "the cells."* It was like a prison cell, but worse.

However, that was not what bothered me. No, what *disturbed* me, viscerally, was…*what* was lying on the floor in the middle of the room. I would not have recognized it…her…had it not been for the vibrant, cobalt blue with splashes of bright red, orange, and yellow that taunted me—*Cobalt-blue-sari lady!*—now more like, pitifully-pathetic-lady. My heart went out to her, whilst simultaneously shrinking back in repulsion.

She was lying on her left side, her body facing us, in a loose, fetal position. She was moving faintly, in her own smeared blood and foam for she was frothing at the mouth. It appeared she had been bleeding and frothing for a long time as it was drying on the floor and on her body. Her long, long hair, which had been in a sleek, tight bun this morning, was undone, wild, clotted, like an animal's, partially matted to her face. Her still-gorgeous, cobalt blue sari—an incongruous contrast to the mood of the room and her behavior and appearance—lay half off her body. Luckily, her choli and petticoat were still on her, but they were rumpled, dirty, and had splotches of blood on them. She held a japa mala in her hand, unused, unnoticed, by her. Dully, she was banging her head on the floor, murmuring to no one in particular, in a flat, raspy voice, *"Kali...Kali..."* The sound of her voice...the very sight of her...of *what* she had become chilled me to the bone, scared me, horrified me, hurt my heart...*disgusted* me. A plethora of emotions surged through my body. All of this held me arrested at the door, my hand still grasping the handle.

"Premabhakti!" Clyda barked sharply at me. "Come on and help me!" My attention snapped to her—*What's she doing near that...?* "I need you to help me tie her up! I chose you because I thought you could handle this." I heard an edge of frustration in her voice. "Come on! Now!"

I hurried in and closed the door behind me. Right then, the woman's moans turned into a high-pitched, ululating whine that ended in a grav- elly, deep, guttural, "KALI!" So gutteral and deep it should have come from a heavyset, barrel-chested man. She had lifted her head and was looking at Clyda with wild eyes full of unspeakable fury and rage. Foam, speckled pink with blood, was around her mouth and was dripping onto the floor. Her forehead was bruised and slightly bloody from the hours of banging it on the cement. (Why it was not bloodier given the hours of banging was a mystery.) The cement underneath her was wet from her blood and foam- ing mouth.

Again, a chill flew down my spine, colder than the first time. I wanted to run; but my body was frozen in place.

"Let's get her!" Clyda ordered as she quickly moved toward the woman, pulling out a length of thick rope from a pocket in her work belt. *Where in the world did she have the rope hidden? And how in the world can she run up to this mad woman...like she's done this plenty times before?!* These thoughts shot through my mind as though fired from a pistol and although my entire being strained to be out the door, it unwillingly followed Clyda toward the woman. I could not believe I was moving—*voluntarily!*—toward a madwoman.

As we closed in on her, she began to growl in a rough, gravelly voice and flail about frenetically. "Grab her legs and I'll grab her arms!" Clyda commanded as she snapped a length of the rope crisply between her hands. "Watch out and don't let her get close enough to bite you!" *Bite me?!* I had seen only one real human-on-human bite in all my life. (When I was in high school, I had watched the shortest-lived fight ever between a boy and girl. He had picked it. She was desperate. Before he knew what was happening, she had grabbed his face and bit into his cheek. The bite had been yucky and ragged. For some reason, I was pretty sure the bite of a frothing-at-the-mouth madwoman would be much worse.) *Ugh! Bite me?* I faltered. My resolve was in no way up to the challenge.

"C'MON NOW!" Clyda demanded. I jerked into motion, again. We quickly moved in. I reached for the madwoman's legs but she was kicking too hard. Before I even thought about it, I dropped down on one knee, sinking it heavily, unmercifully, into her stomach. That pinned down her midsection. I leaned forward, grabbed her legs, and held them down. Clyda grabbed her arms and twisted them roughly behind her back. I winced. *I hope she doesn't break them!* I thought to myself well aware of the amount of force we were using with the woman. But, it took every bit of our might as she struggled powerfully, insanely, against us. Clyda finished tying her hands behind her. We rolled her over and tied her legs with the same rope as her arms so that she was bent backward into a grotesque backbend.

Even as I busily helped bind her, thoughts coursed through my mind—*How did this happen?! She is so ugly!* How true! She was no longer beautiful. There was absolutely nothing lovely about her (except her sari). She was ugly. Everything about her was hideous. Repulsive.

The moment we were done binding her, I jumped away from her growling, vainly jerking body. I did not want to stand too close to her. I wanted to run away. A part of me, a deep, unspoken, unnoticed part of me was afraid that whatever was going on with her was contagious. A contagious disease of some sort...that made a person roll around on the ground in mindless oblivion. I backed toward the closed door, fascinated by the hoarsely breathing woman...*thing*. She stared at us with malevolent, *unhu*-man eyes.

I looked down. My sooty skirt was damp with her blood and froth; in some places the soot, blood, and froth had caked together. I was sweating and trembling. I looked at Clyda. She was standing in her usual John Wayne stance. Her demeanor was calm and steady; and her clothes were still neat and white, as if she had done this plenty of times before and had mastered the technique a long time ago. My mind wanted to think on some crucial point concerning all this...but deep inside, I dared not.

"What happened to her?" I whispered to Clyda, as I stood against the door.

"You haven't heard about her?!" Clyda threw me a wide-eyed look.

I shook my head, my eyes still riveted on the woman. "I remember her from this morning..."

"You haven't heard about her brother, either, then?"

"No, I didn't even know she had a brother..."

"Yeah..." Clyda drawled as she leaned against the door beside me, thumbs hooked in her work belt. She was looking at the woman as though she were an animal in the zoo—purely entertainment. She continued— her voice conversational and pleasant, "Apparently, she and her brother came last night. He had been drinking. The high energy of this place and alcohol were a bad mix. He went crazy last night. Did you hear someone screaming last night, 'Kali! Kali!' in a guy's voice?" Clyda did not wait for me to respond, "Well, that was him. He lost it. Went cuckoo...bonkers... we had to put him in a cell last night. He's in the cell across the way. He stopped screaming and yelling some time early this morning. Now he's just quiet, moaning and growling to himself."

Clyda took a few steps toward the woman and looked her over. "I think she's messed herself up much worse than him..." She hitched her head, indicating to me to move out of the way. When I did, she opened the door and walked out. "C'mon. We're done."

I followed her, looking back one more time at the once beautiful and so-well-put-together, now completely insane and hideously ugly woman. My heart hurt for her. She was pitiful, moaning, "Kali...Kali..." I knew her mind had been destroyed forever. Some treacherous "sensation," some precarious "feeling" seized me deep inside. I could not, I would not...I *dared not*...look at it or even acknowledge it. I tried to push "it" to the back of my mind and leave it there as I walked out of the room.

I headed back to the kitchen to check on the soup. When I was done stirring it, I sat down to think. What had just happened, coupled with Clyda's words, sent a frigid chill down my spine of pure, unadulterated fear...the cause of it unrecognizable, dangerous, which made it all the more frightening. I was getting glimmerings of something, some phenomenon that was much greater than I was, and much, much more deadly—*This is not fun ashram life in India anymore*. It was young men dying and anguished, devastated wives staring at the burning pyre. It was men going crazy and women losing their minds and banging their heads on cement floors. It was blank-eyed girls, who were once innocently beautiful, yet now so corrupted and denigrated that they blended into the nasty décor of a public toilet. It was the loss of deep significance to a human life, the loss of what makes a human a *person*, and nobody cared except to speak of the person as an anecdote and curiosity. Even I was guilty of it.

I did not know, at the time, that I would be continually haunted by the image...the *specter*...of a once-beautiful woman gone hideous and crazed. I did not know that I would never forget the foaming mouth, the bloody forehead, the mindless banging of her head, the angry and rageful and altogether *un*human eyes. I did not know that I would be plagued by recollections of binding her feet, of sinking my knee into her stomach as another viciously twisted her body and bound her hands, all actions that do not settle well with the human soul.

The next morning, I walked around the corner of the ashram building into the back area of the brahmachari huts. Near the temple building was a white car. I asked one of the gawking bystanders what was going on and was told that help had come to take care of the woman and her brother. I was told that they were to be admitted to the nearest mental institution and that no one expected them to ever get better. (Months later, when I thought to ask after them, I received no real answer. I continued asking around the ashram. Finally, I asked Bri. Lakshmini, who informed me that they were still the same—they had permanently, irretrievably, lost their minds. Just like Kartika. The "rarefied" air of the ashram, the vibrations, the "high" energies could cause incurable insanity, Lakshmini told me, not at all bothered. I, however, was intensely perturbed and spent a great deal of time trying not to think about it; instead, I buried my thoughts deeper and deeper.)

Later that evening, I ran into Karuna near the brahmacharini huts. I told her the rest of the story about cobalt-blue-sari lady. I tried to voice my concerns, my fears, and worries. Karuna smiled and nodded; but I could see that my concerns did not have much of an impact upon her. Perhaps because she had not seen her...most definitely because she had not taken part in tying her up. *I'll never forget that!* We walked along the edge of the temple and up the back staircase. We stopped on the balcony of the women's dorm. Our way into the dorm was blocked by large piles of clothing that lay heaped on the floor of the balcony.

"Who did that?" Karuna asked, nodding her head toward the piles.

"I don't know..." I responded, puzzled. My mind flew back to the conversation I had had with the brahmacharini, Parvati, at the washing stones months ago when she had told me not to hang my clothes out after dark. *Does it have anything to do with that? I wonder what it means...*

"Namah shivaya," Karuna stopped a British woman who was walking by, "Why are all the clothes on the ground?"

The woman shrugged nonchalantly and rewrapped her shawl around her shoulders. "One of the swaminis came by a few minutes ago and took the clothes down."

"Why? They're all dirty now." I was curious but not upset, since they were not my clothes.

The woman shrugged her shoulders again. "I don't know. All they said was that Cha Ma says, 'No clothes hanging after sunset.' She sent them to take them down." She gave a flimsy, disinterested smile and strolled off, chanting her mantra.

I kept rolling the conversation I had had with Parvati around and around in my mind—*What's up with that? I wish she had told me more...*

Marie
United States

I have to pray...not for myself, but for Maya. Marie blinked her eyes, nothing changed—black spots continued dancing before her eyes. *How long before the spots turn to webbing?* Of the two, she disliked the webbing more than the spots. There was something sinister about the webs. They made her feel as if *something* were wrapping itself about her, wrapping thin, wiry fingers or long, viselike tentacles around her. Intending to suffocate her. Kill her.

Marie, although she prompted herself, did not start praying; instead, she started worrying. *My eyesight is growing steadily worse. Sometimes I can barely see—between the black spots and the webbing. Am I going to lose my eyesight altogether, like the doctors have suggested might happen?* Her heart started pounding faster. Even the thought of losing her eyesight scared her, maybe even more than death. *What would that be like? I never thought I'd go blind.* The throbbing behind her eyes suddenly, horrifically, spiked, as if someone had shoved daggers into her eyes. *My head hurts constantly. And now this! Lord! What is going on? Even in my sleep, the pain's at me. Maybe if I lay down, my headache will ease...of course, it won't....*

Marie lay down on the bathroom floor. The cold tile felt cool to her hot, paining face. Although it felt good, it did not bring relief to the pain in her head. *Weeks later and the doctors still have yet to find an answer. They're sure it's a brain tumor, but they just can't find it. I know I've got to stop thinking about this...*Marie was certainly going around and around in her own head. *I know worrying doesn't help me...but I can't seem to stop myself. A brain tumor...a brain tumor... And they tell me I'm going to die if they can't find the tumor because my condition is worsening so quickly. How can it be that I'll probably die before I ever see Maya again? Would she even care now? What does she think about all this?*

Marie's mind went over her attempts to call Maya in India. *Thank good-ness she finally sent her address and phone number to me.* Marie had started trying to call her a little less than a month ago in order to tell her about her condition—that she was dying (Clearly, some part of Marie had accepted the possibility stated by the doctors as fact.)—but she never got through.

Most of the time, her call was relayed from one operator to another until it was dropped. However, a couple of times, her call made it to the ashram only for her to be told that there was no Maya living there.

What if I die before I see her? With that thought, Marie felt tears of pain and hurt welling up. Frustration seemed to press through her insides and up into her head. She could not distinguish if she was crying from hurt or from frustration and anger. Her tears made her head throb. Stabbing pains shot through her eyes to lodge deep within her head. It felt almost as though someone were shoving red-hot irons into her eyes.

Marie could not see—standing beside her was Jovial. He wanted to act; but she was giving him nothing upon which to act. She needed to pray— she *had* to pray something more than her worries in order for the Lord to release him. But, she had not, so Jovial stood beside her, shifting restlessly. *Just one word!*—he urged silently. He could not say anything aloud—he did not want, was not permitted, to create a suggestion in her mind.

He dared not open his mouth for he knew that any word from him would become a suggestion in her mind…sometimes permissible when there was intercession that called for it, but in situations like this—times of testing, no. Suggestions were not permitted. The Lord's Law demanded that humans originate prayers from their hearts, from their desires; not that angels create them out of their own angelic will, even if it was in line with the Lord's Will. Free will. This is where the dark angels manipulated and usurped—suggesting, hinting…planting an idea in a human that the human would then believe was his or her own. (Humans were so quick to own a thought, never once considering the origin of the thought and if it was even their own.) *Direct violation of the Lord's Law*—Jovial thought to himself as grimly as his nature would allow. He looked around and allowed another grin to pop out as he placed his mind on other things—*Even two seconds contemplating the dark ones is two seconds too long.*

He placed his mind back on the Lord's plans for her. The Lord wished to reveal what lay hidden deep in Marie's heart—the good and the bad.

The bad needed to be seen in order to be destroyed. The good, that which was pure and righteous in her, needed to be drawn to the top in order to be reclaimed by Him, so that one day He could magnify it and cause it to shine before the world. In the Lord's realm, in the dimension where time and space did not exist and all was perfectly as it should be, she was already wholly reclaimed—pure and righteous. In that place, all that was righteous and good within her had already been magnified and caused to shine for all eternity.

Even in the waiting, he exuded the attitude that gave him the name, Jovial. Joy, exuberant and unchanging, was coupled with an intrinsic, unquenchable proclivity toward laughter and humor. A slight smirk of delight danced across his mouth. *Pray, Marie! Pray! Go to church. Do something other than sitting here making yourself depressed. See the joy of the Lord. Count it all joy. Pray! Help me to help you!*

Marie thought of her husband, Paul, who was sure to be in the den— *In the dark, no doubt.* Marie knew he was praying. She had grown to learn that when he sat alone he usually prayed and talked to God. Whatever it was he said to God, she did not hear. He spoke so quietly, under his breath. Here and there, she would hear snatches of his conversation with God, "Lord, please…" or "Father, if…" or "I just don't…"

This night, she tried to pray. To no avail. *It's Wednesday…I'll go to church.* She pushed herself up from the bathroom floor. Her head throbbed so violently she felt nauseous. She clamped her jaws together, not that she would throw up. She never did. *It would almost be a relief to throw up…maybe ease some of this pain or, if anything, make me focus on something other than this headache. Oh Lord, please…*

She went to the hall and called quietly, trying to baby her headache, "Paul! I'm going to church. You want to come?"

"Sure, OK."

She headed to their bedroom as she massaged her temples.

As they drew nearer to the church's front entrance, Marie could hear strains of the music. It seemed to swell through the wooden structure itself. The church was a cluster of buildings. All of the buildings were wooden and put one in the mind of a grouping of variously sized log cabins. The main sanctuary was the largest. For Paul and Marie, it was spiritual home. The Lord was there. Always. They loved to worship God, spend time before Him, enjoy Him. Just the sight of the buildings lifted her spirit.

Paul pulled open the door of the main sanctuary to allow her to enter—the music poured outside. It was slow and powerful, deep and rich. *They're already in worship? That's unusual.* They were early, as usual. Paul liked to be on time. Marie recalled the time Maya had joked that Paul, in heading out to Sunday morning church, would have left Jesus behind if He had been late. Marie took several deep breaths as they walked through the foyer, into the sanctuary, and down the center aisle. Immediately, her headache began to ease.

The sanctuary was comfortably full with at least 500 people. The crowd was mixed—blacks and whites, Asians and Latinos, elderly and young. Most everyone was engaged in worshiping—their eyes closed, heads thrown back singing, arms raised—saluting, greeting, reaching for God. Whenever she walked into the sanctuary, she could not help but think, every single time—*This is what Heaven looks like!*—It was a thought that was so welcome and comforting.

She led the way down the center aisle and found two open seats next to the aisle near the front. Once there, she just stood, still, listening...feeling... Tears began to well up inside of her.

The praise and worship team had shifted into a song of spontaneous worship. The worship leader nodded to the guitarist who began playing from his heart, thrumming his love for the Lord. The pianist and drummer stayed with him as they all melded together into a fluid, passionate song of worship. The band flowed in the Spirit, as if on a river, carrying the congregation along with them.

The worship leader began to sing an impromptu song from her heart. Her voice was rich and earthy.

"We hear You, Lord…

We hear You.

We love You…love You…

Adore You.

You are everything to us. You are everything to us.

Nothing…no one…is lovely like You."

Underlying her voice, others started singing harmoniously in the Spirit. Their voices wove in between the melodies of the guitar and drums, the violin and piano. A flutist played and the notes of the flute floated atop all the other sounds—reaching and straining toward God. Underlying the harmony and melodies was the beat. So deep and full, it seemed the heartbeat of God. The music rolled along, powerfully, deeply. A massive river. As the music grew fuller and stronger, the congregation's singing in the spirit grew more passionate and richer—melody wove harmoniously upon melody. The congregation pressed with the worship team straight up into the Throne Room.

Engrossed with them in the worship was a myriad of angels—all of differing duties and services. Ministering angels were present and stood intermingled with the people. Larger and brighter than the humans. Guardian angels were dispersed throughout the congregation, too, worshiping beside the person to whom they had been assigned from before the beginning of time. Of the angels, they came the closest to appearing human. So often, needing to intervene in human activity, so often, needing to appear to a human, God allowed them a similarity to the humans. But, even with such a likeness, they were still supernaturally vibrant and glorious. If they did not remember to "dial down" their splendor when appearing to humans, they tended to cause the frail beings to faint upon sight of them. Warrior angels stood around the perimeter...within and without the building, not fully minding physical laws. They dwarfed the humans. Their swords were sheathed (for the passionate worship had caused every demonic entity to flee). In fact, that was the reason Marie's headache and nausea had disappeared. The weapons and armor of the warring angels glinted with silvery white and bright golden flashes. Angels, whose sole purpose was to worship the Lord, descended from Heaven...hundreds... not minding any physical laws. They stood...floated...wherever they chose, within and without the sanctuary. And though not attentive to the physical laws of the earth, they were ever mindful of the Laws of the Lord—their ranks maintained perfect order and form and beauty. They joined in the worship, singing with all their hearts. As they sang, their entire beings shifted into living instruments as melodious sounds emanated from them.

No matter the duty of the angels, all of them were thoroughly enwrapt in the worship. Like the humans, their arms were raised. Soft, gentle light radiated from their bodies. Divine, luminous light streamed from their eyes and hands and soared upward, piercing the sky. Their eyes stared into Heaven because they could see...the Lord, Jesus, responding.

He arose from His Throne at the right side of His Father...*the Father...* and stepped down from Heaven...and if any human had had eyes to see... Oh! How joyously did the laws of physics, light, and sound play within Him. All was nothing but a dance to Him! He existed within a particle, so minuscule that one particle was like a universe about Him. He was so vastly diminutive that quarks and mesons existed for an eternity in His eye and was so intricately aware that each one danced slowly before, and particularly for, Him and was acknowledged, in return, by Him. Simultaneously, He was so massive that He could consume the entire universe with a single indrawn breath. The universe was less than a quantum to Him so immeasurably great and vast was He. Yet and still, He heard and saw everything that was within that universe which fit in the span of His hand from the tip of His thumb to the end of His little finger. He saw every beat of every sparrow's wing through the ages, He heard the sound of every tree that fell in every forest, and knew every plant and organism that had been and would be affected and would grow from it. He heard and saw all.

So, it was no extraordinary thing that He was watching Marie and Paul within that church. He attentively listened to each one of the notes they sang. He caringly willed each one of their heartbeats. Had He not, had He been neglectful for even a nanosecond, they would have perished in that instant. Such was the case for every human alive. In fact, the entire universe hinged dependently, breathlessly, upon His conscious Will and ardent Desire—in every instant for all time, He breathed life into all things that ever existed.

Jesus heard their song. He listened to their prayers. Even more deeply, He saw the prayers of their hearts. And He responded. Within those minutes of worship (each moment to Him as long and full as an eternity, each moment that ever happened ever present to His awareness—past, present, and future folded in upon itself—as He noticed, watched, and attended to incalculable beings, not merely those human), He nodded to an angel, a six-winged seraphim who served within the Throne Room.

The angel tenderly…reverently…lifted a clear, delicate bottle that was etched with a fine filigree of gold. Bowing, he handed the bottle to the Lord. The Lord opened His hand—His infinitely immense, yet sub-molecularly-sized hand—and allowed the angel to place it in His palm. The vessel sat nestled comfortably there. Flames rose from His palm, His nature—all-consuming fire, He whose jealousy burned brighter and hotter than any flame—could not be denied. The flames grew brighter and hungrily licked at the vessel and its contents; what remained was a more transparent vessel that contained a beautiful, fragrant liquid. The flames had merely refined and purified the vessel and its contents.

The Lord stepped forward and as He moved into and through the human dimension, He gathered time and space about Himself. Time bent, warped, and wove around Him. Space sparked and danced to suit Him. Some ethereal similitude of human substance knit about Him. He continued forward…drawn by the pure worship of imperfect vessels. Always He could not resist—He dwelled among those who worshiped Him. Their worship and adoration pierced Him, suffused Him, infused Him. No, He did not *need* their worship, but oh how He responded to, and *reveled* in, it. And in receiving it, Who He was—love and kindness and goodness itself—poured and rolled out of Him.

As He came forward, the seraphim of the Throne Room remained and called aloud His nature down through the path He created through the heavens, "Holy! Holy! Holy!" Their words wove and flowed down from Heaven, touching the angelic and human worshipers. Facing Him, drunk in the magnificent glory of Him, the Creator and Master of all things, were the humans (completely unaware of the glorious scene that was unfolding in the supernatural) and the angels. Innumerable angels—ministering and guardian angels who walked amongst the people in the church, warring angels who stood around the periphery of the sanctuary, angels of worship whose nature it was to praise and worship the Lord were thoroughly engrossed in the worship. A majestic, yet passionate sound of worship roiled the atmosphere—human and angelic adoration meeting and melding; entwining and magnifying. And that sound sparked and flashed and became light. Vibrant, dancing light. Living and powerful. Hot and fiery.

The Lord of the universe, vast and infinite, now condensed into an ethereal, divine Man—awesomely beautiful and magnificent in His Perfection, altogether lovely—leaned forward, His face *so close* to Marie's, and gathered the tears that fell from her eyes into a quivering drop that pooled on the tip of His index finger. Attentively, He held His finger above the delicately filigreed bottle that He cradled in the palm of His other hand, and allowed the drop of tears to fall into the bottle. His actions were full of care and love. His face, inches from hers, shone passionately with adoration for her. With every tear that was lovingly collected in the bottle, the golden network of filigree warped and morphed and grew more elaborate and beautiful. It was *her* bottle of tears. Every human had one, but each person's bottle was different—highly personal, etched and engraved by the tears of his or her own trials. Never had a single tear been lost.

As He leaned forward and caught her tears, He whispered to the pastor, Pastor Goodson, "Now is the time for healing…" His glorious voice, which only those spiritual could hear, sounded like thousands of delightful waterfalls and finely tuned bells.

The angels grew quiet, their voices hushing; yet undulating hums and melodies continued to emanate from deep within their beings. They had no choice but to worship—it was their nature to worship—it would have been impossible to stop their adoration. The undulating harmonies of the sounds that manifested from deep within them wove into the background. It seemed that the air itself was breathing in and out…rhythmically, melodically—the atmosphere was worshiping. The sanctuary grew hushed as the people sensed the shift in the Spirit.

A sweet heaviness descended. Pastor Goodson spoke quietly, although his voice carried to the back of the sanctuary. "I feel as if the Lord is telling me that now is the time for healing. If you want to be healed, come forward." Many of the people in the sanctuary stepped forward. Marie was one of them.

She stopped in front of the altar. The Lord leaned over and murmured to her, "Not right now, my darling…I will make you strong!" He tenderly kissed her head. A delicious warmth flooded her body. Soothing heat flowed from the top of her head, down through her chest and out to her arms, into her belly and down through her legs to her feet. The Lord touched her cheek, lightly. "I don't want to see you suffer. Oh! But for the Glory that shall come of this!" A tear dropped and landed on her eyes. A tear of God. Everything good and righteous and holy and lovely flowed into Marie. That solitary tear, that tear of the Lord, engulfed her. She felt herself falling. All consciousness disappeared.

Before her, in her mind's eye, with the eyes of her heart—so much more real and tangible than anything she had ever experienced before—stood the Lord. Her Lord. It was a flash. A momentary flash. Of His lovely face. Golden. Burnished. Eyes of fire—ablaze with the flame of His divine, all-consuming love. He was smiling at her—tenderly, lovingly. His eyes spoke to her an understanding, a planning, a *pointed, meticulous deliberateness* to everything she was going through. She *knew* that He knew and that He was entirely in control. Every part of her being strained to be with Him.

To go with Him. To leave everything behind and remain forever in worship before Him. Everything within her yearned to just *remain* and *be* in His Presence.

"Remember I am God and I am always with you." His words rolled over her—a vast waterfall of melodious sound. He caressed her cheek, again, and she came to. It seemed but only a moment. Only a moment that she had been in the Presence of the Lord—His lovely, golden, all-luminous Presence and she was forever, indelibly changed. Fire. She opened her eyes.

Where am I? She was disoriented. The dimness of her surroundings (made even more dim after the unimaginable brightness of the Lord's Presence) made it difficult for her to discern exactly where she was. Finally, she realized—*I'm in church.* With the realization of her whereabouts, she remembered the events of the evening. She peered about.

Behind her, sitting in a chair, was her husband. Eyes closed. Lips moving softly in prayer. They were the only ones around. She moved to get up; Paul opened his eyes and jumped up to assist her.

As he helped her to stand, she asked, "Where is everyone? What time is it?"

Slowly, they began to walk down the aisle to the exit. "Everyone's gone," he replied, "with the exception of the cleaning crew. You've been down for a long time."

"Really?" Surprise was apparent on Marie's face. "It felt like just a moment."

"No." He shook his head. "It's been a few hours. Do you remember going to the front?"

"Yes, Pastor Goodson called those who wanted healing to come forward."

Paul let out a little chuckle, "People came up from all over and began to go down under the power of the Holy Spirit. Pastor didn't even touch most of you." He laughed aloud. "He certainly didn't touch you. The moment you got to the altar, you just flopped down. You fell out so quickly no one could catch you." Paul laughed, again. Marie joined him.

Smiling, she remarked, "I can just imagine what I looked like." They laughed afresh.

Paul asked, "So, what happened?"

"Oh Paul! I wish I could say in words..." Marie let out a long exhalation. Joy danced through her body. "All I know is that I was in the Presence of the Lord and He *is* altogether lovely and beautiful and understanding and powerful. I've never felt so good and so loved and so cared for in all my life." Paul remained quiet as he held the door open for her. She drew in a deep breath of the night air before adding, "But, I didn't get healed..."

Paul hurried forward and gripped her hands. "What do you mean? After all *that*...you didn't get healed?"

"No...I don't know why I didn't get healed." Marie's voice trembled as the vague hints of doubt tried to press in. *Why didn't He heal me? I know I felt Him. Maybe I was wrong? Maybe I didn't feel Him? Maybe He wasn't with me and He didn't speak to me? What have I done wrong that He won't heal me?* Marie set her chin, "But I can handle whatever comes our way." She sounded much more confident than she felt. Through her mind snaked half-questions and partial-doubts—*Why didn't He...? Why doesn't He hear me?*

Her thoughts echoed her husband's, though he never would have admitted it. *Why doesn't God heal her? What are we doing wrong? Where are we going wrong? First our daughter...she'll never come back...and now, it doesn't seem He's going to heal Marie either.*

Doubt, Depression, and Despair descended upon them as they walked out of the entrance. Marie's constant companions, Sickness, Illness, and Disease, who had been waiting at the door, also pounced upon her the moment she stepped outside. Sickness stuck a vomity, pinkish tentacle into her head, creating a headache. Illness took some of the green, frothy gooze that was his exo-skin and rubbed it into her eyes. Immediately, webbing began to etch over her field of vision. Intently, they strove to reassert their version of the situation—hopelessness and despair, loss and death.

No, after all that—Marie sighed—*I definitely didn't get healed. Why, Lord?*

KALI'S GREAT BLESSINGS

Maya
India

"Namah shivaya! Miss…miss…" A middle-aged Indian man, wearing a white dhoti and shirt, walked up to me as I stood over by the Indian canteen drinking chai, talking with Karuna and Chandy. I recognized him as being one of the guys who worked in the telephone office. The telephone office was located in one of the small rooms on the opposite side of the temple, facing the brahmacharini huts. It quartered all of the telephones in the ashram—all two or three of them and from what I heard, they were none too reliable.

"Namah shivaya?" I queried, curious as to why he would be calling me. Karuna and Chandy turned to him with an expectant air.

His head bobbled, "Phone call for you…"

"For me? Really? Are you sure?" I asked. I could not believe I would be receiving a phone call.

"You are...Maya...?"

"Yes," I interrupted him, my curiosity rising. *He used my real name, not my Kali name. It must be my mom.* I felt my heart harden within me. *I don't want to talk to her.*

"We must hurry," he urged, his thick accent almost making his words unintelligible, "before we lose the connection." He headed into the direction of the telephone office.

"OK, sure," I said, following behind him, feeling more reluctant than I sounded.

"I'll see you when you're done," Karuna called after me. "I'm going to try to get another cup of chai from Raju!" She headed back into the canteen.

"Me, too!" Chandy sang. "I want chai! I want chai!" She and Karuna walked off giggling. *I wish I could walk off*—I thought desperately.

The telephone-office-man hurried toward the telephone office, which was on the opposite side of the temple from where we had been drinking chai. Once there, he picked up a phone that was off the hook.

"Here!" He thrust the receiver at me with great gusto.

I took it slowly, with some resistance, not really wanting to talk to anyone not in India...especially my mother. "Hello?" I mumbled. Silence. I heard clicking and whirring and a noise that sounded like the ocean in the background. I tried again, "Hello?"

And then, "Maya? It's your mother..." My heart sank with the knowledge that it *was* her. I did not want to hear from her. It was enough that I had caved one day a couple months ago and had sent her my address and phone number in a letter. I had no clue as to why I did it...guilt maybe... maybe for "just in case" situations. And now, here she was calling.

"Hi, Mom. How are you?" I tried to be civil, although a wave of anger and something that felt dangerously close to hatred roiled up from within me that was awful and made me want to throw up. It was so strong it felt almost physical.

"Maya, that's why I'm calling…" I strained to hear her. The connection was bad. "I've been trying to get through to you for a few weeks now…"

I thought snidely—*A good sign then that you weren't supposed to get me!* I kept the thought to myself.

"But, I couldn't get through the operators. The couple of times I did get through to the ashram, the men who answered said there no one named Maya." *Yeah, because I'm not Maya anymore! I'm Premabhakti!* "But, finally, this last man was very nice."

"OK," I responded coldly. *Somebody needs to talk to him about his "niceness."*

A pause.

"Well?" I demanded rudely, not caring that I was being ugly.

"Well, I went to the doctor because I've been having episodes of my vision going out. The doctors say that I have a brain tumor. The fluid caused by it is giving me headaches and making me lose my vision. They're trying to locate the tumor; but the problem is that they can't seem to find it and it's getting progressively worse," she said all of this in a rush, as though she feared that if she did not get it out quickly she might not be able to get it out at all. Another pause, longer this time. I did not say anything. "The doctors say I may not have long to live, if they can't find a solution. It's very severe. They say I have…"

The telephone man was gesturing for me to hang up. "We have another call coming through. You must hang up."

I interrupted my mother. I felt a frigid chill flooding through me. "I have to go…"

"…two months, at most six months, left to live!" she rushed it out.

"Mom! I have…"

"I'm believing God to heal me!"

"…to go!" I hung up the phone. *Sure! Let your God heal you.*

I could not distinguish if the anger-turned icy-cold-rage was because of the man rushing me or because of mom calling me in India—*Reaching into my world!*—or because she said she was believing God. I was in a chaos of confusion and violent emotions. As I was walking away from the telephone booth to the canteen to find my friends and more chai, I realized—*Not one of my feelings for her is sad.* I had not an ounce of empathy or caring about her. I felt proud of my dispassion and detachment—traits Hinduism urged because it meant one was not so attached to worldly things (much easier to reach enlightenment when a person was not so burdened down by emotional ties).

And then, quietly, I allowed myself to hear the whisper deep within. Too awful to admit to myself, let alone to anyone else—*If she died, I would get part of her insurance money…enough to ensure that I would get to live in the ashram for the rest of my life! I could give it to Cha Ma!* My mind danced happily around these thoughts. *Kali! I never would have thought that you would bless me with the means to live here in the ashram for the rest of my life! Kali!*

In all my calculations, I did not give a thought to my father—as if he would ever give his renegade, uncaring, unloving daughter a penny of his dearly loved, surely-to-be-missed wife's insurance money! Give her money to stay in India for the rest of her life? Not a chance! But I never considered that obstacle. All that kept going through my mind was—*I'll get the insurance money! I'll be able to live in the ashram for the rest of my life!*

I turned the corner and leaned against the wall of the ashram. I had to catch my breath. I was so excited. I had to tell someone my good fortune—I was about to be greatly blessed by Kali! I skipped off to find Karuna and Chandy, even as I contemplated what I would tell them, I purposed in my heart not to show how glad I was at the prospect of my mother dying and that I would get her insurance money—some things were not to be admitted!

Majesty and Awe stood in the air watching Maya. Awe was frowning, "Sometimes I just don't understand humans…" He shook his head as he crossed his arms over his massive chest.

Majesty nodded in agreement, "They are truly some of the most unusual and fascinating of God's creatures. They can sink to such unspeakable, inconceivable lows…and also, rise to unimaginably glorious heights. Yet, no matter what they do, no matter how far they sink, or how perverse they become, there is still hidden deep within their hearts a spark, a yearning…a *cry*…that at times, only God can see and hear. A cry that only God can fulfill and redeem. Is it not amazing how He can redeem and make beautiful the most pernicious soul? Make glorious the most depraved life?"

"I cannot wait to see what He does with this. She is sinking to such a low," Awe said. He shook his head again.

"I agree. But, He is the Lord, the Maker of the universe, and He makes all things beautiful in *His* time. In His established time for her, this, too, will be beautiful. All of it will be beautiful and will proclaim the Glory of the Lord." As Majesty spoke, he looked upward and grinned.

"Premabhakti! Will you come here?" Bri. Sita called to me from the other part of the kitchen. I was in the fry kitchen. I was standing beside the rusty, old furnace that looked like it was an antiquated relic from the fifties. I had just positioned a big cooking pot underneath the hot water spigot. It could easily have held 25 gallons of water.

"Just a second!" I called. "First let me fill up this pot with water." I needed it full in order to begin cooking the pumpkin chunks. I liked starting the process of cooking with hot water because the cooking would go much faster. Heating up cold—*OK, nasty, tepid water*—over a wood fire took much too long. It easily added an hour to my cooking time, which meant I would miss bhajans. I preferred to cut corners so that I could participate in the evening singing.

"Oh! Don't worry about it! Just come for a second! I need you to tell me if I've cooked the beets long enough! If you think they're soft enough!" Sita called from a few yards away. She was just on the other side of the wall in the part of the kitchen with the steamers, chapati stove, and iddly equipment.

"OK! I'm on my way!" I lifted the handle of the spigot and watched as boiling hot water from the furnace ran into the pot. It was filling up slowly, as usual. The spigot would not allow any more water out than a thin stream. It would take a good three or four minutes to fill up the pot. After lifting the handle and watching the water leisurely fall into the pot, I headed into the other part of the kitchen.

Sita was not more than five or ten yards away from me, staring into the first steamer—the largest of them. The water was a rich maroon from the juice of the beets. They had been chopped into little one-inch cubes. Sita fished a couple of beet cubes out for me. *She's always cooking with beets!* "Try these...tell me what you think. Do they need to cook longer?" she asked as she proffered the spoon to me.

I picked up the cube from the spoon and stuck it into my mouth. It was fine. Soft, but not too soft. I told her so. "Oh yeah, this is fine. I'd drain the water out, pour them into a big pot, and get on with the rest of my meal if I were you."

Right then I heard my name bellowed, "PREMABHAKTI!" I whipped around and hurried back toward the fry kitchen as it seemed like the place where my name had originated. It sounded like Cha Ma calling me, but it could not have been, not before bhajans. She rarely came into the kitchen, and in the months I had been a cook, she had *never* come in during the afternoon. The last time she had been in (the time of my scolding for wasting the rotten tomatoes), it had been late at night.

I turned the corner and BAM! There she was all right...Cha Ma! Standing beside the furnace with a furious look on her face. She was pointing at what had to be my pot of water—but I could not see it—already, a group had formed around her, cutting off all visibility.

She called my name again, "PREMABHAKTI!" and rattled off in a fierce, staccato Malayalam. Her voice sounded loud and deep like a well-oiled machine gun—such was the depth of her voice and the quickness with which she spoke. She sharply bobbled her head as she talked. Quite angry. I pushed, and alternately, was shoved through the crowd. When I had made it to the front of the crowd and was standing before her, I saw that yes she was pointing to my water pot. My *overflowing* water pot—the water was gushing over the sides as though the pot had been sitting under a full throttle spigot for hours. I glanced at the spigot—still a trickle. *How…?*

Chamunda Kali's anger flashed through Cha Ma's eyes. Easily she had pushed herself into Cha Ma's body. Cha Ma was so open to her—she actually enjoyed Chamunda's presence. "Come!" Chamunda whispered to a group of demons who were standing in the shadows. Hatred and Anger stepped forward. Despair hovered nervously around the edge; he would take Maya when the others were done with her. "We must crush her spirit!" Chamunda sneered as she returned her focus to Maya. The four of them circled Maya and began to whisper hateful insults, vile words, and curses at her. Their words, their curses, shot straight into her and pierced her innermost being, assaulting her heart.

Out of the corner of my eyes, I could see the people moving in closer. Indians and Westerners alike—50 or 60 people—stared. The Westerners were wide-eyed, mouths agape. The Indians stared—their hands covering their mouths out of respect, and in this moment, fear. Their eyes as round as saucers. Heads bobbling rapidly from side to side as they listened in rapt attention.

More and more demons began to circle about Maya…circle about the entire group…screeching and shrieking curses and invectives at her. The air grew yellowish and foul—but not in the visible spectrum. The effects were imperceptible to the humans. However, to anything spiritually aware or made of spirit, the effects were obvious. The words thickened the atmosphere, making it dense and putrid. They started chanting, "Go! Go! Go!" alternating with "Die! Die! Die!" Although they circled around the entire crowd in a grotesque dance, they stared at Maya, and focused all of their annihilating rage and bellicose hatred at her. Their frustration with the Lord's angels, with her parents' prayers, and with the Lord's bidden Presence poured and oozed out upon her.

As they circled, they fed upon the fear and fright of the crowd. Their bodies grew denser, thicker, heavier. Their colors grew richer and more putrid—shifting into a pukish pink, into a dense, saffron-like brownish yellow, into a rich, disgusting brackish brown-black.

As soon as Cha Ma was done yelling at me in Malayalam, she pointed at the door and spat at me, "Go!" her voice hot and venomous. Her eyes blazed. *Gray!?!* Her face was set with an intensity and anger that exceeded the situation.

She said go. So, I went. I pushed through the crowd, my eyes threatening tears, tears that burned the back of my eyelids and chokingly coagulated in my throat. I swallowed hard and then hard again, trying to push down the burning mass of embarrassment, shame, and *upsetness*. Every fiber of my being ached to cry. I was not too sure why. I was not even aware of the aching…

The demons howled and chanted macabrely, thoroughly enjoying themselves. Chamunda Kali appeared to grow in the atmosphere—the hatred and anger and ugliness of the situation, of the emotions, fed her otherworldly body. Her frame remained skeletal, yet it grew and towered over the humans. Her "skin" hung off her gaunt body in thick, rippling black waves. She whirled her weapons about, causing them to glint fiery red with evil light. She stalked behind the fleeing girl—a rabid animal intent upon the kill. She wove around the bodies of the humans in pursuit of Maya, although it was not necessary as she was not made of the same "material," and whispered into her ear, "Premabhakti...the roof...to the roof...throw yourself off..."

As she whispered the words, Suicide joined the group. Suicide, along with the others, picked up her incendiary chant, "The roof...to the roof... throw yourself off...the roof...to the roof...throw yourself off..." Rhythmically, they chanted and suggested into the girl's weak mind.

A bloodlust...no, a vicious, voracious *spiritlust* had commenced. A spiritlust so malicious and destructive that human bloodlust monstrously paled in comparison—a spiritlust borne of millennia separated from God, the life-giving, refreshing, rejuvenating One, a spiritlust that came from having to feed upon the spirits, souls, and psyches of others as they were relegated to parasitic scavenging the instant they rebelled—such a spiritlust rose up powerfully, uncontrollably within them.

They left the crowd and followed Maya, some of them attaching themselves to her, chanting in hushed tones, others screeching virulently, "The roof...to the roof...throw yourself off..." And then, two others, Deception and Delusion, began to whisper the lie, "If you throw yourself off the roof, you'll get enlightenment. Show everyone how much you want enlightenment. Get release from this cycle of rebirth." On and on they spoke *at* her. Her mind was too weak and impressionable, and too injured, to resist. Every word, every curse, they uttered took root in her heart, in her soul.

Outside of the kitchen, I felt the tears streaming down my face. *When had they begun? How humiliating!* They did not help the burning in my throat. My legs took me to the temple. I ran into the darkened, desolate building and up the inside stairs to the meditation roof. To my relief, it was deserted—everyone who was awake was with Cha Ma. *Watching me be scolded! I am sooo stupid!*

Before I even had a moment to think about it, I found myself on the edge of the roof. I ached to jump. *Just to jump, to show my desire for enlightenment. To reach enlightenment…release…freedom from this horrible existence, from this never-ending cycle of rebirth. As the great masters say, "Enlightenment comes when the desire for it far exceeds one's desire for life."*

I stared, unseeing, at the ocean. My toes protruded over the edge by a couple of inches. I felt the warm, moist wind blow by my face. My clothes moved gently in the wind. It all felt so familiar—*How many times have I found myself here, right here?* I asked myself. *Night after night…*Within and without myself, I heard—*Lean forward…lean forward…all I have to do is lean forward.*

The demons danced around Maya. The key ones—Chamunda, Suicide and Despair, Hatred and Anger, Depression and Deception—surrounded by a band of lesser demons and imps. A large roiling mob of evil ones had joined the girl on the roof. She was oblivious to their overwhelming, albeit *intangible* presence. They chanted at her, "Lean forward! Lean forward! Lean forward!"—goading her, pressing her, urging her on. They frothed at the mouth. Spittle putrid and acidic in dark, nasty colors—foamy brackish brown, pussy mustard yellow, vomitous pink—dripped down and soaked into the floor of the meditation roof, tainting even the inert, "unliving" concrete. Their skin had deepened in hue as they had fed off the crowd's worship and fear of Cha Ma and its enjoyment of the girl's scolding and humiliation; and now it continued to deepen from her anguish and shame, from her confusion and pain. The girl's emotions and their outrageous spiritlust affected the atmosphere, causing it to darken and coalesce into a hazy, brownish-yellow vapor, which thickened and grew like a ravenous fog.

"Just jump!"

How they anticipated the moment when she would go hurtling over the edge! For they would have won. At least with one. Not the war. No, not the war, but one skirmish. They would have snuffed out what they knew was a bright light, a marvelous and special creation. All of God's children, His "Loves" in weak, fragile vessels, were bright and marvelous and special. How they hated that most of all! Humans were something they would never be. "Lean forward! Lean forward!" Suddenly they stopped, their voices fading away one by one as each of the demons saw *them. Felt* them.

Majesty, Awe, Brilliant, and His Strength appeared, seemingly out of nowhere. The Lord's angels were lovely and glorious—even more strikingly so in close proximity to the demons. Large, beautifully muscled. Fierce and mighty in their loveliness—even beauty—godly, righteous beauty—is a weapon. Light radiated from their bodies and brightened the area. This living, powerful light pressed upon and began consuming the suffocating, saffron vapor. It reached out toward the demons, active and aggressive, fueled by prayers and the Presence of the Lord. It caused the demons to shudder back. Further, the demons stepped back because of the pure, unassailable authority with which the Lord's angels appeared. The Lord had told them to carry out this particular mission. The intent and authority of the mission was imprinted upon their beings. The demons could not thwart them.

"But, we can try…" hissed Chamunda. "Kill her! Kill her!" Quickly, the evils ones refocused upon the girl. For although the evil ones feared and respected the Lord's angels, although they burned from being in such close proximity to the angels, and although they could not gainsay the Lord's express authority, the lure of a human on the brink was simply too much. They could not back away from a possible (in their eyes—probable) kill. They were too far gone. Spiritlust reigned in them—they *needed* it!

They formed a half-circle around Maya, facing the Lord's angels. Chamunda leaned in close to Maya's ear and whispered, "Jump…just jump! Free yourself from this cycle…" she whispered and hoped, for she understood free will (at least, in part). She understood the rudiments: that every second of every day…every single moment, humans must choose: life or death. That was the nature of the human condition. If Maya *chose* to jump…

The others took up her urgings, "Jump...jump! Free yourself."

Maya, tears streaming down her face, shook her head vigorously—surely looking like a person who had lost it. Her mouth moved frantically, whimpering silent words that only the supernatural could hear, "Jump...jump! Free myself." She leaned forward a little more.

Brilliant positioned himself in front of Maya, standing naturally, effortlessly in the air. He stood strongly, legs spread. Slowly, he allowed his eyes to cut a wide arc—passing through the human girl as though she were a sheet of crystal clear glass—as he smiled enigmatically at each of the evil ones present. They froze as his gaze pulled them into their true, natural realm, outside and beyond time.

Then, he spoke to them...*into* them...as they were helpless to resist the words that slammed against their minds, "You do not understand... You never will. It is our lot, as angels, to ponder the mysteries concerning the humans and our Lord. As an angel of the Lord, I, at least, can *perceive* when a mystery is in operation...in this case, that of free will *and* intercession. Through the Lord's Grace, I can, at times, understand glimmers of the workings of the mysteries. However, you, as those who have rebelled against the Lord, will never ever perceive, let alone understand, any of the mysteries. You have not the eyes to see nor the ears to hear. You have forever separated yourselves from our Lord. You will never understand anything of the Lord. You will never transcend what you are. You will only continue to fall. How I pity you." He smiled again, leisurely, at each of them. Finally, he let his eyes rest upon Chamunda, who unconsciously · shrank back from his gaze. When he looked away, they rejoined time and its flow in the human dimension.

He turned his gaze kindly, lovingly, to Maya. He stretched his right arm out to her, allowing his index finger to extend a little farther so that he was just barely touching her chest. Just enough to keep her body from tumbling off the roof. Simultaneously, the other three formed a semicircle around her, facing Satan's minions. As they moved into position, battle armor arose from their bodies and solidified—shining, glinting, silver with gold edging—smooth and seamless. Breastplate. Shield. Gauntlets. In a movement of precision borne of one mind, their right hands went to their swords on their left hips. They drew them out partially. The swords rattled against scabbards. Sparks shot out in all directions. They were ready for battle.

The evil ones were not. They shifted. Calculating. *To battle?* Spirit-lust deluded them—how they ached to battle and push through and secure the girl's death. (They could not understand that she was *not* going to commit suicide this night. Their eyes were darkened. Their ears were stopped.) Yet, they were distracted. Bothered. Impossible to focus. Something caused the hackles to rise up on their backs. They looked about, bewildered. What was it?

Sweet, gentle, epiphaneous words. Powerful words. Words that wafted through the air, floating as though upon gossamer wings. Sound so subtle and powerful. Sound that was also living, vibrant light—though not light visible in the human spectrum. The prayers and worship of Maya's parents, and many others, danced across continents and oceans and wove through the atmosphere. Sound full of the essence of God.

The angels of the Lord, even as they stared at the evil ones, spoke into the wind, matching the light-words that blew gently by. The delicate, epiphaneous words were so powerful that they instantly caused the demons to diminish. The evil ones stepped away from Maya, drawing in upon themselves. They pulled into the shadows...their arms and appendages clutched about themselves. The burning that they had been feeling ever since the angels of the Lord had arrived months ago, the burning that had multiplied this night when the Lord's angels had appeared, the burning that they had been able to ignore in their mad spiritlust, now increased multi-fold. They could no longer stave off the burning. They ran.

What if... What if...? Silence. Abruptly, silence. I listened intently but all I heard was silence. I did not hear the insistent, demanding drone in my head to throw myself off anymore. Still...I was in this place, this position, where I had been almost every night since I had come to the ashram. I allowed my mind to play with the idea. *What would it be like if I leaned forward enough to fall?* I allowed myself to lean forward a little more. Or rather, I intended to…I tried. Truly, I *tried*. However, it felt as if the wind gently, but definitely, opposed me. Or, it felt as if some presence… some *thing*…were pressing decidedly against me ever so gently, almost imperceptibly, yet most decidedly. I continued to lean forward and whatever it was continued to press, ever so lightly, against my chest. I stayed this way for quite some time. Tears streamed out my eyes. I could barely see. But, oh! How I burned inside for enlightenment, to be set free from the maddening cycle of samsara. *Oh! How I want to be free from the hurt and the pain, the shame and humiliation. And on top of it, I'm a coward. I can't jump…*

Brilliant kept her from falling. If she had looked down and if she had been in a rational frame of mind, she would have noticed that it was not physically possible to stand where and *how* she was standing on the ledge and not fall off. Her body leaned precariously, dangerously far into the air, on the diagonal. However, Maya was too upset and too disturbed to notice.

The evil ones had been disarmed and rendered useless—for the time being—by the Lord's angels, who were ready for a good battle, and by the ethereal sounds that floated by, heavenly nectar to the Lord's angels but worse than fingernails on a chalkboard to the evil ones. Unlike mere fingernails upon a chalkboard, these sounds were substantive and powerful as they rendered the evil ones ineffectual and powerless, whilst simultaneously empowering the Lord's angels.

"Look!" whispered Majesty, in less than an instant he was beside Maya, his body armor melding seamlessly, indistinguishably, back into his body. In its place appeared his shimmering tunic and pants, which glided beautifully over his massive, muscled body. He touched her cheek gingerly with one hand and lifted her face upward. With the other hand, he pointed toward the moon, the beautiful moon. "Look deeply and enjoy," he ordered with a tender smile, his eyes full of love. His invisible-to-human-eyes hand cradled, dwarfed, her chin. "The earth…oh yes, the earth and the heavens proclaim the beauty of the Lord. The very nature and purpose of nature is to praise Him. See its praise of the One True God!"

The crescent moon, unearthily white and vibrant, cast a wan light over the ashram, the palm trees, over the ocean. Its light shimmered on the surface of the ocean, dancing and playing. The trees, the ocean, even the air seemed to be expressing delight. The beauty of it all began to draw my attention. Yes, I burned; but the intense desire to "remove" myself forever was gone. At some point, I found I was no longer leaning against a nothingness that opposed me and kept me from falling off. I was not leaning forward at all. I was standing upright on the edge of the roof.

"You don't want to be there on the edge," the Lord's angels whispered in unison. "Step back. Sit down."

Brilliant, still facing Maya, leaned forward until he was not even an inch from her face. Smiling into her unseeing eyes, he whispered, again, "Look deeply…look deeply and enjoy."

Suddenly…strangely…I just did not want to be there—there, on the edge of the roof. I wanted to be sitting safely on the deck, comfortable and warm, gazing at the fantastic view in front of me. I stepped back from the edge a couple of feet, arrested by the beauty all around me. I gently lowered myself to the ground, careless of all the warnings that I had heard against sitting on cold, hard cement to meditate. Right then, I just did not care. I drew my legs up against my chest and hugged them. I put my chin on my bent knees and stared and stared. Hope began to course into my heart. Life began to hold a little promise. If only for that moment.

Maya had not, could not, have seen the evil ones when they had slunk away. The Lord's angels had—they had won that battle. They smiled at each other. They looked up into the sky and saluted the Lord with a rousing shout of triumph. Then, they sat down in a semicircle around Maya and enjoyed with her, the awesome scene before them. Light radiated from them—more luminous and radiant than that of the moon. Their light bathed the meditation deck in a pale blue illumination that gently pulsated in all directions.

I looked all around. *This is incredible! Where is this light coming from? Tho moon? It's so beautiful! This light! It seems almost living....*The meditation deck seemed bathed in a faint, almost imperceptible light blue luminosity. The darkness of the palms was offset by the moonlight that was faintly reflected by the foliage. The ocean was alive and vibrant, the white light of the moon tripped delicately over its surface as though the light and water were playing tag with each other. *Wow!*

ASHRAM DAYS

*A*nother day…cooking…by this hot fire—I half-mused, half-complained to myself as I sat on my rock by the wood fires outside of the kitchen. I was watching another soup boil. By the time I was done, resident darshan and meditation would be over. It would be an hour before bhajans and then time for dinner. My life had settled into a steady routine, and excusing the random emergencies and "situations," it had grown comfortable in its odd predictability.

When I was certain that the pot was boiling well and that the fire would not burn out, I went into the kitchen. I figured I could check on the carrots in the steamer. Sita was steaming them for a salad. *I wonder what type of salad she's making for tonight… a carrot and mung bean salad, maybe. At least, no beet salad tonight.* As I walked into the fry kitchen, I caught a quick glimpse of Manoj through the doorway that led to the other part of the kitchen. He was wielding his machete, hefted high above his head, as if he were ready to strike someone.

Sita approached me, "Come see!" I followed her through the fry kitchen into the main kitchen area. It was in its usual state—dim, hot, smoky, very humid. We stopped in between Manoj and the steamers. "Look down!" she ordered.

I did. That is when I saw a black bug-thing, a rather *large*, black bug-thing. It was about five inches long and an inch wide. Shiny, hard, jet-black exo-skeleton. Tons of little legs.

"What is it?" I asked, a grossed-out chill coursing down my spine.

"A centipede," she informed me keeping her distance from the thing. She held up the skirt of her sari as though she were afraid it would skitter up her clothes.

I moved in for a closer inspection, "Is it dangerous?"

"I don't know…" She squinted down at it, though not stepping closer.

Manoj interrupted us, "Step back! I'll kill it!" He swiftly lunged past us and, before we could blink, swung down hard, deftly hacking the creature in two with his machete. He used the edge of his machete to sweep the halved-pede into the gully that ran behind the steamers. Sita leaned over and turned on the water spigot that ran behind the boilers—the dead two-piece centipede flowed out of the kitchen with the water.

"Ahhh! There's nothing like a little excitement!" Manoj exclaimed, his cheeks vibrant from the excitement and exertion. "I've seen a couple of these things. They're poisonous, but not deadly. Just if they bite you, you won't feel too good. Now, you, Premabhakti…*you* really need to be careful…" He stuck his machete under the running water to wash off the centipede guts from its blade.

Why me *be careful?* "Careful? Of what?" I asked, curious and dreading what those things could be.

"You know," he answered distractedly, "there are centipedes in the woodpile." Briskly, he swung his machete back and forth to shake the water off it.

"CENTIPEDES IN THE WOODPILE!" He had freaked me out faster than you could say...could say...anything! "I...I...I've never seen anything..." My voice trailed off. I know I did not sound secure in my own knowledge.

"Oh yes! There's centipedes and snakes. One must be careful! Especially you, since you are always climbing around in the woodpile. Keep your eyes open and always be ready. You don't want to be bitten." He swung his machete again, this time hacking downward as if at an invisible...something...near his shins.

Sita chimed in, "That reminds me of a story I heard about Cha Ma. The story goes that one day while Cha Ma was in the kitchen cooking..."

"Cooking?" I interjected. I had never seen her cooking.

"Oh yes! She cooks," Manoj affirmed as he ran his fingers along the blade of his machete. "She used to cook much more often when the ashram was smaller and the people were fewer." He flashed me an engaging smile. "One day while she was cooking, she went to the woodpile in order to get some wood for her cooking fire. When she reached into the pile, a centipede bit her. Everyone expected her to swell up, to hurt, to be affected by the venom. But, they say that nothing...nothing at all...happened."

"Did she ever say anything about it?" I was fascinated and repulsed at the same time.

"Yes, she says that she was burning our karma for us by accepting the bite. She says that, particularly, she was taking on the karma of the person for whom that centipede was intended. That's what she says. I don't know if I believe it." He winked confidentially to me, swung his machete again, this time as if he were slashing through some high weeds, and strolled out of the kitchen.

Later that evening, right before bhajans, Chandy, Karuna, Sandi, and I were sitting on Chandy's bunk, talking. *Gossiping.* Most of the women were in the dorm relaxing or preparing for the evening bhajan session. The atmosphere was relaxed and laid-back. I enjoyed this time of day immensely because my cooking, for the day, was finished. And this day, I did not have pots to wash nor the seva desk to work.

"Shhhh! Cha Ma's coming!" Alice rushed into the women's dorm, grayish-white sari, crumpled and rust-stained, as usual. Anneshwari was right behind her as they were doing their "usual" thing—"stalking the avatar"—but apparently it had backfired on them: Cha Ma was coming up the stairs. They had had to about-face and hustle hard to get out of her way. Being Anneshwari or Alice and moving too slowly while in her path was a good way to get smacked. I could hear the hustle and bustle preceding our guru. Sandi, Karuna, Chandy, and I immediately ceased talking. *Gossiping.* Karuna and I jumped up from Chandy's bed and headed for the doorway.

Why is she coming? In the months that I had been at the ashram, she had not come into the women's dorm before. *Highly unusual.* Even more unusual was the time. Rarely was she out at this time of day. It was right before bhajans and usually she was in her room preparing. I did not have much opportunity to wonder why as she was on the last landing before the dorm. Quickly, I stepped back, in part, out of habit (I liked to stand in the background and watch the drama), in part, so that I would not get yelled at, and in part (the greatest part) because Alice and Anneshwari pressed backward against me. Cha Ma stepped through the open door. Swami and Swami Shivaramananda were a couple of inches behind her. One at each shoulder. Looking wide and orange in their swami robes. Behind them crowded a large group of bewildered, but curious, brahmacharis and -charinis—hands over their mouths in deference, eyes wide. *How many people can you cram onto a narrow staircase?*

Cha Ma threw us a withering scowl and headed back out the doorway. Swamis, brahmacharis and -charinis scrambled to move their bodies out of her way. Given the gross lack of space, they somehow managed to make way for Cha Ma who kept moving undeterred by the obstacles of bodies. She was like a tugboat cutting through turbulent water. Alice and Anneshwari pushed in close behind her. I kept my distance and cast a quick, questioning glance at Karuna, who was by my arm—she did not like drama any more than I did. She shrugged her shoulders, her eyebrows hiked up in an "I don't know…"

Right outside the door, Cha Ma stopped short and started yelling in Malayalam. In the amount of time it took for her to halt and start yelling, her skin had turned jet-black. Her face was fierce. She strode over to the clotheslines that crisscrossed the balcony. Clothes, as usual, were hanging haphazardly on them. As she yelled in her deep, guttural voice, she snatched the clothes down piece-by-piece and flung them to the ground. She was furious. I shrank back—I surely did not want to be one of the ones at whom she yelled.

As she spoke, her head bobbled angrily from side to side. One of the brahmacharinis in yellow who was standing near Karuna and me leaned toward us, her hand over her mouth, and whispered a translation, "Cha Ma says, 'She has told you to take your clothes down. Many times. Now you must wash them all over again...to get the spirits out!'"

My first reaction, overwhelming and frightening—*SPIRITS?! Get the spirits out? What kind of spirits?*

Cha Ma jerked the last piece of clothing down. She was done! She continued yelling; but the brahmacharini did not interpret any more for us. Cha Ma wheeled around on her heel and cast all of us who were standing nearby yet another castigating glare, this one even angrier than the first. We cowered back, with the exception of Anneshwari, who never seemed afraid of Cha Ma and just beamed at her with a dull expression of adoring idiocy.

With that, Cha Ma headed back down the steps. The swamis, brahmacharis and -charinis scrambled to get down the steps and out of her way. Alice and Anneshwari trotted down the steps behind the group, Anneshwari pressing against the brahmacharis and -charinis in order to get close to Cha Ma.

I just stood there, Karuna still by my side. Sandi and Chandy headed down the steps after the crowd of people. Other Western women rushed to the balcony to pick up their clothes. After a good minute had passed, Karuna and I turned, headed back into the dorm, and sat down on my bunk. None of our clothes had been hanging on the line. We tended to wash our laundry first thing in the morning, either by the brahmacharini huts or in the bathrooms. Then we laid them on the black rocks over by the brahmacharini huts. Sandwiched between the rocks, all the hotter because of their color, and the tropical rising sun, our wash dried within an hour or two.

Early on, I had heeded the unsolicited advice of the brahmacharini, Parvati, given to me over a washing stone. It had stuck with me and was one of the first things I had passed on to Karuna when she arrived. Being that I never liked—no I *abhorred*—confrontations with Cha Ma, as did Karuna, we made sure our laundry was down well before the sun set.

Sitting on my bunk, we resumed our conversation—*gossip session*—but, in my head, I kept hearing over and over, "Now you must wash them all over again…to get the spirits out!" I was bewildered—*and freaked out!*—and wanted an explanation. However, Karuna could not give me one. She knew even less than I did.

That day, I asked around but the more I asked the more it seemed that no one knew anything. My answer did not come until many days later during residents' darshan.

AN INFORMATIVE
DARSHAN

"Cha Ma is giving darshan! Cha Ma is giving darshan to the residents!" said one of the brahmacharinis who worked in the kitchen to me as she rushed out of the kitchen, intent upon getting to resident darshan.

Oh well! I'll probably miss it. . .not that I care. I quickly squelched any desire I had for a hug and prasad. *I have to finish cooking this soup.* I stayed with the soup as it gently boiled over the open fire, watching the blackened kettle that sat upon it grow even blacker with soot. I sat on my rock, getting up only to stir the soup now and then, and sang bhajans to myself.

Finally, the soup was done; rather the potatoes and carrots had turned into a smooth, baby food-like consistency—they barely maintained any shape, looking like irregular, mushy lumps. The fire had burned down to almost nothing. I could leave.

I headed into the temple and up to the top floor meditation hall where Cha Ma usually gave resident darshan. It was a wide-open space. Airy. A warm, humid breeze blew through. It was late afternoon. The sun was still shining, but it had not the burning intensity of the middle of the afternoon. About 500 of the ashramites were sitting around Cha Ma—a sea of white with specks of yellow here and there. Of course, men and women were separate. The atmosphere was light. Everyone was watching Cha Ma, laughing at her antics and jokes. A few Westerners sat at the back meditating. I walked over to the women's side and sat in the back, not wanting anyone to smell me as I reeked of soot and smoke.

A brahmacharini in white was kneeling before Cha Ma. Like all the others, she was beautiful. She looked to be in her teens. She had her head in Cha Ma's lap and was crying hard tears. Cha Ma rubbed her back in apparent consolation. At the same time, Cha Ma grinned up at a man who was leaning over the girl. He was trying to whisper to Cha Ma behind his hand. I watched the scene, curious as to the drama that was unfolding.

Someone sat down beside me. It was Radha. "Do you know about this girl?" she asked. I shook my head. Radha leaned over, talking in hushed tones. "Her name is Priya. She's fourteen years old. She came to Cha Ma two years ago." Radha paused. I thought to myself—*not anything too interesting*—and began looking around at all the other residents present. Maybe there would be something of interest elsewhere. Raucous laughter—Cha Ma's laughter—pulled my attention back to the scene at the peetham.

"The man, there…standing over her…is her husband," Radha continued. "He's way older than her. I've heard thirteen years or more."

Fourteen years old and with a husband! A husband who—I calculated in my mind—is at least twenty-seven years old! Now, THAT is interesting! I scrutinized him. He did appear to be in his late twenties or early thirties. "What's up with them? Why are they here?" I asked, intrigued.

"They were an arranged marriage many years in the making. I've heard they were arranged since she was five years old."

"Five?" I observed the couple intently. "He would have been fifteen… no, at least eighteen years old when they were first set up! Yuck!" The idea of arranged marriages went completely against my Western sensibilities, as did the age difference at her tender, young age.

"I know!" Radha agreed, smiling. She lapsed into silence as she stared at the scene with Cha Ma.

"Well, what happened?" I prodded.

"When she was twelve, which was two years ago, they were married. Immediately, she ran away from him and came to Cha Ma. Cha Ma took her on as a brahmacharini. Now, she must stay with Cha Ma for the rest of her life. If she leaves her, she will be ruined because she left her husband." I watched the girl staring up at Cha Ma with such hope, her cheeks wet with tears. The man was still leaning over her, talking into Cha Ma's ear. Cha Ma just nodded and smiled sweetly at him.

"Cha Ma's like a mother to her," I remarked.

"Yes, her own family disowned her when she left him. They won't speak to her. Cha Ma is like a mother to her."

"So, what're they doing with Cha Ma now?" Sometimes I wished I spoke Malayalam so that I could understand what was being said.

"He comes every few months to beg Cha Ma for his wife." Somehow…bizarrely…the drama had shifted: the man was crying, his head in Cha Ma's lap, while the ex-wife-teenager—*too weird!*—was no longer crying. Rather, she was beaming up at Cha Ma, head bobbling in delight. "As you can see, he's in love with her, which is strange because she's so much younger than him…"

"Yeah, with her fourteen, he must be at least twenty-seven." I wrinkled up my nose. It sounded even worse spoken aloud. *YUCK!*

"I know, gross, huh?" Radha asked.

I thought for a moment. "But, it's not the age difference that's the big problem. It's just that she's so young plus the age difference."

"Yeah, if she were older…"

"…a *lot* older…"

"It would be fine."

I nodded in agreement.

We sat in silence, watching him cry and talk—it looked like plead-ing—to Cha Ma, who just kept smiling mischievously as she bobbed her head. The girl, still beaming, continued to stare at her with such hope.

Radha spoke, "He really, really does love her. Somewhere during it all, he really did fall in love with her. But, she's not in love with him. Never has been. She's too young really, to even be in love."

"Do you know…did they ever?" I could not even say what I won-dered. I hated the idea.

Radha understood. "From what I've heard, no. Even then, he loved her and didn't want to force her. And then, she ran away within days of their getting married…." Radha lapsed into silence. Finally, she added, "Soon, Cha Ma will tire of this and send him away."

We sat in silence with the other ashramites and watched. After a few minutes, Radha picked up, "Even though she's disowned and her family doesn't know her anymore, she gets the better end of the deal, if you ask me…"

"How so?"

"While she's with Cha Ma, she'll go to school. You know how Cha Ma believes in Indian girls being educated. With her family, she was given only a little schooling, not even beyond the elementary level. With him, she was getting nothing, except time in the kitchen and life as an Indian wife, no future at all. Now, she's back in school. And if she wants, after she finishes high school, she can go onto college for computers or business. She could move up very high and one day even be a swamini, if that's what she wants to do.

"Her prospects are so much greater now: there are all of the different ashrams she could live in, all the different schools she can go to. Easily, she could end up managing one of the ashrams or schools. Cha Ma is so different from Indian society, in that men and women can, and do, hold equal power in ashrams and schools. Look at Swamini Ma—she's up there, right beside Swami, in terms of power, maybe having even more..." Radha fell quiet. She was done.

So, too, was Cha Ma, which was made apparent when she pushed the man off her lap. For a moment, she smiled sweetly at him, and then she looked away dismissively. She was done with him. He turned and walked away, head hanging dejectedly, his face wet with tears; however, no one seemed to notice or care anymore—Cha Ma's attention was gone, thus, everyone else's was, too. All except me. I watched him—fascinated by the entire drama. He stopped at the entrance of the meditation roof and looked back at his girl-wife who had happily rejoined the dense group of brahmacharinis, now indistinguishable from the others. A terribly wistful look was upon his face. He was still wifeless. He had lost his love, that much was obvious—he had lost her to the guru.

I felt conflicting emotions. On the one hand, I was glad for the brahmacharini—14 was much too young to be married. In addition, married to a man in his late twenties or early thirties, whom she did not even love—yes, she was much more fortunate. But, I felt sorry for him—his face evinced desperation for her. It was evident that he loved her, loved her tremendously. *Passionately. However that can be! What an awful situation all around.* I sighed and, resolving within myself—*It's none of my business anyway,* closed my eyes intent upon meditating.

I slipped easily into a deep state and would have gladly stayed there. But, after a short while, Cha Ma's voice broke through. She was speaking to Bri. Durgamma, who was kneeling to her right. She was speaking loudly and as she spoke, she looked about the room as if she were addressing all of us. Bri. Durgamma's head bobbled rapidly back and forth. Her hand covered her mouth in the deferential way.

I looked at Radha to explain, but she was deep in meditation. *Don't want to disturb her and chances are she won't be able to tell what Cha Ma's saying anyway.* Radha did not speak Malayalam. So, I looked around for someone else to tell me what Cha Ma was saying. No one, who spoke Malayalam, was within leaning distance. *Oh! There's Bri. Lakshmini!* She was sitting near the door. *I'll ask her.* I got up and moved within a foot of her, well aware that I reeked of the kitchen. She was watching intently, shaking her head back and forth in agreement. She smiled at me as I deposited myself beside her.

"You have been working in the kitchen?" she whispered. I nodded, ashamed of my smell.

"Namah shivaya," I apologized. She bobbled her head in understanding of my apology. "What's going on? What's Cha Ma saying?"

"Cha Ma is scolding us about our laundry." She was quiet for a moment, listening. Then she continued, alternating between whispering to me and focusing upon what Cha Ma was saying, "Cha Ma says that we must take our clothes down before the sun sets." Pause. Listening. "She says that many of the ashramites, particularly the Western women, are leaving their clothes hanging. But, now even the brahmacharinis are doing it. Some of the brahmacharinis are washing clothes and hanging them before sunrise. We must stop." She paused, listening. I sat waiting. After a minute or so, I prompted her.

"Why? Is she saying why we should take our clothes down?" Even as I asked, I was so glad that I was not one of the offenders. *Don't want to make Cha Ma angry.*

Lakshmini bobbled her head in assent. "She says that at the changing of the day—at sunrise and at sunset—the door between this world and the spirit world is most open...that is why we meditate and do archana at sunrise..." She paused.

"Yes...?" I prompted.

"Yes, during these times the doorway to the spirit world is most open. When clothes are hanging up, spirits get into them. When we put the clothes on, we put the spirits on that have gotten into them. Many of us are putting on unknown, unwanted spirits. They come. They attach. They are hard to remove."

She listened as Cha Ma solemnly gazed around the room, speaking in her gravelly voice. When Cha Ma paused, she picked up, "She says that...

some days you are feeling fine, you are happy…and then you get dressed. You do not know that because your clothes were hanging up at sunset, a spirit got into them. Now you are sad and depressed and you do not know why. It is because the spirit has attached itself to you. Some of us are getting spirits and they are staying with us."

Cha Ma said one more thing, shaking her head fiercely. Lakshmini interpreted, "She says that there will be no more clothes hanging up at sunrise or sunset. At that time, we must meditate, do archana, or some sort of tapas."

Cha Ma was done. She positioned herself into the lotus position, placed her hands into a mudra in her lap, and sank into meditation. I stared at her in wonder. Her body had grown profoundly still. She seemed so…gone.

I noticed that the sun was beginning to set. Sunset. *The doorway is open.* I felt a creepy-crawly feeling travel up and down my spine. Fear. *I wonder who has clothes hanging up?* I looked about in curiosity, though the predominant feeling that snaked through me was fear of the spirits that Cha Ma had been talking about. The room was hushed—many were wondering the same thing.

A couple hours later, I found myself resting on my bed, my mind swirling around the darshan. *Spirits in clothes! I don't want any spirits in my clothes. Do they really enter people through their clothes? Do they really attach themselves to people so easily? Is it so hard to get rid of them?* As these thoughts roamed around in my mind, I drifted to sleep.

I dreamt dreams that bordered on the fringe of normality. Sepia toned. People I knew and people I did not know coming in and out of them. Some looked normal; some looked oddly misshapen. I was climbing up the back stairs of the ashram. The sky seemed so far away and as I climbed, it receded farther and farther away from me.

I found myself on my favorite deck on the roof. I was staring out over the ocean—inky black. Something vast was approaching. I could feel it deep within me, pressing against me. I could not tell what it was. Nor could I tell from where it was approaching. Then, I felt something…*else*…

rising up from underneath me. *What is it?* It worried me…scared me… dark and nameless. Devouring. Consuming. Suddenly, I felt as though a million little insect legs were crawling all over me. I tried to look down to see what it was, but I could not! Something strong and viselike held me immobile. I wanted to scratch and rub them away, push them off me… whatever they were! But they…the sensation…would not go away. I became frantic but could not do anything about it. I struggled within an invisible net or barrier. I wanted to scream to get them off me, but I could not find my voice. I could barely breathe.

I awakened! Bugs were all over my bed, all over the walls, swarming me. *Where did they come from?* Frenetically, I batted at them. Ineffectually. I began to panic. *What am I going to do about all of these bugs?* They weren't biting me or anything. Just crawling all over me. Still, I wanted to scream; but the sound was stuck in my throat as if hundreds of the bugs had clogged my throat.

I awakened a second time! I found myself on my knees, batting against the wall. I swung a couple more times as it took me a while to realize that I had been sleeping, dreaming about bugs crawling on the walls and all over me. *Was that a dream within a dream? What do they say about dreams within dreams?* Even as I realized that I had been dreaming, I could not escape the unnerving sensation of bugs crawling all over me, overrunning the bed and walls. I could not bring myself to lie back down. I could see that nothing was there. I just did not want to lie back down.

I forced myself to sit on the bunk, cross-legged, and looked around the dimly lit women's dorm. Everyone was sleeping. The room was hushed. The atmosphere subdued. *All except for me with my crazy batting at imaginary bugs!* I tried to chide myself. It didn't work. I simply could not shake the feeling of bugs all over me. I continued to peer around the dorm, unnerved and uncomfortable.

Finally, I felt the heaviness of sleep overtake me. I lay back and let my head slump onto my arm, as I had no pillow, and was soon fast asleep. This time my sleep was dreamless and full of brownish-yellow nothingness.

ARE YOU GOING?

"Are you going on the India tour?"

"Are you going north with Cha Ma?"

Everybody who was anybody was asking everybody else if they were going with Cha Ma while she visited her temples scattered throughout India.

"I don't think so," I responded unwittingly the first time I was asked. I was sitting on the women's side of the temple watching Cha Ma give darshan. I was only a few feet from Funeral Swami as he sat on the men's side with just the middle aisle separating us. A few Western women were sitting near me. A couple hundred Indians were scattered around on the floor—either having received darshan or still waiting for their turn. The atmosphere was relaxed and comfortable— just a bunch of devotees enjoying watching their ishta-deity.

"You're not going!" Alice retorted. Astonishment was evident in her voice, on her face, and in her body. She plopped down beside me. (A little too close to me if I could say so—*How is it*

she's like the Indians with the personal space thing?) "Oh! But you have to! Everybody will be going!"

"I know everyone'll be going," I responded with a nod of assent, not taking my eyes off Cha Ma. "I figure it will be one of the few times that I'll be able to enjoy any peace and quiet here. Girl! You know how this noise gets to me!"

"But, you always wear earplugs! How can it get to you so much?" Alice grabbed my elbow for emphasis, leaning against me as she spoke.

"I dunno, but it does and I think it would be nice just to be alone… give me an opportunity to meditate a lot…" My voice trailed off. Something about her whole demeanor was changing my mind. She probably did not have to say a word to start convincing me, but she plunged right on.

"Oh! But you've got to go, Prema." She nudged my shoulder with hers (not that she had to stretch too far to do so as she was practically sitting on top of me.) "It's so much fun. We, Westerners, get to run around wild. It's the only time we can talk to the brahmacharis and not get in trouble. And it's the only time they will actually talk and play with us."

"Us? Us who?" I asked, confused, finally giving her my full attention. She looked so earnest (and odd without her peanuts).

"Us women, especially us Western women. It's a different story with the brahmacharinis, who're not allowed to fraternize with guys at all, no matter where they go. They're locked up tight, even on the trip. But, we're not. Prema, you've got to come! It'll be so much fun!"

"OK, I just might," I responded as I shifted my gaze and attention back to Cha Ma giving darshan. I hated to admit it, but today it was boring: the brahmachari and -charini helping Cha Ma pushed the devotees along; the devotees bobbled their heads and said things to her; she smiled sweetly as she hugged and whispered to them in their turn—nothing very exciting at all.

A couple of hours later, I found myself climbing the stairs to the balcony. Darshan was over   *boring darshan*—and I figured I would stop by the Western shop. I had a hankering for some cookies, some permitted fats and solids—*The idea of permitted fats and solids still bugs me for some unknown reason*—Indian cookies. *Nothing like some killer cookies*—I chuckled at my own joke—*to drown out the tediousness of a boring darshan session.*

As I began to walk around the almost empty balcony, Radha poked her head out of the door of the Foreigners' Office and called, "Prema! Come here!"

I detoured with my heart instantly rising up into my throat—*He has to be in there. How is he going to act toward me? Surely, like a freak!* In no time, I had traversed the space between us and found myself standing in the doorway of the Foreigners' Office. Br. Narayanan was there, sitting at his desk, his chair tipped back on two legs, his heels propped up on the desk. Karuna was there, too.

As I stepped into the office, I caught a mischievous smirk pass between Karuna and Radha. *Oh no! They're up to something and I can bet what it concerns.* They loved to tease me about Narayanan and I sensed they were going to do so to his complete obliviousness. I stood uncomfortably by the door as Br. Narayanan kicked his feet back underneath him and thumped his chair down so that it sat on all four of its legs. He opened a desk drawer, pulled out a newspaper, and snapped it open. An air of irritation immediately settled about him.

"Hey Prema, were you just watching darshan?" Karuna asked innocuously. Narayanan began to study his newspaper.

"Mmm-hmm," I mumbled, as I warily watched the two jokesters.

Just then, I heard behind me, "Namah shivaya, guys! What're you doing?" I turned around to see Alice stepping into the already crowded office. I took a step farther in to allow her space.

"Nothing, just chatting," Radha answered nonchalantly as she leaned against the desk. Karuna nodded. Narayanan did not even bother to look up.

I studied him for a moment while his head was down. *His hair's growing out nicely.* It had grown out about three or four inches since his sannyasi ceremony. *My, his hair grows fast! Can't be the food. Must be the climate or maybe the radioactive isotopes in the sand.* I did not think about the fact that mine had been growing fast, too. It was several inches long and beginning to hang down nicely.

"Oh! Well, I've been asking all the Westerners if they plan on going on the tour with Cha Ma," Alice volunteered. "Are you guys going?"

"I am," Radha replied. "I have to."

"I'm not too sure," Karuna answered, shrugging her shoulders. "I haven't decided, yet." She gave me another sly grin, which caused me to suspect her of something. "What about you, Prema?" Quickly, I saw Narayanan's head shoot up and then he looked back down. *Could he be…? No…*

"I don't know. I was thinking no, but then Alice has been talking me into it. She's been saying that everyone's going."

"That's true," affirmed Radha. "None of the Indians'll be here." She nudged Br. Narayanan's shoulder. "You're going, right?" Narayanan looked up at her and smiled, nodding his head. His eyes darted over to me and his smile evaporated. He snapped his newspaper again and resumed reading, quickly picking up his air of diffidence.

Impossibly, my heart sank at his cool antagonism toward me, while it rose at the quick glance he had shot my way over the question of whether I would be going on the tour or not. The contradictory emotions made me feel psycho. I noticed smirks on Karuna and Radha's faces as they elbowed each other.

"Well, let's go…" Radha announced as she jumped up from the desk. "See you, Narayanan!" she called airily as she led our group out of the door. Karuna elbowed her, again.

Alice, having no couth, asked, "What's so funny? Why are you guys elbowing each other? I want to know what's so funny!"

At her question, Radha and Karuna burst out into loud guffaws. I wanted to be swallowed up by the floor—yet hope buoyed me. *Maybe I*

will go on the India tour. Maybe it'll be fun. And if everyone's going, even…especially…
Narayanan…

As we walked down the balcony toward the women's dorm, Radha turned to me, "Oh, Prema!" Her voice was all innocence. "Would you mind running back to the Foreigners' Office? I forgot my tin."

"Sure," I responded, eager to have a chance to see Narayanan again, hopeful of his possible kindness, yet dreading the aloofness and meanness that I often got from him. Highly unpredictable. *Freak!*

When I turned back, I noticed that he was standing in the doorway of the Foreigners' Office, leaning against the doorjamb, arms crossed, ankles crossed. Watching us. As I approached him, my heart fluttered in nervous anticipation—*Will he be kind or a jerk?* He was so random with me. Again, I caught myself wishing that he and I had an easy, relaxed relationship like he and Radha. *I wonder if he likes her…* Just the thought made my heart clench up with an ugly, green jealousy and a faint trickle of despair.

"Namah shivaya, Premaaaabhaktii!" The way he spoke my name sounded like a song. *His voice is so lovely.* "Again." He gave me a boyish grin.

"Namah shivaya," I answered, sounding breathless. *Yuck! I sound like a simpering high school girl. Get hold of yourself!*—I chastised myself. "Radha asked me to come back and get her tin."

"Ah yes!" He gestured into the office. "It's on the desk."

As I stepped in, I brushed past him, as he had not moved from the doorway. The light brush caused a jolt to course down my arm as though someone had prodded me with an electric brand. My heart lurched. Stop that I ordered myself! I walked to the desk and picked up the only tin sitting there. I was insanely conscious of him in the doorway. *Is he watching me? No, probably not.*

I turned around to leave and almost ran into him. He had followed me into the office and stood right behind me. My heart lurched again as I looked up at him. Unconsciously, I examined his face. The bareness of his jaw (he had kept himself clean-shaven ever since his sannyasi initiation) only worked to accentuate his high cheekbones and…his eyes. I gazed into his eyes. Almond, liquid. Expressive. *He is so beautiful.* He was uncomfortably close, yet he did not step back. I could smell him. He smelled yummy—like a combination of temple incense and sandalwood, and maybe a hint of rosewater and jasmine. I had never thought that rosewater and jasmine could smell so masculine; I was wrong. I caught myself breathing in his fragrance.

He stared down at me, still uncomfortably close. His eyes looked dark and fathomless—with something unnameable glinting through. "So are you, Prema?" he asked softly. His accent made my name gorgeous.

"Am I what?" I asked, sounding stupid even to myself.

He smiled a tender smile that made me hold my breath. "Are you going on the tour?"

Why is he asking if I'm going on the tour? Why does he want to know? I caught myself asking 50 million questions in my mind until I realized that I had not answered him. Still staring into his eyes—*Like a deer before headlights!*—I nodded dumbly. *I hope my mouth's not hanging open like some goober.*

"Good," he whispered as his eyes searched my face. He began reaching with his right hand toward me—*How'd he end up standing so close?* It seemed he was even closer than the "uncomfortably close" of a few seconds ago—pausing with the tips of his fingers an inch or so from my face. His eyes shifted to my hair. "Do you mind?" he asked so quietly I had to strain to hear him. I shook my head—no, I did not mind, whatever he was going to do. He reached past the small distance between us and touched a lock of my twisted hair that hung down by my ear. I felt him gently caressing it. I watched his face as he touched...*played with*...my hair. His eyes were gentle and expressive as he looked down on me. A smile played about his mouth. *What is he thinking?* I felt a slight tugging on my hair; and then he let go.

His eyes slowly searched my face again. He gave me another smile—secret and private—his face much too close to mine and whispered, "Namah shivaya...Prema."

"Namah shivaya, Narayanan." But I did not move. Nor did he. We just stood there. *Pull yourself together girl and walk out!* I snapped at myself. Gathering all the self-control I could, I walked around him, again brushing against him because of the closeness of the office, and out the door. My heart thumped around erratically in my chest. With as much composure as I could muster (and the permitted fats and solids cookies looooong forgotten), I walked toward the women's dorm. Unconsciously, I reached up and touched my hair where he had been playing in it. He had unraveled a lock! I sighed. *Just like he's doing to my heart.*

At the door to the women's dorm, I ventured a glance backward. He was standing in the doorway of the Foreigners' Office, leaning against the doorjamb. Relaxed. Watching me. I sighed again. *Yes, I'll definitely be going on the tour.*

GLOSSARY OF TERMS

Adiparashakti (ah-DEE-pah-duh-SHUK-tee)—according to Hinduism, the ultimate energy that powers the universe, within her everything (Brahma, Vishnu, and Shiva) is contained.

Antyeshti (AHN-tih-YESHH-tee)—Hindu funeral rite, intended to release the soul from the body and send it on to its next life or into enlightenment (souls improperly sent off or not sent off at all remain on the earth as ghosts). The body is placed atop a pyre, and after certain chants and actions, the pyre is set on fire. Three days after the ceremony, the ashes are collected in an urn and sent down the Ganges or another river believed to be sacred.

Arati (AH-dah-tee [rolled quickly off the tongue])—a Hindu ceremony in which a lit lamp is waved before the god, goddess, or guru being worshiped. Particular songs are sung, which praise the deity or guru during the waving of the lamp.

Archana (AR-chuh-nuh)—a session of focused chanting of the names of, and to, a god or goddess. It is believed to purify the chanter, burn off karma, bring great spiritual power, and take one to extraordinary heights.

Asana (AH-suh-nuh)—meditational sit mat, usually made of cotton or wool or in special cases, animal hide.

Ashram (AH-shrum)—Hindu version of a monastery where many spiritual seekers live, usually as monks (brahmacharis, sannyasis, and swamis) and/or nuns (brahmacharinis and swaminis). The ashram life is centered upon the worship of, and service to, a particular deity. In the case of Cha Ma, who was believed to be an avatar, worship was centered around her and Kali. In India, men are usually the ones who take on brahmacharya and the vow of sannyasa, which is avowed celibacy and lifelong dedication to the guru. However, in the case of Cha Ma's ashram, women also vowed celibacy and a life dedicated to the guru or deity.

Avatar (AH-vuh-tar)—a human incarnation of a god or goddess. Hindus believe that gods and goddesses will take on a human form in order to come down and help humanity when humanity is most in need.

Bhajans (BHUH-juhns)—Hindu religious songs, usually of, and to, various gods, goddesses, and their consorts (i.e., Shiva, Kali, Ram, Sita, etc).

Bhakti (BUHK-tee)—intense love and devotion to a god or goddess, guru or satguru.

Bindi (BEN-dee)—(sometimes called a tilaka when it has religious significance) adornment on the forehead. It may be made of powder, paste, or more contemporarily, jewelry. The area between the eyes symbolizes the ajna chakra and/or the third eye. The bindi (or tilaka) is believed to contain the energy that comes to the ajna chakra when the kundalini shakti rises. It also is believed to help open the third eye.

Brahmachari (BRAH-mah-char-ree)—a devout, unmarried, celibate boy or young man who lives in an ashram (brahmacharini is the female counterpart). His life is dedicated to whatever deity he worships. Our Western equivalent would be a junior monk or nun. After the stage of brahmacharya, the next step a brahmachari would make, if he was dedicated enough and progressed far enough, would be to take the vow of sannyasa. The vow of sannyasa is a formal vow of celibacy and service to the deity or guru for the rest of his life.

Brahmacharini (BRAH-mah-char-REE-nee)—female brahmacharis.

Brahmin (BRAH-men) thread—a woven thread consisting of three strands. It is tied to make a loop. Generally, it is worn over the left shoulder, crosses the chest, and loops generously under the right arm. It is positioned differently for varying occasions or ceremonies (for example, it is worn over the right shoulder during antyeshi).

Chai—spiced tea. In India, it is often called masala chai. It is made of black tea, lots of cream and sugar (honey), peppermint, cinnamon, cloves, ginger, cardamom, black pepper, and masala tea spice.

Chapati (Chah-PAH-tee)—a thin, round, flat bread, unleavened. Cooked on a stove.

Chappel (CHAH-puhl)—sandals, usually made of thin, cheap plastic.

Choli (CHOE-lee)—a little half-top worn underneath a sari. It is usually form-fitting, with buttons up the front. It is made in a fabric that complements the sari. However, in the ashram, cholis were usually big and baggy so that little was revealed.

Dalit (DUH-leet)—lowest caste, often called the untouchables. They are considered social outcasts.

Darshan (DAR-shun)—the viewing of a guru, satguru, god, or goddess. It is considered a very great blessing.

Devi (DAY-vee)—another name for goddess. It is a general term used for all female deities (Durga, Kali, Lakshmi, etc.).

Dhoti (DOE-tee)—a form of traditional dress for Indian males and is worn instead of pants. It is a long, rectangular piece of cloth that is wrapped around one time and tucked into itself at the waist in order to stay on.

Durga (DUR-guh)—one of the goddesses of Hinduism.

Enlightenment—when a person is free from the cycle of reincarnation. One is bound to the cycle of reincarnation, to be born over and over and over again for eons, until one's karma, whether good or bad, is completely exhausted or burnt off.

Ghee (Ghee)—highly clarified butter used in religious rituals. ·

Guru (GOO-doo)—spiritual teacher (It is believed that the satguru will take a person to moksha, enlightenment.).

Householder—a person who follows a guru or devotedly worships a deity but lives a family life. He/she may marry, have children, etc.

Iddly (IHD-lee)—a food native to Southern India. It is made of ground rice that has been fermented overnight. The resulting batter is put into an iddly tray and steamed. Cooked, it is approximately four inches in diameter and one inch thick. It is eaten with many things, particularly sambars, chutneys, curries, dahls, and curd (yogurt).

Ishta (ISH-tuh)-deity—favorite deity or god.

Japa (JAH-puh)—repetition of a mantra or a name of a deity. It is believed to increase spiritual power, purify the chanter, and remove karma. Different mantras have differing effects.

Kali (KAH-lee)—one of the Hindu goddesses. She is considered the most malevolent of all the gods and goddesses. She is usually depicted as jet-black, with dreadlock-like hair and her tongue sticking out. She has four or more arms (the more arms the more malevolent). The arms hold different weapons (machete, sickle, sword, etc.). One of the arms holds a severed head. Another arm holds a bowl with which to catch the blood. Kali has different names and personalities. Bhadra Kali is a favorite and is considered sweet and cute. Chamunda Kali is the most pernicious of all her forms. She is thin and emaciated. She looks perpetually hungry and is depicted as living in a cemetery.

Kali Leela (KAH-lee LEE-lah)—the play of the universe, believed to be whimsically orchestrated by Kali. In this series, it means, specifically, Cha Ma's special darshan nights when she reveals more of herself as Kali.

Kanji (KUH-nee)—rice and water gruel, which is usually used as a base to curries and pickles. Of a thin, soupy consistency. Salted to taste.

Karma (KAHR-muh)—according to Hindu philosophy, thoughts and actions that a human accumulates over many lifetimes. All karma, whether good or bad, must be depleted (or burned off) before one can attain moksha.

Kimini (KYE-men-nee)—small hand cymbals. One cymbal is held in each hand and is banged against the other. They make a high, ka-ching ka-ching sound.

Kitchen ammas (ahm-MAHZ)—kitchen mothers, the older women who work in the kitchen and oversee all the food preparation.

Kovalam (KOE-vuh-lum) beach—located approximately 8 miles (13 kilometers) south of Kerala's capital city, Thiruvananthapuram (Trivandrum). It is situated along the shoreline of the Arabian Sea. It is a popular tourist and domestic spot.

Krishna (KRISH-nuh)—one of Hinduism's major gods. He is believed to be an avatar of Vishnu.

Kumkum (KOOM-koom) powder—a powder used for religious reasons. It is made of either turmeric or saffron, which when compounded with calcium hydroxide (lime) turns the yellow powder red.

Kundalini shakti (KUHN-duh-lee-nee SHUHK-tee)—is the Sanskrit word for "coiled (like a serpent)." Hindus believe that it is a dormant spiritual energy that lodges in the root, muladhara, chakra. Once it is awakened and then energized through spiritual practices and/or contact with the guru, it will move upward along the seven chakras. The final state, enlightenment, is when the kundalini shakti passes through the sahasrara chakra, the last chakra at the crown of the head, and merges back into Brahman. Kundalini shakti is often viewed as a goddess.

Ladu (LAAH-doo)—a popular sweet made of gram flour, which is ground chana dahl (chickpeas), sugar, and saffron (for coloring). It is approximately the size of a golf ball.

Lakshmi (LUCK-shmee)—one of the goddesses of Hinduism.

Loka (LOW-kuh)—world, realm, or dimension on planes or in dimensions different than our own. The Puranas (Hinduism's main texts) state that seven lokas exist. While in the ashram, I was taught there were nine.

Lotus position (half and full)—a yoga posture and meditative position. In full lotus (padmasana), the practitioner sits cross-legged, with each foot sitting upon the opposing thighs. In half lotus (ardha padmasana), the practitioner sits cross-legged with only one foot on the opposite thigh.

Mahasamadhi (MAH-hah-suh-MAHD-hee)—when one consciously and permanently leaves the body during meditation; intentional death. It is considered a special ability of those who have attained enlightenment or who came to the Earth enlightened (avatars).

Mala, or Japa mala (JAH-puh MAH-luh)—a string of beads used for keeping count of the number of repetitions when doing japa (repetition of a mantra or name). Usually made with 108 beads or some numeric derivative thereof.

Malayalam (MAH-lay-yahl-lum)—a Dravidian language and one of the predominant languages spoken in Kerala.

Moksha (MOKE-shuh)—means enlightenment. It is the Sanskrit word for freedom from the cycle of rebirth (reincarnation).

Mudra (MOO-druh)—hand positions, movements, and gestures used in Hindu religious ceremonies and in meditation. They are believed to have differing spiritual effects given the particular mudra used.

Murti (MUHR-tee)—a replica or three-dimensional, physical representation (statue) of a god or goddess and is used in worship to that deity. It can be made of metal, porcelain, sandstone, or any other material.

Namah shivaya (NAH-muh SHEE-vay-yuh)—is derived from one of Hinduism's fundamental mantras—Om namah shivaya. "Namah shivaya" means salutations to, I bow to, I salute the Shiva in you. It is a way to say hello, good-bye, thank you, excuse me, what did you say, etc., depending upon the context of the phrase.

Om chamundayai namaha (OHM CHAH-mun-dye-yay NAH-muh-huh)—salutations to Chamunda Kali.

Om maha kalyai namaha (OHM MAH-huh KAH-lee-yay NAH-muh-huh)—salutations to the great goddess Kali.

Om para shaktyai namaha (OHM PAH-raah SHUK-tee-yay NAH-muh-huh)—salutations to the ultimate primordial energy of the universe.

Om shiva shaktyaikya rupinyai namaha (OHM SHEE-vuh SHUK-tee-yay-kay ROO-pin-yay NAH-muh-huh)—salutations to the union of Shiva and Shakti. One of the many phrases chanted during archana.

Pada puja (PAH-duh POO-juh)—worship of the guru's feet. It is done by "washing" the feet with various substances.

Peetham—a low bench, usually only a few inches off the ground.

Pranam (PRUH-nahm)—to bow. A full-pranam is to lay prostrate on the stomach, forehead touching the floor. A half-pranam is to get on one's knees and bend over, touching one's forehead to the floor. Both gestures are a sign of reverence for, and honor to, the deity, guru, satguru, or teacher. Sometimes, children pranam (bow) to their parents as a sign of respect. Another version, but not really pranaming, is to touch the feet of the guru, satguru, teacher, parent, etc. with the hands. This, too, is a gesture of respect and reverence.

Prasad (PRUH-sahd)—anything (usually sweets) that is offered to a deity or guru. It is often given later to devotees. It is considered to contain that deity's or guru's blessing.

Premabhakti (PREY-muh-BUHK-tee)—divine love. Prema means ultimate, divine. Bhakti means love.

Pujari (POO-jar-ree)—Hindu priest who performs the pujas.

Puju (POO-juh)—ceremony of worship to a god, goddess, or guru, usually done in a temple or shrine.

Punjabi (POON-jah-bee)—traditional Indian clothing for females, particularly favored by girls and young women. It is a two-piece set with baggy pants and a matching top that extends to the knees or calves.

Radha (RAHD-hah)—Krishna's consort.

Rajasic (RUH-jah-sik)—describes food that is of a lower vibration than sattvic food and should be eaten in limited amounts. This type of food is called rajasic. Hindus believe that rajasic food influences people to be excessively energetic, easily angered and upset, overly passionate, and attached to things of this passing, illusory world. Rajasic foods include tomatoes and spicy and hot food.

Raktabija (RUHK-tuh-BEE-juh)—According to Hindu lore, at one time demons (called asuras) began rampaging throughout the Earth led by their demon-general Raktabija. None of the male deities had what it took to control them, so out of Durga, Kali arose in order to defeat Raktabija and his demons. Kali wiped out the demons effortlessly and turned to battle Raktabija. She wounded him gravely and from every drop of his blood a demon, called a raktabija, was spawned. His raktabija army grew rapidly. She wiped out the raktabija army, along with Raktabija, and drank his blood (symbolized by the long, red tongue). She was so intoxicated by the blood and destruction that she whirled about annihilating everything in her path (humans included). In order to stop her, Shiva laid down in her path. The moment she trod upon him, she stopped—thus the image of Kali standing upon Shiva.

Ram, Lord Ram (Raahm)—one of the gods of Hinduism.

Samadhi (Suh-MAHD-hee)—very high level of meditation in which the one meditating is completely absorbed in a trance. It is usually signified by no awareness of the external world, diminished heart rate, slower rate of breathing, etc.

Samsara (SAAHM-saah-duh)—the karmic cycle of death and rebirth.

Sannyasa (Sun-YAH-suh)—stage of religious devotion in Hinduism where the person takes a formal, solemn vow of sannyasa, which is a vow of life-long celibacy and a life lived solely for the guru or deity. It comes after the stage of brahmacharya. The sannyasi wears yellow and is considered a true and earnest Brahmachari or Brahmacharini. The next and highest stage is that of swami. At that stage the clothing is orange.

Sannyasi (Sun-YAH-see)—one who has made a vow of sannyasa.

Sanskrit (SANS-skrit)—an ancient Dravidian language. It is the basis of much of Hinduism's foundational texts, chants, mantra, and songs.

Sari (SAH-dee)—traditional Indian dress for women. One piece of cloth, usually several yards, is wrapped around and around a woman's body. The trailing edge is hung over the shoulder and down the back, most of the time (Gujarati style is tucked into the front). Underneath is a petticoat and choli (form-fitting, half-top, although in the ashram, the brahmacharinis wore their cholis large and very loose).

Satguru (SUHT-goo-doo)—the "ultimate" spiritual teacher. Hindus believe that out of all the teachers, in all the lifetimes, the satguru is the one who will, definitely, take the person to enlightenment.

Sati (SUHT-tee)—the Hindu practice of self-immolation, in which the widow throws herself upon the burning funeral pyre of her husband in order to die. It is a practice that is illegal in contemporary India.

Sattvic (SUHT-vik)—according to Hinduism, this describes food that is of the highest vibration. It is believed to influence people to be calm, focused, controlled, able to meditate, and inclined to a higher spirituality. Such foods include milk and milk products, nuts, potatoes, carrots, raisins, and certain other foods.

Seva (SAY-vuh)—volunteer work. Selfless service that is offered up to the guru or deity. It is believed that seva purifies the person (leaving only the higher nature) and burns off karma.

Sevite (SAY-vite)—someone who does seva.

Shakti (SHUHK-tee)—the underlying force, the fundamental power, the ultimate energy of the universe. This force is seen as feminine.

Shiva (SHEE-vuh)—considered one of "the three" major gods—Brahma, Vishnu, and Shiva, respectively the creator, the sustainer, and the destroyer.

Shudra (SHOO-druh)—the servant class. They are second to the lowest on the class scale. They are one step higher than the dalits, the untouchables. They are treated much more poorly and are significantly more impoverished than the servant class in many other nations.

Siddhis (SID-dees)—thought to be spiritual powers that are attained as one progresses and garners spiritual power and knowledge. Included in them are mind reading, astral projection/travel, levitating, etc. It is believed that it takes many years of intense, single-minded effort to attain them and that most people never will.

Sita (SEE-tuh)—Ram's wife in Hindu lore.

Swami (SWAH-mee)—a high position and a great honor. It means that the man has mastered his lower nature and is free from all karma. In the hierarchy of brahmacharya, sannyasa, and swami, swami is, by far, the highest honor and position. Only a few ever attain this level.

Swamini (SWAH-men-nee)—female swamis.

Tamasic (Tuh-MAAH-sik)—food that is believed to be of the "lowest" tier and should be avoided altogether. Such food causes the eater to be slow, dull, lazy, completely uninclined toward anything spiritual, and drawn to negative thoughts and activities, at times even verging on violence. Tamasic foods include onions, garlic, and meat.

Tapas (TAH-puhs)—spiritual disciplines or disciplines meant to subdue the lower nature so that the higher nature will dominate. Also, meant to increase one's spiritual power and/or burn off karma.

Thali (TAHL-lee)—round, steel plate generally used for eating.

Trivandrum (Trih-VAN-drum), Thiruvananthapuram (Teer-doo-vuh-nan-thuh-poo-dum)—the capital of the Indian state of Kerala. It is located far southwest on the Indian sub-continent.

Tulasi (TUHL-see)—the various parts of this plant are used for medicinal and religious purposes. The wood is made into japa malas. Often it is ground into a powder and used for ayurvedic purposes.

Turmeric powder—used for medicinal and religious purposes.

Upanishads (Oo-PAHN-nee-shahds)—philosophical scriptures that developed around 1000 BC. They are considered a compilation of religious and spiritual thought and consist of 13 essential principles. It espouses the principles of Brahman, karma, reincarnation, meditation, yoga, etc.

Vibhuti (VIH-boo-tee)—sacred ash, often from a puja. It is believed to have spiritual power.

Vishnu (VISH-noo)—considered one of "the three" major gods—Brahma, Vishnu, and Shiva, respectively the creator, the sustainer, and the destroyer.

Yagna (YUG-nuh)—fire ceremonies performed by pujaris, in which various substances are offered into the fire. These ceremonies have very strict guidelines for what can be offered, when, and in what manner.

CHARACTERS

Anneshwari
(Uh-NESH-shwuh-dee)

Brahmacharini Durgamma
(BRAH-mah-char-REE-nee DUR-gah-mah)

Brahmacharini Lakshmini
(BRAH-mah-char-REE-nee LUCK-shmee-nee)

Brahmacharini Sita
(BRAH-mah-char-REE-nee SEE-tuh)

Bredano
(Bre-DAH-noe)

Cha Ma
(Chah Maah),
Chamundamayi Ma
(CHAH-moon-duh-MY-ee MAH)

Chamunda Kali
(CHAH-moon-duh KAH-lee)

Chandy
(SHAN-dee)

Clyda
(KLYE-duh)

Dar-Rek
(DAAR-wreck)

Devi
(DAY-vee)

Gangama
(GUN-guh-mah)

Hachao
(Huh-CHAH-oh)

Karuna
(Kuh-ROON-nuh)

Manoj
(MAN-noejh)

Narayana
(Nuh-RYE-yuh-nuh)
aka Brahmachari Narayanan
(BRAH-mah-char-ree Nuh-RYE-yuh-nan)

Premabhakti
(PREY-muh-BUHK-tee)
aka Maya
(MY-yuh)

Priya
(PREE-yuh)

Radha
(RAHD-hah)

Raju
(RAH-joo)

Rukmini
(ROOK-mee-nee)

Salaa
(SAH-laah)

Swami
(SWAH-mee)

Swami Shankarapranatman
(SWAH-mee SHAWN-kah-dah-PRAWN-naht-mahn)

Swami Shivaramananda
(SWAH-mee SHEE-vuh-rah-mah-NAHN-duh)

Swamini Atmapranananda
(SWAH-men-nee AHT-mah-prahw-nah-NAHN-duh)

Swamini Ma
(SWAH-men-nee MAH)

JOVAN JONES
Ministry Contact Information

WEBSITE:

www.jovanjones.com

MAIL:

Jovan Jones

P.O. Box 58302

Fayetteville, North Carolina 28305

EMAIL:

jj@jovanjones.com